1/03

BEFORE
THE CREEKS
RAN RED

BEFORE THE CREEKS RAN RED

CAROLYN REEDER

HarperCollins*Publishers*

Acknowledgments

*This book could not have been written
without the help of historians at Fort Sumter
National Monument, the Maryland Historical
Society, and The Lyceum in Alexandria—or without
the willingness of scores of Civil War reenactors
and other experts to answer my questions.*

Library of Congress Cataloging-in-Publication Data
Reeder, Carolyn.
Before the creeks ran red / by Carolyn Reeder.
    p.   cm.
Summary: Through the eyes of three different boys, three linked novellas explore the
tumultuous times beginning with the secession of South Carolina and leading up to the
first major battle of the Civil War.
Contents: Timothy Donovan's story, Charleston Harbor, South Carolina: December
20, 1860–April 15, 1861—Joseph Schwartz's story, Baltimore, Maryland: April
18–May 15, 1861—Gregory Howard's story, Alexandria, Virginia: May 16–Late June,
1861.
    ISBN 0-06-623615-0 — ISBN 0-06-623616-9 (lib. bdg.)
    1. United States—History—Civil War, 1861–1865—Juvenile fiction. 2. Fort
Sumter (Charleston, S.C.)—Siege, 1861—Juvenile fiction. 3. Baltimore (Md.)—
History—Civil War, 1861–1865—Juvenile fiction. 4. Alexandria (Va.)—History—
Civil War, 1861–1865—Juvenile fiction. [1. United States—History—Civil War,
1861–1865—Fiction. 2. Fort Sumter (Charleston, S.C.)—Siege, 1861—Fiction.
3. Baltimore (Md.)—History—Civil War, 1861–1865. 4. Alexandria (Va.)—History—
Civil War, 1861–1865.] I. Title.
PZ7.R25416 Be 2003   2002023841
[Fic]—dc21   CIP
                                                                          AC

Typography by Larissa Lawrynenko

1 2 3 4 5 6 7 8 9 10

First Edition

NOTES ON THE LANGUAGE IN
Before the Creeks Ran Red

The German spelling of the name Joseph is *Josef*, but in the second story I have written it as *Yosef*—the way his family pronounced it.

Lena, Belle, and Deborah's dialect in the third story is patterned after that recorded in oral history interviews of freed slaves (except for the substitution of "gonna" for the awkward spelling commonly used for the dialect form of "going to") and on linguists' studies of Black English.

For Susan Grigsby

ABOUT THE THREE STORIES . . .

At first glance, Timothy Donovan, Joseph Schwartz, and Gregory Howard seem to have little in common. Timothy is an orphan and the bugler with the U.S. Army in Charleston Harbor, Joseph is a working-class Baltimore boy with a scholarship to a private academy, and Gregory is the son of a privileged family in Alexandria, Virginia. But their stories are links in a chain of events that begins with South Carolina's secession in December 1860 and leads to the Civil War's first major clash of arms along the steep banks of Bull Run in July 1861.

During the seven months between the secession vote in Charleston and the eve of that deadly battle, the boys in these stories find their lives turned upside down as the nation moves toward war—and as ordinary people must decide where they stand in the controversy swirling around them. Though Timothy, Joseph, and Gregory never meet, the resolution of the events in each boy's story sets the stage for what happens in the one that follows—and for the inevitable battle that lies ahead.

CONTENTS

★ ★ ★

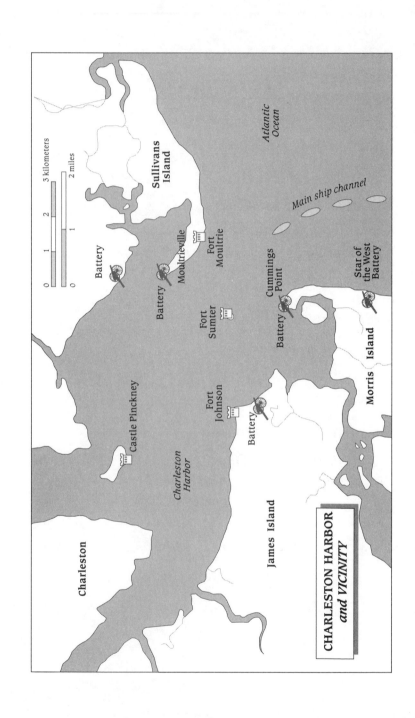

CHARLESTON HARBOR *and VICINITY*

★

Timothy Donovan's Story

★

Charleston Harbor, South Carolina: December 20, 1860–April 15, 1861

★

CHAPTER ONE

★　　　★　　　★

TIMOTHY DONOVAN stared across the harbor toward the city. "A hotbed of treason," he whispered. That's what the captain had called it, and he'd said it was filled with fire-eaters. Timothy wished he could be there now—in Charleston, where exciting things happened every day—instead of here at Fort Moultrie on Sullivan's Island, waiting to sound the next bugle call.

The faint sound of church bells floated across the water from the city, and almost immediately, the bells in the island's town of Moultrieville began to ring, too. Then came the low rumble of cannon firing in measured cadence in the distance. Glancing up when young Private Norris joined him on the parapet, Timothy said, "That sounds like a salute. I wonder what's going on over there."

"They're celebrating South Carolina's own private Independence Day," Norris told him. "You could have figured that out for yourself if you ever read the newspaper—or if you just kept your ears open. It's all anyone's been talking about lately."

Timothy scowled. He hated it when Norris acted so superior, when he talked like he was twenty years older instead of only four—almost middle-aged instead of eighteen.

"You *do* know that South Carolina's been threatening to secede from the Union, don't you?" Private Norris asked. "Well, delegates from all over the state are meeting in Charleston right now, and from the sound of things, they've just voted themselves out of the U.S.A."

"I guess that makes us foreigners, then," Timothy said. He meant it as a joke, but Norris took his comment seriously.

"Yes," said the young private, "and you can bet the people of South Carolina aren't going to allow any foreign forts on their soil."

Shaken, Timothy stared at him.

"Don't tell me you never noticed the local militia units drilling at the far end of the island—and other places around the harbor, too. They've been at it since before last month's election."

"When Lincoln was elected without the votes of a single southern state," Timothy said, trying to show that he wasn't completely uninformed. "Of course I'd noticed they were drilling—I just hadn't thought much about it. Are you saying they'll make us leave here?"

Norris squared his shoulders and said, "They'll try to, but they won't succeed. Fort Moultrie belongs to the United States, and Major Anderson has orders to defend it."

Timothy's eyes widened. Was Norris serious? There were more hired laborers working to repair the run-down fort than there were soldiers to safeguard it! How could sixty-some men and their officers defend Moultrie against all of Charleston's militia units?

The salute from the mainland boomed on and on, and

Timothy gazed across a mile of open water to the unfinished fort near the mouth of the harbor. Its high walls rose from a rocky, man-made island, and it looked indestructible. *That* would be a place a small garrison like theirs could defend.

Timothy was about to ask Norris if he knew when the bricklayers and stonemasons were supposed to be through with their work on the new fort's interior, but his friend's grim expression made him change his mind. The young artillerist looked as if he'd just heard Major Anderson give the order to defend Fort Moultrie to the last man.

Timothy didn't want to think about that. "It's almost time for me to sound Drill Call," he said, and he headed for the stairs that led down to the parade ground.

Timothy took his place on the bench outside the guardhouse and brushed a speck of dust from his sleeve. He had a good life now. An easy one, too. He thought back to his last day as a printer's apprentice, when he'd spilled a tray of type for the second time in less than a week. That half-deliberate mistake had brought Old Man Martin to the end of his patience. Almost before Timothy realized what was happening, instead of learning the printing trade, he was being trained as a bugler for the army—which was a lot more to his liking.

Life as a musician in the U.S. Army might not be very exciting, but it was a hundred times better than his apprenticeship at Martin's Print Shop back in New York. Sounding the bugle calls that organized the soldiers' day at Fort Moultrie beat setting type and inking presses by a mile. He looked a lot snappier in his red-trimmed blue uniform than in a printer's apron, and the camaraderie of the fort's mess hall and barracks was the next best thing to being part of a family. What an improvement over the silent meals at the Martins' table and his dusty room in their attic!

And on top of all that, South Carolina was an agreeable place to live. Timothy raised his face to the afternoon sun. Here it was, almost Christmas, and the days were still mild. The sea breezes kept Sullivan's Island comfortable in the summer, too. So comfortable that rich people who lived in Charleston had cottages here, some of them crowded right up to the back wall of the fort. A lot of the families had opened their cottages for the Christmas holidays, but they'd all gone back to the mainland today—and now he knew why.

Timothy gave a start when the order came. "Bugler Donovan, sound Drill Call."

Putting the conversation with Norris out of his mind, Timothy stood up, raised his bugle, and let the clear notes ring out. Perfect, as usual. What would Old Man Martin think if he knew that Timothy Donovan, the "worthless incompetent" he'd turned over to the army recruiters, had mastered all the bugle calls and knew when to play each one?

Timothy lowered his instrument and watched one company of soldiers head up the stairs to the artillery guns trained on the harbor while the other company gathered on the parade ground for the afternoon musket drill. Ever since Major Anderson had taken command of all the U.S. forts in Charleston Harbor a month ago, Fort Moultrie had become a lot more military. Timothy liked the changes. Even though the daily drills the major insisted on had become routine now, they were still fun to watch. With all the noise and the clouds of dark smoke, he could imagine he was witnessing a real battle—except that no one ever fired back.

But now they might. Timothy hoped Norris had been wrong about the South Carolinians trying to make the garrison leave Fort Moultrie now that the state had voted itself out of the U.S. "Seceded," he whispered, remembering the word the young private had used. Shaking off the uneasy feeling that had crept over him, Timothy turned his attention to the musket drill. As he watched the men respond to the commands their officer brayed out, he knew he would hate doing exactly the same thing, over and over again, day after day. The artillery drills looked more interesting—the artillerists had to practice every one of the six positions on every type of cannon, and they had to learn to work as a team.

I've got the best job of all, Timothy thought—and the easiest. Nobody else is spending the afternoon sitting in the sun.

"Bugler Donovan, sound Recall!"

Timothy scrambled to his feet and brought the bugle to his lips. This was one call the men were always glad to hear, because it signaled the end of the drill. As soon as the notes of the call faded away, Timothy headed for the stairs.

From the parapet, he glanced toward the city. Then his eyes scanned the harbor and came to rest on the seashore, where the wives of two of the soldiers were walking with their children. The women waved, and Timothy waved back, but when the little boys beckoned to him, he had to shake his head. Not long ago, he would have jumped down onto the bank of sand that had blown against the fort's wall, slid his way to the beach, and given them each a quick piggyback ride. Afterward, he would have run back up the slope of drifted sand and used the crevices in the fort's wall for fingerholds and toeholds to reach the parapet again. But that was before hired laborers had shoveled away the sand banks and filled in the cracks in the crumbling brick.

Timothy frowned. He'd never thought about how easy it would have been for an enemy to climb into the fort the same way he did, because there hadn't been any enemies. That must be why the forts around the harbor hadn't been kept in better shape, why Fort Sumter had stood unfinished for so many years. But now, if Norris was right, the people of South Carolina—even people right here on Sullivan's Island—might become their enemies. No wonder so many workmen had been hired to repair Fort Moultrie and finish the interior of Sumter, the huge fort in the mouth of the harbor.

I should have figured something was going on when Captain Foster brought all those bricklayers and stonemasons from Baltimore, and when Major Anderson came to replace our old commander. Norris probably knew right away what it meant.

Timothy looked down from the parapet when one of the little boys called, "Timothy! Look what a big seashell I found."

"Good for you, Peter," he called back.

Peter raced off, the shell clutched in his hand. The same kind of shell Timothy had picked up the first time he'd ventured outside Fort Moultrie's walls. And beefy Private Hanson, on his way back from Moultrieville, had ridiculed him for collecting shells, had said he was better suited to the nursery than the garrison of a U.S. fort.

"I shouldn't have answered back and said he was better suited to a sideshow in the circus," Timothy muttered. "I should have just ignored him, like Corporal Rice is always telling me to." He'd made himself an enemy that day. At least he got along well with the rest of the men, though except for Private Norris and the young lieutenants, they were more than twice his age. Maybe even three times his age, he thought, eyeing a nearby sentinel.

At first some of the men had called him Baby Blue Eyes, and others had called him Goldilocks or Curly Top. Now, though, they called him Bugler Donovan and treated him like a younger brother. Except for Hanson, of course. Hanson called him sonny boy and treated him like dirt.

"Hey, bugler! How long till you sound Guard Mount?" the band's cornet player called from the shore.

"About twenty minutes," he called back. He checked the timepiece that had been his father's. *Exactly* twenty minutes. Before he put it back in his pocket, he held the timepiece for a moment longer, remembering how Ma had pressed it into his hand just before she died, almost three years ago. It was his only link to his parents—the father he had no memory of, and the mother who had worked as a dressmaker to pay the rent for their cozy home.

Better get down to the parade ground, he told himself.

Maybe listening to the band play for Guard Mount would raise his spirits.

After darkness fell, Timothy climbed to the parapet and joined men from the garrison who were looking across the harbor toward Charleston, hoping to see the fireworks that would surely be part of an independence celebration on the mainland. As he gazed toward the city, curls of smoke began to rise. First he saw a glow, and soon flames leaped upward—a bonfire! For a few heartbeats, there was silence, and then one of the men spoke.

"The fires of secession will spread through the South. You mark my words."

Another soldier pointed to the trail of sparks from a rocket that had been set off in the city and said, "It won't be long before the night sky is streaked with flares like that."

Corporal Rice turned to Timothy and explained, "He means we'll be tracing the paths of artillery shells by the glow of their fuses."

Artillery shells? I thought he was talking about fireworks from other independence celebrations.

Private Evans cracked his knuckles and said, "I still don't see why the government won't send us the men and guns we need to defend this place against these secessionist rebels."

For such a pale, scrawny little man, Evans certainly was full of fight, Timothy thought. That must be why he was treated with respect in spite of his unpopularity. No one else would get away with asking a question that had been answered so many times before—and always with the same words. Timothy's lips moved as Corporal Rice said,

"Our leaders in Washington are concerned that those rabble-rousers in Charleston would see it as a hostile move if we mounted more guns or reinforced the garrison."

That was easy enough to say if you were safe in Washington instead of just a few miles from the rabble-rousers, Timothy thought, forgetting his impatience with Evans.

"What's the matter, sonny boy—scared?"

Timothy gave Private Hanson an innocent look. "Scared?" he echoed. "Should I be?" He hid a smile when Hanson turned his attention back to the bonfire and didn't answer. Tossing his hostile questions back to him almost always worked. Timothy had learned that trick by watching one of the girls whose family summered on the island respond to her brother's teasing, and it worked as well with Hanson as it had with the spoiled young boy.

Remembering what Norris had said about keeping his eyes and ears open, Timothy listened to the conversation going on around him.

"I hope those fools on the mainland don't think that because we're outnumbered we'll hand over Fort Moultrie without a fight," one of the men said.

"Some of the folks in Moultrieville seem to assume we'll do just that," Corporal Rice told him. "They say it will all be very civilized—Major Anderson will take down the U.S. flag and they'll put up that palmetto tree flag of theirs, and everybody will shake hands all around."

"That's because they know Major Anderson's a southerner," Evans said. "They know he used to own slaves."

Timothy was shocked. He hadn't known that.

"Major Anderson took the same vow to protect the Union that we all did, Evans," Sergeant Zell said, his voice cold and disapproving. "It's true he's from Kentucky, but he puts his country before his state."

And the people of South Carolina put their state first, Timothy thought. He stood quietly, his eyes on the glare that lit the night sky, but his mind raced as he wondered what would happen next, wondered what would become of him. Moultrie might not be much of a fort, but it was home. And being bugler for the First United States Artillery suited him just fine—in spite of Private Hanson.

Still, it didn't make a lot of sense for the garrison to put up a fight to keep Fort Moultrie if they were sure to lose it anyway. *And probably lose our lives, too.*

Hours later, Timothy awoke to the murmur of voices and strained his ears to catch what was being said. Often the late-night talk in the barracks where the unmarried men lived was about their exploits in the war with Mexico more than a dozen years before—the war his father had fought and died in. But this time, the men weren't talking about the past. Hanson was saying, "I know they've always been our friends, but I still don't trust 'em. The windows of those cottages lined up along the back of the fort would be perfect places for their sharpshooters to pick us off one at a time."

"Or they could fire on us from one of the sand hills farther back," someone else said.

Timothy felt a chill. He was relieved to hear the calm voice of Corporal Rice in the bunk below him say, "I can't believe that people who have been our friends would do that. Men we've fished and clammed with. Men we've sung hymns with at church."

Men who have brought their families to watch our dress parades and listen to our band concerts, Timothy added silently.

"Maybe the men from Moultrieville wouldn't, but could they stop militia units from the city from taking advantage of cottage windows that look down on our parade ground?" Hanson's voice again.

When Corporal Rice didn't answer, Timothy's heart began to pound so hard he almost missed the next speaker's comment. "—a lot of talk in the city about taking over the U.S. forts around the harbor, starting with this one."

Now Timothy's heartbeat was so loud he had trouble hearing anything else.

"—still don't see why Washington hasn't sent us more men or—"

"—funds to strengthen our defenses."

"This fort is an embarrassment!"

Again Corporal Rice spoke. "Captain Doubleday says the War Department in Washington won't do anything that might stir up trouble with the locals."

From across the room a voice growled, "Why don't you fellows turn in? Every night, you keep me awake with the same conversation."

Timothy was glad he'd never heard it before. He stared into the darkness, worrying about sharpshooters. Maybe they wouldn't bother to "pick off" a bugler. But maybe they would.

CHAPTER TWO
★   ★   ★

YESTERDAY WAS THE best
Christmas since Ma died, Timothy thought as he buttoned
his uniform coat. Not only had he enjoyed a festive meal
in the mess hall, he'd even had presents—homemade
fudge from Mrs. Reilly, the cook's wife, and a copy of *The
House of Seven Gables* from Sergeant Zell's wife. He'd
eaten the fudge right away, but he hadn't had much time
to read yet because the garrison had spent the day packing up just about everything in the fort that could be
moved. Timothy hadn't minded the work, but he hated
being ordered to do something without being told why.
That was the worst thing about the army.

In the darkness, he felt for his bugle, hanging by its cord
from a peg in the wall by his bunk. He slung the cord over
his head and across his chest, put on his hat, and went
outside, wondering if Evans was right about the reason for
their hard work the day before—that Major Anderson
probably planned to send government goods away and
blow up the fort instead of surrendering it. Timothy hoped
that was true. It would be a way to keep Moultrie from
falling into the hands of the secessionists without risking
a single life. And as for what would become of the garri-

son—well, he'd worry about that when the time came.

The frosty grass crunched under his boots on his way across the parade ground to the flagpole. There, he drew in a deep breath and raised his bugle. The clear notes of the morning's first call broke the stillness and floated through the morning darkness. "Perfect," he whispered. It was a good start to the day.

Free for the quarter hour before time to sound the call that would bring the men to the parade ground, Timothy turned away from the barracks. He'd learned the hard way that few just-wakened soldiers have a kind word for the bugler. He glanced up at the parapet and saw the dark shapes of sentinels silhouetted against the midnight blue of the sky—more men on duty now that South Carolina had voted itself out of the United States.

Timothy ran up the stairs and stood on the parapet, looking out over the water and enjoying the hint of salt in the damp air. No stars broke the gradually lightening sky, but the harbor lights still burned brightly. His eyes rested on the beacon that shone high above unfinished Fort Sumter at the mouth of the harbor. He hoped Private Hanson had been trying to scare him when he'd announced last night that the secessionists would no doubt take it over and turn its guns on Moultrie.

A rose-colored streak faintly shone on the horizon, and Timothy checked his timepiece. After one last look toward Sumter, he headed for the parade ground to sound the next call.

He was playing the last notes when the men stumbled out of the barracks to line up so the sergeant could take the roll. Timothy waited for them to form ranks, wondering why grown men willingly put up with this kind of life—following orders, answering roll call three times a day, and on top of all that, inspections and rules, rules, rules. It was worse than being a schoolboy.

At breakfast, one of the men asked, "What do you think about the major's announcement that he's chartered schooners to move the wives and children over to Fort Johnson later today?"

Private Evans said, "Most likely he's sending them to safety because he expects the secessionists to pay us a call."

Or the sharpshooters to start picking us off. Timothy's stomach tightened, but he forced himself to keep eating, sure that Private Hanson would be watching his reaction to what Evans had said.

"Say, I'll bet they'd let you go along with the ladies and their little ones if you asked real sweet, sonny boy," Hanson said from across the table.

"Why would I want to go across the harbor to Fort Johnson?" Timothy hoped he'd managed to sound puzzled, hoped his face didn't show how much he'd like to do just that. His heart sank when Hanson leaned forward to answer. This time, tossing the question back at him hadn't worked.

But Private Hough said in his lilting brogue, "Keep the holiday spirit alive, Hanson, and let the boy be."

Timothy flashed Private Hough a grateful look, then turned his attention to spooning up his porridge. Each swallow seemed to enlarge the lump he could feel forming in his stomach at the thought of secessionist militiamen and sharpshooters.

"Too bad all our guns face the harbor," Private Evans said. He cracked his knuckles and added, "If they faced inland, we could blow those secessionists to smithereens."

"Moultrie and the other harbor forts were built to defend Charleston against an attack from the sea," Corporal Rice reminded him. "Nobody expected an attack from our own people."

Evans narrowed his eyes. "You mean 'from the mainland.' Those secessionists aren't 'our own people' anymore."

In the silence that followed those words, Timothy found himself wishing that the boats would sail back and pick up the rest of the garrison after the wives and children had been taken across the harbor to safety. He forced down the last of his porridge and tried not to think about what might happen next.

At least today everyone knows the reason for what they've been told to do, Timothy thought later that morning. He'd lost track of how many trips he'd made, carrying boxes and bundles from the families' living quarters to the fort's wharf, where laborers were loading the boats. But he was glad for a chance to do something active for a change, glad the band's elderly drummer had taken his place outside the guardroom, ready to beat the Long Roll to call the men to their battle stations if the secessionists threatened the fort.

Timothy set down the two carpetbags he'd been carrying and said, "Hey, Norris. Look at all those barrels of flour and pickled salt pork on the wharf—that's more than the wives and children could eat in a year." Frowning, he added, "I hope the major kept back enough for us."

"I heard some talk about delivering provisions to feed Captain Foster's laborers at the fort in the harbor," Norris said. "Look, here comes Private Evans, carrying nothing but a pillow, the slacker."

"You need some help with that?" Timothy called.

Evans glared at him and said, "I didn't join the army to fetch and carry for the ladies. I'll leave that sort of thing to the tall, dark, and handsome fellows like Private Norris. Fellows with Virginia manners."

"Well, I'm short, blond, and ordinary-looking with New York manners, and I'm—"

"Let's go, Bugler Donovan," Norris interrupted. "We have work to do."

Timothy was adding "laziness" to his mental list of things he didn't like about Private Evans when Norris said, "Keep that up, and you'll turn Evans against you, too. It was your big mouth that got you off on the wrong track with Private Hanson, after all."

Sure that Norris had no way of knowing about that first exchange with Hanson on the beach, Timothy said, "If you mean the time he told me to 'go tootle your flootle,' all I did was explain that I play the 'bugle,' not a 'flootle,' and that the correct pronunciation of the instrument he'd mentioned was 'flute,' not 'flootle.'"

"Yes, and now dozens of times a day, each time you sound a call, Hanson's reminded of how everybody laughed while you went on and on about the 'long, skinny instrument that sounds a bit like a fife' and the 'looped-around instrument that sounds a lot like a trumpet.'"

Timothy's smile faded. "Is *that* what he holds against me?"

"Partly. He also thinks you became an army bugler because the job comes with free room and board, not because you wanted to serve your country."

And he's right. Old Man Martin gave me the choice of the poorhouse or the army. Shaken, Timothy asked, "How do you know all that?"

Norris looked smug. "You learn a lot if you keep your eyes and ears open and your mouth shut."

They were almost back to the families' quarters when Timothy said, "I guess if Private Hanson knew that you ran away and joined the army because you hated your stepfather, he'd have it in for you, too."

"It wouldn't make a bit of difference to him. I was a good drummer when I was your age, and I'm a good artillerist now. That's what counts with Hanson."

"Then how come it doesn't count that I'm a good bugler?" An excellent bugler, even, Timothy added silently.

Private Norris glanced down at him. "Because that's all you are, Donovan. Before you came here, I not only beat out all the calls you play, I pitched in without being asked

19

whenever I saw something needed to be done. And I didn't do such a clumsy job in the kitchen that the cook asked for somebody else to be assigned to help him."

"I'm a musician, not a—"

"You're a *bugler*, Donovan. The men in the regimental band are musicians. They can read music, and their instruments play more than five notes."

Stung by his words, Timothy retorted, "I think you're just sore because you aren't the one sounding the calls now."

"I only signed up as a drummer because I was too young to be a soldier. I'd been asking the captain to let me train as an artillerist for a long time, Donovan. When you came, he finally agreed that I'd be more use helping defend Moultrie than beating out calls."

"As if one more artillerist is going to make lot of difference," Timothy said. He picked up a wooden box from the pile outside the quarters and headed toward the wharf without giving Norris a chance to reply.

Half an hour later, Timothy and Norris had just stopped to rest, setting down the medium-sized trunk they were carrying between them, when Hanson appeared. "I'll take that the rest of the way," he said. "You boys can trot on back and bring a couple of hatboxes or something." He hoisted the trunk onto his shoulder and walked away, whistling.

Norris pursed his lips and said, "I didn't join the army to carry heavy trunks. I'll leave that for louts like Hanson, with his Minnesota farmhand manners."

Timothy decided not to mention that Corporal Rice, who was always courteous and kind, had also grown up on a farm in Minnesota. He stepped aside for an officer's ten-year-old son lugging a rocking chair, then followed Norris back to the pile of goods that still had to be hauled to the wharf.

At last everything was loaded, and it was time for the wives and children to board one of the chartered schooners. Timothy's eyes were on Sergeant Zell, walking beside his wife with their toddler riding on his shoulder, when Mrs. Reilly stopped to give him a hug. "You take good care of yourself, Timothy," she said.

"You too, Mrs. Reilly." *Now there will be no one left who calls me by my first name.* Timothy was wondering why the cook wasn't here to tell his wife good-bye when Private Reilly caught up to them, still wearing his apron. Timothy saw Mrs. Reilly's face light up the way his mother's always had when he came home from school, and he felt a wave of sadness as he stepped back to stand with Norris again.

"Look at that pair coming over from the vacation cottages," Norris whispered. "I wondered when the locals would get curious."

One of the men gestured to the wives and children, who were being helped aboard a schooner and asked, "What's going on here?"

"Major Anderson is sending the married men's families across the harbor to old Fort Johnson," an officer answered.

The secessionist looked satisfied. "Good idea. They'll be safer somewhere else," he said, exchanging a knowing look with his companion. Timothy's stomach tightened until he realized that civilians wouldn't still be here on Sullivan's Island if their militia was about to attack the fort.

Once all the wives and children were aboard, the married soldiers lined the wharf, waiting to wave good-bye, and Timothy followed Norris and the bachelors back to the fort. The sound of martial music came from the upper end of the island, where a local militia unit drilled, and Timothy wondered if it was true that the secessionists were mounting cannon there. Well, he wasn't going to worry about that until after the Charleston families spending the Christmas holidays in their beach houses went back to the city.

The sun was just setting that evening when Captain Doubleday burst into the barracks. "We leave the fort in twenty minutes," he announced, unable to hide his excitement. "Get ready, men."

Relief flooded over Timothy. Now he wouldn't have to worry about sharpshooters anymore—or about being massacred if the secessionists attacked the fort.

The barracks was a flurry of activity as the men grabbed their knapsacks and rolled up their blankets. When everyone had assembled on the parade ground, Major Anderson stood before them, his slim figure erect. Timothy didn't think he looked at all like a man who was about to abandon his fort without a fight. "I'm moving the garrison to Fort Sumter," the gray-haired officer announced. "Even though it's not finished, we'll be able to defend it against the South Carolinians."

We're going to the fort in the harbor!

"Follow me, men," the major said. "I don't need to remind you that our departure must be made in silence." He tucked the carefully folded U.S. flag under his arm and led the garrison out of the fort.

Timothy's chest was tight as they marched past the seaside houses nearest Moultrie, their footsteps muffled by the sand. *What if someone sees us?* The families must be at supper, he realized, but what would happen if the locals challenged them? True, the soldiers were armed, but could any of them shoot someone they knew? Someone who had been a friend? Evans probably could.

Timothy scanned the water for a glimpse of the chartered schooners. But he saw only the distant lights of Charleston and the navigation light at Castle Pinckney, the small fort on an island near the city. The beacon at Sumter burned brightly, but it seemed farther away than Timothy remembered.

He guessed they had walked a quarter of a mile when they came to three six-oared boats partly hidden by a crumbled seawall. Was *that* how they were getting to Fort Sumter? In rowboats?

After whispered orders, Captain Doubleday's company was assigned to the boats, with the brawniest men at the oars, and Captain Seymour's company settled down to wait for the next crossing. Timothy found himself in the third boat to leave, sitting opposite Hanson and Private Hough, who had been chosen as two of the oarsmen. The boat rocked as the men on shore shoved it into the water, and Hanson whispered, "Don't puke on me when you get seasick, little landlubber." Timothy clutched his stomach and leaned forward, pretending to retch, and was rewarded by Hough's quiet chuckle when Hanson drew back his feet.

From behind Timothy came Captain Doubleday's voice, low and authoritative. "Row your hardest, men. Pull straight for the fort."

The boat began to move with a great splashing, and the captain commanded, "Muffle those oars! And coordinate your movements. Can't you match your rhythm to your partner's, Hanson?"

Timothy fastened his eyes on the dark hulk of Fort Sumter at the mouth of the harbor and wondered how long it would take to row a mile. Hanson's oar splashed water into the boat, and the captain asked, "Haven't you ever rowed a boat before, Private Hanson? Lean forward as you bring that oar up, then lean back as you pull on it. Watch Private Hough, and adjust your movements to his."

Timothy would have enjoyed Hanson's upbraiding if he hadn't felt so nervous. He told himself he wasn't scared, he'd just never been out on the water at night. Never been so *close* to the water. The boat rose with the swells and then settled back, rose and settled, rose and settled. Timothy gripped his bugle and willed himself not to be sick.

"Confound it!" the captain exclaimed. "Can't you fellows row any faster?"

Timothy's heart raced when he saw a beam of light that pierced the near darkness and shone on the channel ahead of them. *The secessionists' patrol boat!* He'd heard it had more than a hundred militiamen on board, enough to prevent Fort Moultrie from being reinforced—or to keep its garrison from moving to Sumter.

A low murmuring told Timothy that the others had seen the patrol boat, too, and he saw that ahead of them, the small boats carrying the major and the rest of Captain Doubleday's company were changing course to avoid its bow light. But the captain said, "We'll make a run for it. Pull on those oars, men. *Pull!*"

Everyone was so quiet that Timothy could hear water drip from the oars as they were brought forward, could hear the rasp of the men's breath as they rowed. But the fort seemed no closer, and the distance to the patrol boat was shrinking. What if they couldn't cross in front of it before the beam from its lamp fell on them? Or what if they were swamped by its wake? The image of water closing over his head made Timothy shudder.

"We aren't going to make it," the captain said, his voice tense. "Take off your hats and coats, and cover your muskets. With a bit of luck, the secessionists will think we're a group of laborers going back to Fort Sumter for the night."

The boat rocked sickeningly as the men obeyed. Timothy unslung his bugle and wrapped it in his coat. Maybe the secessionists' steamer would cross their path without anyone on board seeing them. Maybe— But its paddle wheel stopped a hundred yards away, and the boat slowly turned toward them as it drifted.

"Keep rowing," the captain said, his voice low. "Act as though we're simply going about our business. Remember, they're used to seeing workmen row between our forts in boats like this."

Caught in the beam of the patrol boat's lamp, Timothy imagined its captain training his spyglass on them. *We're laborers on our way to the fort. We're laborers going about our business.* He faced the ray of light shining from the boat, silently repeating the words, until the paddle wheel began to turn again and the patrol boat continued toward Charleston.

The murmur of relief that filled the rowboat told Timothy that the others had been as worried as he was. And then Captain Doubleday said, "Many of the workmen at Sumter are bound to be secessionists. I assume that some of the bricklayers and stonemasons Captain Foster brought here from Baltimore are loyal Americans, but he hired scores of local men, too. We'll hold them all at gunpoint until Major Anderson arrives."

A surge of energy seemed to run through the boat as the men put on their hats and buttoned their coats. No longer at the mercy of the secessionist patrol, now they were soldiers with a job to do.

By the time they arrived at Sumter, the hired laborers had spotted them and were gathered on the wharf. At first, Timothy was glad he didn't have to drive the unsuspecting workers back through the fort's huge gates and hold them at gunpoint. But when he saw how many of them wore blue rosettes pinned to their hats to show their secessionist sympathies, and when he heard them mutter hostile comments about "enemy soldiers," he was grateful for Captain Doubleday's plan.

Timothy stationed himself on the wharf to watch for the boats that had detoured to avoid the secessionists' steamer. It wasn't long before he spied them in the moonlight and ran to tell Captain Doubleday that the major and the rest of Company E were in sight.

Now, though, the oarsmen would have to row back to Sullivan's Island for Captain Seymour's men. Timothy was glad he hadn't had to wait over there all this time. He frowned, thinking of how different that long, sandy island with its village and vacation cottages was from this so-called island that surrounded Fort Sumter. "Just a few feet of rubble outside the walls," Timothy muttered. For all he knew, even that would be covered at high tide, though he figured the paved walkway that stretched along the wall behind him would always be above water.

Much later, Captain Doubleday joined Timothy on the wharf and silently scanned the dark water as they waited for the boats to return from Sullivan's Island with the men of Company H. Finally the officer put his spyglass in his pocket and said, "Seymour's company should be here soon, Bugler Donovan, but I want you to watch for our rear guard. When you see their boat, come inside and let me know so I can tell O'Malley to fire the signal shots."

"Signal shots?" Timothy repeated.

The captain nodded. "It will be safe then to bring the families here to Sumter."

"You mean they didn't go to Fort Johnson after all?" Timothy was embarrassed by the hopeful note in his voice.

Captain Doubleday's face relaxed in a smile that made him look almost handsome. "They sailed across the harbor to James Island, but they never went ashore. Once all our men have arrived safely, the families will rejoin the garrison. After the schooners are unloaded, we'll put the secessionist laborers aboard, send them over to Fort Johnson, and keep them there until we can bring the rest of our supplies from Moultrie to Sumter."

Of course! That was why the garrison had spent Christmas Day packing up the commissary goods and quartermaster's stores—and why so many barrels of flour and salt pork were on the wharf this morning, too. "And then we'll blow up Fort Moultrie?" Timothy asked. In the moonlight, he saw the captain's eyebrows rise.

"Major Anderson has no authority to destroy the fort, bugler. After the last of our supplies are loaded, the men will drive spikes through the barrels of the cannon and set their wooden carriages afire so the rebels won't be able to turn our own guns against us."

Timothy's scalp prickled at the image of Moultrie's guns trained on Fort Sumter. Had they traded sharpshooters' muskets for artillerists' cannon? Refusing to think about that, he stared across the harbor, his eyes searching the darkness for three small boats.

CHAPTER THREE

★　　　★　　　★

IT TOOK A moment for Timothy to remember where he was when the corporal of the guard woke him the next morning. *Fort Sumter.* He dressed quickly and found his way outside to sound the call that would wake the garrison.

In the murky darkness he crossed the cluttered parade ground to the flagpole, raised his bugle, and let the notes ring out. After a quick glance around, he made his way past sheds and piles of building materials toward a stair tower. Timothy climbed past the unfinished second tier to the top level of the fort, the one he'd heard the captain call *the barbette.* He was surprised to see how crowded it was—besides the sentinels on duty, dozens of men had risen early to inspect their new surroundings. Even Private Norris, who usually wasn't fully awake till after breakfast, was there. Timothy joined him on the parapet and looked down at the water a dizzying distance below.

"How high are these walls, anyway?" he asked, moving back from the edge.

"Forty or fifty feet, at least," Norris told him. "Maybe even sixty feet."

So Norris doesn't know everything after all, Timothy thought. One thing was sure, though—standing on the edge of Moultrie's parapet had never given him this unsettled feeling in his stomach.

"Look there," Norris said, pointing, and in the gathering light, Timothy saw the secessionists' patrol boat steaming toward the mouth of the harbor.

"Just wait till they spot us up here," Evans said.

While Timothy watched, the boat's paddle wheel stopped turning, and its crew stared up at the soldiers on the fort's ramparts. The captain peered at them through his spyglass, then snapped it shut and shouted a command. The paddle wheel began to churn the water again, and the boat steamed toward Charleston to spread the alarm. The men on the parapet were still cheering when Timothy checked his timepiece and headed for the parade ground.

On his way to the flagpole, he surveyed the fort, which was in the shape of a pentagon, with the officers' quarters that housed the entire garrison along its base and unfinished barracks angling off on either side. It was light enough now for him to see the arched entries to the cavernous gun rooms along the two faces of the fort that met opposite where he stood. "Two tiers of gun rooms and the barbette tier, but hardly any guns are in place," he muttered.

His eyes swept the parade ground in the fort's center and came to rest on a long row of unmounted cannon. It didn't look as though there were enough of them to fill all the gun rooms—but with a team of six needed for each gun, there weren't enough artillerists in the garrison to man all the cannon they did have.

Timothy looked from the cluster of temporary buildings to the heaps of sand, piles of brick, and coils of rope that were scattered about. He hadn't thought Sumter would be like this. From Sullivan's Island, it had looked so grand. Oh, well. At least they didn't have to worry about sharpshooters here, he reminded himself as he raised his bugle.

That morning, one of the schooners Major Anderson had chartered to transport the families brought over more supplies from Moultrie. The soldiers and the Unionist workmen who had remained at Fort Sumter worked side by side to unload the goods and bring them inside the walls. Timothy had never worked so hard in his life. He couldn't manage the heavy loads the men carried, but he was quicker and made more trips. He hoped Norris noticed he was doing his part.

When the last boatload of supplies arrived, a lieutenant came ashore and reported that the cannon had been spiked and that his men had set their wooden carriages afire and chopped down the flagpole. Puzzled, Timothy turned to Corporal Rice and asked, "Why did they chop down the flagpole?"

"Because they didn't want the secessionists to run up that palmetto tree flag of theirs where the Stars and Stripes had flown for so long," the corporal explained.

Bearded Sergeant Zell paused as he passed and said,

"Be ready to sound Assembly, bugler—the major has planned a flag-raising ceremony."

"Yes, sir," Timothy said. "I mean, yes, *sergeant*." He noticed Sergeant Zell's frown and was glad he had an excuse to hurry away. Everyone knew that in spite of Sergeant Zell's stern expression and solemn manner, he was both fair and kindly, but he was also a stickler for following army regulations to the letter. Timothy scowled. I know as well as anybody else that only commissioned officers are addressed as "sir," he thought as he headed for the flagpole.

By the time the last notes of Assembly died away, the band members were heading for the stair tower with their instruments, and the soldiers, their families, and the workmen were gathering around the flagpole on the parade ground. Timothy stood at attention while the band played "Hail, Columbia!" Then, along with the others, he took off his hat and bowed his head while the chaplain prayed, giving thanks for the safe crossing to Sumter and ending with a plea for the country to be quickly united again.

After the chorus of amens, Major Anderson knelt at the foot of the flagpole and took the halyards in his hands. As the flag he had brought from Fort Moultrie soared upward, his clean-shaven face seemed to glow. Timothy craned his neck to watch the flag unfurl at the top of the pole, high above the parapet, and the band struck up "The Star-Spangled Banner" the moment it caught the breeze. The men began to cheer, and Timothy joined in the rousing shouts, feeling more a part of the garrison than he ever had before.

After the clamor died down and they had been dismissed, Private Hanson declared, "No dishonor will come to that flag while I have breath. I will protect it with my life."

"And I, too!" cried one man after another.

Timothy raised his eyes to the flag snapping in the wind. Protect it with his life? But it was *cloth!* Turning toward the quarters, he saw Captain Doubleday watching him.

"You have a good head on your shoulders, young man," the captain said.

Confused, Timothy said, "I—I don't understand, sir."

"I noticed that you didn't vow to defend the flag with your bugle." A slight smile softened the officer's face, and he added, "I always respect a man who isn't swept along by the enthusiasm of the crowd."

Timothy didn't know what to say. No one had ever told him they respected him, or even shown him much respect. And he certainly didn't feel like a man.

Timothy set down the load he was carrying across the parade ground when he saw men on the parapet looking off to the northwest. He ran up and joined a group of privates from his company. "What do you see out there?" he asked.

"It looks like the secessionists are about to take Castle Pinckney," Private Hough told him. "Here, have a look." He handed Timothy a spyglass and added, "I bought this at a pawnshop on my last trip to the city." The men grudgingly made room for the young bugler, and he pointed the glass toward the small fort that stood on a marshy island near the city. The patrol boat was heading toward it, and Timothy could see uniformed men massed on the deck.

"Let somebody else have a turn with that, bugler," Evans said, holding out his hand, but Timothy returned the spyglass to Hough, who took another quick look before he passed it on. Timothy waited impatiently for another turn with the glass, listening to the men's conversation.

"—certainly didn't waste any time—"

"—always knew they'd take it first because it's closest to the city."

"—no garrison—"

"There's a caretaker to keep the light—"

"—and Captain Foster's workmen, but—"

"Let's hope the gates are sturdy, and—"

At last it was Timothy's turn with the glass again. Scarcely breathing, he watched the Charleston militiamen stream from their boat like ants and darken the shore outside the curved wall of the fort. "They aren't going in. I think the gates are locked," he said, careful to pass the glass along before anyone complained.

"That won't stop them," Evans said, raising the spyglass. "They've probably brought scaling ladders. Yes, they're dragging them over to the wall now."

Timothy wished he could watch the Charleston militiamen climb the ladders and swarm over the wall. And then he had a terrifying thought: What if they used those ladders here at Sumter? What if they climb into the fort through those openings in the gun-room walls—Norris had called them *embrasures*—where no cannon were mounted yet? They wouldn't even need a ladder to reach the ones on the first tier.

"There's nothing to see now that the rebels are inside," Evans said, returning the spyglass to Private Hough.

Farther along the parapet, Norris beckoned for Timothy to join him, and they waited together, eyes on the U.S. flag that waved over the distant fort. A murmur that was almost a groan rose from the men around them when the flag was lowered, and a familiar voice shouted, "An act of war, that's what it is!"

"Evans," Norris said as other voices joined in.

One of the lieutenants stood nearby, peering through his spyglass. "This is strange," he said. "The rebels are lowering the flag on their patrol boat. I wonder what they're up to."

Timothy and Norris exchanged a puzzled look, and Timothy thought wistfully of Private Hough's spyglass.

The lieutenant gave a scornful laugh. "Looks like they forgot to take along a flag to raise over the fort, so they have to use the one from the *Nina*."

Timothy made a mental note that the patrol boat was named *Nina*. He'd show Norris that he could keep his ears open, too. Hadn't he already learned that the top tier of the fort was the barbette and the windows in the gun rooms were embrasures?

"The secesh will probably take Fort Moultrie next," Norris said.

"Secesh?" Timothy repeated.

"It's short for 'secessionist,'" Norris explained. "A good name for them, don't you think? It shows just the right amount of disrespect."

Secesh, rebels—Timothy didn't care what the South Carolinians were called. He was just glad Major Anderson had moved the garrison to a place that could be defended against them. But then he remembered the rebel militiamen with their ladders, and his heart beat faster. No wonder so many sentinels were on duty!

For once in his life, Timothy was glad when Sunday came. Usually the Sabbath-afternoon calm made him fidgety, but after three days of exhausting work, he was glad to have a day of rest. Ever since they'd arrived at Sumter, everyone who wasn't on guard duty had pitched in to make the fort defensible, working alongside the laborers who had stayed on. And tomorrow, they would all be at it again. But for now, the men were relaxing in their quarters—except for the sentinels, of course.

Timothy looked up from *The House of Seven Gables* when the silence was broken by a low rumbling sound. "That sounds like cannon fire," he said.

"And what would the likes of you know about cannon fire, sonny boy?" Hanson asked, glancing up from melting sealing wax onto the envelope he had just addressed.

"He's watched our drills often enough to know a little about it, don't you think?" Corporal Rice asked.

Hanson didn't answer, and Timothy shrugged into his

uniform coat and headed for the door. Outside, he ran to join Private Norris, who was hurrying toward a stair tower. "What do you think they're saluting this time?" Timothy asked when he caught up.

Norris held up a hand to silence him, and Timothy realized that his friend was counting. When the firing stopped, he announced, "Thirty-two guns."

Timothy was puzzled. He'd heard of fifty-gun salutes and hundred-gun salutes, but he'd never heard of a thirty-two-gun salute.

"This morning I heard one of the lieutenants say it was just a matter of time till the rebels took over the U.S. arsenal in the city," Norris said as they climbed the stairs. "That's probably what happened," he added. "We surrendered the arsenal, and the South Carolinians let us salute our flag as it was lowered."

"But why thirty-two guns?" Timothy asked as they reached the top tier and joined the men looking toward the city.

"Use your head, Donovan," Norris answered. "One for each state left in the Union. We'll have thirty-three again when Kansas becomes a state next month."

How does Norris know so much?

They stood on the parapet and looked toward the city, but there was nothing to see. Another shot was fired, and Timothy waited expectantly, ready to count, but that was all. "A *one*-gun salute?"

"For the one state that has left the Union, apparently," Sergeant Zell said, pausing on his way toward the stairs.

"A state that now can arm itself against us," he added, the frown on his somber face deeper than usual.

Then Norris was right—the South Carolinians had taken the arsenal. And that meant all the weapons that had been kept in the huge storehouse were in the secessionists' hands! Now their state flag flew over the U.S. arsenal as well as Castle Pinckney and Fort Moultrie. The rebels had taken Moultrie the night before, and Fort Johnson would probably be next. Timothy raised his eyes to the Stars and Stripes waving above him and wondered how much longer it would be there.

TIMOTHY SCOOPED a shovelful of sand from the pile on the parade ground and added it to the mortar Norris was mixing. He tried to ignore his empty stomach, tried not to think of still another meal of pickled salt pork and bread. Who could have imagined that the governor would be so angry about their move to Sumter that he'd refuse to let them buy food in the city? The women were fretting about the lack of vegetables in the garrison's diet, and Mrs. Reilly had said her husband was "quite morose" about not having the supplies he needed to prepare decent meals for the soldiers and their families.

Hanson paused on his way past with a wheelbarrow load of bricks and said, "You must be getting used to this place, sonny boy, 'cause you don't look half as worried as you did when we came here last week."

Before Timothy could reply, Corporal Rice said, "Our officers must have been worried, too, because they didn't waste any time ordering us to brick up all the embrasures on the second tier."

"And the ones we won't be using on this level, too,"

Hanson agreed. "If I'd wanted to be a bricklayer's helper, I wouldn't have joined the army."

A bandsman carrying water to add to Norris's mortar set down his buckets and said, "When I volunteered, nobody ever said anything about hard labor. I'm up to it, of course," he added quickly, "but it's a bit of a strain for Corporal O'Brian, our drummer."

The dampness here must be making the old man's rheumatism worse, Timothy thought as he dug his shovel into the sand pile. "I wish this work would go a bit faster," he hinted when he saw Private Evans loading bricks into a wheelbarrow one at a time.

"How can it, when guard duty uses up so much of our manpower?" Evans asked. He looked up at the sentinels keeping watch from the parapet.

Norris gave the mortar another stir and said, "Well, according to the Charleston paper, we should be getting reinforcements any day now. And provisions, too."

"Provisions?" Timothy echoed. "I hope they get here soon."

"How did you get hold of a newspaper?" Evans asked.

"I didn't. One of those secesh laborers who rowed out here to collect his pay had a copy of today's *Mercury*, and he was showing everyone the headline. I'm surprised neither of you saw it."

Timothy added his shovelful of sand to the thickening mixture Norris was stirring and said, "I don't like it that the secessionists—the secesh—know more than we do about what the government plans for Sumter."

"And I don't like it that the secesh leaders keep coming over and demanding that we leave here and turn the fort over to their so-called republic," Norris said, "especially—Hey!" A rubber ball had knocked off his hat and would have bounced into the mortar if Timothy hadn't caught it.

"Sorry!" called one of the young boys playing near the officers' quarters. "We're trying to see if we can make the ball go as high as the parapet."

Timothy wondered if he could do that, could throw the ball in such a steep arc that it would rise above the fort's high wall and curve down to land where the children stood. Leaning back so far that he could see the patch of sky directly above him, he hurled the ball with all his might. It sailed upward, seemed to hang in the air just above the barbette tier, then plummeted to the ground.

The little boys cheered and raced after it, and Timothy was feeling pleased with himself until Hanson stopped and grinned down at him. "Is that the best you can do, sonny boy?" He left his loaded wheelbarrow and called, "Toss me that ball of yours, Johnny."

Across the parade ground an officer shouted, "We're waiting for that load of bricks, Private Hanson!"

"Yeah, Hanson," Timothy said, "what kind of laggard are you?"

His broad face flushing with anger, Hanson called back, "Be right there, sir." He threw the ball to Johnny, then glared at Timothy and said, "You'd better hold your tongue, sonny boy, or—"

"Like this?" Timothy interrupted, sticking out his tongue

and grasping it between his thumb and forefinger. "Ith thith ri'?"

Evans and several of the hired workers laughed, and when Hanson's heavy brows drew together to form a mirror image of his drooping mustache, it was hard for Timothy to maintain his look of studied innocence. The man took a step toward him, then checked himself. With a smothered curse, he turned and trundled his wheelbarrow over to the gun room where Captain Foster was supervising the bricklayers filling in the embrasure.

Timothy was silently congratulating himself for getting the best of his tormenter when Corporal Rice set his empty buckets by the pile of sand and said quietly, "I think you owe Private Hanson an apology, bugler."

"For what?" Evans asked. "Can't Hanson take a joke?"

"Nobody likes to be the butt of a joke, but that's not what I meant," Corporal Rice said, his eyes on Timothy. "You shouldn't have called Hanson a laggard. He's probably the last person here who would ever shirk his duty, and you ought to apologize for what you said."

Timothy could hardly believe his ears. "Is that an order, corporal?" he asked.

"No, it's a suggestion made with your best interests in mind."

An awkward silence followed the corporal's words, and Timothy kept his eyes on the ground. He felt a sense of relief when Corporal Rice finished filling his buckets with sand and headed back to the second tier.

"Order or not, you'd better do what he said, Donovan,"

Norris told him.

Who does he think he is, anyway? "I'll tell you what," Timothy said. "If you can get Hanson to say he'll let me be, I'll gladly go over there and apologize to him. Agreed?"

Norris shrugged and turned his attention back to the mortar. "I think this needs another shovelful of sand," he said.

Timothy scowled as he dug into the sand pile again. The corporal's reprimand and Norris's unwelcome advice had taken the pleasure out of getting the best of Hanson.

Timothy had made climbing to the top tier after the morning's first call part of his daily ritual. He liked watching the stars fade as the eastern sky began to lighten, liked to savor this quiet part of the day before the garrison's relentless work on the fort began. He always felt reassured when he saw the sentinels on duty and knew that Sumter needn't fear a surprise attack. He felt safer when he saw officers with their spyglasses keeping track of the progress the South Carolinians were making on their defenses, too.

Today, though, the lookouts—and Captain Doubleday—were all gazing out to sea. Timothy leaned into the wind and made his way along the parapet, careful to stay away from the edge, and he soon saw that everyone was watching a ship moving slowly toward the harbor.

Standing far enough from Captain Doubleday not to seem presumptuous, Timothy watched, too. Several months before, the captain had stopped him and said,

"I've been meaning to ask you, bugler, if by any chance you might be Timothy Donovan, *Junior*? I knew a Tim Donovan in Mexico, and . . ." Ever since then, in some unexplainable way, Timothy felt less of an orphan when he was near the captain.

Without lowering his spyglass, Captain Doubleday said, "It looks like this might be a lucky day for Sumter, young man."

Timothy moved closer and asked, "Why is that, sir?"

"I've had my eye on this ship on the horizon for some time. It's flying the U.S. flag, and I'm fairly certain it's the *Star of the West*."

"The warship that's supposed to be bringing us provisions and reinforcements?" Timothy asked eagerly, remembering what Norris had said the day before.

The captain lowered his glass and turned to face Timothy. "It's the ship some of us have been expecting, but it's not a warship, bugler. Sending a U.S. naval vessel would no doubt provoke those hotheaded secessionists on Morris Island to open fire, but there's a chance they'll allow an unarmed merchant ship into the channel." He raised the spyglass again, adding with satisfaction, "If the *Star* does get through with the reinforcements and supplies, Sumter will be in good shape."

Timothy glanced from Morris Island to Sullivan's Island. Lying on either side of the entrance to the harbor, they guarded it like a pair of sentinels. Would the secesh artillerists let the *Star of the West* pass between them? To the south, the Morris Island battery that overlooked the shipping channel was out of sight, but to the northeast Timothy could see Fort Moultrie, its silhouette low and menacing against the dark gray of the sky. After one last look at the ship moving toward the harbor, he turned and hurried toward the stair tower. For once, he had some news for Norris instead of the other way around.

At breakfast that morning, the mess hall was almost deserted, except for the enlisted men's wives and children at their usual places on the far side of the room. A few men from Captain Seymour's company were clustered at the end at one long wooden table, and Evans sat alone at another.

"I'm surprised you aren't up on the parapet, watching with everyone else," Evans said when Timothy sat down opposite him.

"I already saw the ship, and besides, I'm hungry."

Evans pushed away his half-empty coffee cup and said, "Boys always are."

Timothy ignored the comment and said, "I sure hope the ship gets through."

"Not much chance of that, bugler. Not when the rebels had advance notice that it was coming. If you ask me, President Buchanan is a lot less interested in getting men and supplies to Sumter than he is in keeping things as calm as possible until he leaves office and turns this whole mess over to Lincoln."

And the inauguration wasn't until March 4—almost two months away. Timothy's heart sank. They might be able to manage without more men, but they badly needed the supplies the *Star of the West* was bringing. How much longer would those barrels of flour brought over from Fort Moultrie last? He'd been hoping the new provisions would include fuel so the barracks wouldn't be so cold and damp, and candles so the nights wouldn't seem so long, but now he would settle for more flour and salt pork.

Timothy had almost finished his breakfast when he heard the boom of a cannon in the distance: *Ka-POW!*

The mess hall fell silent for an instant, and then from across the room where the families sat came the wails of a small child. Outside, a drum began to beat a call Timothy hadn't heard since he was training to be a bugler, and his heart almost stopped. *The Long Roll—the call to battle stations.*

The few soldiers who had appeared at breakfast raced to the door, and Evans knocked over a bench in his hurry to leave the table. Half terrified, half excited, Timothy followed him. On the parade ground, he ran past the band's elderly drummer, whose beating of the Long Roll provided an ominous background to all the activity, and dashed up the stairs to the barbette tier. There, Timothy joined the crowd watching the artillery teams in position at the three guns facing Morris Island.

"The secesh fired a warning shot across the ship's bow," Norris said, his voice tense.

"You don't think they'll fire again, do you?" Timothy asked.

Before Norris could answer, a puff of smoke rose from

the dunes on Morris Island as a second shot was fired from a battery there, and the *ka-POW!* echoed across the harbor. An angry murmur ran along the parapet where the men were watching, and Timothy waited tensely for the fort's own guns to thunder. He could see the artillerymen beside them, waiting for the command to fire.

Another puff of smoke above the dunes, another echoing *ka-POW*. The men on the parapet fell silent, and Timothy held his breath as he watched the iron ball skip across the water. He could see Captain Doubleday's agitation as he gestured toward Morris Island with one hand and pointed to the fort's guns with the other. But Major Anderson shook his head. Why didn't he give the order to fire?

"She's hit!"

The cry went up as the shot struck the steamer, and Timothy stared across the water, heart pounding, and waited for it to sink. But Private Hough said, "Don't worry, bugler. It sounds like they're firing 24-pounders, and at that range, there shouldn't be much damage." Timothy's dismay turned to relief, but all around him, the men were becoming more agitated as Sumter's guns remained silent.

"Why doesn't the major—"

"—firing on an unarmed vessel!"

"— going to let them get away with that?"

" What's the matter with Anderson? Can't he see—"

"— insult to our flag!"

"Are we supposed to just stand here and watch like

some kind of —"

The men made no effort to keep their voices down, and in the hubbub Timothy caught the words *cowardly* and *traitorous*. And then Private Evans, his voice louder than the others, raged, "The flag of the United States has been fired on, and yet he does nothing. Didn't I tell you he was a southern sympathizer?"

But he isn't. I saw his face the day he raised the flag. Major Anderson is as patriotic as anyone here.

The Morris Island battery fired again, and Timothy held his breath until he saw the iron ball sink harmlessly behind the ship. "Why doesn't the major give the order to fire?" he wondered aloud.

Norris didn't answer, but Private Hough explained, "We won't be able to reach that battery of theirs till our heavier guns are mounted. Still, I wish we'd fire on Morris Island anyway. It doesn't seem right to stand here and do nothing."

Now Fort Moultrie's guns began to fire, and several of the artillerists made derisive comments as the first shot missed the ship by half a mile.

"Finally!" Norris exclaimed. "Now maybe we'll see some action."

Following his gaze, Timothy saw that one of the lieutenants who had been speaking with Major Anderson was leading a group of artillerists toward the stair tower. "What's happening now?"

"They're going down to the first tier to man the guns that face Moultrie," Norris said. "The guns the secesh would have used on us if *they'd* taken over Sumter."

He had barely finished speaking when the crowd erupted in pandemonium and the men swarmed along the parapet toward the gun teams, shouting and waving their arms. Private Norris cried, "She's turning back! The *Star of the West* is heading out to sea!"

"Turning back?" Timothy cried. "With all our *supplies*?"

"And with a couple hundred men for the garrison, too, assuming the Charleston newspaper got it right," Norris reminded him.

Fort Moultrie's guns thundered again, and Timothy saw the iron ball skip across the water behind the *Star*. "Wait a minute," he said, "I thought our rear guard spoiled Moultrie's guns."

"They *spiked* Moultrie's guns and burned the carriages," Norris said, "but it looks like the secesh have mounted others."

"Can you see what's going on over there by our guns?" Timothy asked, wishing he was taller.

"Anderson's heading for the stairs," Norris reported, "and it sounds like the men are threatening to open fire on Fort Moultrie on their own."

"Do you think the ship would turn around again if they did?" Timothy asked, his hopes rising.

"Don't you know anything, Donovan? An artillerist who fired without orders would face a court-martial! Haven't you ever heard of mutiny?"

Timothy had heard of it, and now he understood how it could happen. "Maybe it's the major who should face a court-martial," he said.

Behind them, Sergeant Zell said sternly, "An officer's commands must be obeyed, whether we agree with him or not, Bugler Donovan. That's a soldier's duty. Remember, obedience and duty are the cornerstones of the army." He hurried ahead without waiting for a response.

What must he think of me? "How much do you think he overheard, Norris?"

"I wouldn't worry about it. He's obviously got more important things on his mind than the opinion of the company's bugler. Just be glad Hanson didn't hear what you said. He'd never let you live it down."

Timothy thanked his lucky stars that Hanson hadn't heard his thoughtless comment—and that Norris was too much of a gentleman to repeat it.

★ ★ ★

"THIS FORT IS beginning to feel like a prison," Timothy grumbled. "It seems like we've been here three months instead of only three weeks." He huffed a warm breath onto his bugle and polished away the moist spot that appeared on the metal. Somewhere in the building, the bandsmen were rehearsing, and Timothy envied them. Since he had finished *The House of Seven Gables*, he felt at loose ends unless he was working. "I'm not surprised some of the laborers decided to leave here," he said.

Evans looked up from blacking his boots. "If you ask me, that artillery fire from the rebel batteries last week scared them off, the cowards. We don't need the likes of them."

"We need every man available to help make this fort defensible," Corporal Rice said. "I'm sorry they're gone."

Timothy wondered whether the forty or so workmen who had stayed would be enough to do all the work that still needed to be done, but instead of asking, he said, "I wish the rain would stop."

"Yes, we'll all feel better when it does," Corporal Rice

agreed. "This weather's dismal, even for January." He bent over his book again.

Timothy wondered how the corporal could see to read in the dim light. "We'd have candles, if our provisions had gotten through," he said.

"And soap," added Evans, who had gotten a smudge of boot blacking on his hand.

The corporal looked up and said, "Yes, we'd have soap and candles—"

"And we wouldn't have to drink that foul half-strength coffee," Evans said.

"—and plenty of coffee," the corporal continued, "and the country might very well have a war on its hands. Don't you think it's worth a few sacrifices on our part to preserve the peace?" He broke the embarrassed silence that followed his words by saying quietly, "We'll all be in a better frame of mind once this infernal rain stops."

Timothy hoped that was true. He could hardly believe he'd turned into a worse complainer than Evans.

The rain ended during the night, and the next day the garrison was hard at work again. Timothy forced the end of a crowbar under one of the huge flagstone slabs that paved the parade ground, then leaned his weight on the tool's handle. He was breathing hard by the time he had pried the slab out of the dirt, but there was no time to rest. Now he had to drag the flagstone over to the wheelbarrow Private Hough was loading. This was the hardest work Timothy had ever done, but he knew it was important. The major had ordered the paving removed so any mortar shells that landed on the parade ground would sink into the dirt rather than ricocheting off the hard surface and sending up a shower of rock-chip shrapnel.

Timothy had loosened another flagstone and was dragging it away when Hanson's voice startled him. "Two hands for beginners, I see," the burly private taunted. He gestured to a stack of paving stones with dimensions not much larger than a bread loaf and said, "Maybe those are more your size. Come along, sonny boy. We'll take some of them to Captain Seymour up on the barbette."

I'd better do it so he can't accuse me of being a laggard. Timothy was surprised at how heavy the stones were, but he figured they would be less awkward to carry than the flagstone slabs.

"Load me up," Hanson said, making a cradle of his arms.

Timothy arranged a row of three stones across Hanson's arms and stepped back.

"Don't stop now, sonny boy."

Impressed in spite of himself, Timothy loaded on an additional row of the paving stones and then picked up two to carry himself, painfully conscious that Hanson was watching him, a scornful expression on his face.

As Timothy trudged up the spiral staircase behind him, his load seemed to grow heavier with each step. By the time they reached the top tier, his arms ached almost unbearably. *How can Hanson carry so many?* He had added his paving stones to the small stack beside Captain

Seymour and was rubbing his cramped muscles when Hanson said, "You can unload my stones whenever you're ready, sonny boy."

"I'm ready now," Timothy said, but he took his time doing it, placing each one neatly on the stack before he removed the next.

"Another couple of loads ought to do it," the captain said as he carefully placed the stones in a barrel, one at a time. Noticing Timothy's puzzlement, he explained, "I've packed a cannon cartridge in the center of this, and I'll rig it so when we push the barrel off the parapet, the cartridge will explode at chest height and throw bits of rock every which way."

"Like a gigantic grenade?" Timothy asked.

The officer nodded. "Exactly. Lining the parapet with these ought to take care of any rebels who think they can storm this fort, don't you think?"

"The secessionists may have all the weapons they stole from our armory, but we've got ingenuity," Hanson said.

Captain Seymour turned to Timothy and explained, "He means we can figure out how to invent whatever we need."

"I'll bring up another load of stones," Timothy said. He'd prove to Hanson that he could pitch in as well as anybody. As well as Norris had when he was drummer.

This is the dreariest place I've ever lived, Timothy thought as he climbed to the top tier for a taste of sunshine late the next morning. He hated the way the fort's high walls blocked the winter sun for all but a few hours, hated the sense of gloom that seemed to fill the long passages of cavelike gun rooms.

Timothy felt his spirits lift as soon as he stepped out onto the barbette level. Even in late January, the stone floor and brick parapet held the sun's faint warmth. Enjoying the contrast to the cold dampness of the fort's interior, Timothy wished someone had thought to load a supply of coal on the boats that brought goods over from Moultrie. Already two of the construction sheds on the parade ground had been torn down and their boards used for the cooking fires.

A shout from one of the sentinels stopped Timothy's brooding. A boat with a white flag at the prow was approaching the fort. What was going on? He dashed down the stairs and across the parade ground to join the soldiers streaming out onto the wharf.

Two of Captain Seymour's men came toward him, each carrying a bushel basket. One of them called, "They brought carrots! And cabbages!"

"They're unloading fresh beef back there, too," the other added.

Timothy headed for the end of the wharf to see for himself. Some of the workmen had gone on board the boat and were handing down baskets filled with sweet potatoes, onions, turnips, and more cabbages. This was the best thing that had happened since they came to Sumter! Timothy was thinking that the garrison would feast that night when one of the men on the boat swore under his breath.

Following the man's gaze, Timothy saw the soldiers returning with the baskets of provisions. Behind them came Major Anderson, his expression somber and determined.

The boat's captain greeted the major by name and said, "Our quartermaster sent over some groceries for your garrison, with the governor's compliments, sir."

"Tell him I appreciate his generosity," the major replied, "but the United States Army must purchase its provisions as provided by regulations. I would be most grateful if the governor would use his influence to make it possible for us to do so again."

Silently, the men began to reload the provisions onto the boat, and Timothy strode along the wharf toward the gates. Sending back all that food was even worse than not firing to protect the *Star of the West*! And this time the major couldn't explain his decision by reminding the garrison that his orders were to defend the fort but not take aggressive action. "This time, all he had to do was say 'thank you,'" Timothy muttered.

One of the wives bustled up to him when he reached the parade ground. "Young man, is it true someone from the city sent over a boatload of fresh meat and vegetables and Major Anderson refused to accept it?"

"Yes, ma'am," Timothy said, removing his hat. He didn't trust himself to say anything more.

"Why on earth would he do a thing like that?" the woman asked. "Doesn't he know the children need more than bread and pickled pork?"

Captain Doubleday paused on his way to the officers' quarters. "I couldn't help overhearing your question, madam," he said. "Major Anderson is keenly aware that our rations leave much to be desired, but the United States Army doesn't accept charity from its enemies. I'm sure you wouldn't want to accept favors from the very people who have voted to separate themselves from our sacred union."

The woman raised her chin defiantly. "If it were a choice between my pride and a child's health—*children's* health—I would accept whatever favors I was offered."

"That is as it should be, madam, because above all else, you are a mother," the captain said, "but you must understand that above all else, Major Anderson is a soldier and a representative of the United States government." He bowed and continued on.

The woman's shoulders slumped, and she turned away. Timothy drew a deep breath as he replaced his hat. He was glad the captain didn't know how much he'd been looking forward to a decent meal—and to eating his fill for the first time in weeks.

After mail call that afternoon, Timothy climbed the stairs to the top tier so he wouldn't have to watch the men read their letters from home. He was looking across the water toward the city when someone called his name. He turned and saw Norris hurrying toward him, clutching several envelopes.

"Hey, Donovan! Wait till you hear this—it's a newspaper

article my grandfather sent." He unfolded the clipping and read the first sentence aloud: "'The House of Representatives today voted approval of Major Anderson's bold and patriotic act.'"

"What are they talking about?" Timothy asked, thinking of the major's refusal to fire in defense of the *Star of the West*.

"About moving the garrison from Fort Moultrie to Sumter. Everybody up north thinks we're heroes."

"It was bold, all right," Timothy said, "but what was so patriotic about it?"

Norris found a paragraph farther on in the article and said, "Listen to this: 'On New Year's Day, scores of northern cities fired salvos of artillery for the officers and men who are bravely holding Fort Sumter, defending the honor of their country and their flag.'" He glanced up and said, "Defending the honor and flag of the United States is about the most patriotic thing you can do, Donovan."

"I guess 'salvos of artillery' must be some kind of salute," Timothy said. "Too bad they don't send us supplies instead of shooting off a bunch of cannon in our honor," he grumbled. He couldn't keep from asking, "Did they list our names in the article?"

Norris nodded. "Have a look. They're at the end."

And there they were, in smaller type. Timothy scanned the list of names until he found Musician Timothy Donovan. He'd never had his name in the paper before—and it said *musician* instead of *bugler*. He handed back the clipping and said, "By the way, I noticed something strange this morning—the rebels have painted their patrol boat black."

"They've screened her light, too," Norris said. "Last time I was on guard duty, the sergeant warned us to keep a good eye out for her—he thought the secesh might be planning to let her drift up to our wharf some moonless night and land troops."

"Storm the fort, you mean?" Timothy asked, alarmed. He hadn't forgotten how the rebels had swarmed into Castle Pinckney.

Norris nodded. "Since I heard that, it's been a lot easier to stay alert on watch."

"I guess that's why Captain Foster has the men burying those explosives along the end of the wharf and the walkway outside the gates," Timothy said.

"The captain has them *laying mines*, Donovan."

Timothy hated it when Norris corrected him like that. What difference did it make whether he said "explosives" or "mines"? Whichever word you used, the idea of something so deadly hidden under rocks along the outside wall made him nervous. They weren't supposed to explode unless they were triggered by someone in the fort—but what if one did? He was about to ask why the "barrel grenades" on the parapet weren't enough to keep the secessionists from storming the fort, but he figured there must be some official name for those, too, and he'd already had his vocabulary lesson for the day.

In the mess hall that evening, the conversation was about the announcement Major Anderson had made at afternoon roll call. The men had been silent when they learned that he'd arranged with Charleston authorities to send the wives and children to Fort Hamilton, in New York, but now almost everyone had an opinion on the subject.

"I guess he figures that with fewer mouths to feed, our food stores will hold out longer," Timothy said, unwilling to admit how much he would miss the families—and motherly Mrs. Reilly most of all.

Corporal Rice looked up and said, "It's more likely that the major doesn't want ladies and youngsters subjected to the bombardment when it comes."

Bombardment. The word struck Timothy like a blow. "Bombardment" sounded a lot more dangerous than "defending the fort," and Corporal Rice had said *when* it comes, not *if*.

"With the families gone, it will be easier for all of us to do our duty to our country and our flag," the corporal added.

Timothy forked up a piece of pickled meat and thought of the Stars and Stripes waving high above the fort. Seeing it there always raised his spirits, but he still didn't understand why the men seemed so willing to give up their lives to protect it. If he died in the bombardment, it would be *because of* the flag flying over Sumter, not *for* it.

Timothy was checking his timepiece the next morning when someone said, "Good morning, bugler."

Sergeant Zell. Timothy had managed to avoid him during the three weeks since the *Star of the West* had turned back and the officer had overheard his rash comment about the major. "G—good morning, sergeant," he said, and trying to hide the awkwardness he felt, he asked, "Do you know what boat the families will be leaving on?"

"No, but the major said the South Carolinians will have some sort of vessel at the wharf to pick them up by eight." The sergeant took a deep breath and added quietly, "I shall miss my wife and babe, but we all know it's for the best."

Timothy nodded. "We wouldn't want them here during the bombardment," he said. Five weeks ago, when the women and children had sailed away from Moultrie, he'd wished he could go with them, but now he was more than a bugler playing the role of company clock. Now he was another pair of hands working to make the fort safe. Helping to defend United States property. And—

"What are you thinking about so seriously, sonny boy? As if I couldn't guess."

"If you've already guessed, why did you ask me?" Timothy asked, adding silently, And what's the idea of sneaking up behind me like that?

Hanson gave Timothy a knowing look and said, "I just like to see you squirm, sonny boy."

"You do? Then watch *this*," Timothy said, and he began rotating his shoulders and wiggling his hips. He grinned when Hanson turned and walked away.

Sergeant Zell gave Timothy a long look and said, "I hope you know what you're doing, bugler. I'd rather have Private Hanson for a friend than an enemy."

"He's been my enemy since the first time he laid eyes on me. Nothing I could do would make him my friend." Timothy glanced at his timepiece, then raised his bugle to sound Breakfast Call.

Later, as he helped carry the families' belongings to the boat sent from the city, Timothy thought again of the day the wives and children had left Fort Moultrie. This time, though, they really were leaving—headed first to Charleston, where they would transfer to an oceangoing ship for the trip to New York.

When the boat was loaded, Timothy watched the smallest children cling to their fathers, watched the men trying to be cheerful and the women trying to be brave. He felt a hollow sadness, partly for the loved ones about to be separated and partly for himself. It was three years ago today—February 1, 1858—that his mother had died.

• • •

Without the women and children at the family tables, the mess hall seemed strangely empty at noon. The husbands all seemed ill at ease, as if they weren't sure where they should sit now, and Timothy noticed that Sergeant Zell looked even more solemn than usual.

Corporal Rice called to him, saying, "We have room at our table, sergeant," and Timothy slid over to make a space for him, moving farther away from Hanson in the process.

Once the sergeant was settled on the bench, there was a moment of strained silence, as if no one knew quite what to say, and then several men began to speak at once. When they all fell silent again, Sergeant Zell said, "It's not like there's been a death, you know." Repeating what he'd told Timothy earlier, he added, "I'll miss my little family, but it's for the best."

Hanson nodded. "Now that we don't have to worry about the safety of the ladies and youngsters, it will be easier for us to be steadfast about our duty." He glanced over at Timothy and asked, "Do you need someone to explain what 'steadfast' means, sonny boy?"

"I'd like you to explain it to me, Private Hanson," Timothy said. "What *does* it mean?"

A look of surprise flashed across Hanson's face. "It means faithful," he said. "Faithful and loyal. You understand those words, don't you?"

"Yes, but there's something I don't understand," Timothy said. "How did having the families here keep you from being faithful and loyal? I don't think the ladies and children made anyone else unfaithful or disloyal."

"That's enough, Bugler Donovan," Corporal Rice said quietly. "We all know that Private Hanson is one of our most faithful and loyal men." He turned from Timothy to the sergeant and asked, "How long do you think the families' trip north will take?"

Timothy was chagrined that Corporal Rice had reprimanded him, but he couldn't help feeling pleased that for once the corporal had come to Hanson's rescue instead of his.

In the quarters that evening, Private Hough mused, "Already, Sumter seems a grim place indeed without the ladies and their bairns."

There were murmurs of agreement, and then Timothy asked, "Was it the Brothers Grimm or Hans Christian Andersen who wrote the 'The Steadfast Tin Soldier'?" The men who had heard the exchange between him and Private Hanson in the mess hall chuckled, and Timothy sensed Hanson's glowering rage. *This is twice in one day I've riled him.*

Evans grinned and said, "Hanson, you may not be one of the Grimm Brothers, but right now you look like a grim soldier."

"Hey, we can call him the Steadfast Grim Soldier," Timothy said. A burst of laughter followed his words, and soldiers who had been immersed in a card game on the far side of the room wanted to be let in on the joke.

"Tell them, bugler," Evans urged.

Timothy said, "It's not a joke—it's a nickname Private Hanson has earned for himself. From now on you can call him the Steadfast Grim Soldier."

The laughter stopped when Hanson roared, "That's *enough!*" Shaking with rage, he said, "Any man who calls me anything but my own name will regret it. And *you*"— he pointed at Timothy—"you will regret trying to make sport of me." He headed for the door, and a sobered group of men turned back to the feeble light of their makeshift lamps.

I didn't just try to make sport of him—without Corporal Rice here to stop me, I succeeded in doing it. And Hanson's empty threat doesn't scare me one bit.

Long before the steamship taking the families from Charleston to New York neared the mouth of the harbor, the entire garrison was waiting on Fort Sumter's parapet.

"Look there," Evans said. He pointed to a barge loaded with sandbags that was moving slowly past the fort. "I think it's criminal that Major Anderson allows it," he continued. "The rebels go back and forth under our very noses, fortifying their artillery batteries on Morris Island, and we sit here, our guns idle, just watching 'em." He cracked his knuckles and added, "We ought to blast those batteries right out of the harbor before the secesh have a chance to use their guns against us."

There were murmurs of agreement, and then the shout went up, "Here they come!" and all eyes were on the ship steaming toward them. The men waved their caps in great, sweeping arcs and cheered as it passed the fort, and the wives let their handkerchiefs flutter in the wind.

One of the barbette guns fired a salute, startling Timothy even though he'd been expecting it, and Hanson said scornfully, "What's the matter, sonny boy? Did the big noise scare you?" Timothy pretended not to hear. He waved and cheered, walking along the parapet with the others, keeping pace with the ship.

When the flutter of handkerchiefs could no longer be seen and the cheers had died away, the unmarried men began to leave the barbette tier. "Come along, bugler," Corporal Rice said. "Leave the husbands to watch the ship out of sight and wonder if they'll ever see their loved ones again."

Timothy followed the corporal down the winding stairs, surprised at the sadness in the man's voice, wondering if he, too, had lost someone dear to him. Someone he missed but never spoke of.

"We haven't had a meal like this for six weeks," Timothy said as he finished the noon meal the next day. "Fresh beef with gravy, carrots, and potatoes."

"It's good, all right," Evans agreed. "What there is of it."

Timothy wiped up the last of the gravy on his plate with a piece of bread, aware that he could have eaten that much again. But he hadn't had a second helping of anything since he'd lived at home with Ma. He put that thought aside and asked, "How come the secesh finally decided to let us buy groceries?"

"One of the major's friends in Charleston made arrangements to buy fresh meat and vegetables for us. He has it all delivered to Fort Johnson, and then brought here to Sumter," Corporal Rice explained.

"First the secesh tell us to pick up our mail at Fort Johnson, which saves us rowing all the way to the city for it, and now they deliver our groceries to our wharf," Timothy said. "I don't understand it."

Sergeant Zell said, "They're trying to avoid trouble. Men wearing the uniform of the United States Army wouldn't be welcome in the city, and if any of our men were set upon by a crowd, we would have to take some kind of action."

"We would take vengeance," Evans declared, his eyes hard.

Sergeant Zell turned to Timothy and said, "I think you can see why it's best that our men stay away from the city, bugler."

"And yet any secessionist who wants to can come and poke around our fort," Evans complained, his voice rising. "Remember that last group of workmen who came here insisting that Captain Foster still owed them wages? Well, I stopped one of 'em from going into the powder magazine. If you ask me, no one from the city should be allowed inside our walls. They're spies, every one of 'em."

"You're forgetting that the gentleman who is responsible for the fine meal you just enjoyed had visited the major here at the fort," Sergeant Zell said, his deep voice a welcome contrast to Evans's nasal twang.

Timothy thought of how Major Anderson had refused the boatload of fresh food sent over as a gift several weeks before. Hadn't he said something about how the garrison had to purchase provisions according to regulations? Maybe the major agreed to this new arrangement his friend had set up because the army was paying for it. Or maybe—

"A meal like this lifts the spirits," Private Hough said, and everyone within earshot raised his coffee cup and said, "Hear! Hear!" Everyone except Sergeant Zell.

He misses his wife and baby, Timothy thought, and for the first time, he felt anger toward the secessionists rather than fear of what they might do. It was their fault that the men here were separated from their families, their fault that the garrison was cooped up in this cold, gloomy place instead of living comfortably at Fort Moultrie. Timothy frowned. We have more reason to hate the secesh than they do to hate us, he thought, but I can't imagine wanting to "set upon" them or "take vengeance" against them.

Keeping my eyes and ears open helps me find things out, but it doesn't help me understand them.

CHAPTER SEVEN

THE BEST THING about being a bugler, Timothy thought, was knowing that when he sounded his first call each morning, he'd be waking Private Hanson from a deep sleep. Even halfway down the hall, he could hear the man's snores. He felt his way down the stairs and along a hallway to the outside door and stepped onto the parade ground.

At the base of the flagpole Timothy raised the bugle to his lips, but instead of sounding the notes of the call, his cheeks puffed out and he felt a fierce pressure in his ears. *Something's wrong with my bugle.* He reached as far as he could into the bell end of his instrument but felt only the smooth coolness of metal. His sense of urgency growing by the second, he shook the bugle vigorously, but nothing fell out and there was no telltale rattle. With trembling hands, he removed the mouthpiece and poked a finger into the tube. Nothing. Someone—and he could guess who—must have rammed a wad of paper so far in that it couldn't be reached from either end. Somehow, he had to dislodge it.

Timothy took a huge breath, put his mouth over the tube, and blew with all his might. A rush of air whooshed from the bell end, and he stared down at the instrument. *Then it has to be the mouthpiece—but how is that possible?* He ran a finger around the inside of it. *Wax! With all the candles gone, where would anybody get— Wait a minute! Hanson always drips sealing wax on the flaps of his envelopes—as if he's afraid somebody might steam them open and read what he's written.*

"You'll pay for this, Private Hanson," Timothy muttered. Without wasting any more time, he raced back to the quarters, felt his way down the hall to the kitchen, and cried, "Quick! I need hot water!" The startled cook pointed to a steaming cauldron, and Timothy filled a nearby ladle and dropped the mouthpiece into it. While he watched, the wax plug melted and formed a greasy smear on the surface of the water. But how could he lift out the mouthpiece without the whole thing becoming coated with a thin layer of wax?

Behind him the cook said, "Bugler, if you tell me what you're trying to do, maybe I can help." He listened to Timothy's explanation and then gestured to a bucket. "If you leave the mouthpiece in the ladle and lower the whole thing into that cold water, the wax will harden on the surface," he said.

Holding his breath, Timothy did as he was told. "It worked!" he cried, lifting off the skim of wax and then fishing out the mouthpiece. He reached for the towel the cook offered, dried the mouthpiece thoroughly, and twisted it onto the bugle. "Thanks for your help, Private Reilly," Timothy called over his shoulder.

He ran all the way to the flagpole on the parade

ground. For the first time since he'd arrived in Charleston Harbor, he was late! Timothy raised his bugle and sounded the call.

It was the worst he'd played since he was a beginner. One of his high notes squawked, and he ran out of wind and had to breathe before the end of a phrase. Mortified, he muttered, "Hanson will pay for this." But it looked like *he* might pay for it, too—Sergeant Zell was headed toward him, his expression dark as a storm cloud. Timothy's mouth went dry.

Frowning down at him, the sergeant said, "Sounds like you need a refresher course, bugler. And a lesson on the importance of performing your duties in a timely manner. What do you have to say for yourself?"

"I—I'm sorry, sergeant. Something was wrong with my bugle."

"Don't make excuses, Donovan. What could possibly go wrong with a bugle?"

Somehow, Timothy managed to keep his voice steady. "A plug of sealing wax had closed the mouthpiece, and I had to melt it out."

The sergeant gave him a long look and then mused, "Sealing wax, eh? I know of only two people here who use it, and one of them is Major Anderson. I'd say this was the work of the Steadfast Grim Soldier."

How does Sergeant Zell know about that?

"I want you to make very sure nothing like this happens again, bugler."

"I will, Sergeant." From now on, he'd sleep with the bugle under his blanket. Hanson wouldn't get another chance to sabotage his instrument.

By the time for the next call, Timothy had calmed himself, and he played with his usual precision. But the grins on the men's faces as they assembled on the parade ground told him he wouldn't be allowed to forget his humiliating performance earlier. Their joshing started as soon as the company was dismissed.

"Hey bugler, next time you let us sleep in, make it a bit longer!"

"Yeah, that wasn't near long enough to make up for abusing our ears like that, bugler."

"Come on, it weren't you makin' that terrible racket earlier, was it?"

Humiliated, Timothy turned and walked away, but Norris caught up to him. "Yeah, Donovan—who got hold of your bugle this morning?" he asked, grinning.

His voice shaking, Timothy retorted, "You ought to be asking who got hold of it last night."

"So that's why Hanson looked like the cat who swallowed the canary!"

"I need you to help me figure out a way to get back at him," Timothy said after he'd told Norris what happened.

"If you're smart, you'll forget about that idea."

"*Forget* about it?"

Norris nodded. "You got what you deserved, Donovan," he said. "It looks like Hanson decided to show you what it feels like to be embarrassed in front of the whole garrison."

"Now wait a minute! I never—"

Cutting him short, Norris said, "Anything that happens

in this fort is public knowledge in minutes, and you know it."

"Well, what Hanson did is a lot worse than making a wisecrack."

"I think he's warning you to leave him alone, Donovan."

That was a new idea to Timothy. "Well, he doesn't scare me. I'll find a way to get even with him."

"And then he'll have to do something to you that's worse still. If you find that bugle of yours wrapped around the flagpole some morning, you'll know why," Norris said.

Timothy's hand moved to the instrument that hung at his side. "I'll wind the cord around my wrist at night so he can't touch it without waking me," he said. "Whether you help me or not, I'm going to make Hanson pay for tampering with my bugle." After all, what could he possibly do next that would be half as bad as what he'd already done?

This is the worst job I've been given yet, Timothy thought as he stood outside the powder magazine with the five others who had been assigned to sew cartridge bags and fill them with black powder.

"Any questions?" asked the young lieutenant who had been instructing them. "All right then. Remember, without cartridges, our guns are useless."

Timothy felt a chill. Rebel guns were aimed at Sumter from all directions, and the fort's guns might be useless? Why hadn't somebody noticed the shortage of cartridge bags two weeks ago, before the families were sent away, so the wives could have done the sewing? He barely heard the lieutenant ask each of them to make sure he was wearing nothing metal that might cause a spark and set off an explosion. "No coins in your pockets?" the officer persisted. "What about that timepiece of yours, bugler?"

Sheepishly, Timothy took it from his pocket and handed it over.

"I'll leave this in the guardroom for you, along with your bugle," the lieutenant said. "Now go inside and get started. Everything you'll need is ready for you—cloth, needles and thread, scales to weigh the powder charge to fill the finished bags. And remember, each of you is responsible for making sure your needle isn't misplaced. Those six needles are all that stand between a successful defense of this fort and surrender to the secessionists."

The little group filed through the entrance of the powder magazine, a small compartment at one end of the building that housed the officers' quarters, mess hall, storerooms, and offices. Once inside, Norris said, "Now I know why the quartermaster was taking a stack of new shirts out of the storeroom this morning—somebody's cut them up for us to stitch into cartridge bags."

"So not only are we short of cartridges, we're short of what we need to make them with—including needles," Evans said.

Timothy had never been inside the magazine before, and he glanced around before he took his sewing supplies from the counter along one wall. "At least there's plenty of powder," he said, eyeing the kegs stacked in ceiling-high rows.

"More than enough to blow us all to Kingdom Come

and save those rebs the trouble," Evans grumbled.

Why doesn't he shut up? Timothy sat on one of the benches and threaded the needle, something he had often done for his mother. He set to work, carefully doubling back on his stitches the way the lieutenant had showed them, so there would be no chance of the powder leaking out. Powder that could blow them all to—

"I hate to be in here sewing when men like Hanson have been carrying up solid shot for those guns we winched up to the top tier—and when they've been doing it for sport, after a full day's work," Evans said.

"We didn't 'winch' them up, we used a block and tackle," Norris said under his breath.

What a know-it-all.

"Do you have any idea how much each piece of that spherical shot weighs?" Evans went on.

Without looking up, Norris said, "One hundred twenty-eight pounds."

Timothy had watched the men shoulder those huge cannonballs and head for the stair towers with them, and all he could think of was that he couldn't manage anything heavier than three paving stones. "Too bad the guns that fire that heavy shot weren't in place when the *Star of the West* was trying to get here last month," he said. "*They* could have reached that battery on Morris Island."

But Evans ignored Timothy's attempt to change the subject. "Hanson will never let any of us live it down that we're *sewing*," he said. "Especially you, Donovan."

"If Hanson mocks you, bugler, just tell him that working with black powder is a dangerous job that deserves respect," said Corporal O'Brian, the band's drummer and the oldest member of the garrison.

That didn't make Timothy feel any better, though he knew O'Brian meant well.

Suddenly, a musket shot rang out. Timothy gave a start, and the others laughed uproariously—until they saw O'Brian struggle to his feet and leave the powder magazine at surprising speed.

"He must think they'll be ordering him to beat the Long Roll," the cornet player said. The cartridge detail worked in tense silence, but instead of a drum calling the artillerists to their battle stations, they heard sounds of confusion from the parade ground as men tried to find out what had happened. It wasn't long before O'Brian returned to the magazine.

"That shot was a sentinel firing at the rebels' guard boat when it came too near our wharf," he explained. "Major Anderson is sending a messenger to the city with a protest."

"All writing and no action—that's our major," Evans complained, jabbing his needle through the cloth.

"Last time I was assigned to the mail boat, one of the rebels at Fort Johnson told me Major Anderson sends a report off to Washington almost every day, but he never hears a word back from the capital," the band's cornet player announced.

"I wonder what the major puts in those reports of his," Evans mused, pulling his thread tight.

Timothy said, "I hope he asks for the government to send us provisions—including more needles."

"Not more *needles*—more cartridges," Evans said, and raising his voice above the chorus of agreement, he added, "I didn't join the army to be a tailor. I joined to fire artillery guns at the enemy—to batter their forts and scatter their forces."

An artillerist who hadn't spoken before looked up from his work and said, "Then you'd better sew faster, Evans, 'cause like the lieutenant said, without cartridge bags, we won't none of us be firing any artillery."

That should shut Evans up for a while, Timothy thought. He threaded his needle easily in spite of the dim light in the magazine and began to stitch again. When you came right down to it, this wasn't such a bad job. It beat hard labor, and it kept him out of Private Hanson's way.

Timothy felt the usual stir of anger at the memory of the terrible morning a week ago when his bugle had been sabotaged. Most of the men had finally tired of kidding him about it, but they seemed to be watching him as if they were wondering when—and how—he would seek vengeance on Hanson. Come to think of it, Hanson seemed to be keeping an eye on him, too.

Timothy's mind was even busier than his fingers. *Maybe that's the answer—Hanson expects me to get even, so he has to keep up his guard, but until I strike back at him, he has no reason to strike at me again. All I have to do is keep Hanson guessing, keep him waiting and wondering. I can win without doing anything at all!*

And that's just as well, Timothy thought, since I haven't been able to figure out how to make Hanson pay for what he did—until now.

TIMOTHY STARED at Hanson across the mess hall table, willing him to look up. At last he did, and when their eyes met, Timothy let what he hoped was a mysterious smile play around his lips for a moment before he looked down at his plate. He sensed that Hanson was still watching him, so he glanced up again.

"How come you're always looking at me like that, sonny boy?"

"No reason, Private Hanson. No reason at all." When Timothy looked away this time, the smile he suppressed was a real one. His plan was working better than he could have imagined. For more than two weeks now, he'd kept Hanson on edge, sure that he was up to something—and now the other men thought he was, too. Timothy could almost feel their expectation in the sudden silence.

At the next table, the officers were talking quietly, and he strained his ears, listening. Maybe he could surprise Norris with a bit of news when he came off guard duty.

"This is an unfortunate turn of events," Captain Doubleday was saying. "These rebel militiamen are amateurs, but with the new Confederate government sending Pierre Beauregard to take command, that's likely to change."

"He'll whip them into shape," Major Anderson agreed. "Beauregard was my student at West Point, and I've never known a better artilleryman." There was a brief silence before the other officers joined the conversation.

"I've counted a few new batteries along the shore—"

"And the rebels seem to be drilling harder than ever—"

"—boats loaded with building material passing here any time you look, day or—"

"—and hundreds of slaves working around the clock to protect their batteries with sandbags and bales of—"

Timothy was glad when one of the men at his table began to wonder aloud what Lincoln had said in his March 4 inaugural address.

"When I rowed over to Fort Johnson to get the mail, one of the secesh told me it was warlike, all about how the government's going to take back its forts and other property in the Confederate states," Private Hough said.

Evans snorted. "Then the government's going to be busy, because Sumter and that fort off the Florida coast are the only United States property I know of that these Confederates haven't helped themselves to."

Ignoring that comment, Corporal Rice pulled something from his pocket and said, "One of my friends in Charleston sent me a copy of Lincoln's speech in today's mail, and—"

"Well, read it to us, man!" Hanson urged.

Surprised at how eager he was to hear what the new president had said, Timothy watched the corporal unfold the newspaper clipping.

"Listen to this part, where he's talking to the South," Corporal Rice said, and he began to read. "'We must not be enemies. Though passion may have strained, it must not break our bonds of affection. The mystic chords of memory, stretching from every battlefield and patriot grave, to every living heart and hearthstone, all over this broad land, will yet swell the chorus of the Union, when again touched, as surely they will be, by the better angels of our nature.'"

Listening to the president's words, Timothy felt the same stirring of emotion that had filled him the day of the flag-raising ceremony. "How could anybody think that was warlike?" he asked when the corporal finished reading.

"That was only one paragraph, sonny boy," Hanson said. "Read us the whole speech, Corporal Rice."

The men at the table listened intently as the corporal read, and when he'd finished, Sergeant Zell said, "I don't think any part of the president's speech was warlike, Hanson. President Lincoln even came right out and said he wasn't going to interfere with slavery."

"You aren't reading between the lines the way the secesh did, sergeant," Hanson argued. "Lincoln said he wouldn't interfere in the states where they already *have* slavery, but that's not the point. The South wants people in the territories and any future states to be able to own slaves. And you must have missed what Lincoln said about revolutionaries. Read that part to us again, Rice."

Timothy couldn't help but be impressed. Hanson was almost as smart as he was mean.

Corporal Rice ran his finger down the column of print until he found what he was looking for. "It says here that 'acts of violence, within any State or States, against the authority of the United States, are insurrectionary or revolutionary, according to the circumstances.'"

"That's not warlike?" Hanson's voice was triumphant. "What do you think governments do when somebody threatens a revolution?" He glanced around the table, and his eyes stopped at Timothy. "What do *you* think they do, sonny boy?"

"They put a stop to it." Timothy thought of how the British had tried to put a stop to the revolution of the American colonists, thought of how they had failed.

"That's right," Hanson said. "You're not as dumb as you look."

"Pretty soon you might find out that I'm a lot smarter than you think. A lot more clever, anyway."

In the charged silence that followed his words, Timothy was afraid he had gone too far. He was grateful when Corporal Rice turned everyone's attention back to the president's inaugural speech, saying thoughtfully, "It might have been easier for the government to put a stop to this 'insurrection,' as Lincoln calls it, when South Carolina was the only state rebelling. Before six more cotton-growing states left the Union and this southern Confederacy was formed."

"What do you think the rebels are going to do, corporal?" Timothy asked. "About us, that is."

"The way I see it, they have only two choices—to attack the fort, or to starve us out."

Timothy stared at his empty plate and wondered if the choice had already been made. But Evans said, "The way they've been drilling, I'd say they plan to attack."

For a moment, no one spoke. Timothy figured the men were all thinking about the practice shots the rebel artillerists fired from Fort Moultrie and their batteries around the harbor—and about the shortage of cartridges that kept the Sumter garrison from doing the same.

Sergeant Zell broke the silence. "I'd choose death in battle over starvation, any day."

"Death in defense of our flag," Evans agreed.

But I don't want to die! I never swore to defend the flag with my bugle.

THE NEXT MORNING Timothy was on his way across the parade ground, headed to the powder magazine, when he heard the day's first shot fired from a nearby battery. Moments later, he heard the unmistakable whistle of an approaching shell. Terrified, he ran for the safety of the closest gun room, but instead of the expected crash of metal into solid brick, he heard a splash.

One of the sentinels posted on the parapet shouted down, "It hit near the wharf! They fired it from the battery on Cummings Point." The men dashed to their battle stations even before Corporal O'Brian began to beat the Long Roll. From the safety of the gun room, Timothy watched some of the artillerists race up the stairway to the barbette tier with Norris in the lead, while others began to aim the guns on the first tier toward Cummings Point.

This was it—the attack they'd been expecting. Scarcely breathing, Timothy waited for Major Anderson to give his men the order to fire—but instead, he headed for his office.

One of the men cursed and asked, "What's he waiting for?"

Captain Doubleday joined them, and Timothy heard him say, "At ease, men. The major is writing to the Confederate commander on the Point to demand an explanation."

"An explanation! Those secesh just *fired* on us!"

"Apparently he wants to make sure it wasn't a mistake," the captain explained, his face expressionless.

The artillerists muttered among themselves, and Timothy wondered if the major thought the rebels might have built their forts and batteries by accident.

"Hey," called one of the sentinels. "Somebody's rowing over here under a white flag."

Then maybe it *was* a mistake, Timothy thought. When he saw the sergeant of the guard leave the guardhouse and slip through the narrow opening in the gate, he dashed after him. Outside the fort's confining walls, he crossed the paved walkway to the wharf.

By the time the oarsmen brought the rowboat alongside the wharf, a crowd of curious soldiers and laborers had gathered. At the prow of the boat sat a soldier who looked younger than Norris. He held out an envelope to the sergeant and said, "A message for Major Anderson, from the commander at Cummings Point."

The sergeant took the sealed paper and handed it to Timothy. "Take this to the major, Bugler Donovan."

He hurried to Major Anderson's office and found him at his desk, writing. Timothy hesitated at the open door, then cleared his throat and said, "A message from Cummings Point, sir." He gave his best salute, and as the major returned it, a look of relief spread across his face.

"Thank God I didn't order the men to fire," he said after he had read the note. "The rebel commander has sent an explanation and an apology. Inform Captain Doubleday at once, bugler."

"Yes, sir!" Timothy saluted again and backed out of the room. It was hard for him to imagine apologizing for firing on your enemy. But then, it was hard to imagine the United States and South Carolina—or any of the other former states—as enemies.

After delivering the major's message, Timothy passed a group of artillerists who were still muttering and grumbling about not being allowed to fire. "So what did the note say, sonny boy?" Hanson called.

"The rebels sent over an apology," Timothy told him. "I think it was an accident."

"Next time it won't be no accident," said a private from Captain Seymour's company.

Hanson agreed. "And next time it won't be an apology they send over here. It will be a demand for us to surrender the fort."

Timothy waited until Hanson looked his way again, and when he did, Timothy raised one eyebrow and held the man's gaze for a moment before he headed toward the powder magazine. Behind him, he heard the other private say, "That bugler looks like he's up to something, don't he?"

His plan was turning out to be more successful than he could have imagined. What could be better than keeping

Hanson constantly on edge without running any risk of retaliation? Timothy was still congratulating himself when he reached the magazine, where the five others assigned to cartridge bag detail were already at work. Before they could ask about the major's message, he announced, "The rebel commander sent over an apology and an explanation."

Evans scoffed, "Amateurs! I'll bet they left live ammunition in that gun at the end of yesterday's drill."

"I hear that most of their artillerists are cadets from the military school in Charleston," Norris said without glancing up from his stitching.

"That's right," Corporal O'Brian agreed, reaching for another rectangle of cloth. "They're boys not much older than Bugler Donovan."

Timothy concentrated on threading his needle. He didn't want to think about the young cadets firing artillery guns, about boys who were soldiers instead of buglers or drummers.

That night, most of the conversation was about the shot fired from Cummings Point.

"I say we missed our chance. We're as ready as we're ever going to be, and every day they're improving their defenses—"

"—*and* their aim—"

"—while we're running low on food and supplies."

"—and we sit here and let them do it."

Private Evans raised his voice and announced, "I say the major should have seized the initiative. Sumter was fired on, and he should have ordered us to fire back. I don't know what's the matter with him."

"Major Anderson knows that more is at stake here than this fort and our garrison," Corporal Rice said, interrupting the chorus of agreement. The room fell silent, and he continued. "What happens here in this harbor will affect the course of history. The eyes of the whole country—both countries, if you will—are on Charleston Harbor. If the fate of this fort can be settled peacefully—"

"It won't be," Hanson interrupted. "Sumter has become a symbol for both sides, and it's a matter of pride now. Lincoln can't give it up because he announced in his inauguration speech that he intends to keep it, and the Confederates can't back down after months of preparations to take it by force."

Timothy forced himself to ask, "How much longer do you think it will be before the shooting starts?"

"Hard to say. Neither side wants to be the one that fires the first shot. The one that gets the blame for starting a war."

A war? I thought the secesh were going to bombard the fort, and one way or another, that would settle things. Timothy hoped Hanson was wrong about the war, but he understood now why the major was so reluctant to order his men to fire—and why the Confederates had rowed out to the fort with an apology for the shell that had hit near the wharf.

But if neither side would give up, and neither side would fire first— How much longer were they going to be here, anyway? Sometimes it seemed that the fort's walls were closing in on him, and every day he was a little hungrier, every night a bit more miserable as he lay shivering in the unheated living quarters. Timothy wished the major had never brought the garrison to Sumter, wished they'd stayed at Fort Moultrie and turned it over to the rebels without a fight.

Just look at the fix Major Anderson's "bold and patriotic act" had got them into.

A few days later, Timothy was heading for the powder magazine when Hanson called, "Going to join the other seamstresses, sonny boy? Maybe we should change your name to Nimble Fingers."

"Maybe we should change yours to Sausage Fingers," Timothy called back.

Some laborers working nearby laughed, and one of them repeated, "Sausage Fingers. That's a good one."

Timothy's mocking grin faded when Hanson started toward him, his face flushed with anger. "Didn't I tell you—"

"What's going on here, soldiers?"

At the sound of Sergeant Zell's voice, Timothy's knees went weak with relief. The sergeant looked from him to Hanson, and when neither of them answered, he said, "Aren't your orders to help mount those extra guns facing Cummings Point, private?"

"I'm on my way now, sergeant."

When Hanson was out of hearing distance, Sergeant

Zell turned to Timothy. "I'm disappointed in you, Donovan. After your last misadventure with Hanson, you assured me nothing of this sort would happen again."

"I meant that I wouldn't be late sounding a call because Hanson had tampered with my bugle. It's never out of my sight—except when I'm working in the powder magazine, and then I leave it in the guardroom."

"Since you're standing empty-handed just outside the magazine, I take it you're on the way in there now, so you'd better move along."

"Yes, sergeant." Shaken, Timothy turned away. He could almost feel those sausage fingers closing on his arm. It was worth a reprimand from Sergeant Zell to escape Hanson's anger.

Timothy stepped inside the powder magazine and pretended not to notice when Evans looked up and gave him a sly grin. But when Norris said, "You just don't learn, do you, Donovan?" Timothy glared at him and said, "He started it."

"Better get to work, bugler," Corporal O'Brian said quietly.

Timothy seated himself on a bench and reached for one of the cloth rectangles and a spool of thread.

At first, no one spoke when the morning stillness was broken by rhythmic firing from the direction of Sullivan's Island, but finally Timothy looked up from his stitching and said, "I wonder what they're celebrating this time." March wasn't half over yet, and the rebels had fired two salutes already this month—first when Texas joined the

Confederacy, and again when the new Confederate commander arrived to take charge of the forts and batteries in the harbor.

"They've fired off at least a dozen shots, so the salute isn't because another state voted to secede," Norris said.

He means it isn't because *Virginia* voted to secede, Timothy thought. Norris always insisted his home state would never leave the Union, pointing out that when the voters chose their representatives to the Secession Convention that was meeting to decide the matter, Unionist delegates outnumbered secessionists two to one. But Timothy suspected that his friend wouldn't rest easy until the Convention had made its decision—and unlike the state conventions in the Deep South, it seemed in no hurry to do so.

"It must be nice to have enough cartridges to fire off a salute anytime you want to," Evans said, his voice bitter.

Timothy added another completed bag to the pile in front of him. If he had his way, they'd forget about salutes and save their cartridges for defending the fort. He'd hated it when Sumter had fired its thirty-four-gun salute in honor of Lincoln's inauguration a week ago, and he'd found the last seven shots galling. Firing off a shot for each of the states loyal to the Union was one thing, but having his cartridge bags being blown to bits for the seven states that had seceded was almost more than he could stand. Wouldn't their band concert have been celebration enough?

"This one must be a hundred-gun salute," Corporal

O'Brian said, "because they've fired more than fifty already."

The evenly spaced shots were making Timothy feel edgy. He wished he could stop stitching and press his hands over his ears to mute the sound. When the harbor fell silent at last, he heaved a sigh of relief and said, "I don't think I could have stood that much longer." But the words were barely out of his mouth when a gun from one of the other forts began to fire. It was another salute.

When it finally stopped, Corporal O'Brian said, "That one was only fifty."

Only fifty? Timothy's head throbbed. He joined the chorus of groans that arose when still another rebel battery began to fire.

It was a welcome distraction when Corporal Rice peered into the powder magazine and said, "Bugler Donovan, the mail boat just docked." Timothy scrambled to his feet and ran to get his instrument from the safety of the guardroom.

As he sounded Mail Call, the men gathered on the parade ground, eager for word from the outside world. Lowering his bugle, Timothy realized that Fort Sumter had become his whole world. There was nothing for him beyond this acre of parade ground and the gun rooms and living quarters that enclosed it. Nothing, and no one.

When the mail bag was empty, Norris had his usual handful of mail—and a newspaper. "How do you decide which letter to open first?" Timothy asked.

"Easy. The one from my grandfather in Philadelphia,

because he always writes real news instead of going on and on about his neighbors and the weather," Norris said. "Listen to what he wrote this time: 'The northern papers are still full of articles about the brave men at Fort Sumter who have been abandoned by their government. Some of the editorial writers call for the president to send supplies, and others demand that he surrender the fort.'" Norris glanced up from the page and said, "That's what Lincoln's decided to do, if we're to believe the headline in today's Charleston paper."

"Surrender the fort?" Timothy echoed. *If the major surrenders the fort, there won't be a war—or even a battle. I can stop worrying about the bombardment.*

Norris nodded. "Apparently all the salutes this morning are celebrating the news that the U.S. government has decided to give up Sumter." There was a chorus of questions from the artillerists who had clustered around to hear more, and Norris scanned the newspaper article before he answered. At last he looked up and said, "This says the garrison will be evacuated 'as a military necessity.'"

"Whatever that means," said Private Hough.

"I'll tell you what it means," Evans said. "It means somebody in Washington finally caught on that there's no way we can defend ourselves against all the guns facing us."

"Speaking of guns," Timothy said, "I think they've finally finished the salute."

Sergeant Zell joined them long enough to say, "All right, men. Back to your duties."

Evans frowned. "But if we're going to evacuate the fort—"

"The major has received no orders to that effect," the sergeant interrupted, "and until he does, we are to continue our efforts to strengthen Sumter and our ability to defend it."

The cartridge bag detail headed back to the powder magazine, and Evans grumbled, "It doesn't make much sense for us to keep on improving the fort if the Confederates are going to be the ones to benefit from it. Not much sense to make cartridge bags we'll never use, either."

Timothy glared at him. "That newspaper article could be a rumor, you know. A rumor the Confederates are hoping we'll believe so we'll let up on our preparations and it will be easier for them to defeat us." Evans had no reply to that, and Timothy added, "Besides, we have to follow our orders."

Timothy was glad to be assigned to a work detail on the parade ground later that week. He emptied his wheelbarrow load of dirt and paused to watch the soldiers and laborers bank it against the wall of the barracks. "I still don't see why Captain Foster wants us to do this," he said.

Corporal Rice glanced up and said, "It's to protect the building from artillery fire from the batteries at Cummings Point—their mortar shells will sail right over our outer wall. This fort was built to withstand shelling from an enemy's naval vessels, not from land batteries," he added.

And I thought we'd be safe at Sumter. No wonder the major is making us keep working until he has an official order to evacuate the fort.

"We're going to need more dirt," the corporal reminded him.

Timothy rolled his wheelbarrow back to where several men were removing another layer of soil from the parade ground. He hoped the corporal didn't think he was a slacker.

"I wonder what they're celebrating over there now," Norris said, straightening up to listen to the strains of band music that wafted across the water from the city.

One of the laborers working nearby paused long enough to say, "Don't you recognize an Irish melody when you hear one? It's Saint Patrick's Day. Your friend Donovan should have been able to tell you that."

"No wonder the band has been practicing all those Irish tunes," Norris said. "I'll bet we'll have a concert tonight." He looked up when one of the sentinels shouted something from the parapet. "Did you hear what he said?" he asked.

"It sounded like 'Company's coming from the city,'" Timothy told him.

Some of the men were running toward the gates, but Timothy and Norris raced up to the top tier and stood a respectful distance from where Captain Doubleday and one of the lieutenants were peering through their spyglasses.

"Civilians," the captain announced. "A right cheery

group, if you ask me. Drunk, probably."

"It looks like they're bringing something over here," the lieutenant said. "They've got some boxes in the back of the boat. Did you notice that, sir?"

Captain Doubleday trained his glass on the boat again. "Let's go down to the wharf and have a closer look, lieutenant." Timothy and Private Norris waited until the two officers had started down the stairs before they followed.

The wharf was filled with soldiers and laborers, and the crowd parted to let the officers pass, then closed behind them. Timothy wasn't tall enough to see anything, but he could hear singing.

"Lovely tenor voice," someone said as the boatman's song became more distinct, but Timothy was more interested in what might be in the boxes the lieutenant had mentioned. The singing stopped, and the mass of bodies on the wharf swayed forward a little. The sound of cheering rippled toward Timothy, and then the word was passed along: In honor of St. Patrick's Day, the boaters had brought wine and cigars for the officers.

A private hollered, "Why not some ale and a bit of pipe tobacco for the enlisted men?" There was a chorus of agreement, and in a fake Irish accent someone else called, "Sure and you should of brought a wee something for the rest of us, laddies!"

Timothy joined in the laughter, glad for what the tipsy revelers *had* brought them: a few minutes of distraction, a break from worry and work. While he waited his turn to file through the small door cut into one of the fort's huge gates, Timothy glanced up at the "shooting galleries" that extended beyond the parapet—another example of the officers' ingenuity. If any rebels managed to get this close to the fort's walls, they would either be picked off by marksmen stationed above them or blown apart by the barrel grenades.

So far, though, all the rebel visitors had come in peace—and only a few at a time. "It doesn't make sense," Timothy said. "All around the harbor, the secesh have been working on offensive fortifications so they can attack us, and then these fellows from the city row out here— more than three miles—with presents for our officers."

"They must be feeling generous now that they know we'll be leaving any day," Norris said.

"Maybe so." Timothy wondered when that day would come. He was tired of being cold at night and hungry just about all the time, tired of either straining his eyes stitching cartridge bags or straining his muscles at hard labor. At night, the men talked about what they would do first when they were "back in civilization," and in the mess hall they talked about restaurant meals they would order. But Timothy didn't think any farther than marching through Sumter's gates and down the wharf to board a ship headed north.

CHAPTER TEN

★　　★　　★

"**I**T'S SUPPOSED TO be April showers, not April downpours," Timothy complained. The gloomy weather the first week of the month had been bad enough, but today it was raining as if it would never stop, with huge drops pelting the window panes. And the weather wasn't the worst of it. After weeks of believing that the government planned to surrender the fort and they would soon be leaving, now the garrison had learned that the president had decided to send them provisions and possibly reinforcements. *And* he'd told the Confederates of his decision, warning them not to interfere.

The angry Confederates had immediately cut off the fort's food shipments from Charleston, but so far, there had been no sign of a relief ship. Timothy sighed. He couldn't remember the last time he'd eaten his fill. Ever since they'd arrived at Sumter, he had been ravenously hungry long before the next meal, but now that they were on half rations, his hunger was a constant ache, a dull gnawing deep in his belly.

Silently, he cursed the Confederate general with the

foreign-sounding name who had been sent to take over the rebel troops around Charleston. Besides putting a stop to deliveries of fresh meat and vegetables, now he had told the major that there would be no more mail or newspapers—an announcement that had plunged the garrison into despair.

Timothy could see that for Sergeant Zell and the other men with families, stopping the mail was worse than being put on half rations—even though, as Private Evans had complained, half of not much was hardly anything at all. *Maybe the Confederates have decided to starve us out instead of bombarding the fort.* Timothy turned away from the rain-streaked window and asked, "How long can a person live without food?"

Corporal Ricc looked up from his book and said, "A month at most, I'd say."

A month!

"Listen," the corporal said, "the band is rehearsing."

The musicians warmed up with "Yankee Doodle," and as one patriotic tune followed another, Timothy began to feel a little better. Listening to the music helped keep him from noticing the cold dampness and his empty stomach, helped keep his mind focused on the present instead of worrying about the future.

The minute he awoke the next morning, Timothy knew that the rain had stopped. Eager to escape the gloom of the quarters, he dressed quickly and went outside. Puddles stood on the parade ground, but the air was fresh and hinted that the day would be warm.

"Those secesh have made us miss spring," Timothy whispered. Never again would he take flower beds and blossoming trees for granted. He glanced at his timepiece and saw that he could spend a few minutes on the parapet before he sounded the day's first call, so he headed for the stair tower. This early, he found only Captain Doubleday on the top tier ahead of him—and, of course, the sentinels.

When the officer lowered his spyglass and turned to him, Timothy saluted. "Any sign of a ship, sir?"

"Not yet." He returned the salute, then raised the spyglass again and turned it toward Fort Johnson and the James Island batteries. After he had studied all the Confederate fortifications that ringed the harbor, he snapped his spyglass shut and slipped it in his pocket.

"What did you see, sir?" Timothy asked, alarmed by the captain's grim expression.

The officer hesitated, then squared his shoulders and said, "Thirty guns and eighteen mortars aimed at Sumter."

Timothy swallowed hard. He was glad the captain had said aimed at *Sumter* instead of aimed at *us*. "When do you think they'll attack, sir?"

"Soon, Bugler Donovan. Very soon. But before they do, I think General Beauregard will offer his old friend Major Anderson a chance to surrender."

Timothy felt a glimmer of hope. "You mean they might not attack us after all?"

"They'd prefer for us to withdraw. After all, which would

be more use to them, a fort to protect Charleston, or a mound of rubble on a man-made island?"

Sumter, a mound of rubble? "With all those batteries they've built, I figured they must be spoiling for a fight," Timothy said.

The officer looked down at him. "Would there be the slightest chance that our major would surrender if their guns weren't facing us?"

Instead of answering, Timothy asked a question of his own. "Do you think he *will* surrender? If General Beauregard asks him to, that is?"

The captain trained his spyglass on the iron-clad battery on Cummings Point and said, "His orders are to try to hold the fort until the relief ships you mentioned arrive."

More than one ship, then! Timothy realized. *Well, they'd better get here soon.* Salt pork and a cracker left everyone hungry and didn't provide much energy. The surgeon was worried about scurvy, too. Timothy thought of the morning the *Star of the West* had turned away, and as if reading his mind, Captain Doubleday looked down at him and said, "This time will be different, bugler. This time, the major has been told that help is coming—and the unarmed ship bringing the provisions will be protected by naval vessels." He raised his spyglass again and looked out to sea.

Timothy checked his timepiece and started down to the parade ground, the words "thirty guns and eighteen mortars aimed at Sumter" echoing in his mind.

CHAPTER ELEVEN

Long before dawn the next morning, Timothy lay staring into the darkness, his body tense and his mind churning. It had taken him hours to fall asleep after the garrison had finished last-minute preparations for an attack and bedded down in the gun rooms where they would be safe from artillery fire—and now he was wide-awake again. Like everybody else, no doubt. How could anyone go back to sleep after being awakened and told that the Confederates had informed Major Anderson they would begin shelling the fort in an hour?

Not sure whether his shivering was from cold or fear, Timothy pulled his blanket tighter and felt for the reassuring presence of his bugle. Surely an hour had passed since an officer had come through the crowded gun rooms to wake the men.

Captain Doubleday had been right, as usual. Right that the attack would come soon, and right that Confederate General Beauregard would offer Major Anderson a chance to surrender with honor. But the major couldn't hand over the fort, because he had orders to hold out until the promised shipment of provisions arrived.

Timothy clenched his jaws to keep his teeth from chattering. It had been better when no one bothered to answer the major's letters. If he'd never heard from Washington, maybe Major Anderson would have given up the fort when the last of their food was gone. After all, no one had sworn to *starve* for the flag.

At least if Fort Sumter ended up a pile of rubble, it would be no use to the Confederacy, Timothy reminded himself. He tried unsuccessfully to ignore the fact that if that happened, the garrison would be buried beneath the rubble. *I wish I knew what time—*

Ka-POW!

A shell exploded with a brilliant flash directly above the parade ground, and at once the air was filled with the roar of cannon firing from the rebel batteries and the whistle of approaching shells. Instinctively, Timothy turned over on his mattress and buried his face in his arms. He was amazed to hear the men nearest him calmly begin to comment on the location and size of the guns that were firing at them.

"That was one of our 32-pounders from Moultrie."

"—sounds like mortar fire from Fort Johnson."

"I'll bet that one's from the new rifled cannon they—"

Timothy struggled to a sitting position, and trying to keep his voice steady, he asked, "Aren't we going to fire back?"

"Not until after breakfast," Sergeant Zell told him. "We have to ration ourselves because we're short of cartridges."

Timothy's stomach was so tight with fear he didn't think he'd be able to eat. He wasn't sure he had the breath he needed to sound the morning's bugle calls, either, but he did—standing in a gun room instead of on the parade ground. The notes echoed from the walls and vaulted ceiling, but the voices that answered at roll call sounded only a little different from the way they did in the open. A bit louder, and very determined.

Later, in the mess hall, Timothy managed to chew and swallow his ration of salt pork and wash it down with water in spite of the rumble of guns and the crash of shells slamming into the fort's walls. Hanson looked at him across the table and said, "Well, sonny boy, I guess you'll find some safe corner to cower in with your needle while the rest of us take on the rebels."

"Remember, Private Hanson, without the cartridges Bugler Donovan and the others have been manufacturing, we wouldn't be able to take on the rebels," Sergeant Zell said. "If we're lucky, the relief fleet will arrive and the warships will turn their guns on the enemy before we exhaust our supply of cartridges."

Hanson fell silent, and Timothy wondered why "manufacturing cartridges" sounded like a more respectable job than "sewing cartridge bags."

At seven o'clock, Major Anderson assigned Captain Doubleday's men to the first four-hour shift at the guns and Captain Seymour's to the second shift. "Remember," the major said, "no one is to go above the first tier."

"Even though our biggest guns are on the barbette?"

one of the lieutenants asked.

"That's right," Major Anderson told him. "Those positions are too exposed. There would be too much loss of life."

Timothy saw disappointment cloud Norris's face. He wouldn't be firing any 100-pounder today.

And then the major addressed the men. "Stay in the gun rooms as much as possible," he told them. "Be careful of your lives—do your duty coolly, determinedly, and cautiously. Indiscretion is not valor."

Hearing that, Timothy felt a little better. He'd simply quote Major Anderson if Hanson made any more comments about cowering in some safe corner.

"Will you fire the first shot, major?" Captain Doubleday asked.

Major Anderson shook his head. "I have no desire to be the one to plunge my country into war."

"Then I shall do it," the captain said. "We'll settle the secession question once and for all."

After the artillerists marched off to man the guns, one of the lieutenants divided the extra hospital sheets between Timothy and five of the bandsmen. Then he gave them each a pair of scissors, a spool of thread, and a needle. "When you've turned all those sheets into cartridge bags, I'll pass out blankets," he said.

"Come along, bugler. Let's get started," O'Brian called over his shoulder.

"Thanks," Timothy said, "but I've already picked a place to work." He was glad his voice sounded normal. He didn't want anyone to know how scared he was. Head down, he hurried to the unused gun room where he and some of the others had slept. He rolled up his thin mattress to make a seat of sorts, chose a place toward the front of his refuge where the light was best, and set to work.

The ground trembled each time Sumter's guns fired, and the sound echoed through the vaulted chambers, making Timothy's ears ring. He saw bricks fly from the parapet, saw the dirt spray up around a mortar shell that hit near the center of the parade ground. Seconds later, the shell exploded, and Timothy gasped as the entire fort shook. *This is it. This is the bombardment.*

His hands were so shaky when he began to cut up the hospital sheet that some of the rectangles had uneven edges. He was glad there was no one to notice—he'd been smart to work alone. When Norris had marched off with his teammates, he'd looked excited. Eager. Most of the artillerists had looked staunch and determined, like Sergeant Zell, but Private Evans and a few others looked fierce and ruthless. I'm the only one who's scared, Timothy thought. The bandsmen aren't soldiers either, but they had just looked resigned.

A shell struck a chimney on the officers' quarters and bricks flew through the air, landing on the parade ground. Timothy's heart pounded. More of the Confederates' shots were finding targets now instead of sailing harmlessly over the fort the way they had at first. In the next gun room, an artillerist cursed and said, "We aren't making a dent in their defenses," and another agreed, saying, "It would be a different story if we could fire those 100-pounders up on the barbette."

Timothy finished his first cartridge bag and reached for another rectangle of cloth. He was sewing as fast as he could—and he knew the bandsmen were, too—but with nine of the fort's guns firing, cartridges were being used much faster than they could be replaced. No wonder the major hadn't ordered the men to their positions until after breakfast!

One of the artillerists cursed and pointed across the parade ground, and Timothy was horrified to see smoke eddying from the third-story windows of the officers' quarters.

"Hot shot!" someone shouted above the din. "They're firing hot shot!"

Timothy fought down panic at the idea of red-hot iron balls raining down onto the fort and setting it afire. Now smoke billowed from the windows of the quarters. While he stared openmouthed, some of the laborers and off-shift artillerists formed a bucket brigade. Other men dragged blankets from the mattresses that had been moved to the gun rooms, soaked them, and then ran into the burning building. They were going to beat back the flames!

"Keep sewing, bugler," one of the artillerists called to him, lifting a piece of round shot from the small pyramid near his gun.

Timothy knotted his thread and began another cartridge bag. He was doing his part. No one expected him to run into a burning building—he wasn't a soldier, after all. Of course, neither were the laborers who were fighting the fire.

The next time he glanced up, smoke no longer curled from the windows, and as he dropped the finished cartridge bag onto the growing pile beside him, Timothy saw the hired workers come out of the building. He watched them toss the dampened blankets in a pile near the abandoned buckets and head for the shelter of an empty gun room.

By now, Timothy's hands had steadied, and he'd established a sort of rhythm, covering his ears at each shout of "Battery ready!" and beginning to stitch again after the gun was fired. His eyes turned toward the sound of a splintering crash, and he saw shattered pieces of slate flying from the roof of the barracks where the laborers had lived. Timothy tried to concentrate on drawing the thread through the cloth and pulling it tight.

Automatically, he covered his ears when a sergeant in the next gun room yelled, "Battery ready! Fire!" Timothy wondered what it felt like to yank the cord that fired the cannon—or as Norris would say, to "pull the lanyard that discharges the piece"—when the gunner yelled *Fire!* He began to stitch again, knowing that one artillerist would be sponging out the barrel to douse any sparks so another could safely place a cartridge in the muzzle for the first man to shove down the barrel with his rammer. "To ram home the charge," he whispered.

Timothy told himself that sewing cartridge bags was

important even if it didn't require the courage shown by the firefighters or the skill and teamwork of the artillerists. He reminded himself that artillerymen worked in shifts while he worked continuously. But nothing changed the fact that in the midst of all the action, he sat here in the safety of a gun room, pulling a thread through a piece of cloth. Cowering with his needle, just as Hanson had said.

But what did Hanson expect him to do—stitch his cartridge bags in the middle of the parade ground? Weren't Hanson and the other artillerists safe inside gun rooms, too? "Corporal Rice is right," Timothy muttered. "I shouldn't let Hanson get under my skin."

In the early afternoon, a cheer went up from the off-duty men who had been looking out to sea, and Timothy glanced up in time to see Private Hough dash across the parade ground, spyglass in his hand.

Timothy felt a surge of hope. "I think they've spotted the relief fleet," he said to the band's cornet player, who had come to collect his finished cartridge bags. "How long do you think it will be before the ships are close enough to fire on the rebel batteries?"

"I have no idea," the man said. "Soon, I hope." He shook his head and added, "It seems a pity that those 64-pounders and 100-pounders on the top tier are loaded and aimed at rebel targets, but the men aren't allowed up there to fire them."

"You're right. That just don't make sense," declared one of the artilleryman in the next gun room. He left his position and headed for the nearest stair tower. It wasn't long before Timothy heard the thunder of a huge gun on the barbette, and then another and another, until each of the cannon that faced Fort Moultrie had been fired once.

The daring artillerist returned to the cheers of his teammates, and Timothy noticed that he didn't seem the least concerned about being disciplined for disobeying orders. Maybe he figured the officers were too busy to care. Or maybe he figured— A jarring crash almost deafened Timothy. A shot had hit the wall behind him! He knew he was protected by a massive thickness of brick and stone, but that didn't slow the rapid beating of his heart.

His hand shook as he threaded his needle again, but Timothy took a deep breath and tried to sew faster. Only six of the fort's guns were firing now, and he was sure that was because of the shortage of cartridges.

At last the long day ended, and the men were told to stop firing. "Bugler, sound Assembly," Captain Doubleday ordered.

Timothy raised his bugle, grateful for the familiar ritual in the midst of the chaos and din of battle. He began to play, and the men gathered in the gun rooms to form ranks for roll call. A shell crashed against the fort's wall and exploded with a flash that could be seen through the embrasure, but Timothy's notes didn't waver. When he lowered his bugle, he saw a strange look on Private Hanson's smoke-blackened face.

A short time later, the men agreed that pickled salt pork and water had never looked so good, and after the meager meal, Timothy felt almost cheerful. In spite of the long hours of bombardment from all directions, the fort still stood, and the only injuries were minor ones caused by bricks flying from the parapet.

But then Evans said, "Well, here we sit, a handful of men with almost no food left, forbidden to use our biggest guns, running out of cartridges—"

"Change the subject, Evans," Sergeant Zell ordered, his voice steely cold.

Timothy was glad to escape the recital of the fort's woes. He didn't want to be reminded of how few cartridges they had—or how little material was left to make more with. He hoped the provisions the relief ships were bringing included cartridges, wished they would hurry up and get there, wondered why the warships hadn't come to their rescue.

Later, too exhausted for sleep, Timothy lay on his mattress and listened to the waves crash against the walls of the fort. Someone swore as wind-lashed rain blew into the gun room, and someone else said, "At least this weather will keep the rebels from trying to storm the fort."

"Maybe so, but it's going to keep those ships anchored beyond the harbor from bringing our provisions and reinforcements, too," Evans grumbled.

Corporal Rice said mildly, "The major thinks small boats might be able to get here in spite of the storm."

"Well, I won't hold my breath," Evans told him.

Ignoring Evans, Timothy turned to the corporal and asked, "How does the major expect us to win when we're using just a few of our guns and none of the biggest ones?"

"The major doesn't expect us to win, sonny boy," Hanson said, speaking for the first time. For once, he sounded resigned instead of sarcastic.

Stunned, Timothy echoed, "Doesn't expect us to win? Then how come—"

"His orders are to defend the fort, and that's what we're doing," Hanson interrupted. "We're defending the fort—and our flag."

Sergeant Zell added solemnly, "Our duty is to defend the fort until its walls are breached."

Timothy's mind reeled. How could the Confederates ever breach the wall when more than three-quarters of a mile of open water lay between the nearest battery and Sumter? When the wharf and the walkway along the base of the wall were mined with explosives? "What if they don't breach the walls?" he asked. "What if they just keep pounding us with their artillery?"

"Fortunately," said the sergeant, "the major's orders also say that he is to surrender the fort rather than unduly endanger the lives of his men."

Unduly endanger their lives? Timothy turned the phrase over in his mind until finally he slept.

CHAPTER TWELVE

TIMOTHY LOWERED his bugle and watched the men assemble for roll call the next morning, thankful that the worst night of his life was over. The Confederates had fired every fifteen minutes, sometimes jolting him into startled wakefulness, though all around him, exhausted men slept soundly. Now he felt as groggy as everyone else looked.

By breakfast time, the bombardment had begun again in full force. Blear-eyed, the men chewed their salt pork and sipped their water in near silence. Timothy glanced up when Corporal Rice announced, "Well, those relief boats are still anchored a safe distance beyond the harbor. I had hoped they'd try to make it to our wharf under the cover of last night's bad weather."

"More likely they used the weather as an excuse not to attempt it," Evans said glumly.

"At least the storm is over," Corporal Rice said. He turned to Timothy and remarked, "I see you've worked your needle through the sleeve of your coat for safekeeping."

Admiring the way the corporal had cut off Evans's negative comments without being rude, Timothy said, "That's the easiest way to make sure it doesn't get lost."

When the men in the first shift marched to their guns, Timothy headed off with an armful of blankets to cut up for cartridge bags. Though the shelling from the Confederate batteries seemed even heavier today, he barely looked up from his stitching when fragments of bricks from the barbette tier rained down. But a commotion on the parade ground caught his attention, and he saw that the barracks where the laborers had been quartered was afire and off-duty artillerymen were running toward it. In the next gun room, Evans called to the others, "Those secesh are sending over more of that hot shot. Too bad we don't have the fuel to fire up our furnace and give 'em a good dose of their own medicine."

One of his teammates called back, "If the major would let us onto the top tier so we could use our big guns on them—" His words were cut off by another shower of bricks from the parapet, and Timothy thought the men should be glad they could fire from the safety of the gun rooms. He looked up to see Hanson approaching with an armload of cartridges he'd filled at the powder magazine.

"You scared, sonny boy?"

Timothy shook his head. "Don't have time to be scared—I'm too busy sewing," he said, realizing with surprise that it was true. "Are *you* scared?"

Hanson shook his head. "I'm too busy passing out the major's wool socks."

"The major's *socks*?" Timothy echoed, looking up.

Hanson grinned and explained, "Major Anderson

decided to hand over all his extra socks to use for cartridge bags since you're so slow with a needle." He headed for the nearest gun room, and Timothy watched him place an armful of powder-filled socks in the leather-topped barrel where cartridges were stored.

Shouts from the parade ground attracted his attention, and he caught his breath. The officers' quarters were on fire again, and the flames would soon threaten the powder magazine! Without thinking, Timothy raced to join the bucket brigade that was forming. He gritted his teeth and tried to ignore the shells that crashed into the walls of the fort and sent chunks of masonry flying, tried to think about nothing more than passing the heavy water buckets along the line.

"This don't do no more good than spittin' into the fireplace," the laborer beside him complained.

Before Timothy could answer, another shout went up. The barracks had been hit! Several band members sprinted across the parade ground carrying dampened blankets to beat back the flames. And still the Confederates lobbed hot shot at the fort. Timothy coughed as thick smoke blew in his face, irritating his eyes and throat.

With the fire burning out of control and the flames creeping closer to the magazine, the officers dismissed the bucket brigade and commanded the off-duty artillerists to start moving powder kegs to the gun rooms.

Dodging flying debris, Timothy was hurrying back to his cartridge bags when above the din of crashing shells he heard someone call his name. It was Sergeant Zell, standing outside the barracks and gesturing to the tub where the firefighters soaked the blankets and burlap sacks they used to beat back the flames. *He wants me to refill the tub.* Timothy ran to the water buckets that had been abandoned along with the attempt to save the officers' quarters.

He lifted one of the buckets, grunting under its weight, then balanced the load with a second bucket and struggled toward the barracks. A burning timber sailed overhead and crashed behind him, sending up a shower of sparks. Timothy fixed his eyes on the tub, where a smoke-blackened artillerist was waiting for the water he was carrying.

He had hauled his third pair of buckets and was emptying one of them into the tub when Private Hough came to soak a blanket. Welcoming the chance to rest his aching muscles, Timothy stepped back and asked, "Aren't we firing at the rebels anymore?"

"We're down to one gun, with orders to fire every ten minutes—just often enough to let 'em know the fort is still being defended." Hough lifted his blanket from the tub and headed back to the barracks.

Through the swirling smoke, Timothy could see a constant line of men rolling powder kegs across the parade ground from the threatened magazine to the safety of the gun rooms. He was about to pour the second bucket of water into the tub when a bandsman came to soak his fire-blackened blanket.

"Looks like the shelling's got so brisk they're closing the door to the magazine," the man said, peering through the smoky haze.

"At least there's less chance of an explosion now,"

Timothy said, though he knew that even with the magazine's heavy copper door closed, a spark from one of the fires could be blown through the ventilator and— Making his mind blank, he stomped out the flames in some burning debris that had fallen nearby.

He had just emptied his remaining bucket into the tub when Hanson paused to dip his handkerchief in the water. Timothy was about to say that all the other firefighters were using wet *blankets*, but the weary expression on the man's face made him think better of it. He watched Hanson fold the handkerchief into a triangle and tie it over his nose and mouth.

Timothy was about to do the same when a red-hot ball plunged to the parade ground and bounced across it into one of the gun rooms. His chest tightened when he saw a mattress burst into flame. *What if powder kegs are stored in there?*

"Fire in a gun room!" Timothy cried. As he grabbed one handle of the half-full tub, Hanson took the other, and the two of them awkwardly made their way across the parade ground. Timothy needed two hands to manage his side of the heavy tub, which made running difficult, but he still kept up with Hanson. An artillerist had dragged the burning mattress onto the parade ground, and they quickly doused the fire.

By now, the firefighters had been ordered out of the burning barracks. Dank smoke filled the fort, and Timothy quickly realized there was a greater threat than the flames. Some of the artillerists lay on the floor of the gun rooms where the smoke was lightest, and others clustered around the embrasures, desperate for air. Timothy and Private Hanson stumbled toward an abandoned gun room, and Timothy was horrified to see that the wind had blown smoldering debris inside. He hurried to stamp out the sparks before they reached the powder kegs stored against the wall.

"The wind has changed!" Hanson shouted, and as Timothy continued to battle the sparks and cinders that swirled around him, he heard an officer call, "Get rid of the powder!" Almost at once, a laborer hurried over to help Hanson push the kegs through the embrasure.

"Don't worry, bugler," the laborer said, grunting as he lifted one of them. "We'll save back enough powder to fill the cartridge bags you and the others are stitching."

Before Timothy could answer, a tremendous explosion jarred the fort, and it was closely followed by another, and then another. The stone floor shook beneath his feet, and he stared openmouthed at the sheets of flame that rose higher than the fort's walls. A blast of heat took his breath away and left his throat parched. *This must be what the chaplain means when he preaches about Hell.*

A soot-covered artilleryman shouted to the captain, "It's them powder kegs we just tossed out, sir. Tide's low, so instead of floating off, they're just laying there outside our walls an' the rebs are hitting 'em with hot shot."

Timothy was still staring at the inferno when he heard Hanson say, "Come on, bugler. We're needed at the magazine."

For a moment Timothy was too stunned to move—when had the two of them become *we*?—but then he hurried after Hanson to join the men in front of the powder magazine. As Timothy helped shovel up the dirt from the area in front of the magazine and bank it over the copper-covered door, he noticed that the metal was badly dented and the lock was smashed. He made his mind blank to blot out images of what would have happened if the door hadn't been in place and the rebel shot had struck the powder kegs still stored inside.

They had nearly finished their work to protect the magazine when a series of deafening explosions rocked the fort. Timothy would have run to safety if he'd had any idea where that might be.

"Blimey!" one of the laborers exclaimed. "Now we're shellin' ourselves."

It was true. A spark had set off shells and grenades that had been moved from the fire-threatened magazine to one of the stair towers. Stones rained down from the barbette, and blazing timbers from the barracks crashed onto the parade ground. The crackling flames seemed even more menacing.

Suddenly, above the sounds of shelling came the anguished cry, "The flag! They've shot down our flag!" Other voices picked up the refrain, and it swept through the fort. *The flag is down.* Timothy ran onto the parade ground, where men were lined up along the sides of the huge flag—now ragged and smoke stained—holding it off the ground while a carpenter looked for something to use as a pole.

"Did you see Lieutenant Hart rescue the flag when it fell?" Norris asked, his usually calm voice betraying his excitement. "He singed off his eyebrows when he beat out the flames along its borders."

One of the workmen added, "Them gold things on the shoulders of his uniform, they got so hot he had to rip 'em off. Don't know how he could take the heat!"

Evans cracked his knuckles and said, "When those rebels see our flag flying again, they'll know the men at Sumter can take anything they send over here."

Timothy looked from the flames leaping above the officers' quarters to the weary, red-eyed artillerists and wondered just how much more Sumter *could* take. A shout went up from the men around him, and he saw that the carpenter had nailed the flag to a makeshift pole. Timothy watched the major's aide and two officers head toward the stair tower with it. His stomach knotted. How could they be so willing—no, *eager*—to risk their lives on the fort's top tier as they searched for a place to display the flag?

The words of "The Star-Spangled Banner" popped into Timothy's head, words that told of the flag flying above the ramparts of Baltimore's Fort McHenry in the War of 1812. And now—

More cheers went up, and Timothy saw that the three men had reached the barbette tier. He craned his neck and watched, scarcely breathing, while they struggled to lash the new flagpole to a gun carriage. Shot and shell flew past them as the rebel batteries concentrated their fire on the flag. Bricks from the parapet were scattered in all directions, and one of the huge barbette guns was hit and toppled from its carriage.

Timothy feared what might happen, didn't want to watch, but couldn't tear his eyes away. He felt dizzy and realized he was holding his breath. At last the Stars and Stripes flew proudly above the fort again, and he joined in the cheers for the flag—and for the courage of the men who had raised it.

One of the fort's guns fired for the first time since the flag had fallen, and Timothy turned toward the sound. To his surprise, he saw the artillerists crowded around the embrasure, peering toward Fort Moultrie. He ran to see what they were looking at, dodging around the unmounted cannon barrels on the parade ground. One of the men moved over to make room at the embrasure, and Private Hough passed him the spyglass. "What are they doing up there?" Timothy asked when he saw a line of Confederates standing on Moultrie's parapet.

"I think they're cheering us on," Private Hough said. "When the wind's right, you can hear their shouts."

"Cheering us on?" Timothy repeated. "I don't understand."

Behind him, one of the artillerists said, "To show their respect for our courage, bugler. Courage under fire."

"Or else they're glad we haven't surrendered so they'll have a chance to pour some more of that fire on us," Evans said, holding out a hand for the spyglass.

More of that fire? Timothy sagged down onto the gun

carriage, wondering how much more he could take. What about Major Anderson's instructions? Not the ones about defending the fort till its walls were breached, but the ones from the new president about not unduly endangering the lives of his men. If they weren't unduly endangered now—

A commotion in the empty gun room that had been prepared to receive the provisions from the relief ships attracted Timothy's attention. Hope overcame his fatigue, and he ran to investigate. He was amazed to see an artillerist haul someone in through the embrasure—not one of the hoped-for reinforcements, but a Confederate colonel with a white handkerchief tied to the end of his sword. He must have been rowed over from one of the rebel batteries, but why?

The artillerists surrounded the officer and everyone began to talk excitedly. Timothy caught the words *flag* and *surrender* before one of the lieutenants turned to him and said, "Find Major Anderson and bring him here, bugler."

Timothy hurried to obey. He hoped one Confederate being helped through an embrasure would count as "breaching the walls," because unless the major surrendered the fort soon, there might be nothing left for him to surrender.

CHAPTER THIRTEEN

★   ★   ★

HE WHITE FLAG that flew above the ruined fort seemed to cast a pall over the garrison, and Timothy found himself longing for the tattered Stars and Stripes to be raised again for the salute. He looked at the pile of cartridge bags on the gun-room floor and tried to estimate how many more were needed. "I wish the major hadn't insisted on a hundred-gun salute to the flag," he said. "It seems like fifty would have been enough." Or better yet, just twenty-seven—one for each state that's loyal to the Union, he added silently.

"I never thought I'd be stitching cartridge bags a day after the bombardment ended," Evans said.

Timothy said, "I never thought the smoke would still be hanging over the fort a day later."

"Some of the fires are still smoldering," Corporal O'Brian explained. He had just tossed another cartridge bag onto the pile when Hanson stopped short on his way past.

"Haven't you seamstresses heard about the surrender?" he asked.

"Yes, but the terms of that surrender include a hundred-gun salute to our flag," Timothy said, as if the taunt were simply a request for information.

"Well, keep at it, then."

After Hanson left, Evans said, "At least he didn't say 'Keep at it, *ladies*,' like he used to."

"His heart wasn't in it," Corporal O'Brian agreed.

No one has much heart for anything this morning, Timothy thought. He looked across the heaps of debris on the parade ground to the still-smoking ruins of the officers' quarters and barracks. At least the fort's outer walls had held in spite of the pounding they had taken, and the gun rooms were barely damaged—the rebels' shot and shell hadn't battered Sumter into a mound of rubble.

"It's hard to think of those South Carolinians as enemies even now," Corporal O'Brian mused, breaking the silence.

"They seem to feel the same way about us," Timothy said. "When their officers came over to visit last night, I heard one of them apologize to the major for 'reducing the fort.'"

"He probably felt guilty about firing on his old friends and the flag he used to honor and fight for," O'Brian said.

Evans scowled. "They all ought to feel guilty. It will be my pleasure as well as my duty to make those rebels regret what they have begun here."

The silence that followed his words was broken when Norris and Private Hough came to collect the finished cartridge bags so they could be filled with powder. "Did you hear that the major is finally letting us fire the barbette guns?" Hough asked.

"We'll use some of the 100-pounders for the salute,"

Norris said, his eyes shining.

"You mean they weren't all destroyed in the shelling?" Timothy asked.

"Not all of them, but now that I've seen the damage up there, I'm glad the major kept us on the lower tier," Norris said.

By the time the last cartridge bags were being stitched, Hanson was waiting to collect them. "If any of you ever leave the army, you could set up a tailor shop," he said.

Out of habit, Timothy worked his needle through the wool of his coat sleeve. "I don't intend to take another stitch for the rest of my life," he announced, getting to his feet. How had Ma worked as a dressmaker all those years, sewing the whole day and sometimes into the night without a word of complaint?

"Now that you've finished your needlework, you ought to have a look at those boats in the harbor," Hanson told him.

"You mean the relief boats that never managed to get here?" Timothy asked.

"The *Pawnee* and the *Baltic* and the rest of that fleet are ships, bugler. I'm talking about boats. Rowboats and fishing boats and just about anything else that will float. Looks like every rebel in the state has come out to watch us lower our flag and leave the fort."

After ringing their church bells and firing their guns in celebration hour after hour in the city, the rebels were coming out here now? Timothy was on his way to have a look at the sightseers when Sergeant Zell called, "Bugler Donovan! Sound Assembly."

Timothy stopped and raised his bugle, glad it was time to form ranks for the salute. He looked forward to seeing the Stars and Stripes fly above Sumter one last time—and then to leaving Charleston Harbor.

More than half an hour later, he stood with the rest of the garrison while the battle-torn flag flying above them snapped in the wind. He'd counted only forty reports, and spaced a minute apart— Timothy groaned inwardly. *We'll be standing here for another hour. I hope Norris is enjoying himself up there with his 100-pounder.*

. . . Forty-five . . . forty-six . . . forty-seven— *What was that? It sounded like an explosion.* Timothy's mind raced, trying to make sense of it. He waited for the next shot, but the silence stretched on and on. Finally, there was a flurry of activity at the foot of one of the stair towers.

Timothy caught his breath. An accident! An entire artillery team must have been involved, judging from the number of men being carried down the stairs by their comrades. *I hope Norris is all right—and Corporal Rice.* From the corner of his eye, Timothy saw the surgeon leave the group of officers and men assembled for the ceremony.

The minutes dragged on, but at last a downcast group of artillerists made their way from the shadows of the gun rooms back toward the stair tower. *There's the corporal, and there's Norris. But who—?*

Soon the huge guns on the barbette began to fire again: Forty-eight . . . forty-nine . . . fifty. The major appeared at the foot of the flagstaff, pale and shaken, and as the echo of the fiftieth shot died away, he lowered the flag. The bandmaster raised his baton, and the musicians began to play. Timothy had a hollow feeling in his chest. He'd wished for a fifty-gun salute, but not at such a cost!

After the ceremony was over, the major explained what had happened. The wind had blown a spark onto a pile of cartridges, and the explosion had killed Private Hough and injured the other members of his team, some of them seriously.

Not Private Hough! Timothy fought back tears.

"The surgeon is tending to the wounded," the major added, turning away.

An hour ago, Private Hough was talking to us. He seemed almost as excited as Norris about firing the 100-pounders.

For a moment, no one spoke, and then Evans said, "To think that no one was killed during the bombardment, and now this."

"I guess you could say that Private Hough died for his flag," Timothy said. As soon as the words were out, he regretted them. It sounded like he was making light of the tragedy. But to his surprise, Hanson agreed.

"Yes," he said quietly. "Hough was the first of us to lay down his life for that sacred banner. Though I daresay he had in mind something quite different when he swore his willingness to die for the flag."

Timothy was sure of it. He raised his eyes from the rubble-strewn parade ground to the pall of smoke that hung above the fort and hoped it wouldn't be long before they could leave Sumter forever.

The next morning, Timothy stood beside Norris at the

railing of the Confederate steamer that would take the garrison to the U.S. ship waiting just outside the harbor. He looked up at the rebel soldiers on Sumter's parapet, and a hollow feeling crept over him—part loss, part regret, part resignation.

Evans joined them, but for several minutes, no one spoke. Finally, Norris said, "I can't get that accident out of my mind. All the blood. And Private Hough's arm torn off and lying—" He took a deep breath and said, "I hope I never see anything like that again."

"If you stay in the army, you'll see worse," Evans said, "but you'll get used to it."

Timothy didn't want to think about that. "I was sure we'd be on our way north long before this," he said.

"We would have been, if we'd left on schedule," Evans said. "And then we wouldn't have had to spend the night on this rebel tub, waiting for the tide to come in so we can cross the sandbar and board our ship."

"We wouldn't have had to listen to those rebels celebrate their victory," Timothy said. "Wouldn't have to see them strut around on our parapet."

"On what's left of it, anyway," Evans said.

Timothy frowned when Norris continued to stare silently down at the water. "Come on, Norris," he said. "Let's walk up to the front of the boat and have a look at the ship that's waiting to take us to New York."

"That's the *bow* of the boat, Donovan, not the 'front.' Let's go." Norris led the way, and Timothy followed, relieved to hear his friend sounding like himself again.

"So instead of bringing us provisions, the ship is taking

the garrison north," Timothy said. "At least there should be plenty to eat."

"I heard a rumor about some kind of a mix-up in the fleet's orders," Norris told him. "Some of the ships never got here. And last night one of the officers said it wouldn't have made any real difference if we'd had the reinforcements and provisions."

Hanson was already at the bow, staring out to sea. Without looking at Norris, he said, "When you come right down to it, those ships may have served their intended purpose."

"How do you figure that?" Norris asked.

"They brought an end to the stalemate. Knowing that provisions and maybe reinforcements were on their way to Sumter forced the Confederates to act. Forced them to fire the first shot." After a moment he added, "I heard that the surrender terms Anderson demanded were the same ones the Confederates had offered him before the bombardment."

Private Hough would still be alive if Anderson had accepted them. Timothy forced that thought out of his mind and concentrated on listening to the lap of the wavelets as the tide came in.

Captain Seymour stood a short distance away, absently tapping his spyglass against his hand. Finally he turned to them and spoke. "Well, men, we were able to abandon our post with our honor intact, and we should soon be able to cross the sandbar and put all this behind us."

"What do you think will happen now, sir?" Timothy asked.

After a pause the captain said, "There will be a great swell of indignation in the North at the attack on United States property and a great swell of confidence in the South at their victory. Not a good combination, I'm afraid."

"This means war, then?" Timothy asked hesitantly.

"I fear so," the captain said. "Of course there may still be a chance for peace, although some would say the course for war was set last November."

Hanson glanced toward Timothy and said, "He means when Lincoln was elected with only the votes of the northern states."

Timothy bristled, but then he realized that Hanson's voice had lacked its usual mocking tone, and his face showed no hostility. Keeping his own voice neutral, he said, "I know."

Captain Doubleday came and stood with Seymour as the steamer's crew hauled up the anchor, and by the time the paddle wheel began to turn, the entire garrison was lined up along the railing. The steamer nosed its way into the channel, and Timothy glanced toward Sullivan's Island for one last look at Fort Moultrie, his home for more than a year. If he squinted, he could see Confederate artillerymen lined up on the parapet.

Captain Doubleday trained his spyglass on Moultrie. "They've all removed their hats," he said.

"They have? But why?"

"A mark of respect, bugler. They're showing their respect for our defense of the fort and our flag." The captain's voice rang with pride.

Before Timothy could reply, word rippled through the crowd at the railing that the soldiers at the battery on Cummings Point were standing at attention to honor them, too. Timothy sensed a change in the men around him, saw that they stood a little straighter, held their heads a little higher. He felt proud, too, but mostly he felt lucky to be alive. As the steamer headed toward the ship waiting across the bar, he took a deep breath and said, "I'm glad to be leaving Sumter. I'm ready to stop being a laborer or a seamstress and just be a bugler."

Hanson pointed to the instrument slung across Timothy's chest and said, "I doubt you'll be sounding any calls on the trip north. How come you didn't pack that thing?"

Meeting his eyes, Timothy said, "I keep my bugle with me to make sure it isn't damaged."

Hanson looked away. "You don't need to worry about that anymore."

"That's good." Timothy had figured as much, after yesterday, but he liked knowing for sure. Strange, how his personal war with Private Hanson had ended as his country's war was beginning.

Timothy raised his eyes to the battered flag that flew above them on the "rebel tub." That same flag had flown over both Moultrie and Sumter, and it would fly over the U.S. ship that carried the garrison north, too. He felt a rush of emotion—and a sense of certainty that as long as the Stars and Stripes flew over him, wherever he was would be home.

★

JOSEPH SCHWARTZ'S STORY

★

BALTIMORE, MARYLAND: APRIL 18–MAY 15, 1861

★

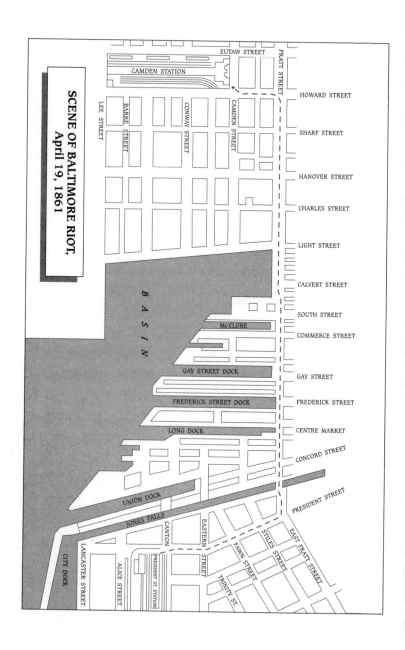

SCENE OF BALTIMORE RIOT, April 19, 1861

CHAPTER ONE

"**H**EY, JOSEPH—we're going to the sweet shop. Want to come?"

Surprised to be invited, Joseph hesitated a moment before he said, "Thanks anyway, Harold, but I'd better get on home." He could hold his own in the classroom or in the school yard, but anywhere else he felt like a fish out of water. What did a scholarship student from the working-class neighborhood near the harbor have in common with boys whose families lived in fine houses and had slaves to wait on them?

Alexander, the one classmate Joseph didn't like, sneered and said, "What's the matter, Joe? Can't afford a penny candy?"

Bristling, Joseph reached in his pocket and pulled out the coins Ma had given him that morning. "I can afford to buy anything I want," he lied. "I could even treat you and Harold."

"Then what are we waiting for? Come on, Joe."

Joseph slung his book strap over his shoulder and followed his classmates out the door and down the hall. Now he'd really gotten himself in a pickle. He was supposed to stop at the butcher shop to buy sausage for supper, and Ma would kill him if he came home empty-handed.

Outside, the April sunshine was bright and the trees were leafing out, but it was the boy hawking newspapers on the corner who captured everyone's attention. "Extra! Extra! Virginia votes for secession! Read all about it," the newsboy called. "Virginia to join Confederacy!"

Harold and Alexander cheered enthusiastically, and Joseph tried to hide his dismay. "That must be the reason for the hundred-gun salute we heard during geography class," he said, figuring that was a safe enough reaction.

His eyes bright with excitement, Alexander declared, "It's about time Virginia left the Union—they waited long enough."

Harold nodded. "Maryland's waited too long. We should secede and join the Confederacy, too."

"And the sooner the better," Alexander said. "Don't you agree, Joe?"

Joseph's heart sank. Until the bombardment of Fort Sumter less than a week before, everyone had hoped the confrontation between North and South would be settled peacefully. But once rebel shots were fired, Lincoln had called on the loyal states to send volunteers to put down the insurrection. And now Joseph's classmates—along with so many others in the city—clamored for Maryland to join the seceded states rather than fight against them. "I think we'd be better off if Maryland stays neutral," he hedged, unwilling to admit he was a Unionist.

"Fat chance of that, when you see Confederate flags just about everywhere you look. If you ask me—" Alexander broke off at the sound of running feet.

Joseph looked behind them and saw a boy zigzagging between the pedestrians on the sidewalk, two men practically on his heels. *Must be a pickpocket.* The man in the lead was catching up, and Joseph waited for him to clamp a hand on the young pickpocket's shoulder. His eyes widened when the man drew even with the boy and then passed him.

Men and a few older boys were running along the other side of the street, too. "Come on," one of them yelled. "We've got to stop them!"

"Let's see what's going on," Joseph said. If they were running, he wouldn't have to answer Alexander's questions—or spend Ma's money at the sweet shop.

Crossing the street, he was jostled by a couple of rough-looking youths hurrying past, and on the sidewalk again he edged around several well-dressed men who had stepped out of a building. Near Howard Street, he became aware of a dull, roaring sound—a sound like rushing water, or maybe a windstorm. Where had he heard that before? *At Monument Square, when the people were heckling a speaker.* It was the sound of a crowd. An angry crowd.

Joseph was breathing hard by the time he saw the wall of people ahead of him. He stopped at the edge of the noisy, shoving mass and asked an older boy, "What's going on?"

"Baltimore's been invaded, that's what," the boy said,

and then he yelled, "Death to the northern oppressors!"

Harold and Alexander ran up in time to hear a scholarly-looking man explain, "The first of the three-month volunteers answering Lincoln's call just arrived at the Northern Central's station. They'll have to march past here on their way to take the B&O rail line to Washington."

Alexander said, "I'm surprised they aren't sneaking through town in the middle of the night," and Harold laughed. Joseph wondered if they would ever stop snickering about how Abe Lincoln had come through Baltimore in the wee hours of the morning two months ago because of secessionist threats that he wouldn't reach Washington alive. And he might not have, judging from the mood of the people here today.

The noisy crowd was growing restless by the time someone shouted, "Here they come!"

Above the crescendo of hoots and hisses, a man yelled, "Down with Lincoln and his hirelings!" And then the air was full of echoing shouts and waving Confederate flags. A small U.S. flag was raised high, but two men tore it from its staff while others in the crowd began to pummel its owner.

"Serves him right," Harold said as the man made his escape, pushing his way past them while other spectators—including Alex—hooted and added their blows.

"He asked for it," Joseph agreed. Didn't everybody know that lately the surest way to start a fight was to raise a flag in the streets of Baltimore? Whether it was the Union's Stars and Stripes or the Confederacy's Stars and

Bars, someone was bound to take offense.

Now the crowd's attention was on the street again. The mass of people surged forward, then stopped so suddenly that Joseph stumbled into the man in front of him. A murmur went through the crowd like wildfire—*Police!*— and Joseph felt a rush of relief. He should have known the mayor would see to it that there wasn't any trouble. Maybe there wouldn't have been any danger to Abraham Lincoln, either.

"Hey, up there!" Alexander called to a group of men watching from an office window. "Can you see anything yet?"

One of them shouted back, "Just a column of troops with a line of policemen marching along on each side."

Raised fists in the crowd ahead of him and the increasing volume of the shouts and hisses told Joseph that the northern troops were passing, but to his disappointment, he couldn't see a thing.

"Next time, I'm going to be where I can see what's happening," Harold declared when the crowd began to break up. He glanced at the clock on the corner and added, "It's too late to go to the sweet shop—I'll see you fellows tomorrow."

Joseph was relieved. "See you tomorrow," he echoed, starting back down the street at a trot to get ahead of the disgruntled crowd. He'd have to hurry to get to the butcher shop before it closed.

On his way past the newspaper office, he paused long enough to read the bulletin that had been posted outside:

FORT SUMTER GARRISON
ARRIVES IN NEW YORK HARBOR;
MEN GIVEN HEROES' WELCOME

Pa would be interested in that news. He'd gone all the way to South Carolina last fall to help complete the brickwork and stonework inside Fort Sumter. For almost three months, he had lived in the unfinished barracks there with other masons from Baltimore, but he'd left soon after the Union soldiers moved in.

That was Pa, all right—giving up good money because he thought it was wrong to be paid for building something he figured would be destroyed almost before the mortar set properly. Ma had hardly spoken to him for days after he'd arrived home. But when the news came that the soldiers who were defending Sumter—and the laborers who had stayed—were running short of food and fuel, Ma had to admit Pa had been smart to leave. Of course, it didn't hurt that by then he'd found work on the docks, loading and unloading merchant ships.

At the next corner, Joseph heard a boy call out, "Buy your evening paper and read all about it! Leaders here say 'Sumter business' is no cause for war."

Too bad it wasn't up to "leaders here" to decide that, Joseph thought as he hurried on. He didn't see much difference between putting down a rebellion and fighting a war.

Pa had sent him to buy a paper when the news of the fort's bombardment came out earlier in the week, and he'd listened to every word. Ma had, too. And the most surprising thing had happened—she'd reached out to take Pa's hand!

"You're late today," the butcher said when Joseph arrived at the market. "Lucky for you I saved back some sausages. How is your mother's sprained ankle?"

"She says it's still badly swollen, and the skin's all purple."

The butcher shook his head. "That must make her life a lot more difficult."

And mine, too, Joseph thought. Since her fall down the stairs several days before, Ma was even more demanding than usual. He took the paper-wrapped package and handed over the coins. Most of the neighbors bought on credit, but Pa refused to. Said he'd go hungry before he'd owe money. Ma said he'd not be hungry very long before he changed his mind about that, but Joseph wasn't so sure. Pa was stubborn, and staying out of debt was important to him.

The sun was casting long shadows by the time Joseph ran up the front steps of the small row house near the harbor. What would his well-off classmates think if they saw where he lived? The downstairs was all one room, with the table where the family ate placed in front of the windows facing the street. Ma's worktable and the coal stove that served for heating and cooking were along the side wall with her rocking chair and Pa's easy chair nearby, and their bed and a chest were against the back wall. The upstairs was divided into two bedrooms, a small one in back that he shared with his older brother, Franz, and one in front for their three sisters. It was hard to imagine that some of the mansions where Franz delivered blocks of ice had twenty rooms or more—and all of them huge.

"So, Yosef," his mother said, giving his name its German pronunciation. "At last you decide to come home."

"Yes, ma'am." Why did his family insist on calling him *Yosef*? And why did his parents' sentences come out just different enough to mark them as foreign-born even though they had both been in America long enough to lose all but a trace of their accents?

From her rocking chair, Ma began the series of instructions he had come to expect. "Put the sausage by my dishpan and change out of your school clothes before you go for the water. After you have done that, Frieda and Erika need help with their lessons." The little girls looked up from their books, faces showing their envy that he didn't have to come straight home from school.

Joseph nodded, hoping his mother's ankle would be better soon so she wouldn't be so grumpy—and so she could do her own shopping. He was pretty sure his classmates' mothers had slaves—or maybe Irish servants—to do their shopping, and their chores, too. But Ma didn't need servants as long as she had him.

Franz no longer had to help around the house because he turned his wages over to Ma—most of his wages, anyway—and fifteen-year-old Anneliese turned over every penny she earned at the textile factory, so Ma never asked her to help, either. But Anneliese helped anyway, and

Joseph had decided that must be because she was a girl. He knew he'd be just like Franz and Pa and would never lift a finger around the house if he had worked all day.

As he climbed the narrow stairs to his room, Joseph thought resentfully of the way Ma never missed an opportunity to remind him that he could be working and bringing home money for the family if he didn't "go to that school with the rich men's sons." She was satisfied once her children could read and write English and had mastered enough arithmetic to keep the shopkeepers from cheating them. But Pa knew there was more to education. Pa wanted him to stay in school so he could work in an office or maybe even a bank instead of laying brick and stone in warm weather and working on the docks the rest of the year.

After Joseph put on a pair of neatly mended trousers and a shirt his brother had outgrown, he hung up his white shirt and brushed the jacket and trousers of his suit. In his school clothes, he looked as fine as any boy at the academy. Better than most, since he was tall and lean— not pudgy like Alexander. And Ma was so skilled with the scissors that no one would ever guess his wavy brown hair wasn't cut by a barber.

Joseph clattered down the stairs, picked up the water buckets, and headed for the pump at the corner. He was filling the second bucket when he saw Anneliese on her way home from work. His sister had loved school, and Joseph suspected that she envied him his scholarship. Franz, though, had gladly gone to work at fourteen—

Joseph's age. He had hated being confined to the classroom and was proud that in just three years he'd moved up from unloading the ice ships that arrived from Maine to loading blocks of ice onto the delivery wagons to having his own delivery route.

Anneliese waved to Joseph, and he waited for her. "How was school today?" she asked when they met.

"Fine," he said. "How was work?"

"The same as always."

Joseph was glad they had only half a block to walk, because he couldn't think of anything else to say. He was ashamed of his silent complaints about the few chores expected of him when his sister worked ten hours a day, six days a week in the textile factory and slipped on an apron as soon as she came home.

Later, at supper, Pa said, "While we were laying new paving stones on Pratt Street, we saw a Confederate flag go up on Federal Hill, and right away we saw it come down again. From across the harbor, we could hear the shouts—'Down with the southern Confederacy!' and 'Hurray for the Union and Abe Lincoln!' We all cheered, too."

"On Howard Street, people were yelling, 'Down with Lincoln and his hirelings,' Joseph reported.

Anneliese said, "That reminds me—I heard the most terrible thing on my way home from work."

"And what was that most terrible thing, daughter?" Pa asked.

Ignoring his teasing tone, she announced, "A mob of secessionists shot at northern soldiers marching to

142

Camden Station this afternoon."

Franz spoke up. "That wasn't shooting, Anneliese, just some fools throwing firecrackers. I know, 'cause I was there."

Ma looked shocked. "You were in a secessionist mob when you should be working?"

With exaggerated patience, Franz said, "It was more of a crowd than a mob, and I wasn't *in* it, I was *watching* it. The street was blocked solid, and I couldn't drive my ice wagon through it."

"It was a crowd with firecrackers this time, but I think before many days pass, we will have mobs with guns," Pa said. "Today our foreman told us the newspaper says folks in the North want Lincoln to take over Maryland to make sure the secessionists—he calls them 'the secesh'—don't vote to join the Confederacy. I think they will make trouble, these secesh."

If they're all like Harold and Alex, they will, Joseph thought.

Franz said, "It wasn't just secesh in the crowd today. I caught sight of a couple Unionists from work. Some of the fellows are worried that northern troops answering the president's call to arms might decide to take things into their own hands when they get to Baltimore."

Pa sighed deeply. "One way or another, we will see trouble before this is over."

"We will if the newspapers keep printing things that make people in the North and the South hate each other," Ma said, passing Joseph the platter of bread.

Franz said, "Well, the news about Fort Sumter has certainly stirred things up. Everyone in the neighborhood is saying the government can't let those rebels get away with what they did. Lincoln's got to show 'em they can't fire on the American flag like that."

"The president's call for volunteers—seventy-five thousand of them, no?—ought to be a fair warning to the rebels," Pa said, spooning sugar into his coffee.

"I think this 'warning' is what led to the trouble here in Baltimore," Ma said. "And it will lead to trouble in this house if you or Franz think that you must go to Washington and volunteer. To join the militia or the City Guard and defend your home and family is one thing, but what happens in the South has nothing to do with us."

Joseph thought of what his history teacher had said about the rising threat of a civil war with Maryland as its battleground, but he decided not to mention that. He was glad when his brother spoke up. "Well, all those people yelling and throwing rocks at the northern troops this afternoon seemed to disagree with you, Ma."

She frowned and said, "Tomorrow, Yosef must stay away from the drunken secesh mobs uptown. It will not hurt for him to miss a day of school."

To Joseph's amazement, his father agreed. "It will be best for him to stay in the neighborhood for a day or two."

Joseph knew it would do no good to object, but he might be able to keep his mother from lining up a day of chores for him. "Then I'll have to study the next chapters

144

in all my textbooks so I don't fall behind," he said.

In the silence that followed his words, Joseph glanced around the table. His mother's expression told him that she saw through his clumsy attempt to avoid helping around the house, and his little sisters' faces mirrored their envy. Both Anneliese and Franz seemed to be avoiding his gaze, but he was sure that they—and maybe even Pa, who was buttering a slice of bread—envied his unexpected day of freedom.

It was bad enough not to fit in at school, but it was worse not to fit into his own family.

CHAPTER TWO

★ ★ ★

"I'LL DO MY studying upstairs," Joseph said when breakfast was over the next morning.

"And ruin your eyes? When Frieda has cleared the table, you will study here, where the light is better," his mother said.

Joseph's spirits sagged. He knew he would feel her disapproval all day even if she never said a word. "I'll get you some more water while I'm waiting," he said, grabbing an empty bucket and making his escape. He hoped the city would be calm today so Pa would let him go back to school on Monday.

Joseph had been studying for almost two hours when Ma exclaimed, "Look what was under your chair!" She held up a spool of blue thread. "I think it fell from Mrs. Brunozzi's sewing basket when she came to visit yesterday."

"I'll take it to her if you want. It won't take long, and I can use a breather." He closed his book and slipped the spool into his pocket, pretending not to hear Ma mutter something about young people who need a breather from doing nothing.

Outside, the spring sunshine warmed the air, and at the corner he glanced across the harbor toward Federal Hill. The budding trees, pale green above the brighter carpet of grass, lifted his spirits. It was peaceful and uncrowded, the way he imagined the countryside must look. What must it be like to live in a house that stood by itself with grass all around it instead of one in the middle of a block-long row with the sidewalk at the foot of your front steps?

Hands in his pockets, Joseph set off toward Mrs. Brunozzi's boardinghouse. He was halfway there when a familiar voice called his name. What was Harold doing *here*? "How come you're not at the academy?" Joseph demanded, noticing the other boy was wearing his school clothes.

"Same reason you aren't, probably—I saw the news bulletin about another trainload of northern troops on the way through Maryland. A whole regiment from Massachusetts is coming in at President Street Station," Harold said, his voice excited.

"What time is the train due?" Joseph asked, realizing Harold didn't know this was the neighborhood he lived in, that Harold assumed he was playing hooky to see the northern troops arrive.

Harold shrugged. "Not for a while yet, but this time I want to be able to see what's happening. We won't be at the back of the crowd again today, right?"

"Right," Joseph echoed. Not that there were any signs of a crowd yet, and besides, the working-class people who lived around here weren't secessionists. Many of them were immigrants or the children of immigrants, proud to be Americans and grateful for the freedom and opportunity they had found here.

Walking at a good pace, the boys soon reached the station. "Listen—I hear a train coming," Harold said. "You think it's the troops?"

Joseph shrugged. "It could be, but it might just be a regular passenger train." Except that no scheduled trains arrived at this time on Friday mornings. When you lived within hearing distance of the station, you knew things like that. "Come on, let's go back to the train yard and see," he said, relieved that Harold hadn't seemed to notice his worn trousers and faded shirt.

By the time they dodged the wagon traffic on the busy street and made their way around to the tracks, the train's engine had been disconnected. A four-horse team was already hitched to the first of the cars, ready to pull it along the track of the street railway to the B&O station a mile to the west. The driver cracked his whip, and as the team set off at a trot, four more horses were hurried into place to be harnessed to the second car.

"It *is* the troops!" Harold cried when the first rail car turned out of the train yard and they could see uniformed men peering from the windows. "It's *them!*" And he let loose with a string of curses that would have earned Joseph a beating from Pa.

If all the secesh felt the way Harold did, it was a good thing the troops didn't have to walk to the B&O station, Joseph thought. And a good thing they had arrived earlier than expected. Even so, three young toughs stood near where the track turned into the street, jeering and shaking their fists. One of them shouted, "Hurray for Jefferson Davis, President of the Confederacy!" To Joseph's dismay, Harold yelled back, "Down with the United States and Abe Lincoln!"

"Look what they're doing," Joseph cried, pointing at the toughs running toward the car as if they intended to jump onto the front platform where the driver stood. They fell back when the driver lashed his whip at them, but they ran along next to the car, taunting the troops inside.

"Come on," Harold said. "Let's run with this next one."

What harm could that do? Joseph had often raced along the sidewalk on Monument Street just for the fun of it, trying to reach the corner before a car of the city's street railway did. He followed Harold, making sure to stay beyond the reach of the driver's whip. Farther up the street, the toughs had stopped to talk to a man on horseback. Joseph couldn't see the man's face but knew he was a stranger. No one who lived—or worked—near the harbor or the rail yard owned a horse.

"Hey, that's my cousin!" Harold exclaimed. "I thought he was going to the secession rally at Monument Square this morning." He waved his arms and shouted, "Hey, Randall! *Ran*dall!"

But Randall gave no sign that he'd heard. "He's headed back the way he came, riding lickety-split," Joseph said.

"On his way to spread the word that the troops came early, I'll bet," Harold said with satisfaction. "Sort of a modern-day Paul Revere, right? But instead of the British, this time it's the Yankees. Come on—let's run with the next car."

Harold began to fall behind after only half a block, but Joseph kept up with the railroad car a little longer. When it began to draw ahead of him, he stopped and raised his eyes to the windows. Some of the faces peering out looked frightened, some curious, and some angry. One soldier shook a fist at him.

Joseph was looking ahead to a group of men waiting at the corner when Harold came puffing up. "Let's rest a minute. We can have a go at the next car when it passes us."

"Right," Joseph agreed. It was good to be outside on a day like this—and on his own territory, he felt more at ease with Harold. Joseph looked back and saw a rail car approaching. Far behind it, another one had just pulled out of the train yard. How many were there? And how long would it take for them all to make the trip to the B&O station?

"Hey, look up there," Harold said. "I guess Cousin Randall spread the word, all right."

A crowd was gathering along Pratt Street, just beyond the wooden bridge. Joseph could hear the men's shouts, and he felt apprehensive. Where were the police this morning? He moved away from the track, positioning himself on the opposite side of the approaching rail car so Harold wouldn't ask why he didn't hiss and shout insults.

Thoroughly enjoying himself, Joseph ran along beside

car after car, keeping up as long as he could, and then dropping back to wait for the next one. By now, both sides of Pratt Street were lined with hissing, jeering men who made threatening gestures when the carloads of soldiers passed. Joseph could hardly believe the number of people swarming down the side streets to join the crowd. And it looked as if there was some kind of commotion opposite the wharf just beyond the next intersection, where a rail car had stopped.

"What's happening?" Harold asked when he caught up.

"I don't know, but that sounded like breaking glass."

"I'll bet somebody threw a rock at that last carful of Yankees!"

"Or maybe a paving stone," Joseph said, beginning to feel uneasy. This was the part of Pratt Street that was being repaired. "Look!" He pointed to a well-dressed man who had raised one of the heavy paving stones above his head and was about to hurl it. *What must Pa and the other masons repaving the street think of this? And where are they now?* Again Joseph heard the sound of splintering glass and a roar of approval from the growing crowd. A third stone crashed through a window of the rail car, and then two more landed harmlessly behind it as it finally pulled away.

Most of the crowd surged into the street and ran after the horse-drawn car, but a few men began to pry up more paving stones and heave them onto the track. Harold pointed toward a bustle of activity on the left and said, "Let's go see what those fellows are up to."

Harold took off at a trot, and glad to be away from the unruly crowd, Joseph followed him. "They're dragging something along the wharf," he said. "It looks like an anchor."

A man with a wheelbarrow full of sand called, "Hey, you two—stop gawking and make yourselves useful!"

"Sure," Harold said enthusiastically. "What should we do?"

"You can help them muscle that anchor at the end of the wharf the rest of the way over here," the man said, gesturing toward a cluster of people on the dock. "And your friend can take this load of sand and empty it on the rails."

Reluctantly, Joseph lifted the handles of the heavy wheelbarrow. *Now* what was he going do? The wobble of the wheel gave him an idea, and he headed toward the track. But when he was still three or four yards away, he raised the wheelbarrow's left handle enough to unbalance the load and spill the sand some distance short of the rails.

His refusal to sabotage the track made no difference, though—except to him—because men had already piled paving stones on the rails and tossed lumber from the docks helter-skelter across them. The quick clopping of hooves and the hum of metal wheels on the rails told Joseph another car was approaching, and he caught his breath. What would happen when the rail car had to stop at the barricade? *Why didn't I think to run back to warn the driver?* He turned and saw that the man had stopped his team to unhitch the horses and was hurrying them to the rear of the car. Good. He was heading back to the station.

But now another car pulled up and blocked his way! While the second driver reversed his team, the men and boys who had lined up along the anchor rope managed to drag their load over from the dock and add it to the debris already on the track. When they saw that the cars had turned back, a few of the men shook their fists and shouted insults, and the rest thumped each other's backs and cheered. Joseph cheered, too, but he was cheering because the soldiers had escaped the wrath of the crowd. For the moment, at least.

"Tough luck," Harold said, eyeing the load of sand Joseph had spilled. "Now you can't say you helped show Abe Lincoln what happens when he tries to send his soldiers across Maryland."

"You can't very well say you helped, either," Joseph retorted. "Those cars had started back before you got that anchor halfway here." He saw Harold's scowl and quickly asked, "What do you want to do now? We'll never catch up to that last car that made it through, and the others have headed back to President Street Station."

His expression brightening, Harold said, "Let's go back there and see what happens next."

The boys sprinted to get in front of the crowd and then walked fast. With the track blocked, the rest of the troops would have to march to Camden Station to catch the Washington-bound train, but Joseph told himself it would be all right. After all, it was one thing to throw stones at a rail car and another to throw them at men armed with muskets.

Joseph walked faster, eager for a better look at the troops who had been so quick to answer the president's call for volunteers to put down the southern states' rebellion.

"Here they come!" Harold's voice was excited, and his usually pale skin was so flushed he looked feverish.

The Massachusetts volunteers marched toward them in columns of four, musket barrels resting on their shoulders, brass buttons and shoulder plates gleaming. Eyes straight ahead, they studiously ignored the howling crowd that surged around them. Where had so many people come from? And why weren't any policemen here to keep the peace? Joseph's jaw tightened when a man carrying a South Carolina flag forced his way to the front of the troops.

"That's rare!" hooted Harold. "He's making Lincoln's troops march behind a palmetto tree flag."

Joseph felt a surge of anger at the secessionist's audacity, and he almost cheered when a Unionist in the crowd pushed his way forward, grabbed the offending flag, and tore it from the pole. But he didn't keep his prize long. The crowd closed in around him, and after a brief scuffle, the torn flag was tied to the pole and held high again, though it was no longer in front of the marching troops. Joseph craned his neck, trying to see what had become of the man who had snatched it, and felt reassured when police raced from the station to rescue him from the angry crowd.

The first of the troops began to pass the boys, and Joseph felt a swell of pride and patriotism he didn't dare show. But by the time the last of the soldiers marched by him, his pride had changed to concern. Separated from the rest of their regiment, the northern men were greatly outnumbered by the howling crowd.

"Come on, let's follow them to Camden Station," Harold said, and he began to strut along behind the troops, much to the amusement of the men nearby.

"I'm going to try to get ahead of them," Joseph said, unwilling to watch Harold's parody of the northern soldiers.

"Good idea. By now, there will be even more people along the route. And this time, there aren't any policemen between us and the Yankees."

They set off at a trot to get ahead of the marching troops. They hadn't gone far when Harold said, "Hey, look up ahead. On the bridge."

Men with crowbars and axes were tearing up the planks and carrying them away! Joseph broke into a run. He stopped just before the bridge and saw that it was still passable, though the water below it was visible in places. On the far side of the span, a rowdy group of men and boys waited, shaking their fists and shouting threats at the rapidly approaching troops. The tramp of feet behind Joseph grew louder, and he moved aside. With a rush of fear, he wondered if the damaged structure would hold the weight of the marching column.

The men started across without hesitation, but their

ranks grew ragged as they were forced to step across the gaps left by the missing planks.

"Just look at 'em," Harold crowed. "They're doing the scotch hop!"

"We'll be doing it, too, if we follow 'em," Joseph reminded him. Jeers and catcalls from the crowd on the other side of the bridge filled the air, and Joseph realized how large the crowd had grown. He thought of his parents' warning the night before, then told himself that they wanted him to avoid the "drunken secesh mob uptown." Well, the route to Camden Station didn't go uptown—it was near the harbor the whole way.

The boys followed the last ranks of soldiers onto the bridge, and Joseph found himself stepping across the gaps where planks were missing, trying not to look at the water swirling below. He saw a group of neighborhood men that included the butcher's oldest son and one of the boarders from Mrs. Brunozzi's. They were shouting, "Go on back where you came from! Stay out of Maryland!"

So the crowd wasn't just the secesh, Joseph realized, and he hollered, "You'll be sorry you ever set foot in Baltimore!"

"It's about time you got in the spirit of things," Harold said. Raising his fist in the air, he yelled, "Death to Lincoln's hirelings!"

Joseph felt a chill. He was relieved when Harold's face lost its fierce expression and he said, "Let's drop back a little. I think I saw my uncle William up there, and I don't want him telling my father I wasn't at school today."

Joseph quickly agreed. He didn't like the looks of the jostling, shouting crowd that almost filled the street ahead of them, barely leaving room for the troops to pass. A boy his age aimed a slingshot and let a rock fly toward the marchers, and someone on the sidewalk threw a bottle that hit a bystander on the shoulder. Farther down the street, a woman flung a water pitcher from a balcony.

"Let's see if we can find something to throw, too," Harold said, his voice excited.

Joseph pretended to search along the curb, glad for an excuse to lag behind. Something sailed over his head, and he looked up to see a man hurling lumps of stove coal from an upstairs window.

At a shouted command, the troops began to march double time, and Harold looked back at Joseph and yelled, "Look at 'em run! I'll bet those muskets of theirs aren't loaded!"

The crowd went wild, and now the air seemed filled with missiles of all kinds—even a wooden stool thrown from a doorway. Joseph thought he heard shots, but he told himself it must be his imagination. He hurried after the troops, and his pulse raced when he saw that the entire road was barricaded not far ahead. *What will happen when the soldiers have to stop?*

A shot rang out in the crowd to Joseph's right, and then he heard a shouted order, followed by musket fire. His mouth went dry when he saw a man in a dark suit clutch his chest and drop a pistol as he crumpled to the ground. *I've just seen a man die.*

Beside him, Harold cried, "Did you see that? They shot him! Those Yankees just up and shot that man!"

"He fired at them first," Joseph protested, but Harold had already pushed his way to the edge of the crowd gathered around the dead man.

Now the northern troops were hurrying along Pratt Street, their muskets held in front of them, bayonets gleaming. The crowd scrambled back to let them by, then closed in behind them, its clamor louder and more abusive. Suddenly, Joseph was afraid. This wasn't a lark anymore—the crowd of protesters had become a mob, and he wanted no part of it.

But there was no turning back. The mass of men behind him carried Joseph along until he managed to stumble into the entry to a shop. He stood there, breathing hard, and watching the crowd surge past—was there no end to it? Two men struggled toward him through the jostling spectators on the sidewalk, half carrying a boy whose face was covered with blood.

"You there," one of the men called. "Hold that shop door open for us."

But shaken by the sight of the boy's limp body and blood-drenched shirt front, Joseph plunged back into the throng. One thought filled his mind: *That could have been Harold—or me.* He grabbed hold of a lamppost and clung to it, eyes closed, while he waited for a wave of nausea to pass. Men shoved their way by, cursing him for being in their way. Then, above the din, he heard someone call out, "It's the mayor!" Almost at once, other voices took up the shout, "Here comes the mayor!"

Mayor Brown will take charge, and then everything will be all right. Joseph opened his eyes and took a couple of deep breaths. No longer feeling ill, he shinnied up the lamppost in time to see the mayor—a known secessionist—shake hands with the officer leading the northern troops and then turn to march toward the B&O station beside him.

The worst of the shouting died down, and from his vantage point, Joseph saw the crowd fall back respectfully. Sensing this change of mood, he felt ashamed of his earlier panic. Someone called his name, and he saw Harold standing in the doorway of a store, gesturing for him to hurry. Joseph dropped to the sidewalk and pushed his way through the crush of sweating bodies toward his classmate.

Harold plunged ahead, weaving in and out of the crowd, and Joseph followed him. When he caught up, Harold asked, "Did you see Mayor Brown shake that Yankee's hand? I can't believe he's protecting the very troops we'll be fighting after Maryland secedes!"

"*If* Maryland secedes," Joseph reminded him as they pressed their way closer to the marching troops. "We'd do a lot better to stay neutral," he added, wondering if that would be possible after today. "Besides, it's the mayor's job to keep the peace in Baltimore, and it's his duty to protect the troops."

Harold frowned and said, "I guess you're right, but I'm not sure he can do it. Look—people have started throwing stones again."

It was true—the crowd was getting bolder. Joseph

gasped when he saw a rioter grab a soldier's musket, wrench it away, and fire it at him. The soldier slumped to the ground, and Joseph cried out, "That's *murder!*" He could hardly make his mouth form the words.

"Soldiers have to be prepared to die, you know," Harold said, his voice shaky.

"In a battle, yes. But not like that." *He was just marching along, and somebody killed him!*

"Come on—something's happening up ahead," Harold said.

Joseph kept up with Harold as they hurried along the fringes of the crowd, dodging a couple of ragged children. It wasn't long before a word came rippling back to them: *Police.*

"My cousin Randall says practically everybody on the police force is secessionist, from the marshal on down," Harold said, his voice excited. "What do you think they'll do?"

"Their job, I hope," Joseph answered as the marshal and more policemen than Joseph had ever seen at one time came running from the direction of Camden Station, revolvers drawn. When they massed between the troops and the mob that tormented them, their tall hats made them look huge, and their expressions made it clear they wouldn't hesitate to use their weapons.

"Keep back!" the marshal shouted. "Keep back, or we'll shoot!"

A rioter tried to run past the solid line of police officers, but the marshal seized him. The crowd began to draw back, and Harold said, "Looks like the fun is over for today." But no sooner had he said it than shots were fired from somewhere in front of the troops. His eyes brightened, and he said, "Let's run up there and see what's happening."

More shots were fired, and Joseph hung back. Pa always said it was foolish to go looking for trouble. "I have a better idea—let's take a short cut to the station. Come on." Without giving Harold a chance to disagree, Joseph led the way down Hanover to Camden Street. As soon as they rounded the corner, they could see a mass of people milling around the station two blocks ahead.

"How did they get here before we did?" Harold asked, slowing to a walk.

"Those must be the people who followed the rail cars when we went back to President Street Station," Joseph said. That seemed a long time ago, but it couldn't have been more than an hour before.

By the time they were opposite Camden Station, the boys could see another contingent of policemen trying to protect the cars of the Washington-bound train and keep the mob from blocking the track ahead of it. "Let's run a ways down the track and drag some branches or something onto it," Harold said.

"I've had enough running for one day," Joseph told him. "I'll just wait here for the marchers."

"Then I guess I will, too," Harold agreed. "Look—here they come."

The boys watched the troops force their way through the crowd that had arrived earlier and head for the cars that would take them to the capital city. Behind the soldiers, the police marshal and his men tried to hold back the mob that spilled into Howard Street and surged toward the station. Stones still flew, and Joseph said, "I wouldn't want to be one of those policemen."

"Neither would I," Harold agreed. "Can you imagine having to protect your enemies? Look—there's Alexander." He raised his voice and called, "Hey, Alex!"

Joseph's heart sank when the other boy began making his way toward them.

"Those Yankees shot one of my neighbors," Alexander said as he crossed the street.

"Just shot him for no reason at all?" Joseph asked.

Alexander glared at him and said, "He'd grabbed their flag, but I don't think that's reason enough to shoot somebody, do you?"

"Is he dead?" Harold asked before Joseph could answer.

"He was hit in the leg," Alexander said. "Last I saw, a couple of men from his office were carrying him off."

They hadn't shot to kill, then. "Sounds like the train's about to leave," Joseph said when he heard the hiss of the engine building up steam.

"Let's give 'em the send-off they deserve," Alexander urged. "You coming with us, Joe?"

Joseph shook his head. "Let 'em leave. I have no quarrel with northern men—provided they don't try to take over Maryland."

"Always playing neutral, aren't you?" Alexander said, his voice hostile.

"Aw, leave him alone, Alex," Harold said. "As long as he's not a Unionist, he's okay, right?"

Alexander gave Joseph a challenging glance and echoed, "As long as he's not a Unionist."

Except he *was* a Unionist. Joseph watched his two classmates dash across the street and shoulder their way through the mass of people toward the station platform. He waited until the locomotive's huge wheels began to turn before he started home, wondering why he felt like such a humbug for going along with Harold. Other Unionists were in the crowd, after all.

"But I never let on that I don't feel the same way Harold does about Lincoln's volunteers," Joseph muttered. The words *As long as he's not a Unionist, he's okay* seemed to ring in his ears, and he thought, I'll be a complete outcast at school if the other boys find out the truth. Maybe Ma's right that people should "stay with their own kind." The trouble is, I don't have anything in common with my old pals in the neighborhood now that they have jobs or apprenticeships. Besides, when I'm free on Saturdays, they have to work, and when they're free in the evenings, I have to study.

Deep in thought, Joseph almost bumped into one of the Pratt Street merchants standing on the sidewalk outside his shop, watching a few stragglers on their way toward the station and remnants of the crowd making their way back uptown. The merchant brushed aside his apologies and asked, "Do you know if the troops got off all right?"

"I saw the train leaving the station. The police managed

to hold back the crowd so the rest of the men could board the cars, but some boys I know were planning to run along the tracks for a ways."

The shopkeeper swore under his breath and then said, "What's wrong with all those southern sympathizers? Can't they see that this city's future lies with the North? Where do they think I buy the goods I sell? And who do they think buys most of what we produce in our factories? If this state secedes, we'll all regret it, mark my words."

"I'll regret it, all right," Joseph agreed. "I think Maryland should side with the Union." How good it felt to say that!

The driver of a passing delivery wagon called out, "Did you hear the news? Virginia troops have taken over the arsenal at Harper's Ferry!"

The shopkeeper swore more loudly this time. "That's where the U.S. government stored its weapons, you know," he told Joseph. "Lincoln might have been able to write off the bombardment of Sumter as the work of South Carolina's fire-eaters, but he won't be able to ignore this. Imagine *Virginians* throwing their lot with the Confederacy!"

Farther down the block, the wagon driver was calling out the news of Harper's Ferry to a small knot of men who had gathered at the corner. "I'd better go," Joseph said, hoping they weren't planning to make more trouble. Slowing as he passed them, he caught the words *over a hundred killed*.

One of the younger men saw him and said, "Hey, here's the boy who spilled that barrow load of sand. Have you heard about the casualties? Those Yankees killed more than a hundred men!"

"At Harper's Ferry?" Joseph asked.

"Here in Baltimore!" the man said, looking at him as though he were crazy. "The next trainload of Lincoln's hirelings will pay for this."

Shaken, Joseph went on his way. A hundred Baltimore citizens dead! Was that possible? Wouldn't he have heard more gunfire—or seen more bodies? At the sound of hoofbeats, he looked up to see Harold's cousin galloping toward him, shouting out to everyone he passed. Still playing Paul Revere, Joseph thought as Randall clattered past, calling, "Troops from New York arriving any minute at President Street Station!"

The next trainload of Lincoln's hirelings will pay for this.

Joseph was staring after Randall when the man who had spoken those words ran past with his friends. "Come on, young fellow," he called over his shoulder. "Didn't you hear about the troops?"

Joseph had heard, but this time he wasn't going to get involved. He'd had enough violence for one day. Maybe even forever. It seemed a long time since he'd left home on a quick errand for Ma. He checked to make sure the spool of thread was still in his pocket, and when he felt it, he headed for Mrs. Brunozzi's boardinghouse.

TWENTY MINUTES later, Joseph was on the way home from Mrs. Brunozzi's when Franz shouted to him from his ice wagon. After he guided his horse to the curb, Franz said, "I thought you'd be at home, studying."

"And I thought you'd be delivering ice in the rich people's neighborhoods," Joseph said, climbing up to the seat beside his brother. "What are you doing in our part of town?"

"The militia's been called out to keep the peace," Franz said. The wagon began to roll again, and he added, "Soon as I take this rig back to the ice company, I'll stop by home for my uniform."

Joseph heard the note of excitement in his brother's voice. "If you want, I can rub down your horse and give her some oats to save you a little time, but it's a bit late to think about keeping the peace. Haven't you heard about the riot?"

"That's why the governor's called out the militia," Franz said. "They're saying the troops killed more than three hundred secesh. Hey, where's everybody going?"

Following his gaze, Joseph said, "To President Street Station, probably. A bunch of New York troops are due to arrive any minute."

"They must already be there. Listen to the shouting."

Joseph frowned. "I didn't hear a train come in, did you?"

"No, but we might as well swing by the station and have a look." Franz urged the horse past a freight wagon and turned toward President Street.

The bleat of police whistles and shouts of the crowd made Joseph's breath come faster. His brother stopped the ice wagon by the rail yard, and Joseph saw that in spite of the efforts of the police, the mob had smashed train windows and men were hurling rocks into the cars. Rioters jumped up and down on the tops of some cars, and a man was trying to beat his way in through the roof of one with a metal bar. Seeing the terrified faces at the windows, Joseph cried, "But those men aren't soldiers!"

A rioter cradling an armload of bricks called over his shoulder, "They ain't in uniform, but they're on their way to Washington to fight for 'Ape' Lincoln, just the same."

Joseph heard galloping hoofbeats and saw the police marshal and a stern-looking older man wearing a military uniform. When the two of them rode into the rail yard, the rioters grew quiet. A few slunk away, but most came closer to hear what the marshal had to say.

After he'd introduced his companion, a general with the Maryland state militia, the police marshal said, "The men in these train cars are unarmed volunteers from

Pennsylvania. They pose no threat to the citizens of Baltimore, but we're going to send them back where they came from anyway. I want all of you to go home so the general and I can make arrangements to do that."

Pennsylvanians, then, and not New Yorkers, Joseph thought as the crowd began to thin. You couldn't believe half of what you heard. He took a deep breath and said, "Boy, I'm glad that's over."

"I'm not so sure it is," his brother said as they headed toward the ice company. "A lot of the rioters are still hanging around. I'll take you up on your offer to look after Nelly so I can report for militia duty a bit sooner."

"Tell Ma I'll be home in a little while," Joseph said. He didn't want to think about what she would say when he got there. He'd already been gone a couple of hours on an errand that should have taken twenty minutes at the most.

After he had rubbed down the horse and given her oats and a bucket of water, Joseph left the ice company stable. He glanced across the harbor to Federal Hill and thought how peaceful it looked. What must it be like to live on one of the estates over there? Or even to work at the hilltop signal station with its view of approaching ships?

Joseph had almost reached the corner of the street where he lived when he heard the thud of running feet and looked back to see a group of laborers from the docks pounding toward him. He pressed himself against the wall of a building to give them room to pass, and then, curiosity getting the better of him, he followed them, sure he would end up at President Street Station—for the third time that day.

Just as he'd thought, that was where they were headed. The train yard was a scene of chaos, and Joseph stood a safe distance away to watch the frightened-looking Pennsylvanians being hurried from the passenger cars and loaded into windowless freight cars. Many of the men were bleeding, and a few were half carried by their companions. A woman standing in her doorway called to Joseph and said, "Some of the ones without uniforms have slipped away. I counted half a dozen."

"Don't much blame 'em," Joseph said, his eyes on the melee. Nearby, neighborhood men exchanged punches with well-dressed men from uptown, and a railroad worker grabbed the arm of a roughly dressed fellow who was about to throw a rock at the volunteers.

Joseph had been in his share of fistfights in the neighborhood, and in the school yard, too. But those were fair fights, and they were fought in anger, not hatred. At least not the kind of hatred he'd seen today. But in spite of the revulsion he felt, he couldn't bring himself to leave. There was something fascinating about seeing grown men completely out of control, something exciting about the violence—and about not knowing what might happen next—that drew him like a magnet.

At last the northbound train pulled out of the station, and the crowd roared its approval. Some of the cheering secessionists waved Confederate flags, and others continued to throw stones at the departing freight cars. People on the fringes of the crowd began to drift away, and Joseph caught scattered phrases: . . . *Close to five hundred of our citizens killed . . . revenge . . . arm ourselves against . . .*

three o'clock at Monument Square . . .

The sound of the train faded away, but Joseph noticed that the din in the station yard had increased. Some of the rioters, angry at being deprived of their prey, attacked the remaining freight cars and began breaking out the windows in unoccupied passenger cars. Pa said vandalism was the coward's crime, and if you couldn't stop it, you shouldn't dignify it by watching.

Joseph turned away in disgust. Maybe he'd walk up to Monument Square and stake out a place where he could hear what the speakers had to say. Squinting, he glanced at the sky. Must be about two o'clock—no wonder he was so hungry. But this was the most exciting day he'd ever had—well worth missing a meal for.

On the way to Monument Square, he saw a crowd of men milling around outside a building and crossed the street to avoid them. When he read the sign over the building's door, he understood: It was the armory of one of the militia units. But were those militia members waiting for their officers to arrive, or were they rioters hoping to break in and take the weapons that were stored there? Joseph felt a chill at the thought of an armed mob raging through the city's streets.

People were already gathering in the square around the monument to George Washington when Joseph got there. More and more men arrived, and the buzz of conversation grew louder, but there was no shouting or name calling. This was an orderly crowd, though Joseph sensed an undercurrent of excitement.

At last the meeting began. Joseph listened while first the police marshal and then the mayor urged the people to stay calm. Finally, a man Joseph didn't recognize climbed to the base of the monument to speak, and a ripple of excitement flowed through the crowd: *The governor!*

Standing beneath the Maryland state flag, the governor, too, spoke of calm. The people packed into the square listened quietly at first, but when he announced that to avoid more bloodshed, he would see that northern soldiers were kept out of Baltimore, the cheers were almost deafening. Joseph cheered as loudly as anyone, and he joined in the roar of approval when the governor declared, "I am a Marylander, and I love my state, and I love the Union, but I will suffer my right arm to be torn from my body before I will raise it to strike a sister state."

How Joseph envied the governor's courage—he'd faced a mostly secesh crowd and told them that he loved the Union. *He* didn't even have the courage to say that in front of the boys at school. But then, *he* couldn't win their approval by promising to keep northern troops out of the city. Or by assuring them that any Maryland troops sent to Washington would be used to protect the city rather than against the southern states.

The crowd had begun to break up, and Joseph turned toward home, feeling a lot better about being a Unionist—and about telling the boys at school he wanted Maryland to be neutral. After all, that was what the governor wanted, and the people had cheered for him.

Joseph was almost home when he heard a commotion

171

behind him. He glanced back and saw a stranger who looked no older than Franz running along the sidewalk on the other side of the street with three older youths in close pursuit. When they passed opposite him, Joseph recognized the young toughs he'd seen at the train yard that morning. *That must be one of the Pennsylvania volunteers they're after!*

The four of them disappeared around the next corner, but Joseph knew the pursuers had caught up to their intended victim by their cries of triumph. At the cross street, he saw that the largest of the roughnecks was holding the stranger while the others pummeled him mercilessly. The struggling youth managed to land a kick on the shins of one of his tormenters, with the result that the two of them began aiming kicks as well as blows at him, while the third gave his arm a cruel twist.

Now the youth no longer tried to resist, but the toughs continued their merciless pounding. *If they keep that up, they'll kill him!* Joseph dashed diagonally across the street and charged head down into the fray, knocking one of the attackers into another. They fell like tenpins, but the third roughneck shoved the limp form of their victim aside and lunged for Joseph.

He ran for his life. *He'll grab me and the other two will catch up and they'll—* Shouts and the sound of running feet told him the toughs were gaining. The rasping breath of the one in the lead was so close Joseph could almost feel the viselike grip of fingers closing on his shoulder.

A lamppost stood just ahead of him, and with an extra

burst of speed, he cut to the right of it, reached out to grab the post with his left hand, and swung around to face the way he had come—and his pursuers. He thrust out a foot and tripped the one in the lead, who crashed to the sidewalk. The second tough leaped over Joseph's outstretched foot and almost stumbled, but the third made a grab for him.

He wrenched away and ran faster than he ever had before, but his pursuer was faster still. The next thing Joseph knew, he was in a stranglehold, and the more he kicked and struggled to free himself, the tighter his captor's grip became. As if in a dream, Joseph saw another figure in front of him, fist drawn back and eyes dark with rage. The grip around his neck was so tight he could scarcely breathe, and his pulse pounded in his ears. *I'm going to die.*

But at the shrill bleat of a whistle, the tough who was holding Joseph shoved him away and yelled, "Police!" All three bullies took off, and Joseph collapsed to the sidewalk, gasping in huge gulps of air.

"Are you all right?" called the young stranger, limping toward him.

Joseph struggled to his feet. "I—think so. What about yourself?"

"It's a good thing you came along when you did," the youth said. "I couldn't have taken any more of their punishment." Already one eye was nearly swollen shut, and he held a bloodstained handkerchief to his badly cut lip.

"If the police hadn't been nearby, those rowdies would

have beaten us both to a pulp," Joseph said. "We'd better get away from here. Come on, I live nearby."

"I'm much obliged," the young man said. "I've not been away from home before, and—"

Another bleat of a whistle, this one much closer, made them both jump. No officers were in sight, but a small boy was watching them from an open window of the house at the end of the row. "Pa got me a pennywhistle," the child said, holding it up. "See?"

Joseph's nervous laugh was cut short by the sound of shouts followed by what might have been a pistol shot. "Quick!" he said, glancing over his shoulder. "Around the corner." He would have raced for home if his companion hadn't been limping so badly. At least they didn't have far to go. "My name's Joseph Schwartz, by the way. I live in the middle of the block."

"Jonathan Engle, from Pennsylvania. My father's a farmer. I'd never been in a city till my militia unit answered Lincoln's call."

"And I've never been on a farm," Joseph said. "Here we are." He led the way up the few steps to the door and opened it. "Ma?" he called, "I'm home, and—"

"Such a long time it took you to return a spool of—"

"This is Jonathan Engle from Pennsylvania," Joseph said, interrupting. "The secesh were beating him up, so I brought him here."

Ma gasped when she saw the young man's ripped and bloody clothing and his bruised face. "The poor boy!" She turned to Joseph's sisters and said, "Frieda, bring warm water from the kettle, and you, Erika, find clean rags and a towel. Joseph, go and get your brother's extra work shirt for Jonathan to wear while his own is washed and mended."

On his way upstairs, Joseph thought, If I hadn't come along, Jonathan would be lying on the sidewalk back there, half dead. And if that little boy's father hadn't bought him a penny whistle— He shuddered.

Joseph took his brother's extra shirt from the peg on the wall and went downstairs, where he found his mother and Jonathan deep in conversation—in German.

"You see, Yosef," Ma said in English, "your Jonathan is not ashamed to speak the language of the old country. And it does not make him less of an American." She turned her attention back to Jonathan and said something that made him laugh, something Joseph didn't understand.

It was nearly dark by the time Ma had cleaned all of Jonathan's cuts, put poultices on the worst of his bruises, and instructed Frieda to wash his shirt in cold water and rub salt into any bloodstains that didn't scrub out. "Anneliese should be at home by now, and so should your father," she said, frowning at Joseph as though he were responsible for their absence.

Anneliese shouldn't be out on the streets alone. "I'll go and meet—"

"You will go nowhere!" Ma said, and Joseph was steeling himself for a tongue-lashing when the door opened and his father and older sister came in.

After the introductions, Pa turned to Joseph and said, "I saw you near Camden Station today, Yosef."

So Pa had followed the rioters, too. "Yes, sir. I stayed away from uptown like you and Ma said."

Ma glared at him from the stove, where she was stirring a pot of stew. "You were supposed to stay away from *trouble.*"

Pa said, "I think Yosef did that, the same as I did. I watched from inside a barbershop, and he stayed across the street from where the trouble was. And when the other lads went to join the mob, I saw him turn away."

Pa wouldn't be so pleased with me if he knew I'd run with the mob—or if he'd seen me pushing that wheelbarrow load of sand.

"And then Joseph got me out of some real trouble," Jonathan said.

Ma began to ladle up the stew. "You see, Anneliese?" she said, glancing at her daughter. "That is how it is with the men. They stick up for each other, no matter what."

"I might be dead if Joseph hadn't stuck up for me," Jonathan said, and he proceeded to describe how Joseph had rescued him. When he finished, Ma's face was pale and Pa's was grave, but Joseph's sisters were looking at him with rapt admiration.

"And then a little kid rescued me," Joseph said, embarrassed by all the attention focused on him.

When he finished telling about the boy with the whistle, his father said solemnly, "This story could have had a different ending for our two young men here."

Pa called me a young man.

"And to think that we kept Yosef home from school

because we wanted him safe here in the neighborhood," Ma said. "I think there is no safe place in these troubled times." She smoothed her apron and said, "But come, all of you. The girls have put the food on the table."

Joseph passed the platter of bread and asked, "Were there still rioters in the streets when you left work, Anneliese?"

She shook her head. "Patrols of militiamen were everywhere, but I was still glad Pa came to walk me home. We saw Franz, by the way. He was standing at a corner with a musket on his shoulder, but he pretended not to notice us."

Pa chided her, saying, "Your brother was on duty, Anneliese. He must not seem to be distracted by a pretty girl, even if she is his sister." Then he turned to Jonathan and Joseph. "You had good luck that only three fellows were in the group that fought you. I hear that bands of older boys, some of them with weapons stolen from the gun shops, are on the streets. But now it seems that things are under control. For the time being, at least."

"And what is this 'for the time being'?" Ma asked. "Is the trouble over, or is it not?"

Pa hesitated a moment before he answered. "Some say northern troops are gathering in Philadelphia and Harrisburg, and that they will come to punish Baltimore for the way their state's unarmed militiamen were treated here. Boys like this Jonathan of ours."

Joseph saw a look of fear cross Anneliese's face. "That might be just a rumor," he said, thinking of how the number of citizens killed in the riot was larger each time he heard it. Erika tugged at his sleeve, and when he leaned toward her, she whispered a question in his ear. "Why don't you ask him yourself?" he whispered back.

Erika turned to the young Pennsylvanian and asked shyly, "If you're a soldier, how come you don't have on a uniform?"

"When we volunteered, they told us we'd be given everything we'd need when we got to Washington," Jonathan explained.

"If those volunteers from Massachusetts hadn't had their weapons, they wouldn't have gotten to Washington," Joseph said. "Not alive, anyway." Before anyone could respond to that, there was a brisk knock at the door, and he went to see who was there. To his surprise, he found himself facing a policeman.

"Some of the Pennsylvania recruits never made it onto the train taking them back home, so we're going house to house, trying to round up the stragglers. Are you harboring any?"

"What are you going to do with them?" Joseph asked, stalling. With their marshal leading them, the police had protected the northern volunteers from the rioters—but what if their Confederate sympathies got the better of them now, unsupervised in the dark streets?

The officer glared at Joseph and said, "We're sending them home, like the mayor said we would."

Joseph's father joined them at the door. "My son has rescued an injured Pennsylvania boy and brought him here to safety. We will walk with him to the station when he has finished his meal."

Joseph heard the note of pride in his father's voice when

he said *my son*, and he hoped Ma and the girls had heard it, too.

An hour later, Joseph and Pa were leaving President Street Station after waiting to see the train steam off for the north. The rubble-strewn train yard had seemed strangely sinister in the darkness, and Joseph was glad he wasn't there alone.

"Thanks to you, Jonathan is better off than many of those young men," Pa said as they headed home. "Some of them looked like they had seen battle."

Joseph thought of Ma's words when she handed Jonathan his washed and mended shirt after Anneliese had ironed it dry: *At least your poor mother will not have to see her boy all bloodied.* "It's hard to believe that something like this could happen," he said, thinking of all the violence he had witnessed that day, remembering the boy covered with blood, realizing that only by luck had he escaped a similar fate.

After a moment Pa said, "What I saw today does not surprise me much. The men who write in the newspapers, they had turned North and South against each other long before Union men moved into that fort in Charleston Harbor. And now—"

"Pa, look." A group of men was coming their way, light from the gas streetlamps throwing hulking shadows far in front of them. Joseph's heart began to pound. What if those toughs had come back and brought their friends? Would they recognize him in the dark? He breathed more easily when one of the shadowy figures called, "Is that you, Schwartz?"

"It is," Pa called back. "And who is asking?"

"Kelly, and some others from the neighborhood. We just stopped by your house."

When they met under a streetlamp, Joseph recognized several of their neighbors with a uniformed man he'd never seen before. The stranger introduced himself and said, "I'm looking for volunteers to come with my unit and stand by in case they're needed for a job that's crucial to the safety of this city."

Mr. Kelly said, "There's threats from the North to send troops to lay Baltimore in ashes—payment for what the secesh did here today."

Then what Pa told us wasn't a rumor.

Frowning at the interruption, the officer continued. "Your son Franz suggested that you and your neighbors might provide some of the manpower we'll need if we get orders to burn the railroad bridges to prevent those threats from being carried out. Will you come?"

"Of course." Pa put a hand on Joseph's shoulder and said, "Tell your mother I will be back when my help is no longer needed."

"Can't I come along, Pa?"

"Tonight your duty is to protect your mother and the girls."

At least he didn't say I was too young, Joseph thought as he watched the men head toward Pratt Street. He weighed the idea of following them at a distance, but the word *duty* hung heavy in the air, and he set off for home.

CHAPTER FOUR

★   ★   ★

JOSEPH STRUGGLED awake the next morning, stiff from sleeping in Pa's easy chair—fully dressed and with the stove poker close at hand. Yawning, he got up and reached for the water buckets. For once, Ma wouldn't have to nag him out of bed to fill them for her and carry in coal for the stove.

Only Mr. Kelly's youngest son was at the pump ahead of him, and while Joseph waited his turn, he glanced across the harbor. Federal Hill was close enough as the crow flies, but it was almost as far out of his reach as the moon. He'd feel no more at ease with the well-off folks who owned estates on Federal Hill than he did with the rich boys at school. *Yesterday, though, Harold seemed just like any other fellow.*

Home again, he dipped water from the bucket into the coffee pot. He was congratulating himself on his thoughtfulness when his mother said, "Next time you are up before me, start the fire before you go for the water. Then the stove can heat up while you're at the pump." She limped to her worktable and began to scoop flour into a bowl. "Do you think you can be back before dark if I ask you to walk Anneliese to work this morning?"

"I ought to be able to manage that," Joseph said, matching her sarcasm with his words but keeping his tone of voice respectful. He half expected a reprimand, but Ma only gave him a sharp look.

More than an hour later, on his way back from walking his sister to the textile factory, Joseph detoured past the newspaper office to see if any bulletins had been posted. Standing at the edge of the group that had gathered to wait for the latest news, he could see only the large print at the top:

TWELVE CITIZENS, FOUR SOLDIERS KILLED IN RIOTING; SCORES INJURED

I knew it couldn't be as many as people were saying. Joseph eased his way closer so he could read more:

BRIDGES BURNED ON ALL RAIL LINES LEADING NORTH

So they'd done it, Joseph thought, glad to know the city was safe from the rage of northerners who had heard about the Union men killed or injured in the riots. He pressed his way forward until he could read the rest of the bulletin:

CITY TO BUY WEAPONS
FOR ITS DEFENSE
Citizens Will Be Armed
To Repel Invaders

He was reading it all a second time when a voice at his elbow said, "What are you doing up so early on a Saturday?"

Harold. Joseph shrugged and said, "Same thing you are, I guess. Trying to find out what's going on. I already knew about the bridge burning," he added. "My father was in on it." Maybe next time Alexander accused him of being a Unionist, Harold would remember that.

"My father was meeting with the mayor and the governor half the night," Harold said. "When I got up, I found a note asking me to check for news bulletins first thing this morning. Listen, I've got to get back—Cook hates it when I'm late for breakfast."

"See you on Monday, then," Joseph said. He remembered that Harold's father had something to do with one of the railroads and wondered if Mr. Porter's meeting had been to decide whether the bridges should be burned. "Rich men make the decisions and poor men carry them out," he muttered as he set off for home.

He'd walked only a short distance before he met another boy from his class. "Going to check the bulletins, Charles?" he asked.

Charles nodded. "My mother asked me to. She's upset because of all the commotion in the city even though it's nowhere near where we live. Well, see you on Monday."

After they said good-bye, Joseph realized that this was the most he'd ever heard Charles say at one time. Unlike the other boys at school, he rarely joined in the arguments and discussions in the school yard. Once Alexander had made fun of him behind his back, but Harold had said, "Let it go, Alex," and it hadn't happened again.

When he passed President Street Station, Joseph saw a man sweeping up broken glass in the train yard and tossing debris into a wheelbarrow. Thinking that this might be a chance to earn a little pocket money, he found the stationmaster and said, "If you're hiring extra help to clean up after the trouble yesterday, I could work for you, sir."

"I could use someone to sort through the baggage cars to see what can be salvaged and whether we can identify the owners. You game for that?"

"Yes, sir," Joseph said, and he followed the stationmaster through the building and out to the train yard where the boxcars were lined up. "The secesh did all this?" He stared at the damaged cars and the debris that surrounded them.

The stationmaster said, "The damage was done by the secesh, but some of the looting was done by folks from the neighborhood." He picked up a flattened object that had once been a trumpet and said, "It's a shame what they did here—pretty much destroyed the instruments of the Sixth Massachusetts Regimental Band. Somebody must have jumped up and down on that drum over there."

Joseph's eyes strayed to an empty boxcar that had its

door pried open and he said, "Looks like they carted off whatever was inside that one."

"It was filled with boxes of muskets and ammunition," the stationmaster told him, "and it was the police who carried it all away. The officers claimed the weapons would be used for the city's defense, but if you ask me, they could as easily end up in rebel hands across the Virginia border." He sighed and said, "Well, young man, you have your day's work cut out for you. Start by sorting things into two piles—one for discards and one for anything that can be salvaged, all right?"

Joseph nodded and set to work, realizing that the stationmaster hadn't said what his pay would be. Well, it was sure to be more than enough to treat his classmates at the sweet shop next time he was invited. And just being out of the house so Ma couldn't order him around all day was worth something.

By midday, he had a large pile of discards and a much smaller one of undamaged goods. He looked up as the stationmaster paused beside him and said, "On your noon break, run up to the newspaper office and see if any bulletins have been posted, would you?"

"Yes, sir!" That would give him an excuse to leave the house again as soon as he finished eating.

Even before he reached home, Joseph could smell the yeasty aroma of freshly baked bread, and when he went inside, he saw steam rising from the stew pot on the stove.

"Set out another bowl, Erika," Ma said. "Your brother will honor us with his presence."

Erika gave him a reproachful look, but Joseph ignored her. "Didn't I tell you I could manage to be back before dark, Ma?" He took his place at the table and asked, "Franz and Pa aren't home yet?"

"Your brother is asleep after his night of patrolling the streets, but your father and the other volunteers from the neighborhood have not come back."

Frieda piped up and said, "Mrs. Kelly thinks they've all been captured by the men from Pennsylvania."

"She was crying," Erika added.

Ma rolled her eyes. "Mrs. Kelly cries just like *that*," she said, snapping her fingers. "Did you forget Franz told us the men did not go to burn those bridges until a few hours before dawn? Of course they are not back yet, Erika! And you need not worry about your pa—he can take care of himself."

"I wish he hadn't gone," Erika said, her voice trembling.

"You are a foolish girl," Ma said. "What kind of man refuses to do what is needed to protect his home and family? Do you *want* angry Pennsylvanians marching into Baltimore? Laying the city in ashes? That is the threat Franz said they made."

Erika began to sob, and Joseph wasn't sure whether it was Ma's scolding tone or her words, but when Frieda burst into tears, he decided it must be the image of Baltimore in flames. "With the railroad bridges destroyed, there's no way for the trains to bring the soldiers here," he said. Then he glanced at his mother and said, "Good stew, Ma."

"It is always better on the second day."

Joseph spooned up the last of it before he announced, "I'm going up to the newspaper office to see if they've posted any more bulletins. The stationmaster asked me to check," he added when he saw his mother's frown. "I'm working for him this afternoon."

Her forehead smoothed. "At last you take your nose from the books long enough to bring home a few coins," she said.

He would have to hand over his afternoon wages, Joseph realized, but he'd hold back what he'd earned this morning.

Just as he reached Pratt Street, a group of uniformed men on horseback rode past. Cavalry! He was still watching them when a barber standing outside his shop spoke to him. "They're from Frederick—I saw their company flag. I hear that a couple of units from Baltimore County have come into town, too."

"Add them to all the city's militia units, and we ought to be in good shape," Joseph said. He noticed that a Maryland state flag flew from the pole over the barber's door instead of the American flag that had been there ever since South Carolina seceded.

The barber nodded. "From what I hear, men all over town are volunteering. It's a madhouse outside the armories."

"Aren't you going to volunteer?" Joseph asked.

The man shook his head. "I'm a Unionist."

"My pa's a Unionist, and he volunteered."

The barber shrugged. "I have a business to run. With all the excitement, not many customers stopped by yesterday or this morning, but when things settle down a bit, I'm counting on the officers of these out-of-town units coming in for a shave."

Joseph crossed the street and continued on his way. He couldn't blame the barber for replacing his U.S. flag, since flying the Stars and Stripes would be a signal for rowdies to vandalize his shop. But it didn't seem right for a man to shirk his duty in the hope of making money from the city's troubles.

Most of the shops Joseph passed were closed, and some had their windows boarded up. But the sidewalks were crowded with men—many of them in militia uniforms Joseph didn't recognize. When he made his way to the front of the group outside the newspaper office, he saw there was nothing posted that he didn't already know:

COUNTY, TOWNS
SEND TROOPS TO CITY
Citizens Rally to Repel
Invasion from North

Disappointed, Joseph made his way back through the crowd to report to the stationmaster. At least it would be fresh news to him.

At the end of the day, Joseph collected his wages and set off for home, the coins jingling in his pocket. He had walked only a block or so when Mr. Kelly caught up to him. "Did you hear?" the man asked. "A mob of secesh are planning to attack Fort McHenry tonight. Probably the same gang that broke into the building where one of the Unionist militia units met. Tell your pa," he called over his shoulder as he hurried on.

Joseph sprinted toward home and was surprised to find Anneliese peeling potatoes when he came in. "They shut down the mill early, Yosef," she said, "and there were notices posted everywhere that the mayor has ordered all the taverns closed."

Pa, who had been dozing in his easy chair by the stove, roused and stretched, and Joseph gave him Mr. Kelly's message about the planned secesh attack on Fort McHenry.

Instantly alert, Pa said, "They are fools! The president cannot lose another fort to southern rebels. If these secesh carry out their plan, Lincoln will send his troops into Baltimore."

Franz clomped down the stairs after sleeping most of the day. "What's this about losing another fort?" he asked. Joseph explained, and Franz said, "Didn't the secesh learn anything from Fort Sumter? Right after the attack, Lincoln called for seventy-five thousand men to put down the rebellion. What do they think he'll do if they try to take McHenry only a week later?"

"Are you going to help protect the fort, Pa?" Erika asked in a small voice.

Pa shook his head. "I will protect my home and family, and I will protect my city, but the soldiers at McHenry must protect their fort without help from me."

"Well, with the reinforcements the government sent to the fort a couple of months ago, they should be prepared for something like this," Franz said. "Besides, a secesh mob—even an armed mob—can't be that much of a threat to the McHenry garrison. Baltimore citizens don't have heavy artillery, you know."

"What I know is that supper is waiting on the table," Ma said. "Come and sit."

Now maybe he could ask Pa about burning the railroad bridges and find out from Franz what went on in the city during the night, Joseph thought. Hearing about it all firsthand would be a lot more exciting than reading the news bulletins.

JOSEPH HAD just stepped outside the next morning when he heard it again—the clamor of a crowd. Now what? He left his water buckets by the steps and followed the sound toward the harbor. The waterfront was teeming with people. What were they doing here at this hour on a Sunday?

"Great news about the troops, ain't it?" said an excited boy standing at the edge of the crowd.

"Which troops do you mean?" Joseph asked.

"The ones that just arrived on the bay steamer *Louisiana*, of course!"

The old man who was with him said, "Seven hundred of 'em, is what we heard. Seven hundred southern boys come to help protect Baltimore from northern aggression."

"But I don't see any soldiers," the boy said.

"I don't see the *Louisiana*," Joseph said, scanning the vessels moored along the docks, looking carefully at the steamboats scattered among the tall-masted sailing ships.

The old man spat on the ground. "Another rumor, I guess, like last night's attack on McHenry that never happened," he said.

Joseph looked across the water toward the mouth of the harbor, where the high walls of the fort rose from the water's edge. A lump formed in his throat when he saw the huge garrison flag that flew high above it—probably the only U.S. flag for miles around. How did the "star-spangled banner" that had cheered Baltimore's people after the 1814 naval battle become such a hated symbol for so many in the city today?

After one last look at the flag, Joseph made his way through the disappointed crowd milling around the street nearest the harbor. Back home, he picked up the buckets he had abandoned outside the door and set off with them. He was sure that Harold's family had water pumped right into their house—not that Harold would have been the one to fetch it if they didn't.

At church later that morning, Joseph noticed that Pa was one of the only men in the congregation. The few other men and older boys who sat with their families were wearing their militia uniforms, and Joseph figured that the rest were on duty or at their arsenals, as Franz was. *Soon as I'm sixteen, I'll join the militia, too.*

Joseph was daydreaming through mass, imagining himself carrying the flag in the Independence Day parade, when a man on horseback rode up to the open door of the church and hollered, "Yankees from Pennsylvania are marching into Maryland—thousands of 'em!"

The stunned silence in the sanctuary was followed by a rustling sound as the uniformed men and boys made their way to the nearest aisle and then to the door. Joseph's eyes followed them, and he wished he dared slip away to find out more. Near the front of the church, a baby began to fret, and the priest raised his voice and said, "Go to your homes, my children. I will pray for your safety and that of our city."

Even before he finished speaking, the people were on their feet and spilling into the aisles. It was worse than the end of the school day. Almost at once, the scuffle and murmuring of the congregation was drowned out by the ringing of the church bell. By the time Joseph had followed his parents outside, the air was filled with the peals of other bells sounding the alarm.

"That would be a pretty thing to hear if you did not know that it meant trouble," Ma said, leaning her weight on Pa's arm.

The family was slowly making their way toward home when another sound reached Joseph's ears—the beating of drums to call out the militia. "If you want, I'll go find out what's happening," he said, hoping he didn't sound as eager as he felt.

"*You* are the one that wants," Ma grumbled.

"Go and find out, Yosef," Pa said, "but this time, come straight home."

Grateful that Pa had let him go, Joseph dashed off. He could feel his mother's disapproving eyes boring into his back, could sense his little sisters' envy of his freedom, and he wondered if Harold chafed at being with *his* family. Was it different if you were rich, or did his

193

classmates feel this same lightness the minute they were off on their own?

Rounding the next corner, Joseph saw men and older boys rushing toward their armories. He had never seen so much activity in the city on a Sunday, and he wished he could be part of it. If only he were sixteen *now*!

When he came in sight of the newspaper office, he saw that hordes of people were there before him. He shouldered his way toward the building until he could see the bulletin posted outside:

3000 NORTHERN TROOPS
17 MILES FROM CITY!

Joseph's throat went dry. It wasn't much more than what the horseman had shouted into the church during mass, but seeing the words in print somehow gave them greater importance. He stared at the bulletin a moment longer, trying to imagine three thousand soldiers marching on Baltimore, and then he raced for home.

He burst into the house and gasped out what he had learned. Pa broke the silence that followed. "Seventeen miles, you say? Then they are near Cockeysville, and if the railroad bridge there had not been burned, three thousand angry Pennsylvanians would be arriving in our city."

"So now you will go with the others to make sure these men do not march into Baltimore." Ma sounded resigned. "Better that you do not leave until you have had your Sunday dinner." She handed each of the little girls a serving bowl, and Anneliese took the heavy platter of *sauerbraten*.

"I think there is no great rush," Pa said, his eyes on the marinated beef roast his oldest daughter was carrying. "We had many hours of waiting before we left to destroy the railroad bridges."

Frieda took her place opposite Joseph and said, "If Franz was here, he wouldn't wait till after dinner. He'd of gone as soon as he heard the Yankees were coming."

Father nodded. "Franz finds all this exciting."

It *is* exciting, Joseph thought, passing along the bowl of boiled potatoes. Not knowing what would happen next was scary, but it made him feel—alive.

Pa finished his meal and pushed back his chair. "Well, I go now to join what they are calling the 'un-uniformed volunteers.' Yosef, again you must look after your mother and sisters."

The door had hardly shut behind Pa when Frieda gave Joseph a challenging look and asked, "How will you protect us from the Yankees, Yosef? With your pocketknife?"

"The Yankees will be too busy burning the city to bother with mouthy little girls."

Frieda's eyes widened, and Erika asked, "Will they burn our house, Yosef?"

"You must ignore your brother when he is teasing," Ma said. "And you must learn that most things we worry about do not happen."

"I'll go see if any more bulletins have been posted," Joseph said. "Just so we can be prepared. I can be back in half an hour."

195

Ma raised her eyes to the ceiling and said, "Go, Yosef. Just go," and he headed for the door.

The sidewalks were even more crowded than they had been earlier, and Joseph sensed an excitement that bordered on panic. At the newspaper office, most of the men stood in clusters, talking about the latest bulletin, though a few stood alone and waited in brooding silence for more news to arrive. Joseph wove his way through the crowd until he could read the most recent headlines:

POLICE CUT
TELEGRAPH LINES
TO NORTH;
CITY CONTROLS
LINES TO SOUTH
SOME VOLUNTEERS
TO BE ARMED
WITH PIKES
Six O'Clock Curfew
Set for Minors

Pa wouldn't much like it if the "un-uniformed volunteers" were given pikes instead of muskets, Joseph thought. He was about to start home when Harold clapped a hand on his shoulder and said, "Isn't it great news about the telegraph lines?" He noticed Joseph's puzzled look and said, "Don't you see? We've got Washington completely cut off from the North—no rail traffic and no news getting through in either direction."

Joseph hadn't thought of that. "Washington's isolated, then," he said as they moved away from the bulletin board. In his mind's eye, he could see the page in his geography book showing the capital city surrounded on three sides by Maryland, with Virginia just across the Potomac River. Angry, rioting Maryland and rebellious, Confederate Virginia. "I sure wouldn't want to be in Abe Lincoln's shoes," Joseph said honestly.

"Once Confederate soldiers march into Washington and capture him and his cabinet, there won't be any question that the South is an independent nation," Harold said. "Maybe *then* the governor will call a convention so Maryland can vote to secede and join the Confederacy."

Joseph didn't answer. He had never dreamed that the rebels might try to capture the president!

"You haven't given me a single reason why Maryland shouldn't join the Confederacy, Joseph—all you ever say is that we'd be better off if we're neutral. I'm beginning to think Alexander's right about you being a Unionist."

"You can think what you want," Joseph said, his voice tense, "but the riot on Friday was a picnic compared to what will happen if we secede. Maryland will be the battle-ground of the war. Don't you see? Northern troops will pour into Maryland and the Confederates will rush here to stop them."

"You don't have to worry about that," Harold scoffed. "One good battle will be enough to make those Yankees decide to move their capital to Philadelphia or New York and let the South go its own way."

Joseph didn't answer. He thought it was obvious that Lincoln had no intention of letting the South go.

"Hey, I was only joking about thinking you were a Unionist," Harold said. "You're not mad, are you?"

"You sounded serious enough to me," Joseph said, surprised to hear the note of concern in Harold's voice. "I'm glad you didn't mean it."

"Of course I didn't. Listen, I've got to get home for Sunday dinner, Joseph. See you at school tomorrow."

I told Ma I'd be home in half an hour. Joseph set off at a run, skirting the crowds gathered outside the armories. But near Pratt Street, he heard a fife and drum, and he stopped to watch a column of militiamen pass. The butcher's small son was marching along beside them, a wooden gun held to his shoulder, and Joseph called, "Hey, Tony! What's going on?"

Without missing a step, the boy called back, "Two more militia units came to help protect the city. They just sailed in on a bay steamer."

But not seven hundred of them, I'll bet. The rhythmic beat of the drum and the high-pitched notes of the fife made Joseph's pulse race as he watched the men march past, the Maryland flag waving above them and sunlight glinting on their bayonets. It was a stirring sight, but the red, black, and gold of the state flag didn't move him the way the red, white, and blue of the Stars and Stripes always had.

Joseph was almost home when an elderly neighbor called from his window and asked in a quavery voice, "Did you see him?"

"See *who*, sir?"

"Jefferson Davis, that's who. The President of the Confederacy. He's on his way here with a hundred thousand southern boys to help us hold off the Yankees."

Somehow, Joseph managed not to laugh. "No, sir. I didn't see him." He ran down the block toward home, aware that his half hour had stretched to at least twice that.

Silence greeted him when he rushed into the house, but by the time he had told about the latest bulletin and described all that he had seen, his sisters were wide-eyed, and his mother was listening with undisguised interest, the tight expression gone from her face.

When he finished, Frieda asked, "Ma, can Yosef take me and Erika to see all the soldiers?"

"Of course not! This is a time for girls and women to stay home."

"It's not fair! Yosef gets to do anything he wants, but we—"

"Don't whine, Frieda," Anneliese said. She looked up from the sock she was darning and added, "That's just the way it is."

Joseph glanced at Frieda to see how she reacted to her older sister's words, and she crossed her eyes at him.

"If you are not careful, your face will freeze like that, young lady," Ma said, just as Joseph had known she would.

"Hey, it would be an improvement," he said. Frieda began to cry, and Erika sent him an accusing look. If Franz had said that, everybody would have laughed, Joseph thought when Anneliese frowned across the table at him and Ma gave an exaggerated sigh. He wondered what Sunday afternoons were like at Harold's house.

Hours later, Joseph was checking over the math problems he'd done Friday morning, half listening to the Bible story Anneliese was telling the younger girls. He glanced up when the front door opened and his brother came in. "Hey, Franz—don't tell me that six o'clock curfew for minors counts for the militia."

"My unit's been dismissed," Franz announced. "You're not going to believe this, but Lincoln has agreed not to send any more troops through Baltimore—and he's telling those Pennsylvanians up at Cockeysville to go back home."

Then the threat to the city is over. But with the rail bridges destroyed, how will Lincoln's volunteers get to Washington?

"I'm starved," Franz said. "Is it long till supper?"

"The girls and I will have it on the table in a few minutes, Franz," Anneliese said, ignoring her sisters' dismay at having their story interrupted. "Don't get up, Ma—stay off that sprained ankle while you can."

"Why do you think Lincoln backed down like that?" Joseph asked his brother, thinking again of what Harold had said about Washington being cut off from the northern states.

"From what I heard, the mayor took the B&O to Washington and convinced the president that it was the only way to calm things down here in Baltimore. And it looks like he was right, too. Soon as people heard the announcement, the crowds in the streets cleared away."

"Then Yosef won't get to stay home from school tomorrow," Erika said, a triumphant look on her face. "It wasn't fair that we had to go on Friday and he didn't."

Ma looked up from her needlework and asked, "And what has made you think life is fair?"

Joseph wished Pa would come home. Erika and Frieda were good as gold when he was here, and Ma wasn't nearly so grumpy.

CHAPTER SIX

★　　★　　★

AFTER ALL that had happened during the past few days, it seemed strange to be setting off for school as usual on Monday morning. Joseph paused at the corner to look toward Federal Hill, rising green and peaceful across the harbor. But that was all that was peaceful. Here it was, barely a week since Fort Sumter fell, and it seemed as though the entire country was up in arms. As Joseph passed the park, he slowed to watch an officer put a group of volunteers through their paces, then hurried on.

The school yard was less crowded than usual. "Where is everybody this morning?" Joseph asked when he joined a group of classmates.

"I guess some of the older fellows are still with their militia units," one of the boys said. "Did you hear the latest? 'Ape' Lincoln has declared a blockade of all Confederate ports!"

"This could make some businessmen think twice about secession," Charles said. "After all, where would Baltimore be without trade?"

And where would our family be? Franz would soon lose

his job if ships bringing in the huge blocks of ice from New England couldn't reach Baltimore, and Anneliese's factory would have to shut down if raw cotton couldn't be brought in from the South—or bolts of cloth shipped out. And if the rebellion lasted till winter, Pa wouldn't be able to find work at the docks.

"Hey, are you all right, Joseph?" Charles asked. "You look sort of pale."

He gave a quick nod. "I was just thinking about what you said. Wondering how long Baltimore could survive without trade."

Harold said impatiently, "You two aren't thinking clearly. The Union blockade makes it more important than ever for Maryland to join the Confederacy and fight for states' rights—and the sooner the better."

"I agree," said another student who had been listening to their conversation. "The governor should call a convention so our legislators can vote for secession and be done with it."

Joseph felt a knot in his stomach. He'd thought the threat to the city was over when Lincoln told the Pennsylvanians marching toward Baltimore to go back home, when he said that no more troops would be sent through the city. But the real danger wasn't soldiers coming from the North—it lay within Maryland itself, because without a doubt, if the legislators voted on secession, they would decide in favor of it.

The nine o'clock bell rang, and Joseph followed the other boys into the building. But instead of concentrating on his lessons, he brooded on the conversation in the school yard—and on his own stupidity. When the train-loads of troops had passed through the city last week, he'd never imagined something like this would come out of it. All he'd thought of was the excitement of seeing them and the exhilaration of being part of the crowd. Then on the weekend, he'd been almost intoxicated by the sense of urgency that had charged the air. He'd never thought about what it all could mean, never imagined that the city's unrest could affect his family's livelihood.

Joseph was brought back to the present by the school-master's voice. "I take it that you do not know the answer, Mr. Schwartz. Perhaps Mr. Wilson will oblige us." Behind him, Joseph heard Charles give the answer *he* could have given if he'd been paying attention, and he felt his face redden with embarrassment.

In spite of Joseph's efforts to keep his mind on his work, the rest of the day passed in a fog, and on his way home, he forgot all about stopping to see if he could work another couple of hours for the stationmaster. In front of the house, his little sisters were skipping rope, but he scarcely noticed them.

Inside, Ma looked up from her ironing and said, "Home so early, Yosef? You are sick, then, no?" Giving him a closer look, she exclaimed, "You *are* sick!" Setting her flat-iron back on the stove she said, "Come, let me feel your forehead."

"I'm not feverish, Ma. Honest, I'm not. But I might lie down for a few minutes." Upstairs, he pulled aside the curtain and looked beyond the roofs of another row of houses to the harbor, with its bay steamers and fishing boats and sailing ships from all over the world. He let the curtain fall back across the window and tried not to imagine the docks as quiet all week long as they were on Sundays.

He was sitting on the edge of the bed, taking off his shoes, when he heard his mother's footsteps on the stairs—limping footsteps. His spirits sank even lower as he thought of the day she'd fallen partway down those stairs with an armload of laundry and sprained her ankle. "You shouldn't have come up, Ma," he said when she reached the landing.

"I would not have to, if you had let me check you for fever when I asked downstairs."

Joseph gritted his teeth and sat still while she laid a hand on his forehead. "I'm fine, Ma."

"You have no fever, but you are not fine," she said, and to his surprise, she sat down beside him on the bed. "I think you have some burden on your mind, son. Are you in trouble for missing school on Friday?"

Joseph shook his head. "Nobody said anything about it."

"So what new rumor has made you like this?"

"It isn't a rumor, it's—" Joseph's shoulders slumped. "President Lincoln has declared a blockade of Confederate ports," he said. "No ships can enter or leave their harbors."

His mother limped to the window and pulled back the curtain. "And so if Maryland secedes . . ." Her voice faded away, and she gazed out over the harbor for what seemed like a long time.

At last Joseph said, "Even if Maryland doesn't secede, we won't be able to trade with the southern states."

Still at the window, his mother said, "Not as many workers will be needed on the docks, then." A moment later she added, "When times are hard in the city, no one builds, and the old paving stones on the streets are not replaced. Our family will not be the only one in the neighborhood that will suffer."

"Well, now you know what got me down," Joseph said. And it was worse than he'd imagined—Pa would be out of a job long before cold weather if there was no work for bricklayers and stonemasons.

Ma was silent for a moment, and then she turned to face Joseph. "Where does your brother keep the money he holds back from his wages?"

How does she know about that? "What do you mean?"

She made an impatient sound. "When I go downstairs, you will find the money Franz has saved. Then you must go to the market and bring back for me a sack of cornmeal and as many pounds of dried beans as you can pay for." At the doorway, she paused. "When you hear bad news, you do not go to your bedroom and lie down. You do what you can to make things a little better."

Smarting from her words, Joseph waited until he heard his mother's halting footsteps on the stairs before he knelt to open the bottom drawer of the bureau. Winter clothes were stored there, and his nose wrinkled at the smell of the dried lavender blossoms Ma had sewed into muslin bags to keep moths away. He found the mitten where his brother hid his savings, put the money in his pocket with the coins he'd earned on Saturday morning, and went downstairs.

"I'm leaving, Ma," he said.

His sisters had come inside, and Frieda complained, "He's *always* going somewhere, Ma, but me and Erika—"

"Enough!" Ma said. "He is going on an errand for me."

Joseph set off toward the market, surprised at how much better he felt. Was it because he was "making things a little better" or because Ma had stuck up for him?

By the time he lugged his purchases back to the house, his sisters were doing their homework at the table and Ma was starting supper. "Write down for me how much you spent, Yosef," she said.

Joseph did as he was told and then handed the paper to his mother. She reached for the pencil and wrote something at the bottom. "Here," she said, handing it back to him, "give this to your brother." He saw that underneath the amount she had signed her name in the ornate script she'd learned as a small girl in Germany.

"I'll put it where he'll be sure to find it," Joseph said. Upstairs, he opened the bureau drawer and slipped the note inside the mitten where the money had been. He hoped Franz would think Ma had discovered his hiding place on her own.

After school the next day, Harold said, "You know those northern troops that camped up at Cockeysville on the weekend? Father told me the city's leaders found out they were short of food, and yesterday they sent a couple of wagon loads of meat and bread up there for them! Can you imagine feeding your enemies like that?"

"As long as we're still in the Union, they aren't our enemies," Joseph pointed out, wishing ordinary citizens would show the same decency their leaders did.

"All the more reason for the governor to call a special session of the General Assembly so our legislators can vote to secede," Alexander said. "Or do you still think Maryland ought to be neutral?"

Joseph heard the challenge in the other boy's voice. "It doesn't matter what I think," he said. "If there's a vote, it will be for secession. Everybody knows the secessionists have a majority in the legislature."

Dropping the subject, Alexander said, "Come on, let's go to the sweet shop."

Joseph said, "Count me out. I'm going to see if any more news bulletins have gone up." Why hadn't anyone realized that by cutting the telegraph lines to the north, they were cutting off the news coming into Baltimore as well as the news going to Washington?

"I'll go with you," Harold said. "I'd like to see if there's anything about the Fort McHenry garrison planning to fire on the city."

"Where did you hear that?" Joseph asked as they set off.

"From my cousin."

Young Paul Revere, Joseph thought. He doubted that the story was true, but it wasn't worth arguing about.

Especially when Harold had just chosen his company over Alexander's.

"Randall says the Yankees at the fort have their cannon pointed toward Monument Square, and every one of 'em's aimed right smack at George Washington's statue," Harold announced. "It wouldn't make much sense for Union soldiers to destroy a statue of George Washington, would it?" Joseph asked, realizing that Harold was waiting for his response.

Instead of answering, Harold said, "Hey, look! They're posting a bulletin now." He set off for the newspaper office at a run, with Joseph at his heels.

NORTHERN PRESS
URGES LINCOLN
TO KEEP MARYLAND
IN UNION AT ALL COSTS
Calls for Occupation
Of Baltimore Increase

The words in the last two lines made Joseph's spine tingle. He called to the printer's apprentice, a boy from his neighborhood. "How did that news get through, Karl? I thought the telegraph lines to the north were cut."

Karl paused in the doorway and said, "The magazine dealer down the street had a fellow ride up to one of the towns near the Pennsylvania border and bring back copies of the northern papers."

At least if the Union occupied Maryland, the harbor

would stay open and—

"Now do you believe that the troops at Fort McHenry have their artillery trained on the city?" Harold demanded, breaking into Joseph's thoughts. "They could fire those cannon anytime they want and claim they were just making sure Maryland stayed in the Union."

"I don't know what to believe," Joseph said.

Harold gave him an exasperated look and said, "Well, while you think it over, I'm going to find Randall and tell him about those headlines so he can spread the word. We've got to be prepared!"

The next morning when Joseph arrived at school, he saw a group of boys standing on the front steps of the building. He hurried over in time to hear the end of what Harold was saying: ". . . so now that they've taken over Annapolis, they can control the Chesapeake Bay. And *that* means Baltimore is cut off from the South."

"What's happened?" Joseph asked Charles, who was standing a little apart from the others.

"Some general from Massachusetts brought his troops into Maryland by rail and then commandeered a ferryboat to take them down the bay to Annapolis. They've occupied the city."

Maryland's capital, occupied?

One of the other boys turned to Joseph and added, "And that's not all. They've repaired the rail line the secessionists had torn up between Annapolis and Washington, and that means Lincoln's troops can get to the Union capital without coming through Baltimore."

Alexander said, "Now *we're* cut off. Where do all our roads lead? To Washington, Pennsylvania, and Annapolis. The first two are Yankee territory, and now that the Union's taken Annapolis—"

"They control the Chesapeake," Joseph said, repeating what Harold had just said. The bay was what mattered, the bay and its harbor here in Baltimore. His family's livelihood depended on ships that sailed up the Chesapeake, and because of that, keeping Maryland in the Union mattered as much for practical reasons as for patriotic ones—the city had to be assured of trade with the northern states. Joseph didn't want to think about a Confederate Maryland under a Union naval blockade. About the Schwartz family with no source of income.

"Bean soup, *again*?" Erika complained that evening. "This is the third time in a week."

Before Ma could scold her, Joseph said, "You'd better be glad Ma stocked up on dried beans, Erika, 'cause there's not much to buy at the market. I guess a lot of the farmers are afraid to come into town and set up their stands for fear of trouble."

Ma said, "The vegetable man's wagon has not come to this neighborhood since before the riot, so I have no more cabbage or potatoes. Not even a carrot."

"I hope the secesh are satisfied with what they've done," Frieda said.

"I hope they like bean soup," Erika said, pushing away her bowl.

Franz said, "Those rich secesh are probably eating

baked ham and sweet potato dinners—or maybe codfish and potatoes with apple pie for dessert. You should see the pantries in some of the houses on my ice route."

Pa said, "I think the rich will begin to suffer a little. With not many ships coming into Baltimore now, men have lost their jobs on the docks, and the landlords will hurt some when these men cannot pay their rent."

"Those rich landlords ought to suffer—as long as they still pay their ice bill," Franz said.

At a lull in the conversation, Joseph took a deep breath and said, "Pa, a boy in my class has asked if I want to go to Frederick with him and his father to see the legislature in session on Saturday. His father can get rail passes, so we'll all ride free."

Before Pa could answer, Frieda wailed, "It's not fair! Yosef is always the one that gets to go places!"

"He is the one the boy invited," Pa said mildly.

"And who is this boy from class?" Ma asked. "You have not brought him here to meet your family."

Joseph's heart sank. He'd give up the chance for a day's outing with Harold before he'd bring him here! "His name's Harold Porter, Ma. The boys at the academy are too busy studying to see each other outside of school."

"Except for this trip on Saturday, I take it," Ma said.

Pa's face had a distant look. "I have heard that you can see the mountains from Frederick town," he said.

He's going to let me go! "We might even be there for the vote on secession," Joseph said, excitement creeping into his voice.

Frieda looked puzzled. "At school, we learned that the General Assembly meets in Annapolis."

"That's right," Joseph said, "but with the Union Army controlling the city, the governor decided it would be better if the legislature met somewhere else."

"Our foreman says the governor wants the meeting in a place that is not full of the secesh," Pa said. "I hear that Annapolis is strongly for the South."

Ma said grudgingly, "I will wash and iron your Sunday shirt so you look presentable, Yosef."

"Thanks, Ma." He could hardly believe his luck! He wasn't sure which was the greatest surprise—that of all the boys in the class, Harold had invited him, or that he was being allowed to go.

CHAPTER SEVEN

★　　　★　　　★

ON SATURDAY, Joseph arrived at Camden Station long before time to meet Harold and his father. The station was almost deserted at this hour—quite a contrast to the week before, when it had swarmed with rioters and police.

Joseph spotted a bench and headed toward it. Someone had left a newspaper behind—a New York paper! *Maybe now I can find out what's going on in the North.* He set down the package that Ma had insisted he bring—*Zimtplätzchen* she had baked—on the bench beside him, sliding it away so he could conveniently "forget" it. Harold and his father were probably used to eating fancy pastries from a bakery and would think it strange if they knew he'd brought along homemade cookies.

Trying to forget how late Ma had stayed up to bake "something to thank your friend and his father for taking you on the trip," Joseph unfolded the newspaper. The first thing his eyes fell on was an article about the ceremony in honor of the Fort Sumter garrison: "The shot-torn flag that flew over Fort Sumter during the bombardment waved from the statue of George Washington in Union Square today as 100,000 New Yorkers honored the brave men who had defended it and shouted their demands for vengeance against the South."

Joseph stared at the words until they became a blur. *If Maryland's legislators vote to secede, then we'll be part of the South. And we'll be the first state to feel the North's vengeance.* He quickly turned to the editorial pages and was still reading when Harold clapped him on the shoulder.

"Hey, Joseph! Father's letting us go to Frederick without him. He has to deal with some emergency at the office. Come on—I've got our passes."

Joseph noticed a paper-wrapped package under Harold's arm. "What's that you've brought?" he asked.

"Sandwiches, so we won't have to waste time buying a meal in Frederick. I see that you brought something, too."

"Just some cookies," Joseph said. He picked up the *Zimtplätzchen* but left the northern paper behind, even though he hadn't finished it.

A few minutes later, the boys had taken their seats in one of the cars, and Joseph was trying to act as if traveling by rail were an everyday experience. Three young men carrying carpetbags passed them, and Harold whispered, "Probably on their way to Harper's Ferry to join a Virginia regiment. My cousin Randall says that's what he'll do if the legislature doesn't vote for secession."

The whistle blasted, and with a lurch, the train began to move, gradually picking up speed. It was much faster than the street railway—noisier and dirtier, too, Joseph thought as ash from the engine's smokestack blew in through the windows. What an adventure!

West of the city, they rode through gently rolling countryside. Joseph had never seen so much land without buildings on it—and he'd never imagined moving at such a speed. "How fast do you think we're going?" he asked, his eyes on the telegraph lines that seemed to swoop past alongside the tracks.

"I dunno. Maybe twenty-five miles an hour."

Joseph was impressed. That meant the trip to Frederick would take less than two hours! He had begun to feel like an old hand at rail travel when suddenly the land seemed to fall away. Joseph caught his breath and leaned closer to the window. Far below he saw the gleam of water—and nothing else.

"Don't look down, or you'll feel giddy," Harold said, adding, "I hate railroad bridges. Say, why don't we have an early lunch?"

The boys made short work of Harold's ham sandwiches and hard-boiled eggs, and then Joseph unwrapped Ma's package.

"What kind of cookies are these?" Harold asked, helping himself.

"They're called *Zimtplätzchen*."

"Sounds German."

I should have just said "cinnamon cookies."

"Mmm." Harold helped himself to several more. "You never mentioned that you had a German cook. What else does she serve you?"

"Oh, things like *sauerbraten*—that's made with beef—

and red cabbage cooked with apples. We all like her sausage and sauerkraut, too."

"You're lucky. Our cook just fixes ordinary food."

Joseph had never imagined that the meals Ma served would make a boy like Harold envious. "Go ahead and finish up the cookies," he said, turning his attention to the window again. He hoped Ma never found out he'd let his new friend think her prized *Zimtplätzchen* had been baked by their "cook." She'd think he was ashamed of his family's German heritage, and he wasn't. But it was just one more thing that set him apart from his classmates.

It didn't make sense, Joseph thought. Most of the recent arrivals to America were for the Union—to them, the word *united* in "these United States" meant just that. It was people like Harold and Alexander, people whose ancestors had been among America's earliest settlers, who were shouting "Down with the United States!" Joseph glanced at Harold, who was brushing cookie crumbs from his lap. *He'd better be glad the U.S. Constitution guarantees free speech. In a lot of countries, people are thrown in jail for speaking out the way he does.*

At last the train began to slow, and Harold said, "Well, here we are. Frederick." He led the way to the door.

"I thought the station would be bigger," Joseph said, glancing around.

"Frederick isn't an important city like Baltimore, don't forget," Harold said. He asked directions to the court house, where the General Assembly was meeting, and the two boys set off.

As they crossed the street, Joseph said, "There sure are a lot of militiamen around the station. And look—more of them are on the next corner. You think they expect some kind of trouble?"

"I think they *are* some kind of trouble," Harold answered. "I don't like the looks of this."

Joseph knew that from Frederick on west, Maryland was mostly Unionist, but that didn't explain all the uniformed men. Still, he was too busy looking at the nearby mountains to worry about it. Federal Hill was nothing compared to the tree-covered slopes that seemed to lie just beyond the town or the soft blue of the mountains rising in the distance.

Before they'd gone very far, Harold said, "That ought to be the court house just ahead."

They had almost reached the door when a militiaman called, "The court house is closed, boys."

"Isn't this where the legislature's meeting?" Harold asked.

"Not anymore," the man said. "It was too crowded here, so they've moved to the building at the corner of Market and East Church Street."

Joseph looked in the direction the man pointed and saw a crowd gathered on the sidewalk in front of a large three-story building.

"Did they vote on secession yet?" Harold asked eagerly.

The militiaman shook his head. "Nope. And they're not going to, either. I don't know about the House of Delegates, but the senators already decided they had no authority to vote on secession issues."

"They decided *what*?" the boys asked in unison.

The man grinned and said, "You heard me. The vote was unanimous."

Joseph was speechless with relief, but Harold laughed and said, "For a minute there, you had us fooled, mister."

The militiaman rocked back on his heels and said, "I'm telling you the honest truth. So if you've come here hoping to watch Maryland vote itself out of the Union, you might as well go on back to Baltimore."

"How did you know that's where we're from?" Joseph demanded.

"'Cause the two of you look like secesh. Now move along."

Joseph didn't have to be told twice. Smarting from being told he "looked like secesh," he turned toward the building where the Assembly was now meeting, but he'd taken only a step or two when the man bellowed, "Not that way, boy—back to the station. We don't want your lot here."

Without a word, Joseph turned and retraced his steps. He walked silently beside Harold, who didn't stop cursing the Union until they were almost to the next corner, where two militiamen stood guard.

After they crossed the street, Harold pulled a folded schedule from his pocket and studied it. "If we hurry, we can catch the next train home. Come on—being around all these Unionists makes me want to puke."

Somehow, Joseph managed not to let his expression

change. He'd have to be more careful than ever about what he said. Now that he'd finally made a friend, he didn't want to lose him.

Neither boy spoke until they were seated in the Gentlemen's Parlor of the small station, waiting for their train to arrive. "I still can't believe every single one of our senators voted not to even discuss secession," Harold said.

A middle-aged man with a secession badge on his lapel looked up from his newspaper. "You don't realize what they were up against," he said. "What would *you* have done if members of the Home Guard threatened to drive you out the window of the Senate chamber at the point of a bayonet if you dared to vote for secession?"

Without waiting for an answer, he gestured to a trio of uniformed men just outside the door and said, "The Home Guard has taken it upon themselves to make sure Maryland stays in the Union, and they don't care how they do it. They patrol the streets day and night, and from what I hear, they're keeping an eye on the legislators as well as any strangers that are in town. Wouldn't let me anywhere near a member of the General Assembly."

"They wouldn't even let us near the building where they were meeting," Harold said.

The train's whistle announced its approach from the west, and the man headed for the platform, leaving his *Richmond Times* behind. Joseph would have liked to read it on the way home, but he was concerned that Harold might think it crass to pick up something that had been discarded.

The train braked to a stop in a cloud of steam, and the boys climbed on. Harold slumped into a seat and said, "What a wasted day. Wake me up when we get back."

It might have been a wasted day for Harold, but it was an exciting one for me, Joseph thought. The train trip, watching the countryside flash past the window, seeing the mountains, finding out that there would be no vote in favor of secession—it was the best day I've ever had, in spite of being told I "look like secesh."

At the supper table that evening, Joseph told everything he could remember about the trip to Frederick, ending by saying, "Harold really enjoyed your *Zimtplätzchen*, Ma."

"And you did not want to take it with you. You thought it was something not good enough for your rich friend."

How did she know? Joseph was glad when his brother spoke.

"I heard something interesting when I was on my rounds today," Franz said. "It seems that a couple of the legislators who favored secession were 'persuaded' to stay away from the Assembly session."

Anneliese's brow creased. "But who persuaded them?"

"Unionist militiamen. The hired girl at a place where I delivered ice this morning said the man of the house was stopped by a group of 'em when he got off the train in Frederick. Soon as they saw the red and white cockade he was wearing, they convinced him to take the next train back to Baltimore."

Pa's eyebrows rose. "How can this be true? People come to America because they hear that such things do not happen here. Because the Constitution protects against it."

221

"Maybe so, but on my way home today, I heard a newspaper boy calling out something about President Lincoln suspending people's rights," Franz said.

"Something about 'suspending the writ of habeas corpus'?" Joseph asked.

Franz's eyes brightened. "That was it!" he said.

"What on earth does it mean?" Anneliese asked.

Joseph said, "It's Latin, and it means the government can arrest somebody without telling them why. Without even having a reason."

After a moment of shocked silence, Ma said, "Are you telling us that Abraham Lincoln will let people go to jail without a trial? How can that happen in America?"

"Because of the South's rebellion, I think," Joseph told her, trying to remember what he'd learned when his class had studied the Constitution.

In a small voice Erika asked, "Will they arrest Pa?"

"Of course not," Joseph said. "They'll only arrest the secesh." The panicky look left his sister's eyes, and Joseph half wished that he could be eight years old again.

O<small>N</small> M<small>ONDAY</small>, Joseph was surprised to see Charles at the center of a cluster of boys in the school yard, but then he realized that it was the newspaper Charles had brought that interested his classmates.

Noticing Joseph on the edge of the group, Charles held up the paper so he could read the headline: **ARREST OF MARYLAND LEGISLATURE**.

"That headline is a bit misleading," Charles said, and he read from the article, "'General Butler, commanding at Annapolis, says that if the Maryland legislature presses an ordinance of secession, he will arrest the entire body.'"

Joseph was speechless, but Harold turned to him and said, "I guess now we know why our senators decided they didn't have the authority to vote on the secession issue."

"I keep telling you, that general is talking through his hat. He can't arrest anybody, much less the whole legislature," another boy argued.

"Actually, he can," Joseph said. "Now that Lincoln's suspended the writ of habeas corpus, military authorities can arrest whoever they want to."

One of his classmates said scornfully, "I don't see why

anyone would want to stay in Lincoln's precious Union if he's taking away their Constitutional rights."

"He didn't suspend the writ everywhere," Joseph reminded him, "just here in Maryland."

"And not everywhere in Maryland," Charles added. "Just 'along a line between Washington and Philadelphia,' according to the newspaper."

His eyes blazing, Harold said, "It's no coincidence that the line goes through the part of the state where people have southern sympathies. Lincoln's taking away the rights of people who might not vote the way he wants them to on the secession issue. Some democracy."

Joseph was glad the bell rang and ended the conversation. It was hard always to be on guard so he didn't say something that showed his Unionist sympathies, like pointing out that the Washington-to-Philadelphia line sounded like the route of the railroad and telegraph, and the president would be foolish not to protect them.

By afternoon, the late April day was so warm the classroom felt stuffy even though the windows were wide open. The Latin teacher droned on, and in spite of Joseph's best intentions, his mind drifted away from the lesson. It was almost as if the riot had never happened, he thought. Less than two weeks ago, the city had been in chaos, and already the telegraph lines had been repaired and the railroad bridges were being rebuilt. Coming back from the noon break, he'd heard a rumor that now the lower house of the legislature as well as the Senate had voted against bringing up the subject of secession, and he hoped it was true.

Joseph was relieved when the Latin master dismissed the class and school was out for the day. He was gathering his books together when Harold paused by his desk and said, "Let's go buy a newspaper and find out what's going on."

They hadn't walked far before they heard a newsboy calling out, "Extra! Extra! Maryland legislature—"

Harold swore when the rest of the sentence was drowned out by the clatter of hooves and creak of wagon wheels. "Come on," he called, sprinting toward the corner.

Several men were clustered around the newsboy, and when Joseph and Harold ran up, the boy said, "Sorry— just sold the last one." A young man who looked as though he might be a clerk held his paper so they could read the headline:

MARYLAND LEGISLATURE
VOTES AGAINST SECESSION

Joseph felt a sense of relief, but Harold's shoulders slumped. "I was sure we'd leave the Union," he said, his voice flat.

"So was I," Joseph said honestly, "until we went to Frederick on Saturday." *Now ships from the North will be allowed to sail up the Chesapeake to Baltimore. The docks will be busy again, and the ice plant and factories will stay open. We'll be able to buy what we need.* "I'd better get on home with the news," he said. Ma would be relieved to hear it.

"I'll have to see if Randall knows yet. He said that if this happened, his whole militia unit would take the B&O to Harper's Ferry, Virginia, and enlist in the Confederate Army."

Maybe Pa was right that one reason the city's been quiet lately is that a lot of secesh have gone south, Joseph thought. "Well, see you tomorrow, then," he said, wondering what would happen next.

"Hey, come look at the badges Alexander brought," one of the boys called, gesturing for Joseph to join them under a tree in the school yard on Thursday morning.

Joseph wasn't surprised when he saw the three broad bars—red, white, red—and circle of stars on a blue field. Confederate flag badges.

"Go on and take one, Joe," Alexander urged. "I've got plenty."

"You know very well that I'm not a secessionist," Joseph said.

Alexander turned to Harold and said, "What did I tell you? I'm surprised he isn't wearing the Stars and Stripes."

"How come you don't have a badge of the Maryland flag?" Joseph asked. "I'd wear one of those."

"If you're so strong for Maryland, you must be for states' rights," one of the boys said, looking puzzled. "But if you're for states' rights, I don't see why you're neutral instead of for the Confederacy."

Alexander gave Joseph a scornful glance and said, "Aw, he's just afraid to take a stand."

It was true, but Joseph hated hearing it. He grabbed the front of Alexander's shirt and pulled him forward until their faces were inches apart. "You take that back, Alex. Or else."

"Lay off! You know I didn't mean anything by that, Joe!"

Alexander doesn't want to fight me. A feeling of power surged through Joseph. "Then take it back," he said, tightening his grip.

"Let go of me—I take it back!"

"Say it, then," Joseph demanded.

"You're not afraid to take a stand!" Alexander gasped out.

Joseph shoved him away. "Make sure you remember that," he said in the menacing tone he'd heard Franz use with a neighborhood bully. He watched Alexander stoop to pick up the badges that had scattered on the ground, noticed that Harold didn't help, and wished he'd put Alexander in his place sooner. "And another thing, Alex— don't call me 'Joe.'"

The school bell rang, and the boys who had gathered with the hope of seeing a fight moved toward the building. Joseph followed them, and when Charles held the door for him, Joseph noticed that he wasn't wearing one of Alexander's badges, either. "Thanks, Charles," he said, but the other boy was already hurrying down the hall.

After school a few days later, Joseph and Harold set off to check the bulletin board at the newspaper office, as they did each day now. Joseph had noticed that ever since the riot, Harold had been spending more time with him and less with Alexander, and he was glad of it. It bothered him, though, that he couldn't be honest about being a Unionist. He'd never actually lied about it, but he *had* deliberately misled Harold, and now that they were friends, he felt guilty.

As soon as they saw the knots of men deep in conversation outside the newspaper office, the boys walked faster. "Whatever the news is, they don't look happy about it," Joseph said. He figured that was a safe enough observation—he'd gotten pretty good at making comments that were true but wouldn't give him away. Still, he was glad Pa didn't know how carefully he walked the thin line between truth and falsehood. Pa would be ashamed of him—and Ma would be disgusted. *But they don't understand.*

When they were close enough to read the bulletin, Harold swore under his breath.

UNION TROOPS STOP TRAINS ON B&O LINE WEST OF CITY; CARS SEARCHED FOR GOODS EN ROUTE TO CONFEDERATES AT HARPER'S FERRY

"It's a good thing Cousin Randall and the other fellows in his militia unit already left for Virginia to join the Confederate Army. Can you imagine how they'd react to having the Yankees stop their train?"

"I sure can," Joseph said, remembering how ordinary citizens had reacted when northern troops simply passed through the city. "And I wouldn't like it any better than they would." Wasn't this supposed to be the land of the free?

An old man who had witnessed their reaction to the news said, "Those Federal troops are in a position to intimidate our legislators in Frederick now. They're General Butler's men, you know."

"Wait a minute," Harold said. "Isn't Butler the one who threatened to arrest the whole legislature if they changed their mind and voted on secession? The one who occupied Annapolis and opened the rail line to Washington?"

The man nodded. "The very one. And he commands the Sixth Massachusetts—the regiment that was caught up in the Pratt Street riot last month."

A shiver ran up Joseph's spine. "Sounds like they're in a position to intimidate Baltimore as well as the legislature," he said.

The door to the newspaper office opened, and everyone crowded around to read the new bulletin as soon as the apprentice posted it:

REPAIRS ON BURNED BRIDGES
NEAR COMPLETION;
RAIL LINES FROM NORTH
TO OPEN TOMORROW

"I guess with General Butler's men so close to the city,

Lincoln's volunteers don't have to worry about crossing town on their way to Camden Station," Joseph said. Now there would be a lot more than a handful of citizens killed if anyone started trouble.

Harold nodded. "I guess we've had our fun," he said. "Well, see you tomorrow."

"See you tomorrow," Joseph echoed. He watched his friend head toward home, wondering how he could think the riot had been fun.

At supper the next evening, Anneliese announced, "The newsboys were crying out something about how Mayor Brown and the city council announced that the people must submit to the federal government. I wish I knew what it all means."

"It means that Baltimore citizens must behave like Americans and support their president even though they didn't vote for him," Pa said.

"But what if they don't?" Frieda asked. "What if people think the southern states have the right to set up their own country?"

Pa turned to her and said shortly, "Then they should go to live in the southern states." When he saw the little girl wilt, his voice softened, and he said, "This country has been good to us, *Liebchen*, and we must support it. All the states united is better than groups of rival states, as we had for so long in our old homeland."

"Still, I do not like the idea of boys like Jonathan from Pennsylvania leaving home to put down this rebellion in the South," Ma said, passing a bowl of sauerkraut to Franz.

"Jonathan and the others will be giving only three months to their country," Pa said. "That is all the president has asked of them."

Joseph said, "But now the president has called for men to sign up to serve for three *years*. I saw the bulletin just a few days ago."

After a shocked silence, Ma asked, "And how many more will he ask for when another week passes? I think Mr. Lincoln's 'rebellion' is becoming a war."

A civil war, Joseph thought. The worst kind. But at least Maryland won't be its battleground. Since we aren't leaving the Union, Virginia will be the northernmost of the Confederate states. He glanced across the table at Franz, who was scowling down at his plate. *I'll bet Franz is wishing he could walk into one of the recruiting stations and sign on to fight for the Union. But three years is a long time.*

JOSEPH STOPPED short when he saw the U.S. flag flying high above Federal Hill on Monday morning—and cannon barrels pointed toward downtown. He raced back home, the empty water buckets banging against his legs.

"The city's been taken over by Union troops!" he shouted. "Baltimore's been *occupied*!"

Franz scowled and said, "I didn't like it last week when that Union general took over the B&O rail line to the west, but this is even worse. Makes you wonder what they might do next."

Before anyone could speculate about that, Frieda asked, "How come you brought back empty buckets, Yosef? Don't you know Ma needs to heat water so Erika and I can wash the dishes after breakfast?"

"News will keep, Yosef," Ma said, "but your sisters must go to school on time."

Without a word, Joseph picked up the buckets and left the house.

On his way to the academy nearly an hour later, he sensed that something was different. It took several minutes before he figured out what it was: No Confederate flags were flying, and no militiamen were in sight. Without militia units drilling, the city seemed strangely quiet.

Ahead of him, several men had gathered to read a sign nailed to a tree, and Joseph ran to join them. They moved over to make room for him, and one of them said, "It's a proclamation from the Yankee general over on Federal Hill."

"So *that's* why there aren't any flags!" Joseph exclaimed when he came to the part that prohibited flying the Confederate colors. Maybe now the Unionists would bring out the U.S. flags they'd taken down the day of the riot, he thought, suddenly aware of how much he'd missed seeing the Stars and Stripes. He considered detouring past the newspaper office to read the bulletins about the occupation but decided there wasn't time for that.

The first thing Joseph noticed when he arrived in the school yard was his classmates' grim faces, and then he saw that the flag badges Alexander had passed out had disappeared from their jackets.

"So you know about the occupation," Joseph said.

Everyone nodded, and several of the boys muttered, "We know." The bell rang, and as they headed slowly toward the building, Joseph matched his pace to theirs.

When he turned into the school yard after the noon break, Joseph immediately noticed a change in his classmates, and as he walked toward them, he sensed an undercurrent of excitement—or maybe anger.

Harold turned to him, his eyes blazing. "Did you hear about Ross Winans?"

"What about him?" Joseph asked, wondering if Harold

knew the rich industrialist and legislator personally.

"The Yankees have arrested him! They're holding him prisoner at Fort McHenry!"

Joseph's eyes widened. "But *why*?"

"For being a Confederate, that's why," one of his classmates said at the same time Harold said, "For his 'secessionist activities.' He gave a lot of money to our cause—and weapons, too."

"I can't believe the president ever intended for an old man like Mr. Winans to be thrown into prison!" Joseph exclaimed.

Alexander turned to Harold and said, "Listen to him—'the president'! I *told* you he was a Unionist. He's no more neutral than you and me."

Harold looked at Joseph. "Is he right? *Are* you a Unionist?"

Joseph's heart sank. "Yes, but—"

"I knew it!" Alexander said triumphantly. "He sure pulled the wool over your eyes, Harold."

Harold's face flushed and he took a step toward Joseph. "You coward. You lying coward. Alexander was right about you being afraid to take a stand."

Joseph was stunned. What could he say that wouldn't make things worse than they already were?

"Lying Unionist coward," Alexander taunted, and other boys gathered around, taking up the chant.

The look of satisfaction and sly superiority on Alexander's face was more than Joseph could take. He stepped toward the other boy and began to roll up his sleeves. "You'll wish you hadn't said that, Alex." The flicker of fear in the other boy's eyes almost made him smile. He'd show these rich secessionists who the coward was!

But Harold forced his way between them and said, "Leave Alex alone. What he said is true—you're a lying Unionist coward."

Joseph's fist swung upward and smashed into Harold's chin with such force that the other boy staggered backward into Alexander, almost knocking him off balance. Breathing hard, Joseph waited, his eyes on Harold but keenly aware of the sullen murmur from the circle of boys who had gathered to watch. *How did this happen? I wanted to fight Alex, not Harold.*

The school bell rang, and the other boys began to move toward the door—except for Harold. One hand on his jaw, he faced Joseph and asked, "Why did you do it?"

Why did he think I did it? "Because of what you said."

"Not why did you hit me—why did you lie about what you believed?"

The mixture of hurt and scorn in Harold's expression made Joseph drop his gaze, and he stared at the ground until Harold walked away. Then, following him with his eyes, Joseph answered silently, Because I wanted to fit in here at school. Because I wanted you to be my friend.

That was the truth of it, but it wasn't something he could admit to. "I was stupid," Joseph whispered as he walked away from the school yard. Stupid to think that a working-class boy could fit in with rich men's sons. Stupid to pretend to be someone I wasn't. And just plain wrong to let Harold think Ma was our German cook. I'll make it up to her. If I ever make another friend, I'll take him home to meet her. I'll ask her to bake *Zimtplätzchen* for us. I'll go to confession and do whatever penance the priest gives me, and maybe then—

"Hey, Joseph!"

Jolted out of his reverie, Joseph turned to see Franz waving from the seat of his ice wagon. "I see you're playing hooky," Franz said when he had brought his horse to a stop near the curb.

Joseph climbed to the wagon seat beside him and asked, "Can I drive?"

"Why not? Nelly knows the route." Franz handed over the reins, and the brothers rode in silence until he announced, "I've told the boss I'm quitting at the end of the week."

Joseph stared at him. "But I thought you liked your job! Have you found one that pays more, then?"

After they rattled across the tracks of the street railway, Franz said, "I'm going to join the army, Yosef."

Half excited, half dismayed, Joseph asked, "Can I come along when you go to the recruiting office to volunteer? Just to see what it's like?"

Franz took the reins to guide the wagon between a delivery wagon and a street vendor's cart, then handed them back. Without looking at Joseph, he said, "I won't be going to the Union recruiting office downtown. I'll be volunteering in Virginia."

"In *Virginia*? You're joining the *rebel* army?"

Franz nodded. "I believed in the Union just as much as

you do, Yosef. Just as much as Pa does. All that business about the rule of law and upholding the Constitution, all those safeguards we were guaranteed in the Bill of Rights. But look what's happened—Marylanders are being thrown in jail without a trial, and soldiers have occupied Baltimore."

"We've been occupied to make sure the rail lines and telegraph lines from Washington to the north are kept open," Joseph said. "They've already been cut once, if you remember."

"Maybe so, but I'm going to fight on the side of freedom," Franz said, and Joseph saw that his brother's face had the same closed, stubborn expression it had worn years ago whenever Ma scolded him. "I know Pa won't like it," Franz went on, "but he'll understand. After all, he's the one who taught us to stand up for what we believe in."

I didn't even admit to what I believe in, much less stand up for it, and Pa will never understand that. "What about Ma? She won't want you to do this."

"I know. But she can't stop me."

"How will you get to Virginia now that the Union controls the railroad between here and Harper's Ferry?" Joseph asked.

"Don't you worry about that," Franz said. "I've already figured out a way."

But he isn't going to tell me because I'm a Unionist. In less than an hour, I've lost my friend and my brother. Joseph blinked back tears, hoping Franz wouldn't notice.

"You haven't said why you're not in school," his brother reminded him.

Joseph told him, adding, "So because I'm for the Union, all the boys at school are against me, and my own brother doesn't trust me enough to tell me how he's getting to Virginia."

"After I collect my pay on Friday, I'll hitch a ride out of town with the vegetable man," Franz said. "His youngest son and I will make our way to Virginia together."

Franz *did* trust him. "Maybe I could ride along with you like this for the rest of the week," Joseph said.

The horse stopped in front of a large brick house, and before Franz climbed down from the wagon seat, he gave Joseph a long look. "If you don't go back and finish out the school year, you'll prove Alexander was right when he called you a coward. And don't take the easy way out by showing up late, you hear?"

Joseph nodded. He stared down at the schoolbooks on his lap and told himself he could take anything for the few days until the term ended. He'd managed a lot longer than that without friends at the beginning of the year, after all. But then it was because he didn't know anyone, and now it would be because of what everyone knew about him.

Joseph was still several blocks from school the next morning when he saw Harold walking toward him. *What's going on? Why is he coming to meet me?* When they were only a few feet apart, they both stopped, and Joseph waited for the other boy to speak.

"Alex has got a bunch of the fellows ready to jump you the minute you walk into the school yard," Harold said.

"You'd better not show up until after the bell rings."

"How come you're warning me?"

Harold shrugged. "We were friends. I don't want to see you beat up."

Were friends. "Thanks, but I'd better face them. Otherwise, they'll just lie in wait for me at noon, or maybe after school. How many do you think they are?"

"Five, maybe six," Harold said, falling into step beside Joseph.

Joseph's stomach tightened. "I'll just have to hope they don't do too much damage before the bell rings." After a few more steps he added, "Look, I'm sorry I punched you yesterday, Harold."

"Forget it. I shouldn't have said what I did."

He shouldn't have said it, but he's not sorry. He isn't going to take it back. Joseph had never felt more miserable. A block from the school, he glanced at Harold and said, "You'd better let me go on ahead so Alex and the others don't see us together."

"Are you crazy? I'm not letting you face them alone!"

Harold is going to stand by me! They were almost to the edge of the school yard when a group of boys who had been sitting on the steps stood up. A lot more than six of them, Joseph saw, his courage faltering. Alexander yelled, "Grab him, Harold! Hold him so he can't run away." He swaggered toward Joseph, glancing back to make sure the others were following him.

"He won't run," Harold called. "He's going to fight you—and I'm going to help him."

Alexander's steps faltered, and he stopped a few feet away. "You are? *Why*?"

"Because ganging up on him like you've planned is unworthy of southern gentlemen."

If Joseph hadn't been so scared, he would have laughed. Unworthy of southern gentlemen? But Harold's words seemed to affect the others. One of the boys said, "He's right, Alex," and another said, "Count me out." Shamefaced, they all turned away.

"If you want to fight, I'll be glad to oblige," Joseph said. "Might as well settle things between us once and for all." He slipped his book strap off his shoulder and lowered his schoolbooks to the ground. He was shrugging out of his jacket when Alexander took a step back.

"I'm not wasting my time on the likes of you—*Joe*."

As Joseph watched Alexander head toward the building, Harold asked, "Why is that ice wagon parked across the street? The driver seems to be looking this way."

Joseph glanced over his shoulder in time to see Franz slap the reins on Nelly's back. His brother had come to help him out if there was a fight! Should he tell Harold that the driver of the ice wagon was his brother? No, the time to be straightforward was long past, and besides, Harold was already walking toward the building with two of the boys who hadn't taken part in Alexander's plan.

So that's the way it's going to be, Joseph thought. Harold stuck up for me because it was the gentlemanly thing to do even though our friendship is over—and it's over not because I'm a Unionist, but because I deceived him. Because

I didn't take a stand. No wonder Harold doesn't think much of me. I don't think much of myself, either.

Joseph was picking up his books when he heard the rattle of drums. He peered down the street and saw a group of Union soldiers marching toward him. Their flag rippled in the breeze, and the sight of it filled him with pride. *How can Franz even think of fighting against the Stars and Stripes? And how could I hide my loyalty to it—and to all it represents?*

Dimly aware of the ringing of the school bell, he stood at attention, his hand over his heart, until the flag passed. It wasn't until he started toward the building that Joseph realized he wasn't alone—Charles was waiting for him. They hurried up the stairs together, and Charles said, "I thought I was the only Unionist here. It sure is good to find out I'm not."

"And I'm glad to find out I'm not the only one who kept my Unionist sympathies to myself," Joseph said, holding the door for his classmate. "I'm a scholarship student, incidentally," he said as they walked down the deserted hallway. "My family lives near the harbor." *There. Now I don't have to worry that he might find out.*

Charles said, "We live uptown. My friends call me Charlie, by the way."

Joseph barely hesitated before he said, "At home I'm called Yosef, because my parents are from Germany, but I go by Joseph here at school."

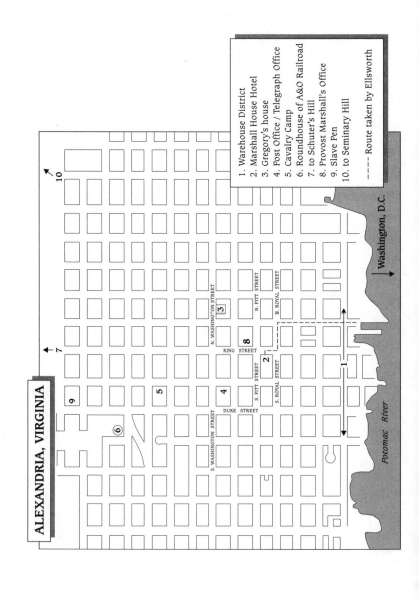

ALEXANDRIA, VIRGINIA

1. Warehouse District
2. Marshall House Hotel
3. Gregory's house
4. Post Office / Telegraph Office
5. Cavalry Camp
6. Roundhouse of A&O Railroad
7. to Schuter's Hill
8. Provost Marshall's Office
9. Slave Pen
10. to Seminary Hill

----- Route taken by Ellsworth

Washington, D.C.

Potomac River

N. WASHINGTON STREET
N. PITT STREET
W. ROYAL STREET
S. WASHINGTON STREET
S. PITT STREET
S. ROYAL STREET
KING STREET
DUKE STREET

GREGORY HOWARD'S STORY

ALEXANDRIA, VIRGINIA: MAY 16–LATE JUNE 1861

CHAPTER ONE

★　　★　　★

GREGORY CLOSED the warehouse door behind him and scowled at the Federal warship moored in the Potomac. He hated the brooding presence of the *Pawnee* with its guns trained on Alexandria, hated the sight of empty wharves on what had been a bustling riverfront. It was hard to believe that only a month ago he had stood on this very spot, admiring the merchant ships lying at anchor and watching laborers roll barrel after barrel into Father's warehouse.

Disgruntled, Gregory turned away from the river. As he headed home, he raised his eyes to the Confederate Stars and Bars flying defiantly over the Marshall House Hotel several blocks from the waterfront. Was it true that Lincoln could see the flag from the White House? Maybe so, since the hotel was four stories high and the pole towered above it. Still, Abraham Lincoln probably had more important things on his mind than a symbol of the Confederacy on a building across the Potomac. Things like sending his northern troops over Long Bridge into Virginia to march the seven miles to Alexandria. Gregory shuddered at the thought.

It was hard to believe that only a few months ago, the worst thing he could imagine was being punished by the schoolmaster. But that was back then. *Before*. He trudged along the deserted sidewalk, his footsteps beating out the rhythm for his silent chant: Before Lincoln was elected. . . . Before South Carolina left the Union. . . . Before the bombardment of Fort Sumter. . . . Before Abe Lincoln called for troops. . . . Before Virginia voted to secede.

Even now, a month after that vote, it was hard to believe Virginia was no longer part of the United States. *Virginia*, where it all began. If George Washington and Thomas Jefferson and Patrick Henry and all those other Virginia patriots were still alive, they'd be shocked. Especially George Washington, who had done business here in Alexandria and had driven into town for church each Sunday. How would he feel if he could see enemy-held territory across the river from Mount Vernon? If he could see the guns of the U.S. fort named in his honor pointed toward land he had owned along the Virginia shore?

He wouldn't like it at all, Gregory told himself, but it would make him—and the others—realize that this was a second War for Independence. They'd understand that the southern states must win their freedom from the tyranny of the North just as the colonies had won their freedom from England. "Abraham Lincoln can't force the Confederate states to stay in the Union any more than King George could force the colonists to stay in the British Empire," Gregory muttered. Too bad Father refused to admit that.

No use ruining a beautiful day by worrying over things that can't be changed, he decided, turning into the alley that ran behind the row of stately townhouses on the block where he lived. He walked between tall fences that hid the backyards with their gardens, summer kitchens, henhouses, and sometimes a cow or goat until he reached the chest-high brick wall that enclosed the yard of his family's next-door neighbor, Miss Lily.

Usually, the tiny, white-haired woman would be cutting flowers for a bouquet this time of morning, but today her slave was working in the vegetable garden. "Good morning, Belle," Gregory called.

Belle put down her hoe and took a pair of scissors from her apron pocket. "Miss Lily, she say for me to cut some forget-me-nots for li'l Miss Mary," she called back, and Greg waited while she bent over the flower bed. He was glad it was only a few steps to his own back gate—he'd be embarrassed if anyone saw him carrying a bouquet.

At the door of the summer kitchen that stood just inside his yard, he greeted Lena, his family's slave, and held out the handful of forget-me-nots. "Miss Lily sent these for Mary."

Lena chose a small white pitcher from a shelf in the summer kitchen, filled it with water, and arranged the flowers. "You spend some time with yo' li'l sister when you take dis up to her, you hear me?" she said, handing him the pitcher. "She lonesome! 'Lizbeth, she still sleepin', an' yo' mama, she out sewin' for de soldiers again."

Gregory heard the note of disapproval in Lena's voice and wondered if Mother spent so many hours working for the Confederate cause to make up for Father being a Unionist. "I'll keep Mary company for a while," Gregory said. It was bad enough that his eight-year-old sister had to stay in bed while she regained her strength after a bad case of rheumatic fever—she shouldn't have to be lonely, too. Besides, he didn't have anything else to do this morning. When school closed a month early because so many students had left town with their families or had been sent to stay with relatives after the secession vote, Gregory had cheered. He'd never imagined time would hang so heavily on his hands.

Upstairs, he found Mary propped up in bed, hands resting idly on her needlework as she listened to the Swiss music box that had been Mother's anniversary present. How small she looked, and how pale. Gregory felt huge in comparison. He and his older brother had inherited their father's large build and their mother's dark hair and eyes, but his sisters were both petite like Mother, with Father's fair coloring.

Sensing his presence in the doorway, Mary turned to him and cried, "I *knew* you hadn't forgotten me, Greg!"

He set the pitcher of flowers where his sister could see them and said, "These are from Miss Lily," but Mary scarcely looked at them.

"Come tell me what's happening, Greg."

He pulled a chair over to her bedside and, "Nothing new at all—just more of the same."

"There must be *something* you can tell me about," Mary begged.

Gregory thought over his day so far. "Well," he said, "when I took Father his mail just now, I saw that enemy warship, the *Pawnee*, still lying offshore with its guns pointed—"

Mary put her hands over her ears and said, "I don't want to hear about warships and guns. Or even about our own brave Virginia boys drilling on the common. Tell me something exciting, Greg."

Exciting? It was all more frustrating than exciting, he thought.

"I know! Tell me about Mr. Jackson and his flag."

"*Again*, Mary?"

She nodded, and Gregory began. "It was April 17, almost a month ago," he began, trying to draw the story out, "and as soon as school was over for the day, Carter and I ran down to the *Gazette* office to see if any bulletins had been posted. A lot of people were already there, 'cause everybody knew the Secession Convention in Richmond was voting on whether Virginia should stay in the Union or secede."

He stole a glance at his sister and saw that she was listening as intently as if she were hearing all this for the first time. "We waited and waited, but nothing happened. Finally, a man pushed his way through the crowd to the building and stood there on the doorstep until everybody quieted down."

"Oh, I wish I could have been there!" Mary cried. "Tell me what happened next."

"This fellow said he knew for a fact that the Convention

had voted for secession, and he reminded everybody about the flag raising at the Marshall House at—"

"That's Mr. Jackson's hotel, isn't it?"

Gregory nodded. "—at four o'clock. For a second or two there was complete silence, and then Carter threw his cap in the air and cheered, and—"

"And then the air was full of caps and hats and shouts and cheers," Mary interrupted.

"Whose story is this, anyway?" Gregory asked, putting on a fierce frown.

Mary laughed. "It's yours, silly. Quick! Tell the rest of it."

"Then Father's friend Mr. Bevin managed to get up to the front of the crowd, and he told the people they were reacting to rumors, and that for all we knew, the Convention hadn't even voted yet. But everybody booed and shouted him down."

"That's because they all knew he was a Unionist," Mary said. She leaned forward a little and asked, "Did you boo and shout, Greg?"

"Of course not! I'd never be rude to a friend of Father's—and besides, what he said made good sense."

"So you and Carter went over to Mr. Jackson's hotel," Mary prompted.

Gregory nodded. "We ran right over and claimed us a spot on the steps of the building catty-corner from the Marshall House. It was a good thing we did, too, because by the time four o'clock came, just about everybody in town was there. A band played 'Dixie,' and we all held our breath while Mr. Jackson hoisted a huge Confederate flag to the top of a pole, high above the roof of his hotel. Everybody cheered, and then the Alexandria Artillery fired a salute in honor of the Confederacy."

"Seven shots—one for each Confederate state," Mary said. "Elizabeth and I counted them."

"And your big brother Martin was the one who loaded the cannon," Gregory reminded her.

"But we didn't know that yet," Mary said. She fell silent, and Gregory wished he hadn't brought it up. He guessed from her troubled expression that she was thinking about what had happened that evening when Martin, their eighteen-year-old brother, had told the family about the small cannon the hotel keeper had mounted in his garden, its barrel filled with shot. Gregory could almost hear Martin describing how Mr. Jackson had asked him and another member of the Alexandria Artillery to aim the cannon at the back door of the hotel. "So he could fire straight down the hall to the front entrance if anyone came to tear down his flag," Martin had explained.

Father had made an impatient sound and said, "The man's a fool, Martin. A fanatic." And Martin had said, "No, Father, the man's a patriot. He's let it be known that if our flag comes down, it will be over his dead body."

Remembering what had followed, Gregory knew it was the words *our flag* that had angered Father so. To him, the Stars and Stripes was "our flag," not the Confederate Stars and Bars. Sometimes Gregory wondered if it was sympathy for Martin, who had been banished from the house that night, that made the rest of the family such staunch

Confederates. Had they turned against the Union that Father held so dear because they couldn't very well turn against Father?

"I wish Papa hadn't said Martin wasn't welcome here anymore," Mary said at last. "I miss him a lot, and so do Mama and Elizabeth."

"I miss him too, Mary. But now that the Alexandria Artillery is camped way out at Manassas Junction, Martin couldn't come to see us even if Father changed his mind." *Not that he would. Father never changes his mind.* Gregory picked up his mother's music box and cradled it in his arms while he wound it, then brushed a speck of dust from the rosewood case before he returned it to the bedside table.

Mary raised the lid, and when the music box began to play, she smiled and said, "That tune is one of my very favorites, and so is the next one." She listened a moment before she confided, "Sometimes when I wake up at night, I hear music. It sounds like band music, but it's very, very soft." She frowned. "Mama always says it's just my imagination, but it isn't. You believe me, don't you, Greg?"

Reluctantly, he nodded. "I've heard it too, Mary."

She leaned toward him and whispered, "Do you think it's ghost music?"

"No, it's just a long way off," Gregory said. "But let's be quiet now and listen to the music box." Mary didn't need to know she'd been hearing bands playing in Yankee army camps across the Potomac, where campfires glowed in the darkness as far as anyone could see. She didn't need to know about all those northern men who had answered Lincoln's call to put down the South's "insurrection," or about the trains that chugged into Washington each day, bringing thousands more volunteers. More new recruits in a single day than all the Virginia militiamen here in Alexandria.

Gregory glanced at his sister and saw that she had fallen asleep. Good. That meant he could leave without feeling guilty. He tiptoed from the room just as Mother was coming along the hall with an armful of lilac blooms and pink tulips.

"Is she sleeping?" Mother whispered.

Gregory nodded. "Those are pretty," he said, breathing in the scent of lilacs. He hoped Mary would show more enthusiasm for Mother's bouquet than she had for the forget-me-nots.

"Would you mind going over to the *Gazette* office to see if they've posted any news bulletins, Gregory?" Mother asked.

"I'll be glad to," he said. If he stopped to watch the militia drill, he could stretch out the round trip to fill more than half an hour. But then he would be at loose ends again. It would be different if Carter were still here, he thought as he left the house. But his friend's family had joined the stream of citizens leaving the city until things settled down, though no one had any idea of when that might be. Gregory hoped it would be soon, but he had a feeling that things would get worse before they got better.

CHAPTER TWO

★　　　★　　　★

GREGORY COUNTED the newly boarded-up shops and offices he passed on the way to the post office the next morning. Abe Lincoln's blockade of the Potomac had been hard on just about all the town's businesses, but Father had fared better than most. A lot of the tradesmen who had left the city had arranged to store their furniture or merchandise in Father's warehouse, and that helped make up for the lack of shipping. Still, he'd had to let his employees go because there was no work for them. Gregory wondered what Father did at his office all day, since there couldn't be much work for him, either.

Inside the almost deserted post office, Gregory bought stamps and began to stick them on the letters he was mailing. Two were addressed in Miss Lily's spidery hand, the ones to Aunt Alice in Baltimore and Martin at Manassas Junction were in Mother's tiny script, and the rest were in Father's bold penmanship—all of them business letters except one to Aunt Adele in western Virginia.

Gregory swept the envelopes into a stack and handed them across the counter to the postmaster, exchanged a few polite words about the weather, and then walked over to the alphabetically arranged pigeonholes to pick up the mail. Good. Miss Lily's sister in Richmond had written, and her issue of *Godey's Lady's Book* had come, too. Nothing from Martin this time, but the weekly letter from his mother's sister near Fairfax Court House had arrived. Father's mail seemed to be all bills and business letters.

On the way home, Gregory raised his eyes to the Confederate flag atop the Marshall House Hotel and thought again of the day he and Carter had stood in the crowd watching Mr. Jackson run it up the pole. The day Virginia had voted to leave the Union rather than send militia units to fight against what the newspapers called "her sister states." That was the beginning of all the trouble, Gregory thought as he crossed a street. His history teacher had traced the roots of the problems between North and South back to the Constitutional Convention in Philadelphia, but Gregory blamed last month's vote of the Secession Convention in Richmond for Alexandria's problems—and his family's, too.

At Miss Lily's house, he accepted a piece of Belle's gingerbread before he took the rest of the mail and went home. Mother was on the way downstairs, wearing her hat, and Gregory remembered that she'd planned to go to the church hall this morning to help sew shirts and uniforms for Confederate volunteers. "You have a letter from Aunt Millie," he said, knowing she would be disappointed that there was nothing from Martin. Obviously, the family thought of Private Martin Howard more often than he thought of them.

"I'll take Father's mail over to the warehouse now,"

Gregory said, glad his mother never pointed out that Father could read it when he came home at noon.

Gregory had barely reached the brick sidewalk when Mother called him back. "Ask your father if you may ride Big Red out to the farm," she said as she slipped her sister's letter back into its envelope. "Your Aunt Millie needs the recipe for Lena's apple cake, and of course she needs it for a party tomorrow night, so she'd like you to bring it to her. I don't know why she always leaves everything till the last minute—or why I always come to her rescue!"

Mother drew on her gloves, adding, "Ask Lena to tell you how she makes the cake—and the icing, too—so you can write it down. You'll only be able to stay one night this time, Gregory. I want you to start home tomorrow afternoon, so you won't be underfoot for the party."

Underfoot? He and his cousins would be outdoors all day, and they'd much rather eat in the kitchen than dress up for a party. Oh, well. It was no use to argue with Mother, and a short visit was better than none.

Less than an hour later, Gregory was on his way to the livery stable where Father boarded Big Red, and for the first time in weeks, he felt almost cheerful. The long ride through the countryside would be fun, and an overnight visit with his aunt's family would help make up for missing Carter and his other friends who had fled the city. His cousin Albert always tried to lord it over him because he was a year older—almost fifteen—but Gregory didn't let that bother him.

A block away from the stable, he saw a cavalry officer riding a handsome horse and leading two others—including one that looked suspiciously like Big Red. It *was* Big Red! "Excuse me, sir!" Gregory called, breaking into a run. "You've made a mistake, sir—that's my father's horse you have there. And the mare belongs to Mr. John Bevin."

The officer looked down at him and said, "There's been no mistake. Our cavalry needs horses, and I'd rather take them from Unionist traitors than loyal Virginians. Now, move aside."

The cavalryman dug his heels into his mount, and Gregory scrambled backward. Big Red whinnied a greeting as he was led past, and Greg's eyes filled with angry tears. *How dare that man take him! And how can I tell Father that a Confederate soldier stole his horse?* There was only one thing to do, Gregory decided. He'd have to go to the cavalry camp and ask one of Martin's friends, or maybe some older man who had done business with Father, to get Big Red back for him.

Gregory started in the direction of the cavalry camp, but he'd gone only a short distance when he saw the three horses tied to the hitching post in front of a coffee shop. He sprinted up to them, and with trembling fingers he untied Big Red and Mr. Bevin's mare. Grateful that the Confederate officer had thought to confiscate the saddles and bridles along with the horses, Gregory mounted Big Red and cantered toward the nearest alley, leading the mare.

What if that cavalryman comes after me? What if he

says I'm a horse thief? Perspiration ran down between Gregory's shoulder blades. The sooner he left town, the less likely he was to be caught—but what about the mare?

The blacksmith! Gregory followed the ringing sound of hammer striking anvil and the stench of a coal fire down a narrow alley to a smithy. The man looked up from his work, and Gregory said, "Do you know Mr. Bevin? I've found his mare."

Pumping the bellows with one hand, the blacksmith said, "That's her, all right. Wandered off, did she? I'll have my boy put her in the yard till I have time to stop by the Bevin place with her."

"Thanks!" Gregory handed the mare's lead to a small boy who came out of the shadows by the forge, and then he was on his way to the farm. He urged Big Red along the Little River Turnpike, hoping the cavalry officer would stay awhile in the coffee shop talking politics, hoping he would look around town for the horses rather than along the pike.

Father wouldn't want him to ride Big Red this hard, especially with a fifteen-mile trip ahead of them, but Gregory didn't slow his pace until he was several miles outside of town. When he came to a shady spot about halfway to the farm, he reined in the horse to let him rest.

Gregory heard a shout, and a man waved to him from a nearby field. "You just come from the city?" the farmer asked when he was within easy hearing distance. "What's the latest news?"

Not knowing whether the man was Unionist or

Confederate, Gregory answered carefully. When he finished, the man said, "Virginia should of stayed in the Union. If I'd had anything to say about it, she would of."

"Well, the vote to ratify secession is next week, so you can have your say then," Gregory told him.

"I would, if we was marking a ballot, but I hear we'll have to declare how we vote, and some official will write it down beside our name. I'll stand up for my beliefs to any man, but I don't want the Confederate government having my name on record as a Unionist. No, I won't be going to the polls on the twenty-third."

But Father will be. A week from yesterday, he'd go to the polls and cast his vote against secession. Gregory's chest felt tight. It was one thing for the neighbors and other townspeople to know Father was a Unionist, but something else indeed for strangers to know. Strangers like the cavalryman who had taken Big Red.

"Well, I have to be on my way," Gregory said.

"Heading for Fairfax Court House? If you hear anything while you're there, stop by on your way home. Not many travelers passing by here these days, you know."

Sure that the cavalryman wouldn't come this far looking for him, Gregory relaxed and enjoyed the rest of the trip. He waved to the occasional militiaman on picket duty along the road and even chatted a few minutes when he stopped to pay the toll with the coins Father had given him. Still, he was hot and dusty by the time he reached his relatives' farm just beyond the village that had grown up around the county courthouse.

"I knew your mother wouldn't let me down," Aunt Millie said when Gregory handed her the apple-cake recipe. She held out the paper to her little daughter and said, "Sally, would you take this to the kitchen and read it to Lucy until she can say it back to you?"

Greg watched the child run off, hoping his sister would soon be healthy again.

"Come on out to the pasture, Greg," said twelve-year-old Robert. "You won't believe how much this spring's foals have grown."

At supper that evening, Gregory was enjoying a second helping of fried chicken when Uncle Matthew turned to him and said, "Well, young man, has that father of yours seen the error of his ways yet?"

"No, sir." He didn't want to seem disloyal, so he added, "Father thinks *we* are the ones in error, sir."

His uncle helped himself to another serving of chicken and said thoughtfully, "Perhaps he is wiser than we think. It will go more easily for him than for his Confederate neighbors when Lincoln's hirelings swarm into the city."

"And that could happen any day, now that Lincoln has the secessionists in Maryland under control and the rail lines to the north protected," Cousin Albert said, watching to see Gregory's reaction to his words.

Uncle Matthew glanced at Gregory and said, "In your father's place, I would send my family to safety. It goes without saying that you would be welcome here."

Who does Uncle Matthew think he is, criticizing Father like this? "My parents agree that the family belongs together," Gregory said, struggling to keep his voice calm. "Mother says she refuses to let fear of the Yankees drive her from her home."

"Those are brave words," Uncle Matthew said. "She would do well to remember—"

"For goodness' sake, let's talk about something more pleasant," Aunt Millie interrupted. She smiled at Gregory and said, "I have a surprise for you, dear."

Grateful for the change of subject, he echoed, "A surprise?"

"What young artillerist would you most like to visit with this evening?" his aunt prompted.

Gregory's heart leaped. "Martin's coming?"

"He usually does on Fridays," she answered. "He should be here by dusk."

"Maybe he can help me decide what to do about Big Red," Gregory said.

His uncle frowned. "You know, it doesn't make sense to raid a livery stable and take only two mounts. It sounds to me more like a misguided attempt to harass the Unionists."

Aunt Millie looked worried. "Then it's no wonder Suzanne's last letter said she was concerned about Roger voting in the referendum. She said the vote was *viva voce*, but I'm not sure what she meant by that."

"'Living voice,'" Cousin Albert said, sounding bored. "Meaning 'out loud.'"

"Then anyone who happens to be there will know how he voted!" Aunt Millie exclaimed. She turned to Gregory and said, "Surely your father doesn't intend to endanger his family by going to the polls and announcing his treason for all the world to hear!"

Gregory wasn't sure whether it was fear or anger that knotted his stomach. "Father intends to vote because he thinks it's cowardly not to stand up for what he believes," he said, his voice tense. "And he thinks *we're* the ones who are traitors," he repeated. The silence that greeted his words made him wonder if he'd been too outspoken. But no matter how much he disagreed with Father, he couldn't let Uncle Matthew imply he was an opportunist or Aunt Millie call him a traitor. He was relieved when his uncle spoke.

"Robert, do you know how the U.S. Constitution defines treason?" he asked, turning to his younger son.

Robert sat up straighter. "Yes, sir. Levying war against the United States or giving aid and comfort to her enemies."

From across the table, Sally asked in a small voice, "Is Mama a traitor because she sends cakes and pies to the militiamen camped in the church?"

"No, sweetheart. A person can only be a traitor to his— or her—own country, and our country is the Confederacy."

Gregory watched his little cousin's pinched expression change to one of relief, but he knew that though his uncle's words had been addressed to Sally, they were meant for him. He felt a sense of relief at the realization that he wasn't a traitor, and neither were Martin and Mother and the girls—no matter what Father thought.

And no matter what Aunt Millie thought, Father wasn't a traitor either.

It was almost dark when Gregory heard hoofbeats on the lane, and he was outside in time to see Martin swing down from his horse. The roughness of his brother's wool militia uniform scraped Gregory's face, and he felt the jacket buttons press into him when Martin gave him a bear hug.

"Are Mother and Elizabeth well?" his brother asked, releasing him. "Is Mary gaining her strength back? And Father—is he as stubborn as ever?"

"Yes," Gregory said. "Nothing has changed much since you left except that Mother just canceled our summer visit with Aunt Alice's family in Baltimore because of the Union occupation there."

Martin scowled and said, "We got word of the occupation today when some new recruits arrived from Richmond with the news."

Gregory wished he could tell Martin how much he missed him, but instead he said, "Aunt Millie had Lucy bake something special in honor of your visit—the first strawberry pie of the season."

"That sure beats what we get in camp," Martin said. He waved to the stable boy who was hurrying toward them. "I won't be long, Andy," he called, "but this fellow would appreciate a rubdown and some oats."

Though Gregory was disappointed to hear the visit would be a short one, he knew his aunt would make sure he had some time alone with Martin. "I have to ask you what to do about Big Red," he said, quickly telling his brother about the cavalry officer's attempt to confiscate horses belonging to Unionists.

Martin swore under his breath. "I figured Father and Mr. Bevin might face some kind of repercussions, and you can bet it will be worse after next week's vote to approve secession," he said as they walked toward the house. "Before I leave, we'll decide how to keep Big Red out of the cavalry," he added. And then in a hearty voice he called out to little Sally, who was waiting in the doorway, "Hey, Sal! Can you spare a piece of strawberry pie for a lowly artillery private?"

Early the next evening, Gregory cut through the alley to the back gate after he left Uncle Matthew's mare, Beauty, at the livery stable. When he passed the open door of the summer kitchen where Lena sat shelling peas from the garden, she cried, "Law, chile! Ever'body been worried sick 'bout you! What you waitin' for? Go on in," she urged when Mary called his name from the upstairs window.

He hurried inside and ran up the back stairs to his little sister's room. She sat on the window seat, her face damp with tears.

"Mary! What's wrong?"

She wiped her eyes and said, "I'm just glad you're home. We didn't know what had become of you!" She raised her voice and called, "He's home, Elizabeth."

"So I see," said sixteen-year-old Elizabeth, coming into the room. "We've all been beside ourselves with worry, Greg. Mr. Bevin stopped at the warehouse yesterday and told Papa a groom at the livery stable said a Confederate cavalry officer from Warren County had taken his mare and Big Red. He said that somebody brought the mare back, but Big Red was still missing—and of course, *you* were missing too! Papa went over to the stable and found out you hadn't borrowed another horse to go to Aunt Millie's, so we didn't know what to think. Where on earth have you been all this time?"

"At Aunt Millie's, right where I was supposed to be."

Mary frowned. "But how did you get there?"

By the time Gregory had explained, his mother had come back home from an afternoon of sewing Confederate uniforms, and he had to tell the story all over again. When he finished, he saw that Father was standing in the doorway, listening.

"If you left Big Red at the farm, how did you get back here?" he asked.

"Uncle Matthew lent me Beauty. I made sure the groom at the stable knew her owner was a Confederate, so he wouldn't get any ideas."

Father gave Gregory a steely look. "You realize, of course, that if anything happens to your uncle's mare, I'll be honor bound to let him keep Big Red."

Honor bound. That's Father, all right. Tied in knots by his idea of honor.

"Where is Papa going?" Mary asked when Father

excused himself and left the room.

Mother said, "I imagine he's going to tell his friend at Confederate headquarters that Gregory is safe at home again, and that Big Red has been found."

Mary looked surprised. "I didn't know Papa had any Confederate friends. Except Miss Lily, of course."

"Why shouldn't he?" Gregory asked. "After all, he has a Confederate wife and four Confederate children."

"One of whom he won't allow in the house, don't forget," Elizabeth said, her voice bitter.

"That reminds me," Gregory said. "Guess what handsome artillery private came to visit when I was at Aunt Millie and Uncle Matthew's?"

CHAPTER THREE

A FEW MORNINGS later, Gregory hesitated outside the dining room. He wasn't sure he ought to blunder in while his parents were arguing, but he decided that would be better than standing in the hall, eavesdropping.

"The subject is closed, Suzanne," Father said, and he turned to greet Gregory.

But Mother said, "Then I shall reopen it, Roger. I think Gregory should be a part of this discussion, since the decision you make will affect him and the girls as well as the two of us."

"My decision is made," Father said. "I shall go to the polls and vote against the secession ordinance." He spread a thick layer of peach preserves on a biscuit.

Gregory cleared his throat and said, "I hear that it will be a voice vote and that each man's aye or nay will be written down beside his name."

Father nodded. "An attempt to constrain the Unionists, of course. Those few of us who are still in town."

Leaning forward, Mother said, "If your vote can't possibly change the outcome, why must you jeopardize your family by going on record as an enemy of the Confederacy?"

Father's eyes blazed. "Because I will not be intimidated! Voting is the only way I can protest the misguided action of the Secession Convention and the hysterical acceptance of that action by the people of Virginia—including, to their eternal shame, members of my own family."

"If you will excuse me, I'll see to Mary," Mother said. "All this thundering and blustering is sure to have upset her." Her back stiff, she left the dining room.

Gregory took a deep breath and said, "I feel no shame in following Virginia in her choice to join the Confederacy, sir." When his father's brows pulled together in a frown, he added nervously, "I'm sorry that you think less of me for it."

"A boy of thirteen I can excuse for such shortsighted foolishness." Father's voice grew harsh as he added, "It is your brother I cannot forgive for taking up arms against the Union that his ancestors fought to bring into existence. At his age, he should have more judgment."

Gregory knew better than to stick up for Martin. He buttered a biscuit, hoping Father couldn't tell how upset he was. Shortsighted foolishness, indeed. Father was the shortsighted one—and the foolish one, too, in spite of his dignified appearance—going off to practically volunteer as a whipping boy for the Confederate government.

Father waited while Gregory choked down the rest of his breakfast. The minute he slipped his napkin into the silver napkin ring, Father stood up and said, "Tell your mother I will go directly from the polls to my office." After a brief hesitation, he added, "You should stay off the streets today—there could be trouble."

Shaken, Gregory watched his father leave the room. *What if there's trouble for Father because of his voice vote for the Union? What if the people set upon him when they hear him vote nay to the secession ordinance? What if they decide to punish him for being a traitor—even though he isn't one?*

Gregory heard the front door open and close. How could he wait until dinnertime to know that Father was safe? Hurrying to the parlor, he pulled back the curtain at the front window and watched Father set off for the polling place. If Father hadn't forbidden him to leave the house—

But wait. Father had said "You *should* stay off the streets today." *Should*, not *must*. His mind made up, Gregory headed for the door. He started along the sidewalk, staying a block or so behind his father.

Everywhere he looked, Greg saw Confederate flags— more today than yesterday, even. Several weeks before, Father had announced at dinner that his friend Mr. Bevin was so incensed by "those counterfeit banners" that he'd gone to Washington to buy himself a U.S. flag. But when Gregory passed Mr. Bevin's house, the Stars and Stripes was gone. Someone had stolen it, he realized when he saw that the flagstaff was broken. He was still staring at the splintered pole when the old man stepped outside and saw him.

"Somebody took your flag last night, sir."

Mr. Bevin shook his head and said, "That happened almost a week ago, just after the groom at the livery stable turned our horses over to that rebel cavalryman. I'm leaving the broken pole so no one will think I was intimidated into removing the flag that symbolizes our country."

Your country, Gregory corrected him silently. He said good-bye and hurried on, thinking of how Father and Mr. Bevin had both said they didn't want people to think they'd been intimidated. That was just about the last thing anyone would think about either of them. Gregory couldn't help feeling a grudging respect for both men. *What if they were the ones who had chosen the right course?* He refused to consider the possibility.

Walking faster now to narrow the distance between himself and Father, Gregory noticed more men on the street than was usual at this hour, and they were all walking in the same direction he was. He sensed excitement in the air and realized they must be on their way to the polls to vote aye to secession.

Several groups of men were clustered outside the door of the polling place, but Father had already gone inside by the time Gregory arrived, and he stopped, not sure what to do now that he was there. He gave a start when a voice said, "Well, now, young fellow. I know you're free and white and male, but I doubt you're twenty-one."

Some of the other men chuckled, and one of them drawled, "The important thing to know is which way he'd vote."

Above the chorus of agreement a familiar voice said, "I can vouch for him," and Gregory saw Mr. Greene, their neighbor. His son Nelson, who had been a classmate of Martin's, was with him, and they were both wearing their militia uniforms and carrying muskets. Taking Gregory aside, Mr. Greene said, "Nelson and I are here to escort your father home after he casts his vote. We'll see that he gets back safely."

Filled with relief and gratitude, Gregory said, "Thank you, sir. I— I was worried."

"And well you might be," Mr. Greene said, frowning at the sudden angry murmur inside the polling place. "Now go along home—no man wants his son to see him vilified by his peers." Gregory waited for the two militiamen to shoulder their way into the building before he ran across the street and ducked into the shadowy doorway of a boarded-up shop. No one would notice him here.

A voice called out, "Traitor! He's a traitor to our cause!" Other voices joined in, and not wanting to show himself, Gregory waited, scarcely breathing. Soon he saw his father pass, walking proudly, as though the shouts of derision were cheers and the uniformed men on either side were companions rather than protectors. Now the crowd spilled into the street, and some of the men tried to overtake Father. Gregory peered from the shelter of the doorway and saw men shake their fists as they jeered and threatened. One of them called out, "We know who you are, don't forget!" and another yelled, "We'll find out where you live, too!"

Gregory felt like an iron band was squeezing his chest. Mother was right—his father's vote had jeopardized them all. Maybe Mr. Greene and his son could protect Father from the crowd on the way to his office, but who was going to guard their house? Greg saw a man throw a bottle, saw it strike the sidewalk and shatter just behind his father.

Father didn't change his pace, but Nelson Greene wheeled around, his musket pointed at the crowd. "That's enough!" he shouted.

The men fell back a few steps, and one of them shouted, "Traitors to the Confederacy don't deserve your protection—they deserve death!"

Gregory's heart pounded. No wonder Mr. Greene hadn't wanted him to witness this! He heard Nelson say, "Maybe so, but not at the hands of a mob."

"He's right," agreed a man in a top hat. "Let the government deal with him—we don't want blood on our hands. Not even a traitor's blood."

The men hesitated and then begin to straggle back to the polling place while the young militiaman watched, his musket cradled in his arms. Nelson was enjoying this, Gregory realized. It was the chance to play soldier, not his friendship with Martin—or Mr. Greene's insistence—that made him willing to defend "a traitor to the Confederacy."

Gregory waited until his father was some distance ahead before he stepped out of the doorway and set off for home. As he walked, questions tumbled through his mind. How could he respect his father for doing what he believed was right and at the same time blame him for putting his family at risk? Why was it that he could understand Father's loyalty to the United States while his father had only scorn for anyone who had a greater loyalty to Virginia? How could he be secretly proud of his father while Father was openly ashamed of him?

It was all Abe Lincoln's fault. Before he was elected, everything was fine.

CHAPTER FOUR

EARLY THE NEXT morning, Gregory woke with a start. Drums? At this hour? He tiptoed to the window, and in the pale morning light he saw one of the local militia companies marching along Washington Street. It had moved beyond his line of vision when Mr. Greene came striding along the sidewalk with Nelson close behind him, still buttoning his uniform coat. *They must be trying to catch up with the others.*

His pulse racing, Gregory pulled on his clothes and ran down the front stairs and out the door. The sound of drumbeats was muted now, but he could see a long column of uniformed men far ahead, turning onto Duke Street. He was standing on the sidewalk, staring after them and wondering uneasily why they were marching away from town, when he heard the faint throb of drums from the direction of the waterfront.

Gregory hurried to the corner and turned toward the river. He had to find out what was happening! A young black boy he'd often seen fishing in the Potomac was trotting toward him, glancing back every few seconds. "Hey," Gregory called. "What's going on?"

Without slowing, the boy said, "Don' rightly know, but

I jus' seen soldiers comin' off ships down at de wharf."

Gregory's mouth went dry. The Union invasion! But would troops have come down the Potomac by ship? *I have to find out for sure before I tell Father.*

As Gregory got closer to the river, the drumbeats grew more distinct, and then he saw the soldiers marching toward him at the double-quick. His heart pounding, he stepped into the doorway of a tobacco shop to wait for them to go by. As the sound of boots striking the ground smartly and the clank of canteens grew louder, Gregory reminded himself that the Yankees weren't interested in him. But his heart still seemed to beat as loudly as their drums.

When the column of men had marched past him, he drew a deep breath and stepped out of the doorway to stare after them. What would they do when they found that the city's defenders had withdrawn? Would they try to catch up with them, or would they—

Surprised to see a handful of soldiers leaving the marching column to follow an officer along Royal Street, Gregory dashed after them. What a story he'd have for Mary today—and for Aunt Millie's family next time he went to the farm. Even Cousin Albert would be impressed by a firsthand account of the Union army's arrival in Alexandria.

When Greg reached the side street, the squad of Yankees was almost to the corner. Where were they going, anyway? Maybe to the telegraph office, to cut the line to Richmond. But at the next intersection, the officer pointed at something, and the others raised their eyes to follow their leader's gesture. *The Confederate flag on top of the Marshall House Hotel—the flag Lincoln could see from the White House.* Walking faster now, the men turned up King Street, and Gregory raced after them.

He reached the corner in time to see the last soldier disappear into the hotel. Slowing, Gregory held his breath, waiting to hear the boom of the cannon in Mr. Jackson's backyard, the one the hotel keeper had asked Martin and his friend to aim for him more than a month ago. But then Gregory realized that with no warning of an enemy's approach, the weapon was useless. He darted down the block, passing opposite the Marshall House so he could watch from the steps of the building where he and Carter had stood the day of the flag raising.

His eyes glued to the huge flag flying high above the roof of the hotel, Gregory waited for it to be lowered. It dropped from sight so quickly he guessed the Yankees had cut the halyards. It was strange to think that most of the city had watched the Stars and Bars go up, but he was the only one here to see it go down. He was about to leave when a shot rang out—and then another. Gregory's stomach tightened. Mr. Jackson had said the flag would come down only over his dead body. Did this mean—?

Suddenly aware of a drum beating double time, Gregory glanced up the block and saw the main body of Yankee troops rounding the corner and heading his way. He fought down the impulse to run, remembering the proverb Father often quoted: "The wicked flee when no man pursueth, but the righteous are bold as a lion." With his heart hammering against his ribs, Gregory didn't feel bold, but he managed to stay put as the soldiers rapidly approached.

"You, boy! Where did that gunfire come from?" demanded one of the lieutenants. Gregory pointed to the Marshall House, and the troops broke ranks and surged toward it. They pounded on the door, but someone inside must have barricaded it against them.

The men's angry voices followed Gregory as he slipped away. The minute he rounded the corner, he began to run and didn't stop until he ducked into the alley behind his house. He was leaning against Mr. Greene's fence, trying to catch his breath, when the throb of drums from the northern part of the city told him that other Union troops had crossed Long Bridge and were marching into Alexandria. *No wonder our militiamen left town. They would have been hopelessly outnumbered.*

Gregory started down the alley, his footsteps dragging now as the reality of what had happened began to sink in: The city and its people were now at the mercy of an army determined to force the South into submission.

Lena was lifting a log from the wood box when he opened the back gate and stepped into the yard. "You look like you done seen a ghos', chile!" she exclaimed. "Where you been already at dis hour?"

"I heard soldiers in the street and went to see what was happening. The Yankees are here, and our militia has left town."

Lena scowled and said, "Yo' mama won't like hearin' dat."

But Father will. "I'd better go inside now," Gregory said.

When he opened the back door, he could hear his father's heavy footsteps on the front stairs, and he hurried along the hall to meet him. "Union soldiers have come into town, Father, and more are on the way. I just saw an officer haul down the flag from the Marshall House roof." Somehow, he couldn't bring himself to mention the shots he'd heard fired.

Before Gregory's eyes, the worry lines in Father's face seemed to disappear. He drew a deep breath and said, "Well, son, no one can say Lincoln didn't bend over backward to be fair to Virginia. He could have acted when the state delegates voted for secession last month, but he held off until the people voiced their approval at the polls yesterday." When Gregory didn't answer, his father added sharply, "Since this was in spite of the fact that Virginia militiamen had taken over the Federal arsenal at Harper's Ferry as well as the U.S. navy yard at Norfolk, I would say that the president showed admirable restraint."

"You mean *your* president," Gregory retorted. "Jefferson Davis is *my* president."

Father gave him a long look. "You are right, of course," he said at last. "My president showed admirable restraint. Now, if you will excuse me, I will be in my library." He went into the small, book-lined room and closed the door behind him.

Gregory couldn't help feeling shut out. Father always rose early and spent the hour before breakfast at the desk in his library, writing in his journal or catching up on his reading—but until today, he had always left the door open.

Breakfast that morning was so tense and strained that Gregory envied Elizabeth her ability to sleep away the hours in spite of the rattle of drums outside. His parents avoided each other's eyes, and he realized that neither of them had said a word about the Union occupation. He hoped the presence of Union soldiers in the city didn't become something else no one dared mention. It was bad enough that by some silent understanding Martin's name was never spoken in Father's presence. Gregory felt a surge of anger—at his parents, at the Yankee soldiers, and at the Confederate militiamen who had fled the city. *This is all Abe Lincoln's fault.*

At last Mother spoke. "Aren't you going to your office today, Roger?"

Father said, "From what I saw of the behavior of the Union troops camped in Washington when I was there last week, they are not a well-disciplined group. I think it best that I remain here today. "

"Thank you, Roger," Mother said, her voice shaking. "Elizabeth and I appreciate that."

Puzzled, Gregory frowned, and Father explained. "In an army of occupation, soldiers are sometimes, shall we say, 'disrespectful' of their enemy's women." Then, meeting his wife's eyes across the table, Father said, "Perhaps under the circumstances you would not object if I were to display the United States flag."

Mother hesitated for a long moment before she said, "You must do what you think best. And now, if you will excuse me . . ."

She left the room, and Father turned to Gregory. "After breakfast, would you be good enough to bring home the flag I have in my office at the warehouse?"

It wasn't really a question, or even a request—it was an order. Gregory didn't like the idea of the Union flag flying outside his home, but how could he refuse whatever protection it would give his mother and sisters? "Of course, sir," he said. He couldn't help adding, "But aren't you concerned the neighbors might think it strange that you didn't fly your flag when the Confederates held the city but you put it out the instant the Union took over?"

Father said, "The neighbors may think what they will. The important thing is the safety of your mother and the girls."

Gregory took the warehouse key and set off for the waterfront. As he crossed Pitt Street, his eyes were drawn to the Marshall House on the corner of the next block, and he saw that the entire King Street intersection was filled with people. *Maybe I can find out what happened.* He trotted up in time to hear a distraught woman say, "Of course they wouldn't shoot a man dead in his house about a bit of old bunting!"

The people standing nearby began to murmur among themselves, and Gregory caught the words ". . . Mr. Jackson's sister."

"Did the Yankees shoot Mr. Jackson?" Gregory asked an older boy at the edge of the crowd.

"There's all kinds of rumors, but nobody knows anything for sure."

A middle-aged man said, "The soldiers won't let anybody inside, but one of the hotel guests called from the window and said they were all being held as hostages."

A boy Gregory had often seen sweeping the street in front of the watchmaker's added, "I heard that the Yankees are threatening to burn the place down."

There was a murmur from the crowd, and Gregory saw a small group of soldiers leave the hotel, carrying a shrouded form on a makeshift stretcher, their faces twisted with grief.

The crowd parted to let the cluster of soldiers through, and they carried their burden toward the waterfront. Now the crowd buzzed with comments. . . . *their leader . . . our flag desecrated by . . . served him right . . . Jackson's last act was to defend . . . a martyr's death . . .* But everyone fell silent when one of the soldiers inside the hotel shouted from the window, "We'll burn this city to the ground to avenge our colonel's death! We'll—"

Without waiting to hear any more, Gregory set off for the warehouse again. He saw the stretcher bearers not far ahead and realized they must be taking the dead officer back to their ship. He wasn't sure it would be right—or even safe—to pass them, so he stayed back a respectful distance.

His eyes were drawn to the two steamships moored at

the wharf, and he wished he could watch the soldiers carry their fallen leader aboard, but with the cry for vengeance against the city fresh in his mind, Gregory made his way to the side door of the warehouse.

He fit Father's key into the huge metal lock and turned it, sensing the movements of the tumblers inside. The door of the cavernous building creaked when he pushed it open, and the morning sunshine slanted in to form a distorted rectangle on the floor. Dust motes danced in the light ray, and Gregory heard a scurrying sound. *Rats*. His skin crawled, and he was glad the door to his father's office was only a few yards away.

The flag stood just inside the office door, where Father could see it from his desk, and Gregory hesitated in front of it. How was he supposed to get it home—march through the streets with it on his shoulder? It didn't take long for him to decide what to do. He slipped the flag from its pole, and began to fold it the way the militiamen did after they lowered their flag in the evening. Then he tucked the compact, triangular bundle under his arm and left Father's office. He locked the warehouse door, and after one last look at the steamships, he started home.

Gregory was still three blocks from Washington Street when he heard the sound of a fife and drum. *More* Union troops. He picked up his pace and reached the wide thoroughfare in time to watch them pass. Wearing dark blue coats and lighter blue trousers, they marched smartly to the tune of "Yankee Doodle," their flag waving proudly. Just three months ago, Martin and the other Alexandria militiamen had stepped briskly to that very tune as they'd carried the Stars and Stripes in the city's George Washington's Birthday celebration. Then, the sidewalks had been lined with cheering citizens, but now only a few faces could be seen at the windows while clusters of black children watched silently from the other side of the street.

The column of marching men was a sharp contrast to the undisciplined troops at the Marshall House, but Gregory reminded himself that they had been orderly at first, too. Clutching his father's flag, he walked briskly home as the blue-clad marchers streamed past him, eyes straight ahead. He was surprised to find the front door shut in spite of the morning's warmth, but when the knob didn't turn in his hand, he understood. Father wasn't taking any chances with the "disrespectful" Union troops. Gregory knocked and waited.

His father opened the door. "Oh," he said. "It's you, Gregory."

Noticing Father's frown when he held out the folded flag, Greg said, "I left the pole in your office because I knew you'd want to hang this from the upstairs window so nobody can tear it down. I guess you know that Mr. Bevin's flag was stolen."

"A good idea, son. I'm pleased to see you still feel some reverence for the flag you were born under."

It was true, but Gregory wasn't going to admit it. "I'll look in on Mary now, sir. She'll want to hear about what's happening." And without waiting for a reply, he climbed the stairs.

Lena was coming out of Gregory's bedroom with her dust rag when he reached the upstairs hall. She glanced across at Elizabeth's door, which was ajar, and then at the closed door to Greg's parents' room. "Miss 'Lizbeth, she ain't up yet, an' yo' mama, she in dere grievin'. Don' know how anybody 'spect me to make de beds when de mornin's half over and folks still in 'em." Gregory had no answer to that, but he knew Lena didn't expect one. She brushed past him, still grumbling, as he reached Mary's door.

His sister was sitting on the window seat looking cross. For once, Mother's music box was silent, and the coverlet Lena must have tucked around her earlier lay on the floor some distance away, as if it had been flung there. "*What* is going on, Gregory?" Mary demanded before he had a chance to speak. "Mama said she was too upset to talk about it, Lena said she didn't know, and Elizabeth's still sleeping."

He crossed the room and sat beside her. "What do you want to know first?"

"I want you to tell me where you went before breakfast, and where you just got back from, and why Papa didn't go to work today."

"Well," Gregory began, deciding not to mention the shooting, "it's a long story, and it all began quite early this morning, while you were still asleep. . . ."

"Where's Mama?" Elizabeth asked as she took her place at the table that noon.

283

Father cleared his throat and said, "I believe she is trying to reconcile herself to the occupation of the city."

"I'll *never* be reconciled to that," Elizabeth said, laying her napkin on her lap, "but I don't intend to miss a meal over it."

In the silence that followed her words, Gregory could hear the mournful tolling of bells in the distance. "You'd think the people in Washington would be celebrating today, but that sounds like a dirge."

Father nodded. "My guess is they're mourning the death of a young officer who lost his life in the shooting at the Marshall House this morning. Mr. Bevin stopped by to say he'd heard it was that fellow Ellsworth, who went around the country giving exhibitions with his military drill team last summer," he added.

"Elmer Ellsworth?" Elizabeth cried. Father nodded, and she whispered, "How can he be dead? He was so young, so gallant—even if he was a Yankee."

Father gave her a pitying look and said, "My dear girl, many young and gallant men on both sides will die before this is over."

But not Martin. Glancing up, Gregory saw his sister leave the table in a flurry of skirts, and he wondered how Lena would feel when she saw that the meal she'd prepared had hardly been touched. Except, of course, by Father.

"You might be interested in a piece of news Mr. Bevin heard from his coachman," Father remarked. "It appears that except for a small group of cavalry, the Virginia militia left safely by train this morning, presumably for Manassas Junction."

"What happened to the cavalrymen?" Gregory asked.

"I presume they were captured."

I hope one of them was the officer who tried to make off with Big Red.

That afternoon, Gregory stood at the window of his room, looking down on Washington Street. It was crowded with vehicles headed south—the farm carts and carriages of Virginia citizens mixed in with a long train of canvas-covered army wagons. He wished Elizabeth hadn't brought Mary in so they could watch with him. He didn't feel much like talking, and the two of them were full of questions.

"But why have all those soldiers come here, Greg?" Mary asked.

"Because President Lincoln feels safer with his own soldiers across the river from Washington instead of our militiamen," he told her.

"Look at all that smoke off to the southeast, Greg—what do you think it means?" Elizabeth asked.

Gregory saw a plume of gray spread across the sky in the distance. "Our militiamen must be burning the railroad bridges behind them," he said. He looked down at the street again and saw that traffic seemed to be increasing. Just below the window was a farm wagon, its high load covered with blankets and roped in place. A cow was tied to the rear.

"Where's everybody going?" Mary asked, leaning forward in the chair Greg had placed in front of the window for her. "And what's in all those covered wagons?"

"They're filled with supplies for the Union Army, Mary," Greg said, answering her second question.

"Like muskets and bullets?" she asked in a hushed voice.

"Like food and blankets and tents," Elizabeth said. "I wonder where so many soldiers are going to camp."

"But why is everybody going the same way?" Mary asked.

Gregory had trouble hiding his impatience. "People leaving to escape the Yankees wouldn't very well head north, would they?"

In a small voice, Mary asked, "Will we leave, too?"

Gregory shook his head. "I think it's mostly the families of our militiamen and the leading secessionists who are going."

"And because of Father, our family's counted as Unionist, even though the three of us and Mama—and Martin, of course—are Confederates through and through," Elizabeth said. "I hate the way men are the only ones who count!"

And I hate being inside with the girls and not knowing what's happening. "I think I'll go down to the newspaper office and see if they've posted any bulletins," Gregory said.

As he passed the parlor, he glanced in and saw his father standing at the double window, hands clasped behind him. "I'm going to the *Gazette* office, sir," Gregory said.

"Perhaps you can find out something that might help us make sense of all this. The editor may even have had time to print up an extra edition by now."

Outdoors, with only the width of the sidewalk between him and all the activity in the streets, Gregory half wished he were still watching from his room. Then, to his surprise, the teamster riding the left wheel mule of a canvas-covered army wagon lifted a hat to him. *Of course—Father's U.S. flag.* Sure enough, it hung flat against the wall below the upstairs hall window. Gregory was surprised at how natural it felt to have it there.

"I see your father didn't waste any time showing his true colors," old Mr. Wilson called from a window of the house across the street.

Gregory's heart sank. This was what he'd been afraid of. "Father never hid his Unionist feelings, sir," he called back.

"Never flew his flag before today, though, did he?"

Gregory glanced at the now-empty place where until that morning Mr. Wilson's Stars and Bars had flown. "Where's *your* flag, sir?" he challenged.

The old man slammed down the window sash, and Gregory felt a mixture of satisfaction and apprehension. "He asked for that," he muttered. Still, it didn't pay to antagonize a neighbor, especially a cantankerous one like Mr. Wilson. And certainly not when Father was watching and listening from the parlor.

Gregory had taken only a few steps when he heard a commotion. As he hesitated, a group of soldiers came around the corner, not marching, but milling along, shouting and shaking their fists in the air. They filled the sidewalk, spilling into the street, coming faster now that they had seen Gregory. Their taunts followed him as he turned back, and he caught the words "burn the city."

He stumbled up the few steps from the sidewalk, and Father opened the door for him. "I think we can get a fairly good idea of what is going on without leaving the house, Gregory," he said as he bolted the door again. "No use asking for trouble."

From outside came a shout. "Lay off, the lot of you. That boy weren't no secesh—his house is flying our flag."

The clamor subsided, but then another voice shouted, "Well, the house next door ain't." Gregory rushed to the sitting room window in time to see one of the unruly soldiers hurl something at Miss Lily's house. He held his breath, waiting for the sound of shattering glass, but jeers from the other men assured him the missile hadn't found its mark.

After the soldiers were out of sight, Gregory said, "I thought there were a lot more of them. Maybe a whole company."

His father said, "A company of disciplined soldiers would seem far less threatening than an unpredictable mob of a dozen or two. You were right to come back when you saw them."

"Thank you, sir." Gregory was about to add that he was glad Father had hung his flag, but he changed his mind. He frowned, realizing that much as he hated the thought of the enemy taking over Alexandria, the presence of Union soldiers in the city meant that Father—and the rest of the family—no longer had to worry about the threats made by the secessionists outside the polling place.

• • •

To Gregory's relief, Mother took her place at the dining room table that evening, though her face was pale and she seemed to be rearranging the food on her plate rather than eating it. Halfway through the meal, the doorbell rang, and Lena went to answer it.

"A gen'leman to see you, sir," she told Father.

He rose from the table, and Mother frowned as if she were wondering what kind of gentleman would pay a call at suppertime. Gregory thought wistfully of the pleasant family meals they'd enjoyed before Virginia left the Union. Back then, if their opinions about the government's handling of the crisis in Charleston Harbor had differed, they'd had animated discussions instead of bitter arguments—or awkward silences. Back then, Father had made sure they saw all sides of a situation, so they would understand what was going on. But the day the Secession Convention voted Virginia out of the Union, that had changed. Ever since then, there had been the Union side and the wrong side, and—

Gregory's thoughts were interrupted when Father returned to the table and said, "Apparently the unrest among those troops we witnessed this afternoon was their reaction to the unfortunate event at the Marshall House just after dawn." He turned to his wife and added, "Both North and South have a martyr now. Jim Jackson murdered a Union officer who cut down the Confederate flag flying from his roof, and one of the soldiers immediately avenged his leader's death by shooting Jackson, fulfilling his prophecy that the flag would be removed only over his dead body."

Her voice shaking with anger, Mother demanded, "When, pray tell, did defending one's home and property against an intruder become 'murder'? If you ask me, Jim Jackson was assassinated."

Father's face flushed, but he said evenly, "It should be no surprise that we have differing interpretations of this incident, Suzanne."

"*Incident?* How can you call the killing of a family man on his own property an 'incident,' Roger?" When Father didn't answer, Mother stood up and said coldly, "You will have to excuse me. I seem to have lost my appetite."

Gregory didn't feel much like eating, either, but Elizabeth seemed unaffected by their parents' quarrel. "Who came to the door just now, Father?" she asked.

"One of the Union officers. He saw the flag and stopped by to assure me that for the protection of the city, Ellsworth's troops will spend tonight on the steamers that brought them from Washington." Father laid his napkin across his lap and added, "The ships will be anchored mid river, by the way."

Gregory hoped his relief didn't show.

"But what about tomorrow?" Elizabeth asked in a small voice. "Tomorrow and the day after?"

"Tomorrow, those soldiers will begin constructing earthworks over on Schuter's Hill. Hard physical work ought to dampen their enthusiasm for making trouble."

"Good," Elizabeth said. "I hope I never have to look at those Yankee heathens again." Noticing her father's frown, she quickly asked, "But what, exactly, are earthworks?"

That was something Gregory could explain. "The soldiers dig long trenches and pile up the dirt behind them to make walls to protect their camp," he said, remembering the diagrams Carter had showed him in a book from his father's library. "They mount their guns—their cannon—just inside the walls they've built, with the barrels sticking over the top."

Elizabeth shuddered and said, "I shouldn't have asked."

Well, you did. This was the worst day Gregory could remember—since the one not quite six weeks before when Father had sent Martin away, anyhow. And that *day* had been fine. It wasn't until evening that everything went wrong.

CHAPTER FIVE

"**C**LOSED UNTIL further notice,'"
Gregory whispered, reading the sign on the door of the
Gazette office on Monday. He had to step back when a
Union officer came out with a stack of printed sheets.

The officer saw Gregory and said, "Here, hold these for
a minute, would you?"

Not sure what else to do, Greg took the papers. His eyes
widened when he read the heading on the top sheet:
PROCLAMATION OF MARTIAL LAW. A wave of anger swept
over him. "Get somebody else to hold your proclama-
tions," he said, spitting out the words as he set the papers
on the sidewalk. "I don't want anything to do with you
and your martial law." He started off, wishing he'd thrown
the papers down, or else tossed them into the air so they
would have come down every which way.

"You come back here, boy. Now!"

The man's commanding tone made Gregory freeze in
his tracks. He stopped and faced the officer, who had finished posting a copy of the proclamation on the door,
right next to the CLOSED sign. The man's face wore the
same expression the headmaster's had when he'd found

Greg and Carter slipping a mousetrap into the desk drawer of an unpopular teacher before school one morning. "Pick up those papers," the officer ordered.

Seething, Gregory did as he was told. "The minute you get your proclamation printed, you close down our newspaper. Haven't you heard about freedom of the press?"

"Under martial law, enemy civilians have no freedoms. Don't you forget that, boy. And the U.S. Army didn't close down your newspaper—the editor shut it down himself rather than print this proclamation for us."

Gregory stared from the stack of papers to the officer. "Then how—"

The officer said, "We printed it ourselves. Don't you think that with all the troops we have in Alexandria, there might be a printer or two in the bunch?" He gave Gregory a long, level look. "You people are going to learn that you bit off more than you can chew when you took on Uncle Sam. Now hand me those papers and get out of my way."

Gregory was staring after him when he heard a commotion inside the building. He glanced back in time to see the door open and several soldiers shove a protesting private outside. The man stumbled, then regained his balance as the door slammed behind him.

"What's going on?" Gregory asked. "It sounds like somebody's tearing the place apart."

"They're upsetting all the type. They put me out 'cause I tried to stop 'em," the soldier told him. "I'm a printer, see, and I have no stomach for what those fellows are doing. I just hope they don't get it in their heads to destroy the presses."

Destroy the presses? "Your officer just left, headed toward Washington Street," Gregory said. "Why don't you—"

"I have to live with them fellows," the soldier said, wincing at the sounds of glee coming from inside the building. "One day soon I'll be fighting next to 'em. You think I'm gonna turn 'em in to an officer?"

"No, but *I'm* going to," Gregory said. He dashed after the officer, sure that such a stern, no-nonsense man would quickly put a stop to his troops' vandalism. At Washington Street, he glanced both ways to see which direction the man had gone and spied him in the middle of the block. He had just stepped through the wrought-iron gate and into the yard surrounding the elegant house that belonged to Carter's family—one of the few places in town where you didn't step out the front door right onto the public sidewalk.

Good. While he waits for someone to come to the door, I'll catch up to him. But before Gregory reached the gate, he saw the empty porch—and the two saddled horses grazing in the front yard.

From the upstairs window of the house across the street, an elderly woman called, "The Yankees have taken over that place. They'll be ruining Miss Julie's floors with their boots, and those horses have already trampled the peonies and iris along the fence." Her voice quivered with anger.

Before Gregory could answer, another officer came out

of the house. His high boots clomped across the porch and down the steps. He was heading for one of the horses when he spotted Gregory at the gate and paused to ask, "Is there something I can do for you, young man?"

"Some soldiers are vandalizing the *Gazette* office, sir. It's not far from here—I can show you the way."

The officer slapped his gloves against his thigh. "Were any horses tied outside the building?" He looked relieved when Gregory shook his head. "Not cavalry, then. Look, I'm sorry about this, and I'll pass on the information to the first infantry officer I see," he said, swinging into the saddle.

He's lying, Gregory thought, *and I was stupid to think that infantry officer inside would care about the property of "enemy civilians."*

The cavalryman looked down from what seemed an enormous height and asked, "Well? Is there something else?"

"N-not really. Just that this house belongs to my friend's family, and those purple iris your horse is trampling are his mother's favorites."

The cavalryman shrugged. "Better to take over an empty house than one where the family is sticking it out, don't you think? I'm sorry about the iris, though," he added. "Those are my wife's favorite, too. Now, open the gate for me, won't you?"

Gregory watched the cavalry officer ride off while the man's words echoed in his mind: "Better to take over an empty house than one where the family is sticking it out." *A house like ours.*

• • •

"Yankee officers are quartered in Carter's house," Gregory announced at the beginning of the noon meal. "Their horses have trampled the plantings in the yard, and their boots are ruining the floors."

Mother and Elizabeth looked shocked, but Father said, "What were you doing inside the house, son?" At Gregory's frown, he added, "I assume you must have been inside if you noticed the floors were being damaged."

"I heard about that from the neighbor across the street," Greg admitted, "but I saw the horses in the iris bed." He went on to say that the *Gazette* office was closed and to tell about the vandalism, adding, "I guess by now everybody knows we're under martial law."

"That was to be expected," Father said, "but what you've told us about the *Gazette* is most distressing."

Mother said, "I heard something even more distressing when I was at the Relief Society this morning." She lowered her voice and said, "The Yankees are threatening to hang Miss Sarah and burn down her house!"

"But *why*?" Greg and Elizabeth asked in unison.

"Because she sewed the flag that flew from the roof of the Marshall House," Mother said. "They're looking for Mr. Taylor, too, since he raised the money and contracted for the flag to be made, but he's at Manassas Junction with the rest of the militiamen."

Elizabeth demanded, "How on earth did the Yankees find out who—"

"Some of the city's Unionists told them," Mother said, interrupting.

"You need no longer be concerned about Miss Sarah's safety, Suzanne," Father said. "The matter has been taken care of."

Mother turned to him. "I—I don't understand," she said.

"Her brother-in-law came to see me at the warehouse this morning and asked if I would intercede with the Union authorities," Father explained. "I supported her defense that she was in the business of making flags, as did Mr. Bevin, and we were able to convince them that Miss Sarah would gladly sew U.S. flags or any other kind of banner she was paid to produce."

"That was good of you, Roger," Mother said, "and I'm sure Miss Sarah is grateful."

"Yes, Papa," Elizabeth agreed, "I'm glad you were able to help the authorities understand that Miss Sarah wasn't responsible for poor Elmer Ellsworth's death, even if she did make the flag he tore down and trampled before he was shot."

Gregory cheered silently. His sister had perfected an expression of wide-eyed innocence that let her get away with comments that would have earned him a reprimand for sarcasm.

Father frowned and said, "The entire country has responded most irrationally to young Ellsworth's death. I heard at Union Headquarters that New Yorkers are flocking to form a regiment called 'Ellsworth's Avengers,' and here in town, churchgoing citizens are expressing pleasure that Ellsworth was killed after he trampled on their flag."

Gregory was wondering how people knew the flag had

been trampled, if it really had been, when his father said, "Nothing has roused the ordinary citizens of both North and South to such a frenzy since the riot in Baltimore last month. Both the people and the press seem to have completely lost sight of the secession issue and the question of whether there will be one nation or two within America's borders."

Right now I'm more interested in what's happening within Alexandria's borders, Gregory thought. Somehow, having the streets filled with Yankees made him forget everything else.

★   ★   ★

"**C**OME SEE what Elizabeth and I are making," Gregory's little sister called when he passed her room several days later.

He stepped through the doorway and saw that her bed was strewn with paper—some of it scraps and some neat rectangles—and Mary was busy with a pencil and ruler. Elizabeth, her watercolor palette on the bedside table, was rinsing her brush in a dish of water.

"What are you two making—besides a mess?" Gregory asked, glad that his older sister was spending some time with Mary.

Elizabeth gestured to the window seat and said, "Have a look."

"Little Confederate flags! What are you going to do with them all?"

With a sly smile, Elizabeth said, "You'll see."

"And so will the Yankees, 'cause she's going to paste our flags all over town," Mary added. She lowered her voice and said, "You won't tell Papa, will you?"

Gregory shook his head. Elizabeth's pranks were none of his business. The sound of voices coming from the backyard attracted his attention, and when he moved to the window, he saw Lena bending down to listen to a little black girl who danced from one foot to the other and gestured as she talked. The minute the child ran out the gate, Lena picked up her skirts and hurried toward the house.

By the time she reached the door, Gregory was there to meet her. He had never seen her so upset. "It dem people!" she cried. "Dem people is comin'!"

"Coming down the alley?" he asked, knowing at once who Lena meant. She shook her head and twisted the skirt of her apron. "Down Washington Street, then?"

This time, Lena nodded. "Dem people is comin' down de street, an' yo' daddy not here to protect us," she wailed.

"It's all right, Lena—they won't come here. Father's U.S. flag will warn them away."

The woman took a deep breath and announced in a shaky voice, "Den I believe de parlor need dustin' 'fore yo' mama come back from her meetin'," and she set off for the front room.

Gregory dashed back upstairs and almost collided with Elizabeth, who grasped his arm and said, "That little girl just came out of Miss Lily's back gate and ran on down the alley. I think she's taking some kind of message to all the servants in the neighborhood. I hope this doesn't mean trouble."

Shrugging off Elizabeth's hand, Gregory said, "She's warning everybody that the Yankees are coming." At the door of his room, he glanced over his shoulder and added, "You and Mary can watch from in here, if you want to."

From his open window, he saw a group of soldiers

300

saunter along the opposite side of the street and stop to pound on the Wilsons' front door. Their elderly slave opened it, and even at this distance, her fear was obvious.

Elizabeth helped Mary to the chair their brother had placed in front of the window. "What's happening, Greg?" she asked, her voice tense.

"They've gone inside the Wilsons' house, but they won't come here because of Father's flag."

Mary asked, "But why did they go to the Wilsons'?"

Gregory ignored her question. He didn't even want to think about that. It seemed a long time before the door burst open and soldiers spilled out onto the sidewalk. The first one through the door was dragging something behind him, and it took a second or two for Gregory to realize what it was. Beside him, Elizabeth gasped and said, "They've taken Mr. Wilson's flag! And they've got that big old musket he always carried in the Washington's Birthday parades, too—the one his granddaddy used in the War for Independence."

"That must be their excuse for harassing secessionists— searching for weapons and Confederate flags to confiscate." A tall soldier paused and pulled something shiny from his pocket to show the others, but Gregory couldn't see what it was.

"Look!" Mary cried, pointing. "They're taking Mr. Wilson away with them!"

Gregory's heart raced when he saw the soldiers hustle the old man along the sidewalk. His hands were bound together in front of him, and the skinny soldier who held the end of the rope gave it a jerk that almost pulled Mr.

Wilson off his feet. Behind them came the slave Deborah, wringing her hands and weeping. Gregory swallowed hard. He didn't want to see this, but he couldn't keep from watching.

Two of the soldiers looked around and shook their fists at Deborah, and she shrank back, but when they ran to catch up with the others, she called after them, "Dis gonna be de death of dat ol' man—an' his sick ol' wife, too."

Mary began to cry, and Elizabeth pulled her close. "Don't just stand there, Gregory," she demanded. "*Do* something!"

Do *what*? "I'll get Father," he said. It was all he could think of.

Gregory ran all the way to the warehouse. Exhausted and out of breath, he stood in the doorway of the office, unable to speak. His father's face grew pale. "What is it?" he asked, rising from his chair.

"Mr. Wilson," Gregory said, still gasping for breath. "They took him away. Because of his flag."

Father reached for his hat and his walking stick. "Have you any idea where they've taken him?"

Gregory shook his head. "No, but they were going south on Washington Street." He followed his father out into the bright May sunlight and waited for him to lock the warehouse door. "Where are we going?" Gregory asked as they set off.

"The provost marshal is the final authority under martial law, so we'll report this at his headquarters," Father said.

"Where is that, sir?" Gregory asked.

"Diagonally opposite the infamous Marshall House," Father replied.

As they drew near, Gregory slowed at the sight of soldiers lounging on the steps of the hotel and clustered on the nearby sidewalk. "Come along, son," Father said. "The provost marshal will no doubt want to question you about the deplorable behavior of his men, but I assure you there is no need for you to be concerned."

"Why are so many soldiers hanging around the hotel?" Greg asked.

"The place has become quite the tourist attraction," Father said, his disgust evident. "I understand souvenir hunters are cutting away splinters from the stairway where Mr. Jackson died."

Gregory swallowed hard, remembering the bloodstains he'd seen on those stairs when he and Elizabeth had gone with Mother—and just about everyone else in the city—to file past Mr. Jackson's coffin and pay their respects to his widow. He remembered Elizabeth's hushed voice when she saw the stains on the landing: "Look, Gregory, we've seen the first blood shed in defense of the Confederate flag."

Supper that evening was the most pleasant meal the family had shared in weeks. Gregory wasn't sure whether it was because Mary was downstairs with them for the first time since her illness or because Father had arranged the release of their Confederate neighbor.

"I wonder how Mr. Wilson felt about being rescued by the very man he's been berating for his Unionist beliefs," Mother mused.

"I think he would have welcomed rescue by Satan himself," Father said. "Those soldiers must have dragged him through every puddle between here and the slave pen. He seems to have missed the irony of the army's using that place to jail the city's white citizens, by the way."

Gregory wished his father hadn't mentioned the slave pen. Ever since he'd learned to read, he had seen ads in the *Gazette* about the slave auctions held there, but he'd never thought much about it since no one he knew—or knew of—bought and sold slaves. Before today, he hadn't known about the small, dark cells inside the whitewashed building, had never imagined what it would be like to be imprisoned there.

Lena had just set a fresh basket of hot biscuits on the table when there was a great pounding at the door. She shrank back and sent Father a pleading look. He laid his napkin beside his plate and said, "I'll deal with this, Lena." Gregory followed him out of the dining room, his heart hammering.

Father opened the door and looked down at the three soldiers standing on the top step. "What is the meaning of this?" he thundered. "I am a loyal citizen of the United States, and you have no reason to be on my property."

"What about the rest of your family?" taunted one of the men. "What about your son in the rebel artillery?"

At those words, Gregory's mouth went dry, but Father didn't flinch. "He is no longer my son," he said. "I have disowned him."

"And have you disowned your wife for sewing uniforms for the rebels?" another soldier asked.

Father drew himself up to his full height. "You are impertinent, sir! I'll thank you to leave at once."

Gregory scarcely breathed. He watched the soldiers glance at each other as if unsure what to do next. Finally the wiry, dark-haired private who had spoken first said, "Sure, mister. We'll leave. But we'll be back—and next time we'll bring some of our friends."

The soldiers sauntered along the sidewalk, and Father stepped outside and stood watching them. They paused in front of Miss Lily's steps but moved on after they glanced back and saw him there.

Father led the way inside. "A pity this had to happen the first time Mary has been able to join us in the dining room," he said. "We won't mention that threat, by the way. I see no need to frighten your mother and sisters." He closed the door and locked it. "Come along, son. Lena's good supper is waiting."

Gregory followed his father back to the table, not at all sure he'd be able to eat. But when he saw Mary's fearful expression, he knew he would have to try.

"What did they want, Roger?" Mother asked, her face pale.

Father spread his napkin on his lap. "Apparently someone had told them that Martin is in the Confederate artillery. They seemed satisfied when I assured them I'd disowned him."

In the silence that followed his father's answer, Gregory tried to forget that the soldiers had said they'd be back, tried not to wonder what would happen if they came when Father wasn't home.

"If it will make you feel better, Suzanne," Father said, "I'll ask the provost marshal to post a guard outside."

"It would make *me* feel better," Mary said.

Father smiled at her. "Then I shall see to it first thing in the morning," he told her.

"How do you think they knew about Martin?" Elizabeth asked.

Father said, "I suppose one of our neighbors must have told them."

Elizabeth scowled. "Then it was Mr. Wilson. He and Miss Lily are the only other people left on this block, now that Mrs. Greene has left for Richmond."

"But how could Mr. Wilson do such a thing after your father got him out of that terrible place!" Mother exclaimed.

He could do it because I made him mad when I asked where his flag was.

Father said, "If he is the one who told them, he undoubtedly did so before I arrived to 'rescue' him, as you put it. You must remember, Suzanne, that what he said is true. And, if I remember correctly, it is something that gives you great pride."

Mother didn't answer, and Mary broke the uncomfortable silence. "I'm not hungry anymore. May I go back to my room now?"

Gregory's eyes met Elizabeth's, and he knew at once that he was not the only one who envied Mary the privilege of leaving the table before the meal was over.

CHAPTER SEVEN

★　　　★　　　★

AT BREAKFAST THE next morning, Mother announced that Mary had spent a fretful night. "Coming downstairs for supper must have been too much for her," she added. "Could you sit with her for a little while, Gregory? Just until Lena finishes the kitchen chores and can take over?"

Before Gregory could answer, Father frowned and said, "I'm surprised that you find your project to aid the families of Confederate soldiers more important than taking care of our own child, Suzanne."

Mother's face flushed. "I refuse to let you draw me into an argument, Roger. But it may interest you to know that when I offered to stay with her, Mary said she would rather have Gregory come up and tell her a story."

Gregory stared at his soft-boiled egg. Mealtime never used to be like this. If he wasn't always so hungry in the morning, he'd pretend to sleep in. His parents didn't seem to mind that Elizabeth never joined them for breakfast.

A series of loud knocks interrupted Gregory's thoughts, and he remembered the parting threat from the soldier the night before. Father was already on his way to the door, and Greg reached the hall in time to see half a dozen blue-clad soldiers force their way inside.

"Now, see here—" Father began, but the dark-haired private who had been there the night before interrupted him.

"Save your breath, mister. We've come to search for weapons and rebel flags."

Gregory stood rooted to the hall floor as soldiers streamed into the parlor and the sitting room, their boots tracking dirt over the rugs. He saw that Father had moved to block the doorway of the dining room, but several of the soldiers simply pushed him in ahead of them. He heard Lena wail, "It dem people! It dem people again!" And then he heard a chair scrape across the floor as it was pushed back, followed by a harsh northern voice saying, "You sit back down, rebel lady. You ain't going nowhere."

How dare Yankee trash that can't even speak proper English talk to Mother like that?

Filled with indignation, Gregory started for the dining room, but at a shriek from upstairs he turned and took the front steps two at a time, reaching the landing just as a red-faced soldier closed the door to Elizabeth's room.

"I—I'm sorry," the young private muttered when he saw Gregory. "Didn't know anyone was in there." At the sound of something heavy being shoved across the floor, he glanced behind him, and then his eyes strayed toward Mary's room.

"My other sister's in there," Gregory warned. He was following the soldier into his parents' room when he heard the stomp of boots on the back stairs. It was two of the men who had come the previous night, and they headed for Mary's room. "Hey, you can't go in there," Gregory called.

"That's what you think," one of the soldiers retorted, pushing open the door.

Gregory dashed across the hall and found the little girl sitting up in bed, clutching her coverlet and staring at the intruders. "My sister's been sick, and now you're frightening her," Gregory said. "Can't you see there aren't any weapons or flags in here?"

"Maybe there aren't any weapons," the dark-haired ringleader said, "but what do you call these?" He held up an open hatbox, and Gregory's heart sank when he saw that it was filled with the paper flags his sisters had made.

"I hardly think that's the sort of thing you're supposed to look for," he said, trying to sound scornful. But to his dismay, his voice shook.

The soldier stood over Mary and demanded, "How do you explain these flags, missy?"

She shrank back from him, and after a long moment the soldier looked away. "Hey, what have we got here?" he exclaimed, and he laid his musket on the window seat so he could lift the music box from the table by Mary's bed. He ran a finger across the inlaid design on the lid before he raised it and listened to a few measures of a popular waltz. Then he tucked the music box under his arm and said, "This will make a fine present for my sweetheart back in Michigan."

"But it's *mine*," Mary wailed. "Put it back!"

"You're no soldier, you're a common thief!" Gregory burst out.

The soldier's face twisted in anger, and he reached for his musket. While Gregory watched in horror, he ran the bayonet through the soft body of Mary's doll. Ignoring the child's shrieks, he was about to smash the doll against the wall and break its china head when the young private who had encountered Elizabeth ran in. He crossed the room in a few strides, yanked the doll from the bayonet, and handed it to Mary. "Come on, Andrews," he said. "It's time to go."

Mary clutched her doll close and sobbed, "Poor, poor Agatha Doll! Why did he do that? And why did he have to take the music box?"

"I'll get it back for you, Mary—I promise."

To Gregory's relief, the little girl's sobs began to subside, but they began again in full force when Mother rushed into the room and gathered the child up in her arms. Gregory was making his escape when he heard his father's concerned voice calling, "Are you all right, Elizabeth?"

He joined his father in the hall outside his older sister's room, and when Father turned to him, his face ashen, Gregory quickly said, "Elizabeth's fine, and Mary's crying because one of the Yankees went off with the music box." He had to raise his voice so he could be heard above the scrape of furniture being shoved aside.

Elizabeth opened the door far enough for them to squeeze into the room. "I'll let the two of you move the bureau back where it goes," she said. She was breathing hard from the exertion of pushing it away from the door.

Gregory was impressed that his slender, delicate-looking sister had managed to wrestle the heavy piece of furniture across the room. "You sure were determined to keep those Yankees out," he said.

"One of them tried to come in, but he left when I screamed."

"I should certainly hope so," Father said, and Gregory grinned, remembering the expression on the young soldier's face.

After Elizabeth's bureau was back in place, Greg led the way across the hall to Mary's room, where Mother was starting to mend the bayonet rip in the doll's cloth body.

"What on earth happened to Agatha Doll?" Elizabeth asked, sitting down beside Mary. "Her stuffing's coming out."

"One of those Yankees tried to murder her with his bayonet—and he took Mama's music box, too." Mary began to sob again.

Elizabeth put her arms around the little girl and held her close. Looking accusingly at Father, she asked, "How you can side with men who would do a thing like that to a little girl, Papa?"

Father's expression darkened. "I have 'sided,' as you say, with the legally formed government of the nation my ancestors fought to establish. I am as appalled as you are at the behavior of the men who have answered Lincoln's call to defend it."

"This legally formed government of yours claims to exist by the consent of the governed," Mother said, "but you overlook the fact that most of the people in the southern states no longer consent to a government in which the votes of their citizens make no difference at all." She took a tiny pair of scissors from her pocket and cut the thread, then smoothed the mended place on the doll's cloth body.

Ignoring his wife's comment, Father said, "Don't worry about the music box, Mary. After the war is over, I'll order another one to replace it."

Mary raised a tearful face and said, "You won't have to, Papa. Gregory's going to get it back for me. He promised."

Gregory heard the confidence in his sister's voice, and regretting his rash words, he said, "I'll do my best, Mary."

After a moment of awkward silence, Father said, "Those brigands made off with my grandfather's sword as well as the music box."

"Oh, Roger!" Mother exclaimed. "I'm so very sorry. I know how you treasured that sword, and it's something that can never be replaced."

Father nodded. "Grandfather carried it throughout our War for Independence, and it was passed down to my father and then to me."

"Maybe Greg can get the sword back, too—after he finds the music box," Mary said, wiping her eyes with Elizabeth's handkerchief.

Father shook his head. "I don't think there's much hope of that, my dear."

He probably doesn't think there's much hope that I'll find the music box, either. And he's probably right.

Father sighed heavily. "I had intended to take our valuables to the warehouse for storage today in case last night's uninvited visitors returned, but obviously I underestimated their determination to make trouble for us as well as the laxity of discipline in their camp." He frowned and said, "Now that I think of it, I don't remember seeing any of our silver leave the house, Suzanne."

"That's because Lena and I hid it all in the summer kitchen after the soldiers took Mr. Wilson away with them yesterday," Elizabeth announced. "Most of it's in the wood box under a layer of kindling, and the rest is in a basket under some laundry that's waiting to be ironed."

Father gave her an approving look. "I am glad to hear that, daughter."

"I made sure the Yankees didn't have a chance to pick these up," Mother said. She reached into her pocket and brought out the silver napkin rings.

"Our table wouldn't seem the same without those, would it, Suzanne?" Father said. "I think it's worth the risk of leaving them behind when I move the rest of the silver to the warehouse for safekeeping later today." For a moment Father's eyes lingered on Mary, who was clutching her doll; then he rose to his feet. "I almost forgot to mention that Mr. Bevin plans to send his slave Jesse to Fairfax Court House with a packet of letters tomorrow," he said. "This would be a good opportunity for you and Elizabeth—and Miss Lily, of course—to catch up on your correspondence. I know how distressed you are that the army has cut off the city's mail service."

Before his mother could answer, Gregory said, "Maybe Jesse could ride Beauty and—"

"I have already thought of that, son. I'll give him directions to your uncle's farm so he can return the mare and ride back home on Big Red."

Mother asked, "Why couldn't Greg make the trip instead of Jesse? I'm sure he'd enjoy the chance to visit with his cousins."

"I'm sure he would, Suzanne, but it's out of the question. He wouldn't be allowed to return to the city unless he swore an oath of allegiance to the Union, and I seriously doubt he'd be willing to do that."

"I'd no more do that than you'd swear an oath of allegiance to the Confederacy," Gregory declared.

After an awkward silence, Father said, "It's past time for me to leave for the warehouse. I'll stop by the provost marshal's office on my way and arrange for a guard to be posted outside." His voice sounded impersonal, as though he were speaking to a group of strangers. Gregory managed a restrained "Good-bye," and as he listened to Father's footsteps on the stairs, he hoped the rest of the day would be an improvement over its beginning.

Later that morning, Gregory stood in the line that inched its way to the door of the provost marshal's headquarters. He and Father hadn't waited nearly this long to arrange for the release of Mr. Wilson the day before. Too bad we didn't let him rot in the slave pen, Gregory thought. It's his fault I'm here on this fool's errand, 'cause if it weren't for what he told those soldiers, they never would have searched our house, and Mother's music box would still be on Mary's bedside table.

At least the old man had the grace to feel guilty about telling his captors that the Union flag hanging below the upstairs window "was protectin' rebels." Not that he'd apologized. But Deborah, the Wilsons' slave, had overheard him admit it to his wife, and Deborah told Miss Lily's Belle, who told Lena, who immediately repeated it to Mother. Gregory wondered what stories Lena told about his family, and whether those stories ever found their way to Mr. Wilson's ears.

At last Gregory made his way into the building and down the hall to the desk officer—the same one who had been on duty the day before. "Your father has already been here this morning, young man," the officer said, peering over his spectacles. "I gave him an order prohibiting searches of your home."

No guard to be posted outside, then. "I've come about something else, sir."

The officer sighed. "All right. Let's hear what's on your mind."

"I'm trying to locate a soldier named Andrews. He's a private, and he's from Michigan."

"Except for the New York troops camped out on Schuter's Hill, all the soldiers occupying the city are from Michigan, and I daresay quite a few of them are named

315

Andrews. You don't know his full name or what unit he's with?"

Gregory shook his head. "I only know that he's infantry, sir. But I have to find him! It's important."

"How important can it be if you know next to nothing about him?"

The officer sounded impatient, but at least he was still listening. "He took something from my sister's room, and I promised that I'd get it back for her," Gregory said in a rush, adding, "It was our mother's Swiss music box."

"Your father has filed a report listing the valuables taken from your home this morning. If anything shows up, we'll see that it's returned," the officer said, obviously losing interest.

Outside again, Gregory faced the fact that Union officials would be no help in getting back the music box. Somehow, he would have to find Andrews on his own.

CHAPTER EIGHT

★　　　★　　　★

GREGORY STARED at the sea of white ahead of him. Huge, cone-shaped tents covered the ground on both sides of Duke Street as far as he could see, and blue-clad soldiers lounged outside them. A man who sat a little apart from the others, reading a small book, glanced up and noticed Greg.

"Is there something I can do for you, young fellow?" he asked.

"Yes, sir. Do you know a Private Andrews?" Gregory asked, hoping against hope.

The man shook his head. "There's no Andrews in our company," he said. "Sorry I can't help you."

"Oh. Well, thank you anyway." Gregory was wondering how he would ever find Andrews when a soldier wearing sergeant's stripes stopped him.

"What are you doing here, boy? Let's see your pass."

Gregory's heart sank. "I—I don't have one, sir."

The sergeant glowered down at him. "No civilian may enter an army camp without a pass. Didn't you read the proclamation?"

"Not all of it, sir."

"Well, get yourself on back to town and read the rest of it," the sergeant said. "And don't let me see you here again without a pass. You understand?"

Nodding, Gregory backed away, conscious of the grinning men who had gathered to witness his humiliation. He hurried back to Duke Street and had almost reached the edge of the camp when he noticed several soldiers crowded around a young black boy. Curious, Gregory paused, and when the boy saw him he called, "Meat pies for sale! Meat pies!"

Greg watched while the soldiers ate theirs on the spot and then each bought another. *That's it!* He turned toward home, making his plans on the way.

When he rushed into the summer kitchen, Lena looked up from the dough she was kneading and said, "Mercy, chile! You looks like dem people been after you!"

"I need your help, Lena," he said when he had caught his breath. "Can you bake me some apple turnovers? Please?"

Lena shook her head. "Yo' mama, she already ask me to make a cake for dis evenin'."

"I didn't mean for the family. I— Well, I'm planning to sell them."

Lena gave him a look he remembered from when he was younger. "Does yo' mama know 'bout dis plan?"

Greg shook his head. "She wouldn't mind, though. I need them so I can get her music box back—you know how much Mary misses it." He watched Lena's expression soften.

"Dat li'l girl, she grievin' fo' it, missin' all dem pretty tune," she said, shaking her turbaned head. "You come back midafternoon, an' I'll have a whole basket of dem turnover ready. An' I won' even ask how dat gonna help."

Elated, Gregory thanked her and went into the house. Since he couldn't carry out his plan till the turnovers were baked, he'd see if he could raise his sister's spirits a little.

"Is that you, Greg? Did you get it back?" she called when he knocked at her open door.

"I haven't found the soldier who took it yet," he said from the doorway, "but I've made some progress." At least I know Andrews isn't in the camp on Duke Street, he added silently. Not in that company with the mean sergeant, anyway. And I know I don't dare go back there without a pass.

Mary looked reproachfully at Elizabeth, who was painting more Confederate flags to replace the ones the soldiers had taken. "See? I *told* you he'd get it back for me."

Gregory looked from one sister to the other, from the trusting blue eyes to the doubting green ones, and his spirits sank. "Well, I'd better be going," he said, managing to sound confident. *What if I can't find the music box? Can't keep my promise?*

Gregory was halfway down the stairs when he heard Elizabeth's quick steps in the hall above him. He waited for her at the foot of the stairs, and she waved him into the sitting room. "Mama's worried about Mary," she whispered. "She's barely eating, and all she talks about is how you promised to get the music box back for her. I've tried to tell her it's like looking for a needle in a haystack, but she won't listen. She really believes you'll find it for her, Greg."

He glared at Elizabeth. "Instead of making her worry that I won't find the music box, you might remind her that I never promised to find it right away."

"I—I'm sorry," Elizabeth said in a shaky voice. "I wasn't thinking straight. Will you let me know if there's anything I can do to help?"

"I can't imagine what it would be." Gregory felt a mean gladness when he saw a flicker of hurt cross his sister's face before she excused herself and left the room. With nothing to do until Lena's turnovers were ready, he sank into a chair and went over his plan again.

At three o'clock that afternoon, Gregory came out of the military office where passes were issued—but only on Mondays. How could he wait till Monday to put his plan into action? Scowling, he set off, eyes on the sidewalk. "Oh, sorry, sir."

"No harm done." The Union officer he had bumped into eyed the napkin-covered basket on Gregory's arm and asked, "What do you have there, young man?"

"Apple turnovers. I hoped I could get a pass to sell them in the army camps, but—"

The officer's eyebrows rose. "Turnovers? I'll buy the lot from you now. How much?"

Gregory backed away. "No need to do that, sir."

But the man took a banknote from his billfold and said, "This should be enough, shouldn't it? Wait here—I'll take these up to my office and bring back your basket."

A whole dollar! Gregory folded it and slipped it in his pocket. He'd just found out two things: He'd have no difficulty selling Lena's baked goods, and if he wanted to peddle her turnovers in the army camps, he'd better not bring them with him when he came back on Monday to get a pass.

Once the officer had returned the basket, Greg set off for home, no closer to finding Private Andrews and the music box than he had been that morning.

"Hey, boy! You selling pies and cakes?" A gangly soldier was reaching into his pocket as he crossed the street, dodging an army wagon.

"Apple turnovers, but I'm sold out. I could bring some out to your camp tomorrow if you tell me where it is." Even with his basket empty, his plan was working!

"We're camped quite a ways out, on the seminary grounds. Know where that is?"

Gregory nodded. "Is Private Andrews in your company?" he asked.

"Johnny Andrews or James Andrews?"

Gregory could hardly contain his excitement. "I'm not sure. I'm supposed to deliver a note, but it's just addressed to J. Andrews, from Michigan," he lied.

The soldier grinned and said, "If the note's from a girl, then you'll want *Johnny* Andrews, 'cause James is an old married man. Tell you what, I'll bring Johnny with me and meet you here 'bout this time tomorrow. That way I'll be sure to get a couple of your turnovers. Our camp is so huge, they'd all be bought long before you could find me."

Gregory agreed and set off for home again. Progress, at last! He stopped at the summer kitchen in the backyard, where Lena was ironing. "Could you make me some more turnovers tomorrow?"

Her face creased into a frown, and she said, "I don' know, chile. I don' know 'bout you sellin' my turnovers to dem people dat force dere way in de house an'—"

"I sold them to an officer, Lena. It's not the officers who search houses. Listen, if you'll bake them for me, from now on, I'll give you all the money they sell for."

Lena's eyes widened. "Well, long as you don' sell 'em to any o' dat riffraff . . ."

"I won't. Thanks, Lena."

The next afternoon, armed with a basket of Lena's apple turnovers and a note addressed to "J. Andrews, from Michigan," Gregory arrived at the corner to wait for the two Union soldiers. After trying without success to write the note himself, he'd asked Elizabeth to write it for him, and he had to admit that she'd done a good job of it—and she didn't rub it in that he'd had to ask for her help so soon after he'd refused it.

"Well, if it isn't the apple turnover boy!"

Gregory's heart sank when he saw the officer who had bought him out the day before. "These are already spoken for, sir," he said.

"A pity. Your mother is a fine cook, young man."

Mother helped Lena with the canning and preserving,

but the closest she came to actually cooking was to plan the meals, Gregory thought as he watched the officer walk away. He heard a shout and saw the soldier he'd met the day before and a sandy-haired fellow he'd never laid eyes on.

"This here's Johnny Andrews," the soldier said. "How much are you selling those pies for? They smell mighty fine."

"Four for half a dollar," Gregory told him, deliberately overpricing them.

The soldier whistled. "That's pretty steep, isn't it?"

Shrugging, Gregory said, "You don't have to buy them." He didn't want to sell out before he had a chance to find out what he needed to know.

The man he'd met yesterday counted out the coins, but Johnny Andrews said, "I'll just take the note you have for me, then." Not knowing what else to do, Gregory handed over the note. The young man read it, shook his head, and handed it back. "This is obviously meant for some other Private Andrews," he said.

"You sure?" his friend asked, looking disappointed.

"The young lady's friend had dark hair."

Gregory was glad his sister had put in the part about "tall, dark, and handsome." He wouldn't like to think of the sandy-haired young man standing on the corner, waiting in vain to meet "An Admirer." The two soldiers left, and Gregory decided to save the rest of the turnovers and try his luck at the camp on Seminary Hill in the morning. That would give him more time to find out if the Andrews he was looking for was a member of one of the other Michigan companies there.

He was almost home when he noticed a rowdy group of soldiers coming toward him. Sensing trouble, he cut down a side street to avoid them, but to his dismay, they followed him and soon caught up. His heart pounded when he recognized several of the men who had searched the house—including Andrews!

"What's in your basket, boy?" one of the soldiers asked as they surrounded him.

"Back off so I can show you," Gregory said, determined not to let them see how shaken he was. He was lifting the napkin when Andrews spoke.

"Hey, that's the cheeky little rebel who called me a thief!"

Rage overcame Gregory's fear, and he glared up at Andrews. "You *are* a thief—and worse! You stole the music box from the table by my little sister's sickbed—and then you ran a bayonet through her doll. Now she's had a relapse, and if she dies, it will be your fault."

An uncertain look crossed Private Andrews's face, and one of the other soldiers shifted his weight and said, "I dunno, Andrews. Maybe you ought to give the music box back. Making the rebels pay for bombarding Sumter is one thing, but taking something from a sick child—"

Gregory's hopes rose, then sank when a soldier who looked younger than Martin said, "He don't have it no more. He lost it to Sergeant Timmons in a card game."

"Wouldn't give it back if I did have it," Andrews said.

"Come on, let's divide up those pastries and get out of here."

Struggling to keep his voice steady, Gregory said, "They're apple turnovers—eight to the dollar."

"Looks like he's got just eight left," said the soldier who had spoken first, and they lost interest in Gregory and his story as they crowded around the basket.

"Mmm, not bad," Andrews said after he bit into one of the turnovers.

A red-haired soldier Gregory hadn't seen before licked his fingers and said, "C'mon, let's go."

"Hey, don't forget to pay for those turnovers."

Andrews grinned and said, "We aren't forgetting, are we, fellows?" A burst of laughter made his meaning clear, and Gregory felt a new rush of rage. *How dare they?*

"You owe me a dollar, Andrews," he said in a hard voice.

"I don't owe you the time of day, little rebel," Andrews said, giving him a shove. "Go on home and hide under your rich daddy's U.S. flag."

His pulse pounding, Gregory waited until the soldiers had almost reached the corner, and then he shouted after them, "Yankee cheaters! Yankee thieves and cheaters!" He turned and ran for home. He cut through the alley, stumbling past some small black children who were playing there, and let himself in the back gate. Lena was sitting outside the summer kitchen hulling strawberries, and when she saw him, her busy hands stopped in midmotion. "What has dem people done to you, chile?" she cried.

Gregory sat beside her on the bench and held the empty basket on his lap. After several deep breaths he said, "I sold four of the turnovers to a private who was a decent fellow, and then—" He took another breath and finished in a rush. "Then the same riffraff that searched the house and stole the music box and Great-grandfather's sword stopped me. They ate the rest of the turnovers and refused to pay for them."

While he struggled to regain his composure, Gregory dug into his pocket. "Here's the money for the four I sold before I met them," he said.

Lena slipped the young private's coins into her apron pocket. "You better think up some other way to get back dat music box, chile, 'cause I ain't doin' no more bakin' fo' dat Yankee riffraff, you hear me?"

"I've got another plan now, anyway." Pass or no pass, first thing in the morning, he would walk out to Seminary Hill and look for this Sergeant Timmons who had won the music box from Andrews in a card game.

At supper that night Elizabeth said, "Mary hardly touched the beef broth Lena brought her at noon, and she didn't want to sit on the window seat. She just lay in bed, holding Agatha Doll."

Mother's expression darkened. "Those Yankee soldiers—"

"What happened yesterday morning was bound to affect the child," Father said, interrupting. "But now that we have an order from the provost marshal making this place off limits, we needn't fear a repetition of that unfortunate experience."

Mother put down her fork. "I think 'criminal behavior' would be a more accurate description of what took place here, Roger."

Gregory held his breath, waiting to hear what his father would say.

"I stand corrected, Suzanne. You need not fear a repetition of that criminal behavior."

Father had actually admitted he was wrong! Gregory stole a look at him, but he was sprinkling salt on his meat as if nothing out of the ordinary had happened.

"I'll reassure Mary that you've seen to it that Yankees will never come here again," Mother said. "That should be a comfort to her."

It might help a little, Gregory thought, but having the music box on her bedside table again would be the best comfort of all.

SEMINARY HILL was so thick with tents the large brick building that stood among them seemed unimportant, almost as if it didn't belong there. Gregory was trying to figure out the best way to look for Sergeant Timmons when someone called out to him, and he saw a sentry with an ill-fitting uniform and an awkward gait approaching.

"You have to have a pass if you've come to visit anybody in camp here," the sentry said.

Gregory's heart sank. "A pass?" he echoed, playing dumb.

The sentry nodded and repeated the same words in the same tone. On a hunch, Gregory pulled out the note his sister had written to J. Andrews and waved it in front of the soldier. "Oh, I've got a pass, all right. I've come to see Sergeant Timmons. Do you know where I can find him?"

The man's face brightened, and he pointed to a row of tents that stood a little apart from the others. "All the officers are up there," he said. "Up on Officers' Row."

I've come to the right place! Gregory headed the way the sentry had pointed, trying not to gawk at the soldiers cleaning their muskets and polishing their boots. The flaps of the tents on Officers' Row were tied back, and when he peered inside the first one, he was surprised to see a man sitting at a desk, writing.

The man saw him and barked out, "Who are you, and what in tarnation are you doing here?"

Answering the second question, Gregory said, "The sentry told me I'd find Sergeant Timmons here, sir."

The man swore. "You'll find *commissioned* officers here—lieutenants, captains, and majors. Your sergeant will be down there, closer to the common soldiers." He muttered something about the army "going to the dogs" and took a swig of steaming liquid from a tin cup.

Gregory was walking back down the slope when he saw a boy who couldn't have been more than eleven years old. Wearing a Union uniform, he sat under a tree, cleaning his fingernails with a penknife. The cylindrical tin case beside him told Gregory that he'd come across the company fifer. "Hey," he said, pausing.

"Hey, yourself!" the boy said. "You joining up?"

Hardly. "I'm looking for Sergeant Timmons. Do you know where he is?"

"Sure! Come on—I'll take you there."

Gregory's spirits soared. It was about time he had a little luck! A few minutes more, and he'd be on his way home with the music box tucked under his arm.

The boy set a fast pace as he led the way to the far edge of the camp where a ruddy-faced sergeant was supervising a group of privates digging a ditch. "Someone to see you, Sergeant Timmons," he said, and stepped back.

The sergeant seemed to welcome a break in the routine. "What can I do for you today, young man?" he asked.

"I've come about the music box Private Andrews gave

you to pay off a gambling debt, sir," Gregory said.

"What about it? You aren't going to tell me it was stolen, are you?"

Gregory nodded. "He took it from my little sister's room."

The sergeant's eyebrows rose and he said, "Isn't that a right expensive item for a child to have?"

"Yes, sir. It belongs to my mother, but she put it by my sister's bed to amuse her while she's recovering from rheumatic fever. Private Andrews came into her room and took it—and then he ran her doll through with his bayonet. She hasn't been the same since."

Sergeant Timmons let loose with a torrent of curses that centered around what he would do to Private Andrews once he got his hands on him. When he stopped for breath, Gregory said, "I promised my sister I'd get the music box back, sir."

"That's the worst of it," the sergeant said. "I haven't got it anymore."

"You *haven't*?" Gregory cried.

The man shook his head. "I sold it to the sutler for a pretty penny. Quite a bit more than that waster, Andrews, owed me. Come on, we'll go over to the sutler's tent and I'll buy it back from him." He interrupted Gregory's thanks with a wave of his hand. "Don't worry, I'll collect from Andrews." He set off, motioning for Greg to follow.

"What's a sutler?" he asked the young fifer, who had fallen into step beside him.

"A storekeeper who sets up shop in an army camp. He sells sweets and all kinds of odds and ends soldiers might want to buy. Our sutler's right over there," the boy said, pointing.

Gregory could see a large tent with its flaps tied back. A rickety table spread with tobacco, playing cards, and other goods was set across the opening, and behind it sat a skinny man with a drooping gray mustache. He put aside his newspaper and stood up when he saw them.

"You coming to sell me some more of your ill-gotten gains, Timmons?" he asked.

But the sergeant wasn't in a joking mood. "I've come to buy back that music box I brought here the other day. That was stolen property, and it has to be returned."

The sutler took a step back and said, "What's gotten into you, Timmons? We both know that everything these recruits gamble away was stolen from the local rebels."

"True, but this time, we know who the rightful owner is." Timmons pointed to Gregory and said, "The music box belongs to this boy's mother, and he's come to get it back."

"My little sister's been sick, sir," Gregory said, "and without the music box to comfort her, she— Well, it's important for me to get it back."

The sutler shook his head. "I wish I could help you, sonny, but I don't have it anymore."

Gregory was speechless with dismay, but the sergeant snapped out, "Then where is it?"

"Pawnshop. The thing is, though, I ain't sure which one." The sutler looked apologetic. "When I was in town last night, I made the rounds—trying to get the best deal, you know—and I don't remember where I sold that music box. Got a good price for it, though. Pretty thing, wasn't it?" Suddenly he snapped his fingers and said, "Say, maybe

I can find the pawn ticket for you—the name of the shop will be on it—and you can get it out of hock."

The sutler disappeared into the tent and returned with a large box. He placed it on the table, opened it, and rummaged through a jumble of pawn tickets until he found the one he was looking for. "Just go to the address on the top of this ticket and show it to the pawnbroker," the sutler said, handing it over.

Before Gregory could find his voice, the sergeant leaned across the sutler's table and said, "Listen to me, and listen good. I want you to give this boy the cash he'll need to redeem that music box."

The two men locked eyes, and Gregory scarcely breathed until the sutler's gaze fell and he disappeared into the tent again, returning to shove a banknote across the table. Gregory was astonished when he saw its value.

"Take it," Sergeant Timmons said, again brushing away Gregory's thanks. "I hope your little sister is better soon."

After Gregory put the pawn ticket and money in his pocket, the fifer said, "Come on. I'll walk you to the edge of the camp." They had gone only a few steps when the boy said, "I guess you're a secesh, right?"

"A *what*?"

"A secesh. That's short for secessionist."

"I guess I am," Gregory said, though he thought of himself as a Virginian. He wondered what the other boy was leading up to.

"So if you're the enemy, how come Sergeant Timmons helped you out like that?"

The question surprised Gregory—he'd just taken it for

granted that the sergeant would help him. "Because it was the decent thing to do, I guess."

"Like when you're on different sides in a game, you play fair with the other players even though you want to win?" the fifer asked.

"Something like that," Gregory agreed. Except that this wasn't a game, and other than the officers, some of the Yankees he'd met didn't seem to have any intention of playing fair.

When the boys reached the road at the edge of camp, they said good-bye, and Gregory began his long walk back into town, whistling.

Aware of the curious eyes that followed him, Gregory walked toward the pawnshop, an unpainted building with three white globes hung above the door. He felt out of place in this neighborhood—too well dressed, and even too well fed.

He stepped through the doorway and stood blinking while his eyes adjusted to the dimness inside the shop, taking in the jumble of goods on shelves and counters. *There it is!* Gregory struggled to hide his elation.

"Never used to see the likes of you in this part of town," the pawnbroker said, looking him over. "Not till all this trouble started and some of the better-off folks lost their livelihood and needed cash. I suppose your mama sent you here to sell some of the family jewels, eh?"

Gregory shook his head. "I've come to buy something back—that music box on the shelf behind you, there."

"Ah, yes. Lovely, isn't it?" The pawnbroker took it from

the shelf, twisted the key to wind it, and raised the lid. Placing the music box on the counter between them, the man cocked his head and listened a moment before he closed the lid again. "So your mama wants this back, eh?"

Gregory gave a quick nod. He didn't like the feel of this place—or the owner's familiar attitude, either. He slid the sutler's pawn ticket and money across the counter, but the pawnbroker peered down at them and said, "This isn't near enough, young man. You'll need another five dollars to redeem this property."

"But it says on the ticket—"

"Come now, young man! How would I make a profit if I didn't charge a little interest?"

"A *little* interest! You haven't had that music box for a full day yet!" Gregory fumbled in his other pocket and pulled out the bill the officer had given him for Lena's first basket of turnovers. He put it on the counter and said, "This dollar is all I have, but it should give you profit enough for overnight shelf space." The old man's eyes hardened, and Gregory wished he could take back the last part of what he'd said.

"You will need four dollars more if you want the item back," the pawnbroker repeated. "Take it or leave it."

I'll take it. Gregory grabbed the music box from the counter and bolted from the shop with it under his arm. As he raced down the street, he heard the pawnbroker's cries of "Thief! Thief! Stop that boy!" But no one made any attempt to stop him, and a scrawny woman sweeping her front steps called out, "Good for you, sonny! That old man's been swindling the lot of us long enough."

The pawnbroker's cries filled Gregory's mind, and no matter how fast he ran, he couldn't outdistance them. As each foot struck the ground, he heard an echo of the word *Thief!* And the faster he ran, the louder the accusation, until he felt his head would burst.

Finally, Gregory slowed and glanced behind him. To his relief, the street was deserted, and he stopped long enough to wipe the perspiration from his face and neck with his handkerchief. He shifted the music box from his left arm to his right and set off again, crossing the street to avoid walking past a disheveled-looking man sitting on the steps of a shabby house a few doors ahead. *I'll be glad when I'm back in my own neighborhood.*

Safely home again, Gregory met Lena at the foot of the back stairs. An almost full cup of broth was on the tray she had brought down, and her forehead was creased with worry lines. "Look," he said, and he held the music box out to her like an offering.

Lena's eyes widened. "You done got it back, jus' like you promise! What you waitin' for, chile? Take it on up to Miss Mary!"

Gregory tiptoed up the stairs and down the hall. Just outside Mary's door, he lifted the lid of the music box, and as he carried it into her room, the notes of his sister's favorite song poured out. "You got it back!" she cried. "Oh, thank you, thank you, thank you!" He placed the music box on her bedside table, and Mary looked up at him and said, "I *knew* you'd keep your promise, Greg, no matter what Elizabeth said."

And no matter if I had to become a thief to do it.

IT HAD BEEN RAINING for three days, and Gregory's mood was as gloomy as the weather. "It's your move, Elizabeth," he said, half wishing he'd never taught her to play chess. His games with Carter had never dragged on like this—not that he had anything else to do. He was glad he'd gotten the music box back, but without the challenge of finding it to keep him occupied, he felt out of sorts, and the pawnbroker's accusing shouts still echoed in his mind.

Finally, Elizabeth reached out and moved her knight— the very thing he'd hoped she'd do. But she kept her finger on it, studied the chessboard for a moment, then shook her head and put the piece back on its original square. Gregory gave an exaggerated sigh, and Elizabeth said, "Look, you're the one who taught me to plan three moves ahead. You'll just have to be patient."

"Patient! You've taken so long I've had time to plan three moves ahead for every move you could possibly make." Gregory was almost disappointed when his sister ignored his outburst. A good argument would have broken the monotony, at least.

Even with the windows closed against the cool dampness, the sound of men's voices could be heard on the street, and Gregory cursed silently. "Don't let them see us looking out," he warned as he followed Elizabeth to the window. He peered through the blinds beside his sister, sensing her relief when the small group of soggy-looking soldiers glanced up at Father's flag and continued on.

"Let's finish our game," he said, turning away from the window.

But Elizabeth cried, "They've stopped at Miss Lily's! We have to do something!" She turned to face him, her green eyes wide.

"I could go for Father, but—"

"There's no time for that. Come on, Greg—we can't let that poor old lady face those brutes alone!"

Amazed at how a girl who thought so slowly at chess could make up her mind in an instant now, he dashed after Elizabeth and caught up with her at the front door. "Wait a minute—you can't go over there."

"Just watch me."

Gregory knew his sister too well to waste time arguing. Besides, she was right. Their elderly neighbor shouldn't have to face the Yankees by herself—not that the two of them could offer anything more than moral support. He hurried through the drizzle behind Elizabeth, wondering what they were getting themselves into.

Before Gregory could knock at Miss Lily's door, Elizabeth pushed it open and went inside. "Miss Lily? Where are you?" she called.

"We're in the dining room, dear."

They reached the richly furnished room just as one of the soldiers moved away from the sideboard he'd been rummaging through and said, "Nothing in here but table-cloths. Where's your silver, old woman?"

Miss Lily said, "You're too late. It's already been made off with." Belle stood protectively beside her and nodded in agreement. If Gregory hadn't known that Father had taken all Miss Lily's valuables to his warehouse the morning after the occupation began, he would have sworn they were telling the truth.

"Well, in that case, we'll have to be content with some of your famous southern hospitality," the soldier said. He pulled a chair out from the table and gestured for his companions to do the same. "You aren't going to keep us waiting for our vittles, are you?" he asked, his voice taking on a threatening tone.

Miss Lily said, "Belle, see what we have in the kitchen that is suitable to serve at this hour."

Gregory watched Belle leave the room, sensing her reluctance to abandon Miss Lily. When he turned his attention back to the table, he saw that the Yankee soldiers were leering at Elizabeth. Was this what Father had meant by soldiers being disrespectful of the enemy's women? He felt a surge of helpless anger, some of it directed at the Yankees and some at his sister. *Maybe next time she'll listen to me.*

"Dear," Miss Lily said, "would you go after Belle and tell her I said to open that last jar of peaches?"

"Of course, Miss Lily," Elizabeth agreed, and she gave the soldiers a scornful glance as she left the room.

Now the men focused their attention on Gregory, and one of them asked, "So what are you and Miss Priss doing here?"

Before he could answer, a freckle-faced private said, "Came to protect 'Miss Lily' from the terrible Yankees, would be my guess," and the others laughed.

"We're not stupid enough to think we could do that," Gregory said, managing to keep his voice even in spite of the anger that welled up in him. "We just came to offer moral support—it didn't seem right for an old lady to have to face a bunch of hooligans by herself."

"Hey, he called us hooligans," the freckle-faced soldier said.

Gregory glared at him. "What else would I call men who break into houses and take what they want and order helpless women to do their will?"

"You could call us conquerors," said an older man who hadn't spoken before. "If you'd studied your history, you would know that this is how conquerors have behaved from time immemorial. This, and worse." He gave Gregory a meaningful look and added, "Leave your sister at home next time you decide to confront the hooligans."

Gregory felt the blood rush to his face. "Marching in and taking over a civilian population isn't my definition of conquering."

"Am I mistaken, or did your so-called defenders run off when they heard we were coming?"

"A tactical withdrawal is a lot different from 'running off.' They were outnumbered almost three to one."

Miss Lily broke in, saying, "Here comes Belle with your—shall we call it your morning tea?"

Belle carried in a tray and set it on the sideboard, then placed in front of each soldier a plate that held a slice of plain cake and small dish of canned peaches. She lifted a pottery pitcher from the tray and said, "All we's got to drink is buttermilk, an' not much o' dat."

"Where's your pretty helper?" one of the men asked, watching Belle fill his glass.

"Her daddy, he di'n't like her bein' here, so he take her on home."

Father would be irate if he knew Elizabeth had come here this morning, but he was at his warehouse. Belle must have sent her home.

"That was real good—what there was of it," Freckle Face said when he'd finished.

"We'll stop by again, same time tomorrow morning," the first soldier told miss Lily. "Have some biscuits and coffee ready for us, so we don't have to wait."

Gregory was still reeling from that announcement when the older soldier he had argued with paused in the doorway and said, "Remember when the rebels bombarded Sumter?"

"You mean when they conquered a fort that was supposed to be unconquerable?" Gregory asked, his voice defiant.

The man gave him a long look before he said, "Fewer

than a hundred half-starved Union men held out for a day and a half against six or seven thousand rebels. Makes being 'outnumbered almost three to one' sound like pretty good odds, doesn't it?" Without waiting for an answer, the man followed the others outside.

Gregory was staring after him when Miss Lily said, "It was kind of you to come to our aid, dear. Belle and I appreciate it."

"Is there anything I can do for you before I go home, Miss Lily?"

The old woman shook her head. "No, dear. We'll just clean up and put this behind us."

Greg thought she was talking about clearing away the empty plates until he saw the muddy boot prints in the hall. "They've tracked up your floor!" he exclaimed. "Don't they know to wipe their feet?"

"I think they choose not to, dear. Look, it's raining harder. You'll have to run, or you'll be drenched."

He dashed for home and found his sister waiting for him in the sitting room. "You were right, Greg," she said. "I should have let you go by yourself. It was positively indecent the way those men looked at me!"

"You never seemed to mind when our militiamen looked at you. In fact, I heard Mother scold you for 'promenading' past their camp with your friends."

"But our men are *gentlemen*. When they look, you feel appreciated rather than insulted."

Mother came downstairs and asked, "Who made you feel insulted, Elizabeth?"

"Yankees, Mama. A bunch of them sat down at Miss Lily's table, bold as you please, and demanded to be fed. I slipped out to the kitchen with Belle and came home."

Gregory wondered how his sister could tell the truth and lie at the same time. He'd make sure to take anything she told him with a grain of salt.

Mother said, "I hate to admit this, but the way things are going, I'm almost glad your father is a Unionist. Having his flag hanging out front makes things a lot easier for all of us."

"That's not a very patriotic thing to say, Mama," Elizabeth said, frowning.

But it was true, Gregory thought. He felt like a hypocrite.

Later that week, Gregory was upstairs telling Mary a story when Elizabeth burst into the room. "I was about to go on an errand when I saw two soldiers coming down the street, so I watched from the door, and when they stopped at Miss Lily's house, I just couldn't keep from running outside and asking, 'Are you going in there to torment that poor old lady?' Well, one of the Yankees whipped off his hat and said, 'No, miss. Lieutenant So-and-so and I are going to board here,' and then he gave a little bow. Before I could think of what to say, Belle opened the door and invited them in. What do you think of *that*?"

"What did they mean, 'board here'?" Mary asked.

"Eat and sleep at Miss Lily's house," Elizabeth

explained. "I remember now that they had their knapsacks. And they wiped their feet before they went inside."

Gregory said slowly, "It might be a good thing, you know. Once word gets out that officers are boarding in that house, the men aren't likely to bother the landlady. I wouldn't be surprised if Father had something to do with arranging it."

"Can he arrange for officers to board here, too?" Mary asked, her eyes on the music box.

"The soldiers won't come here again, Mary," Gregory said. "Remember? Father has an order from the provost marshal that says this house is not to be searched."

"Good," Mary said. "Papa always makes things work out right." She turned to her sister and said, "Don't forget about your errand. Are you sure you have everything you need?"

Elizabeth hid a smile. "Everything is right here in my basket. I'll be back by noon." She threw Mary a kiss from the door.

"She's up to something, isn't she?" Gregory said, and Mary nodded.

"I'm not supposed to tell, but you already know," she said. "Remember? You promised you wouldn't tell Papa?"

The paper flags. That must be what Elizabeth had in her basket. "Don't worry, Mary. All I know is that she's gone on an errand." And that's all I want to know, he added silently.

When Father left for his warehouse after the noon meal, Gregory went out to the summer kitchen, where Lena was pouring a kettle of steaming water into her dishpan. She looked up and said, "There weren't no leftover dessert today, chile."

"That's not why I came. I have to ask you something." He hesitated a moment, and then in a rush of words he asked, "What would you say if I told you I stole back Mama's music box?"

"I'd say, good fo' you, chile, 'cause dem people done stole it first."

Gregory nodded. "That's true," he said. The problem was, he hadn't stolen it from the Yankees—he'd stolen from a businessman, a shopkeeper. That made him a shoplifter, he realized, cringing inwardly. Still, what he'd done hadn't cost the pawnbroker any money—the man had even made a profit, thanks to the dollar from Lena's first batch of turnovers. Gregory didn't understand why his conscience tormented him like this.

Suddenly, he thought of what his little sister had said that morning: Papa always makes things work out. "If anybody asks where I've gone, I'll be at Father's office," he said, pausing at the door of the summer kitchen. His step was light when he slipped through the back gate and started down the alley.

Near the waterfront, Gregory was surprised to see soldiers with shovels strung out in a long row that paralleled the river for as far as he could see. He was wondering how he would get past the ditch diggers when he saw a break in the line. He was walking toward it when a sentry stopped him and said, "No one's allowed beyond this point without a pass."

"But my father's warehouse is over there. He's a Union man—you probably know him. His name's Roger Howard."

The sentry said, "I checked his pass not twenty minutes ago." He gave Gregory a long look and said, "I'll let you through, but I'm keeping my eye on you. Make sure you go straight to his warehouse and come straight back here when you leave. You understand?"

"Yes, sir. I understand." On his way to the warehouse, Gregory felt the back of his neck tingling from the sentry's gaze. At the entrance to the building, he glanced back and saw that the man was still watching him.

The office door was open, but Gregory paused at the threshold and said, "Father?"

Obviously surprised at the interruption, Father raised his eyes from the northern newspaper spread out on his desk and said, "Gregory! I'll have to speak to the sentries about allowing a known Confederate into a restricted area." Smiling at his own joke, he folded the newspaper and said, "Come in, son."

Father motioned him to the chair opposite his desk, and Gregory sat on the edge of the seat, feeling the way he did when he was called to the headmaster's office. "Why don't they allow Confederates to come down here, sir?" he asked.

"I imagine they're afraid of sabotage, or maybe theft."

Theft!

"Huge quantities of goods for the army—including weapons—are unloaded from ships here every day and left on the wharves. Citizens with Confederate sympathies might be tempted to either destroy or make off with them."

Make off with them!

"Apparently, the army plans to put up a stockade fence all along the waterfront," Father continued. "Now then, what brings you here this afternoon, Gregory?"

"I came to ask if you would lend me some money, Father. I'll pay you back."

His father cleared his throat and said, "That is customary, of course, in the case of a loan. It's also customary for the lender to inquire what amount is needed and for what purpose the money will be used."

Gregory could feel the perspiration trickle down his back. "I need four dollars, sir, to—um, to pay off another debt, sir." Father's eyes seemed to bore into him, and he tried not to squirm.

At last his father asked, "Would this by any chance have anything to do with the reappearance of your mother's music box?"

"Yes, sir." Gregory was surprised that he was able to keep his voice steady.

"Why don't you tell me about it, son."

After what seemed like a long time, Gregory managed to say, "I'd rather not, Father. It would make you think less of me." To his embarrassment, his voice wavered.

Father's chair creaked as he stood up. He walked to the window and looked out, hands clasped behind his back. The only sound in the room was the ticking of the clock on his bookcase. At last he said, "How could I not think well of a son who keeps his promises? A son who would rather say nothing than tell me less than the truth?"

Gregory's eyed burned with unshed tears. He took a deep breath and said, "When I told you about getting the music box back, I didn't tell the whole story, sir. I—left out a part at the end."

Without turning from the window his father asked, "Would you like to tell me that part now?"

Glad he didn't have to face his father across the desk, Gregory began. "I left out what happened after I gave the pawnbroker the ticket and the money I got from the sutler." He stopped, wondering how to explain what had happened next, listening to the seconds tick away.

It was Father who broke the silence. "But the pawnbroker said you owed him more," he prompted.

"How did you know about that?" Gregory asked, shaken.

Facing him now, Father said, "I am well aware of the unscrupulous way some pawnbrokers operate. It takes very little imagination to suggest that one of them might demand from an inexperienced young person four dollars more than the amount written on the ticket."

"He wanted five dollars, Father, but I had a dollar in my pocket."

Father gave a bark of a laugh. "So he settled for that and acted magnanimous when he let you take the music box." His desk chair squealed in protest as he lowered his bulk into it.

"The pawnbroker didn't let me take it, Father," Gregory

347

whispered. "I just— I just took it." The silence that followed his words was marred by the clock's mocking *took*-it . . . *took*-it . . . *took*-it . . . *took*-it . . .

Father swiveled his chair a quarter turn so it faced the window, and he leaned back with his hands folded across his vest. It seemed a long time before he swiveled back to face Gregory again. "I would like to meet this pawnbroker of yours," he said.

Not knowing what to expect, Gregory waited for Father to pick up his hat and his walking stick, then followed him out the door. "The pawnshop is on the other side of town, Father," he said after they had passed the sentry post by the ditch diggers.

"I assumed as much," Father said dryly.

Half an hour later, they neared the pawnshop, and a few small boys playing mumblety-peg in a vacant lot stared at them. The woman who had cheered Gregory on as he fled two days ago peered from behind the limp curtain in her front window, and he wondered what she was thinking. "The shop is just ahead, Father," he said.

Father nodded. "I will do the talking, son," he said.

The shopkeeper looked up when they entered. "May I help you, sir?"

"I understand my son transacted some business here a few days ago."

A glimmer of recognition lit the man's eyes when he peered at Gregory. "I believe this is the young man who came to redeem his mother's rosewood music box."

"He is also the young man you attempted to cheat out

of five dollars in addition to your inflated redemption price," Father said. He glowered down at the pawnbroker for a moment before he turned to Gregory and explained. "You see, son, the amount written on the pawn ticket included payment of the interest on the cash the sutler received when he pawned the music box. You owed this man nothing more than that."

Gregory felt giddy with relief. *I'm not a thief after all!*

Father's voice was hard when he spoke to the pawnbroker again. "Not only do you traffic in stolen goods and charge usurious interest rates, you have attempted to take advantage of my son—*and* you have falsely accused him of theft when you, sir, are the thief!"

The man fumbled in his money drawer and drew out a handful of bills. "Your accusations are unfounded, sir, but to further good customer relations, I'll return the lad's money."

"The dollar that you extorted from him after he paid the amount on the ticket will be sufficient," Father said. "That, and an apology."

"I beg your pardon for calling you a thief, young man," the shopkeeper said as he slid the dollar across the counter. Then he turned to Father and added, "But I must protest your charge that I deal in stolen goods, sir. This is a reputable business, and—"

"Father! Look there!" Gregory pointed to a display of swords and sabers that hung on the wall behind the shopkeeper. "Don't you see? It's Great-grandfather's sword! The one the soldiers took from above the parlor mantel."

"I think you're right, son," Father said slowly. His eyes bored into the pawnbroker's, and he said, "I believe that you will find the name 'Gregory Howard' engraved just below the hilt of the sword my son has indicated."

Reluctantly, the man brought the sword to the counter, and Father drew it a few inches from the scabbard to show him the name. "I am reclaiming this piece of stolen property, sir. I'll thank you to wrap it for me and secure the package well with string."

Hands trembling, the pawnbroker did as he was asked. "I want you to know that I bought that sword in good faith," he said meekly.

"I doubt that," Father said. "Good day, sir." He took the package and led the way out of the store. "Well, son," he said after the two of them had walked a few steps in silence, "it appears that I owe your little sister an apology."

"I don't understand, sir."

Father chuckled. "If I remember correctly, Mary suggested that you might be able to find the sword for me, and I told her that wasn't very likely. But as things have turned out, she was right."

Gregory's heart swelled with pride. For the first time in weeks, Father was pleased with him.

CHAPTER ELEVEN
★　　　★　　　★

SOMETHING WAS wrong, and when Gregory's eyes met Elizabeth's across the supper table a week later, he knew that his sister sensed it, too. Mother had barely touched her meal, and though Father had made his way through second helpings as usual, he seemed preoccupied. Well, sooner or later, Elizabeth wouldn't be able to stand it any longer, and she'd—

"Papa, have either Greg or I done something to displease you?" his sister asked.

Father stirred another spoonful of sugar into his coffee before he answered. "No, daughter, I was waiting for an appropriate time to tell you two young people what your mother and I have decided."

Whatever it was, Mother didn't look happy about it, Gregory thought, stealing another glance at her.

Father cleared his throat and said, "On Friday, I will take both of you to the farm to stay with your aunt and uncle."

Gregory was too stunned to speak, but Elizabeth cried, "That's wonderful! But I thought you said the Yankees wouldn't let us leave the city."

"Anyone may leave," Father said, "but only citizens loyal to the United States may return. That wouldn't affect you, however."

Elizabeth's eyes darkened. "How foolish of me. I forgot for a moment that females are not considered citizens."

"Wait a minute," Gregory said. "Does this mean I'll be expected to swear an oath of allegiance to the Union when we come back?"

"You won't be coming back until the occupation is over," Father told him.

"But that could be weeks from now!"

Eyes blazing, Elizabeth said, "First you disown Martin, and now you're sending Greg and me away, and all because we're loyal to Virginia!"

Father said calmly, "I'm sending the two of you away for your own safety and my peace of mind. Whether or not it is true, Elizabeth, the authorities believe that you are responsible for the proliferation of small Confederate flags cut from paper that have been pasted on water pumps and walls on several occasions. And Gregory has made an enemy of a soldier we all know to be vengeful and unpredictable. Your mother and I would rest more easily if the two of you were out of the city and away from the occupying forces."

"I don't like the idea of our family being separated," Mother said, "but I agree with your father that under the circumstances, this is the best thing to do."

Torn by conflicting emotions, Gregory's mind churned. *It's always fun to be at the farm with my cousins. . . . Mary will miss my stories and Elizabeth's company. . . . I'll worry about what's happening at home. . . . Any soldiers I see will be Confederates. . . . Maybe Martin will visit again while we're there. . . .*

"Your mother and I will come for you as soon as Mary is strong enough to make the trip," Father was saying.

"But I thought you said we wouldn't come back until the occupation ended," Gregory said, confused.

Father stared into his coffee cup for a moment before he met his son's eyes and said, "I'm making arrangements to rent the warehouse to the army—and this house also. We will stay in western Virginia until the war is over."

"In western Virginia, where the people are Unionists," Elizabeth said bitterly.

"I believe I just heard you say that you were loyal to Virginia, daughter."

Her voice rising, Elizabeth said, "But now there's talk that the western counties will secede from Virginia and form a new state!"

Father looked amused. "My dear girl, if you claim that the disloyal states have the right to secede from the Union, how can you refuse the loyal part of a state the right to secede from the Confederacy?"

For once, Elizabeth was at a loss for words. She slipped her napkin into the silver ring and said, "If you will excuse me, I have a letter to write."

Gregory hated his father's satisfied expression. Turning his words against him, he asked, "If Lincoln claims the southern states had no right to secede from the Union, then why does he welcome the idea of the western counties seceding from Virginia?"

"That's a fair question, son, and one I believe the president himself answered when he said that he would do anything necessary to preserve the Union."

"Is he saying that the end justifies the means?"

"Yes, I believe he is, Gregory. And in this case, I have to agree."

Dropping the subject, Gregory turned to his mother. "I thought you said you would never let fear of the Yankees drive you from your home."

Mother said quietly, "It's concern for the welfare of my children, not fear of the enemy, that has convinced me to go along with your father's plan." She hesitated a moment, then added, "Mary has nightmares about Yankee soldiers nearly every night."

Father cleared his throat and said, "Sometimes changes in the situation one is facing can lead to changes in one's attitude, son."

"Does Lena know that we'll be going to western Virginia?" Gregory asked.

"Lena knows, but she won't be coming with us. Your mother has decided to manumit her—to give her freedom."

Shaken, Gregory turned to his mother. "But how will we get along without her? She—she's *raised* us."

"Lena has been with me more than half my life," Mother said, her voice trembling. "She was a wedding present from my grandfather in North Carolina."

Gregory hadn't known that. "Maybe she'll come with us and work for pay," he said, unable to imagine leaving her behind.

Mother shook her head. "She wants to stay in Alexandria with Jesse."

"With Jesse?" Gregory echoed. "Mr. Bevin's Jesse?"

Mother nodded. "That's why I decided to manumit her. I couldn't bring myself to separate them." She paused a moment before she added, "You see, Lena had to leave her first husband behind when Grandfather brought her to Virginia."

Gregory's mind reeled. He hadn't known that Lena was married, had never even imagined that she might have another life beyond this house and his family. With an effort, he forced himself to listen to Father explain that Jesse would drive them to the farm in Mr. Bevin's carriage, and that they would leave early in the morning to allow the horses a rest before the trip back to town.

Father's voice droned on and on, but at last he finished outlining his plans. "May I please be excused?" Gregory asked, pushing away his unfinished slice of pecan pie. "I need to pack." It was the only excuse he could think of.

Friday morning, Jesse brought the carriage to a stop just before the sentry post at the edge of the city, and Father showed his pass to a young soldier, who waved them on. Gregory glanced about, amazed at the changes in the countryside since he had ridden Big Red to the farm last month. Trenches snaked through what had once been fields and gardens, and a tent city stretched as far as he could see.

From the seat opposite Gregory, his sister said, "I had no idea there were so many Yankees," and beside him,

Father replied, "Nor did I."

Peering ahead, Gregory announced, "I think we're finally coming to the boundary of their camp." A few minutes later they were stopped by another sentry and waved on again. Greg drew a deep breath, glad to be out of Union territory.

They were still several miles from the village of Fairfax Court House when Elizabeth asked, "How long will it be until we all leave for western Virginia, Papa?"

"A week or so, if all goes well," Father said. "Mary is stronger every day, and I would like to be away from this part of the state before the fighting begins."

"There's going to be fighting *here*?" Elizabeth asked.

"That seems a reasonable expectation when tens of thousands of men in opposing armies are facing each other little more than twenty miles apart," Father said. "You understand, of course, that any possibility of settling the secession issue peacefully ended when the rebels fired on Fort Sumter."

Bristling, Gregory said, "Or maybe when Lincoln sent out his call for troops."

Elizabeth gave an exaggerated sigh, and Father said, "I suggest we drop the subject."

Gregory was tempted to point out that it was Father who had brought up the bombardment of Sumter, but instead he leaned back in his seat and contented himself with the thought that General Beauregard, Sumter's hero, was now in command of all the Confederate troops at Manassas Junction. The whistle of a distant train caught his ear, and he was sure it was a troop train. According to the northern newspaper Father had bought from a street vendor last week, soldiers from all over the South were assembling at Manassas Junction, and more of them arrived each day.

And then Gregory had a frightening thought. "Wait a minute! Fairfax Court House and the farm are right on the road between Washington and Manassas Junction!"

"I am well aware of the geography of northern Virginia," Father said, "and you may be sure that I intend to come for you and Elizabeth as soon as possible."

Gregory swallowed hard. He'd been so involved with how Virginia's secession and Alexandria's occupation by Union troops had affected him personally that he hadn't looked much farther ahead than the next day, hadn't thought about the battle everyone said would settle once and for all what Father called "the secession issue." Hadn't *let* himself think about it.

Leaning forward, Elizabeth asked, "When they have the battle, who do you think will win, Papa?"

"It's hard to predict, with both armies inexperienced and both so certain that God and justice are on their side. The Union has more men and better equipment, but the Confederacy has better officers. And, of course, its men are defending their homes and families—and what they regard as their country—against an invading enemy."

Breaking the tense silence that followed his words, Father added, "I daresay it won't be many weeks before we know the outcome of the battle, and perhaps of the war, as well."

"Do you think the Confederates will march out to meet

the Union troops?" Gregory asked. It was hard to imagine the pastureland on either side of the road as a battlefield.

"I expect that they will remain south of Bull Run. The stream's steep banks provide a natural line of defense for them—and for the railroad junction they're protecting."

Elizabeth said, "You'd think our boys would be protecting Richmond instead of guarding a railroad junction in the middle of nowhere."

"They *are* protecting Richmond, Elizabeth. That junction is on the rail route to the city," Gregory said. Hadn't she ever looked at a map?

Father added, "If the Union gains control of Manassas Junction, besides providing transport south for our own men and supplies, we can cut off the flow of men and provisions to Richmond and the Shenandoah Valley." The carriage came to a stop at the Confederate sentry post outside the village of Fairfax Court House, and Father nodded to the soldier on duty. "We'll be visiting at the Oliver place a short distance down the pike," he said.

"Give Mrs. Oliver the warm regards of the boys camped at the chapel, sir. She is kind enough to send over baked goods now and then," the young man said, stepping back.

Once they were on their way again, it wasn't long before the carriage reached Main Street. Confederate flags and gray-clad soldiers were everywhere, and Gregory felt his spirits rise.

When the carriage stopped in front of the post office, Father took some letters from the pocket of his vest and handed them to Gregory. The envelope on top was addressed to Father's widowed sister, and Gregory asked, "Will we stay with Aunt Adele when we go to western Virginia, sir?"

"I daresay she'll be willing to take us in," Father answered, handing him some coins for the stamps.

When he approached the tiny building, Gregory noticed that the sign now read *Confederate* States Post Office. Didn't that prove the Confederacy was a country in its own right? That it was more than "what the secessionists regard as their country"? Whether Father liked it or not, he was in the Confederate States of America now.

Inside, Greg slid the letters across the counter and said, "I'll need seven stamps, sir."

"That will be thirty-five cents, young man," the postmaster told him, and as Gregory counted out the coins, he added, "Can't use U.S. stamps now, and our government hasn't printed any yet." Gregory watched him write "Paid 5" in the upper right-hand corner of each envelope. Reading upside down, he saw that Elizabeth had written to a friend who had fled to Richmond, and Mother had written to Aunt Alice, her sister in Baltimore. He couldn't make out the three addressed in Miss Lily's spidery penmanship, but the one at the bottom of the stack was addressed to Martin—and it was in Father's handwriting!

In a daze, Gregory waited until the postmaster counted out his change. *Father wrote a letter to Martin.*

Back in the carriage, Gregory handed Father the change, and when their eyes met—and held for a moment—he sensed that something more than coins had passed between them. He settled back in his seat, feeling at ease for the first time since the day Virginia had voted to secede—and the night Father had told Martin that the house on Washington Street was no longer his home.

Gregory was glad their early supper was almost over and Father would soon be starting back to Alexandria. Though Aunt Millie did her best to smooth things over, it was obvious that Uncle Matthew didn't like having a Unionist in-law for a guest. It had never dawned on Gregory that his father might not be welcome at the farm.

"I'm sorry you must start home so soon, Roger," Uncle Matthew said, arranging his knife and fork across his plate to signal that he had finished. "Still, I can understand your reluctance to leave Suzanne and little Mary to the mercy of Lincoln's hirelings any longer than necessary."

Aunt Millie flushed and said quickly, "It's been months since I've seen Suzanne—not since before Mary came down with rheumatic fever."

"If things go as I hope they will, you will see your sister in a week or so, Millie, when we come to pick up Elizabeth and Gregory for the trip to western Virginia," Father told her. Then he shifted his attention to his brother-in-law and said, "You might want to consider moving your family out of the path of your enemies sometime within the next few weeks, Matthew."

Uncle Matthew raised his eyebrows. "Oh? Do you have some kind of advance information that the Yankees will head this way? And that it will be soon?"

Gregory felt uneasy. It sounded almost as if his uncle were mocking Father.

Ignoring the tone of the questions, Father said, "If you study the map of Virginia, I think you'll agree that Union forces will have to come this way to do battle with the Confederates camped near the railroad junction. As for the timing, any attack would have to come before the ninety-day enlistments expire for the troops who responded to Lincoln's first call to arms."

Gregory felt a chill. Ninety days was three months, and Lincoln had asked the states to send militiamen to put down the south's rebellion right after Sumter fell. Northern troops began arriving in Washington a few days later—April 19 for the ones caught in the riot in Baltimore. He remembered that because old Mr. Wilson across the street had made a big issue of the fact that Maryland secessionists had fired on "the northern aggressors" on the same date the patriots in Lexington and Concord first fired on the Redcoats.

May, June, July. That meant the army would have to make its move sometime around the middle of July—less than a month from now!

"What's wrong, Gregory? You've barely touched a thing on your plate."

"I—I guess I was wool-gathering, Aunt Millie," he said, picking up his fork.

Uncle Matthew turned to him and said, "Tell me, young man, how does it feel to be out from under the despot's heel?"

Puzzled, Gregory repeated, "The despot's heel?"

"Haven't you read the poem 'My Maryland'?" his cousin Albert asked. "I thought it had been in all the newspapers."

"We don't *have* a newspaper now that the Yankees have taken over," Elizabeth complained. "Not a real one, anyway—just a daily sheet called *The Local News*."

"I'll bet the Alexandrians are the only people in the South who haven't memorized the whole poem by now," Robert said, adding, "Our grandmother in North Carolina wrote out all the verses in one of her letters, but we'd already cut a copy out of the Richmond paper." He elbowed his older brother and said, "Say the first stanza for them, Albert."

Albert glanced at his father and asked, "Shall I?"

"By all means, son," Uncle Matthew said with a sly glance at Father.

Striking a pose, Albert began:

> *"The despot's heel is on thy shore,*
> *Maryland!*
> *His torch is at thy temple door,*
> *Maryland!*
> *Avenge the patriotic gore*
> *That flecked the streets of Baltimore,*
> *And be the Battle Queen of yore,*
> *Maryland! My Maryland!"*

Gregory grinned at his cousin's dramatic recitation, and Robert said, "The rest of the poem is even better. A teacher down in Louisiana wrote it after he heard about those

Yankee troops on their way to Washington firing on innocent citizens in Baltimore."

Father cleared his throat and said, "The northern press called the shots exchanged there 'the Baltimore Massacre,' and the southern papers wrote about 'the Lexington of 1861.' I think there was some truth on both sides."

"And I think we should talk about something else," Aunt Millie said. She picked up the small crystal bell near her plate and rang it to call a house servant to clear the table and bring in the dessert.

Truth on both sides. It had been a long time since Father had said anything like that, Gregory thought. If there was truth on both sides—right and wrong on both sides, too, probably—no wonder he sometimes felt so confused. Maybe that was why he hated the Union occupation but secretly missed being part of a country with a glorious past, why he loved Virginia but felt lukewarm toward the Confederacy.

Now, though, Virginia was about to become a battleground, and nothing could keep it from happening. It was as if a giant wave were cresting, a wave that had begun to form in Charleston Harbor, had risen higher and higher as both sides made their speeches and built their armies, and now was about to engulf the entire nation. And the cresting wave of war could no more be controlled than an ocean wave in a hurricane.

A servant placed a large slice of cherry pie in front of Gregory. His first thought was that the crust didn't look quite as flaky as Lena's—and then he remembered that the night before, he'd left the table with nearly half a piece of her good pecan pie still on his plate.

That night Gregory lay awake, tossing and turning, trying without success to keep his mind blank. It seemed hours since he'd heard the faint notes of a bugle call signaling the troops camped in the village to put out their lights, hours since his aunt had tiptoed up the stairs and he'd seen the flicker of her candle when she passed his open door.

This is all wrong. Elizabeth and I shouldn't be here on the farm while our brother is camped at Manassas Junction and our parents—and Mary—are in Alexandria. We should all be home together. "If only the Yankees weren't occupying Alexandria and their army weren't fixing to march out here and attack our army," Gregory whispered.

The wail of a train whistle floated through the night air, and he tried again to make his mind go blank. He didn't want to think about more southern boys arriving at Manassas Junction, about the inevitable battle. And he didn't want to think about staying with Aunt Adele in western Virginia, either. About his family leaving their home. Becoming refugees.

With a deep sigh, Gregory climbed out of bed and padded to the window. Above the silhouette of a low line of hills, the moonless sky was clear and dotted with stars. As he searched for a familiar constellation, breathing in the scent of his aunt's roses mingled with the fragrance of honeysuckle, he heard the liquid call of a whippoorwill.

It was so peaceful here. So calm. Gregory felt some of

the tension drain from his body, but the sound of the train whistle—fainter, this time—was a reminder that the peace and calm of the Virginia countryside would soon be shattered. "And there's nothing anyone can do about it," he whispered. "Not even Abraham Lincoln and Jefferson Davis. Not now."

A falling star streaked across the southern sky. Gregory was about to make a wish, but he caught himself in time. Wishing was useless. Childish.

Suddenly the floor felt cold to his feet, and he shivered. He turned away from the window and crept back to the bed where he had slept on more visits than he could remember. He pulled the sheet up to his chin and stared at the ceiling. It was stupid to wish for the impossible, but he could hope for the best, couldn't he?

"I hope Martin isn't wounded in the battle," he whispered. "I hope the Yankees march right by the farm. I hope our side wins so the troops will leave Alexandria." *But the troops would leave when the war ended, no matter who won. And if the Yankees won, Virginia would be part of the United States again. And—*

Gregory forced that thought out of his mind. "I hope Martin isn't wounded in the battle," he whispered. "I hope this battle will end the war." He repeated the words, silently, over and over again, until at last he fell asleep.

HOW MUCH OF THIS BOOK IS TRUE?

Timothy Donovan's Story: Timothy's story closely follows historical events, but the young bugler is a purely imaginary character. We know there were two company musicians at Forts Moultrie and Sumter, but we don't know their ages or whether they were drummers, buglers, or fifers. Because the historian at the Fort Sumter National Monument said it was likely that they were buglers, I chose to make Timothy a bugler. But because I found references to beating the Long Roll at Sumter, I created the band's elderly drummer, Corporal O'Brian. (The calls sounded in the story are only a few of the ones that regulated a soldier's life.)

Though most of the other characters are also imaginary, a few represent actual people. Major Anderson and Captain Doubleday were the top two officers at Sumter, and in several instances I have used their own words. Minor characters based on members of the garrison include Captain Foster (who hired the Baltimore masons and others to work on the harbor forts), Captain Seymour (who made the "barrel grenades"), Lieutenant Hart (who singed off his eyebrows saving the flag during the bombardment), and Private Hough (who was killed during the salute).

The details of the garrison's last week at Fort Moultrie, the crossing to Sumter, life there before the bombardment, and the bombardment itself are as close to the truth as I was able to show them through Timothy's eyes and experiences. But because this is a story and not a history book, a great deal that actually happened has been left out, and many unrecorded details were supplied by my imagination.

Joseph Schwartz's Story: Joseph and the other characters are all imaginary, but some of the people mentioned in the story are real, including Mayor Brown, General Butler, and Ross Winans (the elderly legislator who was imprisoned "for being a secessionist"). There are scores of firsthand—and sometimes conflicting—accounts of the unrest in Baltimore at the start of the war, and I used details from many of them in this story, keeping in mind what it would be reasonable for Joseph to have witnessed and understood. I made up most of the bulletins he read at the newspaper office as well as most of the newspaper headlines, but the news itself is accurate—and people really did crowd around the bulletin boards at newspaper and telegraph offices.

Gregory Howard's Story: Gregory and the members of his family are imaginary, as are all the other characters except for the two martyrs, Colonel Elmer Ellsworth and the hotel keeper, James Jackson. The shootings at the Marshall House Hotel are historical events, and poorly disciplined Union troops did harass "the rebels," ransacking their homes, demanding food, and taking whatever they wanted. Often, Unionists in Alexandria interceded with the authorities on behalf of their secessionist neighbors, as

Gregory's father did in the story. Many of the details of daily life in the city were suggested by entries in the diaries of Alexandria citizens.

The *Pawnee*, which had been part of the Sumter relief fleet, really was stationed on the Potomac with its guns trained on Alexandria in May 1861, and Sumter's hero, General Beauregard, was the commanding officer at Manassas Junction, where Martin and the other Alexandria militiamen were in camp.

WHAT HAPPENED NEXT?

In Charleston Harbor: The Confederates holding Sumter were unchallenged for the first two years after the Union garrison's surrender. But between April 1863 and mid-September 1864, Sumter withstood eleven bombardments—including three major ones—as the Union attempted to retake the fort and capture Charleston. (The famous Fifty-fourth Massachusetts Colored Infantry made its assault on Morris Island's Battery Wagner as part of this effort.) The Confederates held Sumter until mid-February 1865, when they abandoned the fort and evacuated Charleston as Union General Sherman approached with his army, determined "to make South Carolina howl."

On the fourth anniversary of the day Major Anderson lowered the Stars and Stripes and led his garrison out of Sumter in defeat, he raised the same tattered flag over the ruined fort in a triumphant celebration. It was a week after Confederate General Lee had surrendered at Appomattox, and hours before President and Mrs. Lincoln left the White House for an evening at Ford's Theater.

In Baltimore: Baltimore was occupied by Union soldiers throughout the war. Because Lincoln had suspended the writ of habeas corpus—the Constitutional right to protection from illegal imprisonment—citizens were jailed in Fort McHenry simply because of their southern sympathies.

In Alexandria: Alexandria remained occupied and under martial law during the entire Civil War. Homes and public buildings were taken over for use by the army, and forts and hospitals were built. The city became a supply center for the Union Army, and the wharves on the Potomac were piled high with supplies brought in by ship to be transported to camps and battlefields by rail.

In mid-July of 1861, a month after Gregory's story ended, the citizens of Alexandria knew that something significant was about to happen: The occupying troops had left their camps, and regiments from the camps in Washington were streaming southward through the city. Then, on July 21, Alexandria's residents heard the boom of distant artillery all day long. It was only after the defeated and disillusioned Union troops began to straggle back to their camps that the citizens learned of the Confederate victory at the battle we know as First Bull Run or First Manassas.

In the Country as a Whole: After the battle near

Manassas Junction, it was obvious that "the secession issue" would not be settled in a single clash of two inexperienced armies. During the next forty-five months, North and South met in combat thousands of times, in actions ranging from raids and skirmishes to major battles. More Americans died in the Civil War—most of them from illness rather than from battle wounds—than in the twentieth century's two world wars combined. Citizens on both sides became disillusioned by the seemingly endless slaughter, and many in the South were demoralized or impoverished by the war's effect on the home front. Scarcely a family in America was untouched by tragedy and suffering in this war that ended slavery as well as preserved the Union.

Though generations would pass before African Americans began to gain the civil rights taken for granted by other citizens, the issue of secession, which had been raised on several occasions before South Carolina left the Union, had been settled—once and for all.